An
Experiment
in Treason

An Experiment in Treason

Bruce Alexander

G.P. Putnam's Sons
New York

G. P. Putnam's Sons
Publishers Since 1838
a member of
Penguin Putnam Inc.
375 Hudson Street
New York, NY 10014

Library of Congress Cataloging-in-Publication Data

Alexander, Bruce
An experiment in treason / by Bruce Alexander.
p.   cm.
ISBN 0-399-14923-6
1. Fielding, John, Sir, 1721–1780—Fiction.   2. Portsmouth
(England)—Fiction.   3. London (England)—Fiction.
4. Judges—Fiction.   5. Blind—Fiction.   I. Title.
PS3553.O55314 E97 2002
813'.54—dc21   2002068365

Printed in the United States of America
1   3   5   7   9   10   8   6   4   2

This book is printed on acid-free paper. ♾

For Chuck Hurewitz

PART ONE

ONE

*In which I visit
Portsmouth as a burglary
is done in London*

I, Jeremy Proctor, must start this narrative of one of the most singular cases of Sir John Fielding, magistrate of the Bow Street
Court, with an admission. To put it plain, I was not present at the
beginning of this case. Indeed, no, rather was I revisiting Portsmouth in the company of Gabriel Donnelly, doctor of medicine and
a surgeon, medical examiner for the City of Westminster, and friend
to us all at Number 4 Bow Street. In the past, I have prided myself
on putting before you each of these cases in toto—that is to say,
from start to finish. Yet, in this instance, I had left London at the invitation of Mr. Donnelly and with Sir John's kind permission that I
might look upon a scientific experiment conducted by one known
throughout England and in all of the great cities of Europe, to wit,
Benjamin Franklin. By an odd turn of fate, Dr. Franklin himself fig-
ured very prominently indeed in the case in question. And so, upon
further consideration, perhaps I was, after all, present at the beginning of the case, for stories can be told from many a perspective
and point-of-view; and what are criminal cases but stories of a certain sort?

Mr. Donnelly and I had traveled down to Portsmouth with an
Arthur Lee, also a gentleman of the colonies, who had something to
do with Dr. Franklin's duties as factor for a number of colonies—
Pennsylvania and Massachusetts, and a couple of others. What that
something was, I have no idea, but it was plain that he was a great
supporter of Franklin in all the latter's endeavors. Indeed he talked
of little else through the length of our journey, so pleased was he at

the prospect of assisting the great man in one of his studies. It should be noted, by the bye, that Lee himself was a man of no little learning. Already a medical doctor (which did account for his acquaintance with Mr. Donnelly), he had come to London to read the law. I knew not, nor did I ever discover, what he planned to do with so much learning in fields so greatly disparate. Yet he seemed to have time enough and money enough to indulge himself in this way. And since he had hired the coach, and I was riding to Portsmouth as his guest, I made no inquiry, and neither, as I noted, did Mr. Donnelly.

We stayed the night at the George. The old inn was filled to bursting. There were many, like ourselves, down from London to see what the famous Franklin was up to, but some of those were not properly respectful—or so it seemed to me. As we ate our dinner that evening, those at the next table talked loudly and with accompanying sneers about "that fool Franklin." And one, I recall, referred to him as "the silly colonial cod." It was all Lee could do to restrain himself from leaping up and challenging the entire table, at which three sat, to a duel in fisticuffs. Fortunately, they had preceded us; they finished early.

"Those are the fools," said Arthur Lee, watching them go. "They know naught of science and care less."

"It is not for his science such men revile him, but for his politics and his fame," said Mr. Donnelly. "They believe he goes too far with that slogan of his, 'No taxation without representation.'"

"And do you believe he goes too far?"

"Naturally not, for I am an Irishman."

"If they only knew," said Lee. "There are many in America who would go *much* further than Dr. Franklin does."

"Perhaps they do know," said Mr. Donnelly, "and that is what they fear."

With that, discussion of the matter ended, and Mr. Donnelly, ever the peacemaker, moved conversation quite gracefully to the matter of the morrow's experiment. There was much of it I did not understand. Or, perhaps better put, I did understand it yet thought it a bit daft.

As Arthur Lee had explained earlier, Dr. Franklin had decided to take the advice of Pliny the Elder quite seriously, and attempt to still rough waters by pouring a quantity of oil over them. This, it was said, had been a common practice by seamen of that time. Franklin had described to Lee incidents which he had experienced, and others that had been related to him that seemed to support this theory. I could not but wonder why, if it had been common knowledge in Pliny's time, it had not been put to the test by Pliny himself, nor by any since his time. Still, it would be tested in the morn with the aid and cooperation of Captain Bentinck.

"Bentinck?" echoed Mr. Donnelly. "What sort of name is that?"

"Dutch, actually," said Lee. "Those on the Continent have ever been willing to give his experiments and theories greater support, and have treated them with greater seriousness, than have those here in England. Why, did you know that this very year, only a few months past, he was elected one of only eight 'foreign associates' of the French Royal Academy of Sciences?"

"Indeed, no, I did not," said Mr. Donnelly.

What followed then was a recitation by Lee of the honors and various forms of recognition Franklin had received from academic bodies in Europe. It was a most impressive list, well annotated by Lee as to the meaning and importance of each item on it. Nevertheless, such was not, intrinsically, of much interest. There was little that we—Mr. Donnelly and I—could do but nod our approval as we chewed at our dinner, and continue nodding as the exacting journey from London gradually overcame us. In short, we near fell asleep there at the table. And though we did not, we came near enough that we were forced to say our good-nights and make for our room promptly at dinner's end. There would be no pleasant tippling for us by the great fireplace in the next room.

Mr. Donnelly and I agreed that, no doubt, Benjamin Franklin had no greater friend nor enthusiast in this world than Arthur Lee. Still, it was true that an excess of praise for any man or matter would surely stifle enthusiasm in others.

Early to bed and early to rise, we were up and about at dawn. After a hurried breakfast of tea, hot rolls, and country butter, we ventured out into the early morn, one typical of that coast in that season. It was blustering, windy, and damp—what the natives thereabouts call a "blowy" day. We looked about for Arthur Lee but saw no sign of him. We had knocked upon his door without result, asked after him at the desk, and looked round and about for him during our brief visit to the crowded dining room. He was nowhere to be seen.

"Well, I suppose we've no choice but to go down to the shore and look for him there," said Mr. D. "I hear a bit of noise coming from that direction. Perhaps Franklin is marshaling his forces there."

And so, we started down the slight hill with a crowd of the curious behind us. Now was it much lighter, and arriving at the shore we had no difficulty discerning a group of three preparing to leave in a bumboat tied up at a wharf. 'Twas I, with the youngest pair of eyes, who perceived Arthur Lee among them. And 'twas Mr. Donnelly, with his great pair of Irish lungs, who hallooed him across the distance. Waving his response, Lee separated from the others and hurried toward us as we jog-trotted to him.

"Ah, here you are then," said he once close enough to be heard without a shout.

"Indeed we are," said Mr. Donnelly as we met. "We knocked upon your door without result. You must have been up very early."

"For hours! I could not sleep; so eager was I to be on with the experiment. You will also play a part."

"Ah, what sort?"

"Dr. Franklin would like you and all others to occupy that point of land on the windward side, out there between the hospital and Jillecker. There you will have the best view of the experiment, and, more important, you will be able to report to us on its success or failure."

"Dear God," said Mr. Donnelly, somewhat intimidated, "are we to have such a great responsibility?"

"Not so great, after all. You need only report as to whether there was or was not a diminishing of the surf in that part of the shore."

"I see. Well, we can certainly do that."

"Of course you can. We'll meet again on the wharf when all is done, and you can make your report. Fair enough?"

"Fair enough."

Lee offered his hand in the way favored by gentlemen of the colonies, and Mr. Donnelly grasped it and gave it a good firm shake.

"Sir?" said I, hoping to hold him a moment longer. "Mr. Lee, sir?"

"That's Dr. Lee, if you please."

"Forgive me, Dr. Lee, but I was wondering, is Dr. Franklin one of the two men on the wharf?"

He turned to look where I pointed.

"The shorter of the two, the stout one," said I, trying to be helpful.

"I'll thank you to keep a civil tongue in your head, young man," said he. "Dr. Franklin is a fine figure of a man, one of athletic capabilities and one most attractive to women."

"Forgive me, sir. I meant no disrespect."

With a great harrumph, *Doctor* Lee stalked off toward the wharf, leaving the two of us staring after him, puzzled and a bit shocked.

"Ah, these colonial fellows," said Mr. Donnelly. "They are as tetchy and mean-minded as any Scotsman ever I met."

"Truly, Mr. Donnelly, I meant no ill."

"Of course you did not. And for your information, Jeremy, the shorter of the two men there, he who is indubitably stout, is none other than Benjamin Franklin, I am sure of it. Now, if you will excuse me, I have an announcement to make to the throng gathered behind us."

And so saying, he turned round and gave notice to the fifty or more who had gathered behind us that we were all to proceed to the point of land some distance ahead from which we might best view . . . et cetera.

The walk to the point designated by Dr. Lee was well over a mile, most of it along the shoreline on a rough, rock-strewn beach. By the time we reached our destination, a long line of marchers stretched out behind us, yet all eventually collected there on the windward side of the point, and there we all waited for the demonstration to begin.

It was, as we had been told, quite the best place to view these singular proceedings. About the time of our arrival, we saw one among the many ships anchored offshore lowering a boat of considerable size, followed by what Mr. Donnelly informed me was a barge: a simple flat-bottomed boat. There were but two men in the barge, while the longboat had a complement aboard. Seamen manned the oars. A line was tossed to the barge and made fast; and in no time the two crafts were off together, the longboat providing the power with its oarsmen, towing the barge at a good rate of speed a quarter of a mile offshore. There was great activity aboard the barge. Two men—was one of them Dr. Lee?—held a large bottle up to the gunwale and from it poured a thick liquid of some sort— presumably oil—in a steady stream over the side.

Something now must be said about the weather. As I said ear- lier, it was a perfectly common sort of day for that part of the coast in that season. Which is to say, it was windy and damp. For a good part of the time we watched the two smaller vessels make their pas- sage back and forth, a light rain blew in our faces.

And if the beach along which we walked to reach our chosen point of observation was notably littered with rocks of up to medium size, then so also was the beach upon which we had col- lected to watch the surf for changes. Indeed, there were rocks everywhere—even, I was sure, in great number beneath the water's surface, as well. I could see two of the largest out from the beach and above the surface, kicking up a great lot of foam as the high wa- ter dashed against them.

The wind drove the water straight at the beach, where it broke, spuming and frothing across the sand and rocks. We watched as the waves broke upon the shore, hoping and even expecting that the surf would slack off in the next moment or two. Yet with the best will in the world we would not honestly say that the surf had diminished in the slightest degree. After near half an hour spent thus, at such time as the longboat and the barge ceased plying the monotonous course I have described, we on the shore turned away and began to talk amongst ourselves of the experiment and how it went wrong.

"I know not why I bothered to come this long way to Ports- mouth," said one of those who had railed at Dr. Franklin the night before. "Such a theory seems pure nonsense. Bound to fail."

"I know why," said his companion. "So that when he is next praised beyond reason at Lady Richmond's table, you will have an interesting titbit with which to counter all that Franklin-mania."

"Ah, will I indeed! All this foolish tittle-tattle of what-will-he- do-next when the fellow is nothing short of a traitor to the crown."

"He'll get what he deserves soon enough, and when he does I daresay he'll . . ."

The voices of the two detractors faded in the wind as they marched off with the rest whence we had come. We watched them go. Soon we were alone on the beach.

"It's just as you said," I remarked to Mr. Donnelly. "They dismiss his science on political grounds." I hesitated just a bit, but then did I plunge boldly forward: "But truly, sir, did not the theory he sought to test seem a bit far-fetched to you? After all, taking a page from Pliny! Hardly what one would call *modern* science."

"Far-fetched? Perhaps, but perhaps not. I'm a medical doctor who happens also to have some skill as a surgeon. I know little of the other branches of science."

"Come now, Mr. Donnelly. You know *little?*"

"Comparatively so. I do, however, know something of human nature. And what I have observed of Dr. Franklin at a distance tells me that he courts celebrity. There were a good many onlookers here today, perhaps some journalists amongst them. I should not be surprised to see reports of this experiment in the *Public Advertiser,* the *Times,* or the *Chronicle,* perhaps in all three. And you may take my word for it, Jeremy, that experiments are best conducted in private—not to say in secret, for there must be a few witnesses to attest to success or failure. Yet Dr. Franklin was so certain of the outcome of this one that he invited many, and the many invited more. What he did not take into consideration is that there were some present, perhaps most, who wished to see him fail."

"All for reasons of politics?" I asked.

"No, not at all. It is one of the burdens of celebrity. One of its dangers, that when you are put above the crowd, the element below wishes you to fall down to its level. In other words, to fail." Then said he with a wink and a nod: "But come along, Jeremy. We ought not to be late to our appointment with Dr. Lee. I fear he might not wait."

With that, we turned round and headed for the wharf which stood well off in the distance. More than a mile we had walked over rocky sand, yet, oddly, it seemed not so far as before, no doubt because we had the wind to our backs, pushing us along. We reached our goal in good time.

And when we did, we saw the same bumboat as had left the wharf an hour before. Yet on this trip it had but one passenger. I wondered at this but said nothing to Mr. Donnelly. As the boat drew nearer I saw that the single passenger was unmistakably Arthur Lee. I supposed that Dr. Franklin had remained on shipboard, yet I knew not why. Upon arrival, the boatman did not even bother to tie up his raft. We, on the wharf, waved our greeting. Dr. Lee who looked quite out of sorts, held tight to the wharf ladder and shouted up at us.

"Well then, what's the report?"

"I fear there was neither rise nor fall in the level of the surf," said Mr. Donnelly.

"You're sure?" Did I detect a note of suspicious doubt in that?

"Of course I'm sure," replied Mr. Donnelly, not in the least intimidated.

"Yes, well, Dr. Franklin kept his spyglass on the beach there at the point, and he saw no change either. I was . . . just hoping . . ."

"I fear not."

"There was a good piece of water between the barge and the longboat that smoothed out proper," Dr. Lee volunteered.

"Well . . . good—but there was no change on the beach where we were," Mr. Donnelly said.

"Yes, but I'm staying on here. I'll be returning with Dr. Franklin. He is weighing the possibility of attempting the experiment a second time."

"And what about us?"

"You can take the hire coach back. Just explain to them that I'm remaining. It's all taken care of."

(Frankly, I was pleased, reader, for I had no wish to return with Lee, having earlier been so sharply corrected by him.)

"Well, all right," said Mr. Donnelly to Lee. I could tell he was not pleased. "Stay if you must. We'll be leaving shortly, I suppose. It was an honor to participate in the experiment, even in a minor role. We thank you for that."

"What? Oh yes, certainly." He returned to his seat in the bumboat and signaled to the boatman that he might proceed. "Good-bye to you then, Mr. Donnelly. I daresay I shall be seeing you soon in London." He waved as the boat pulled away.

"Well, Jeremy," said Mr. Donnelly with a sigh, "it seems that we are on our own."

"It does indeed. Shall we then hasten to claim our coach lest it be taken by some of those who watched with us on the beach?"

"That seems to me an excellent suggestion."

And so, up the hill we went to the George, and there we separated. I went to collect our bags from the room and Mr. Donnelly to settle up at the desk for our stay. I returned to find him, red-faced, in loud conversation with the driver of the coach. I perceived at once that this was no ordinary disagreement but a proper battle, involving the driver, Donnelly, and a third party, Arthur Lee, not physically present yet perhaps the cause of it all.

"Jeremy, do you know what this fellow tells me?"

"Let me guess. That all has not been taken care of as regards the return fare to be paid for this coach-for-hire."

"Exactly. And the worst of it is, I'm inclined to believe the coachman rather than Lee."

"Well, thank God for that, sir," said the driver to Mr. Donnelly, "for I ain't the sort to go chargin' a man for what's already been paid. But I tell you fair, the way back just ain't been paid—not by him, not by anybody. What I was told by Mr.—what's his name?"

"Lee, Arthur Lee."

"That's right. That's him. What Mr. Lee said was, 'Here's for the trip down to Portsmouth. I ain't sure I'll be making it back with you, but the gent who'll be traveling down with me certain'y will. You can get the fare to London from him.'"

"There was never any hint given to me of such an arrangement."

"Oh, I believe you, sir, and if I understand your remark to the lad here a-right, you believe me, as well. That's a good start for workin' out some sort of a deal, wouldn't you say so?"

"Well yes, I suppose I would," said Mr. Donnelly after a moment's careful consideration. "What sort of a deal did you have in mind?"

And with that began a session of hard bargaining there in the lobby of the George, which must have lasted near ten minutes. Gabriel Donnelly was, as Sir John had often said, one Irishman who was as tight with a shilling as any Scotsman. He demonstrated it then and there as he haggled histrionically, at one point offering to walk to London rather than pay such an exorbitant fare. (I hoped sincerely that it would not come to that.) For his part, the coachman was equally dramatic. He alternated demanding with pleading in a manner quite outrageous. He shouted dramatically that he had a wife and children and would not see them starve with such an offer as Mr. Donnelly had put forth. "Have you no conscience, sir?" (This, I'm sure, was said for the benefit of the crowd that had gathered round them in the lobby.)

It came as a surprise, at least to me, that they did at last settle upon a price. Could it be said that the agreed-upon amount was thought by both to be fair? No, say rather that each for his own reasons seemed to think it unfair. Nevertheless, their onlookers were so relieved that the matter had been settled without resort to violence, that quite spontaneously they burst into applause. Caught by surprise, the two negotiators turned to the crowd and acknowledged the response with waves of the hand and nods of the head. Then, obeying the custom, they did solemnly clasp hands on the matter, thus sealing their hard-won agreement before witnesses.

In no time at all we were in the coach and well-begun upon our journey. I know not the cause—perhaps that the load was lightened so by the absence of Dr. Lee (though he was in no wise an extraordinarily large man)—but the journey seemed to go much faster on the return trip to London.

At first, Mr. Donnelly would do not more than grumble that he had been bested in the haggle with the driver, yet it was not long until he put blame where it belonged and began to assess the extent of Dr. Lee's guilt in the matter.

"Why would he do such a thing?" said he to me, honestly seeking some explanation for the fellow's behavior.

"Well," said I, "perhaps he was financially embarrassed and wished to keep it a secret."

"Yes, but to tell the coachman that he would have to seek payment for the return trip from me without ever broaching the matter to me—that does exceed the limit, don't you think? And as for the possibility that he might be, as you suggest, financially embarrassed—well, all of us are from time to time, but, damn his eyes, he should have told me. He should have asked. It would have been the gentlemanly thing to do. But then again, I do not think these colonial fellows are much concerned with proper behavior—no, not even their champion, Dr. Franklin. He, so they say, is no more a gentleman than this man Lee."

That interested me. I wished to hear more. Nevertheless, it was evident that he intended to add nothing. Something in his eyes, as he glanced in my direction, seemed to say that he regretted saying all that he had, and that he would tell no more. Under the circumstances, it would have been rude to pursue the matter. And so, did we lapse into silence. He, for his part, sat staring out the window. I, for mine, looked at the colors of autumn reel by and wondered, as I did so, in what way Benjamin Franklin failed to meet a gentleman's high standard. Could it have something to do with his attractiveness to women? I pondered that for a while, yet could do little with it, for, in all truth, I could not suppose for a moment that a man of such an appearance *could* be attractive to women. But then, having thought long enough upon it, I put it out of my mind and succumbed to sleep.

When I woke, it was dark enough so that I had a bit of difficulty in discovering just where we were. Staring out the window, I saw lights aplenty in the near-distance and realized, after a bit of staring, that the surrounding darkness was naught but that which encircles on all sides as one crosses the Thames by way of London Bridge. We were, to my astonishment, quite near home. Depending upon the number of coaches and hackneys on the streets at whatever hour this might happen to be, we were no more than minutes away from Number 4 Bow Street.

"Ah, awake, are you?" It was Gabriel Donnelly, leaning forward to catch the light in my eye.

I sat up straight, blinking, and then nodded my reply.

"I've no idea how you managed to sleep, the way we were bouncing along on those country roads," said Mr. Donnelly. "You've a talent for it, I do swear."

"A talent for what?" My voice cracked as I tried it for the first time in hours.

"For sleeping," said he.

"Perhaps I do, but so few are my opportunities to exercise it that I fear it may eventually be lost."

At that he merely chuckled.

"Did you sleep?" I asked him.

"Oh, I dozed, little more than that. Unlike most, the movement of the coach upon the road tends to keep me awake."

We were now across the bridge and into the maze of lights. The driver swung left into Thames Street, following a line of hackney coaches. It must not have been long past dark, for there were indeed a flood of vehicles in the street. At such a time, in such a season of the year, London was at its most handsome—certainly the best-lit city in all of Europe; visitors came from all over to admire the oil-burning street lamps that gave light even on the darkest, foggiest nights. The blinking lights of the coaches and carriages added their bright pinpoints to this vivid picture, as did the torches that lit the door of each tavern, inn, and eating-house along the way. I was altogether fascinated.

"Tell me, Jeremy," said Mr. Donnelly, "are you disappointed in our expedition to Portsmouth?"

Pulling myself away from the coach window, I gave that a moment's thought.

"Disappointed in the failure of the experiment, yet not sorry to have been present."

"Nicely put," said he. "I should say I felt the same. I was, however, disappointed in the behavior of our supposed host—but at this point, the less said about that the better."

With that I concurred, and our conversation then drifted aimlessly to Dr. Franklin's political position, a question much discussed during those days. Was his first loyalty to England, or to those colonies which paid him a salary to represent their interests in London? As an Irishman, Mr. Donnelly knew something of divided loyalties, yet he made no reference to his personal feelings in the matter—that would have been quite unlike him.

This took us to Number 4 Bow Street, where the driver came to a halt, and we climbed down. Mr. Donnelly paid off the driver down to the last penny and appeared ready to bid me a good night and make his way home.

"Why not come up?" I offered. "Though they've likely eaten dinner, there's sure to be enough left over to feed us both. You'll have the chance to meet our new cook, Molly Sarton."

He confessed he had no wish to go home and try potluck for

one, nor even less visit one of the rowdy dives surrounding Covent Garden; and so he happily accepted the invitation. We marched up to the top of the stairs and into the kitchen. There at the table sat Molly Sarton and Clarissa Roundtree, who served as Lady Fielding's secretary.

We were in luck. Dinner had been eaten, yet I was expected, and the stew left over for me was more than enough for two. So said Molly, in any case, as she poked up the fire to warm the pot. I sensed an immediate spark between the surgeon and the cook when I introduced them. As she stirred the stew, he stood nearby, telling her of our bootless journey to Portsmouth, yet making of it a great long joke, wherein he himself was the butt of the story. It was evident that he was attempting to charm her. She laughed. She smiled. She glanced neither left nor right but gave to him all her attention.

"Goodness," whispered Clarissa to me, "they've certainly hit it off, haven't they?"

A word about Clarissa: She and I had come to Sir John Fielding's household by way of similar paths. While I was popularly thought to be a "court boy" (one snatched away from a life of crime and put to useful work), Sir John perceived in my appearance as prisoner before him that I stood falsely accused. He opened his home and his heart to me, an orphan, and had treated me ever after more as a son than a servant. For her part, Clarissa was the daughter of one who would sure have been hanged or given transportation had he not been murdered by a criminal far more cruel and ruthless than he. She had escaped from the parish workhouse of Lichfield and would have, in the ordinary course of things, been returned there. Yet Lady Fielding, who had never had a daughter of her own, had formed such a great attachment to her that she would in no wise allow her to be sent back and she persuaded Sir John to allow Clarissa to stay on as her secretary. That was, if you will, a couple of years past, and it has taken Clarissa and me nearly that long to establish a modus vivendi. Now, however, we seemed to have done so. Indeed, our recent trip to Deal, during which we spent a good bit of time together, seemed to have sealed our friendship. In any case, I hoped that this was so.

"Where is Sir John?" I asked her. "Up in that little room he calls his study?"

"Oh no," said she, "he responded to a sudden call from Mr. Bilbo and went off to see him in the company of Mr. Bailey." She hesitated. "Bailey's his name, isn't it? The great, tall man who is chief of the constables?"

I nodded, yet still was I puzzled: "Mr. Bilbo is usually at his gaming club at this hour of the evening."

"Well, no longer, for it seems that he has sold it."

"Ah, so it has happened at last just as I feared it might."

"You know something about this?"

"I believe I met the buyer—a Mr. Slade."

"I know not if he were the one. I heard Sir John say to Lady Fielding that there were a number who were interested in buying the club from Mr. Bilbo, but one who had an advantage over the rest."

"And what was that?" I asked her.

"He had offered the most money."

"Indeed that sounds like the sort of remark Mr. Bilbo would make." Then did I frown and puzzle away at a question which I finally did put into words: "But why sell now? I don't understand."

"You don't?" Clarissa asked with a knowing smile. "Then try this. Lord Mansfield sent word to Mr. Bilbo that the trial date for Lady Grenville has finally been fixed."

"So the French ambassador was finally unable to bring her back to France?"

"It seems," said she, "that our friend Márie-Helene must stand trial in an English court. All would have been well had she not bombarded English soil."

"When must she surrender to the court?"

"I've no clear idea of that. In a day or two, perhaps. I should not be surprised if Mr. Bilbo asked Sir John to come and advise on what, if anything more, could be done to keep her out of court."

And if she appeared in an English court, she—a native of France—would be convicted, as Clarissa and I both knew. Márie-Helene, Lady Grenville, had undeniably been engaged in the smuggling trade with her husband; thus much was known by all. The matter was complicated, however, by the fact that Sir John's great friend, Black Jack Bilbo, had fallen quite hopelessly in love with her and, to keep her out of Newgate, had given his promise that he would deliver her up for trial when the magistrate required. Now, it seemed, he must keep his promise. I wished to ask Clarissa how Sir John was taking all this, but there our discussion ended, for Molly Sarton called me over to collect my bowl of mutton stew.

"Well, Jeremy," said Molly, "you and Mr. Donnelly indeed had yourselves quite an adventure, did you not?"

"Mr. Donnelly has told you all, has he?"

At that she laughed. "Oh, I'm confident that he hasn't. Still and all, from what I have heard, it sounds like the sort of lark my late husband used to love." She did lower her voice to add: "Though not near so dangerous." Then did the smile fade from her face. "Ah, you men," said she with a sad shake of her head.

But Mr. Donnelly would have none of that. He stepped forward, bowl in hand, for his dip into the stew pot. "Jeremy," said he brightly, "you should have told me you'd an Irishwoman in your midst. Had you done, I should have been here in a trice to welcome her to London."

I stammered out an excuse which was no excuse at all: "I . . . I . . . never knew that she was Irish." And having said that, I was reminded that Sir John did hazard when first we met her that she *seemed* Irish.

"But how could you think otherwise?" said he. "Hair the color of fire . . . eyes of cornflower blue . . . freckles . . . Why, she's the picture of Irish womanhood."

"Mr. Donnelly, please, you're makin' me blush," said Molly— and indeed she *was* blushing.

She giggled. I had never before, in the three months of our acquaintanceship, heard her giggle. Nor, for that matter, had I ever seen or heard Mr. Donnelly play the gallant. I was greatly puzzled by their actions. They seemed, ordinarily and separately, to be such sensible people. I carried my bowl of stew back to the table and settled in next to Clarissa. For her part, she seemed quite fascinated— and secretly amused—by their odd behavior. In response to my frown, she gave me a wry smile and a wink.

"Now, I believe," cried Mr. Donnelly from the other end of the table, "that is the best mutton stew that I have ever in my life tasted!"

"Ah, now, please do stop," said Molly to him, blushing still.

There was, it seemed, little could be done to halt him. Yet in a last effort to divert attention from herself, she cried out, "Clarissa!"

"What then, Molly?"

"You must show these two we have our adventures, as well. Tell them how you spent last night, child."

Now was it Clarissa's time to wriggle uncomfortably in her chair. She seemed not so much embarrassed as discomforted. This was clearly something she would prefer not to go into just at that moment.

"Oh, let it go," said Clarissa. "They'll hear about it soon enough—Jeremy will, anyway."

"Do please tell, Clarissa," urged Mr. Donnelly, then added, "I hope you were put in no danger."

"Oh no, nothing like that." She threw an uneasy glance at me. "It's the sort of thing that Jeremy attends to every week—or every day, for all I know."

"Well now," said I, "you must tell us." Though just at that moment I had no idea of what her "adventure" might have been, I would soon find out, for she seemed to take what I had just said as permission to proceed, and she did then begin to tell her tale.

I take the liberty here of retelling it in my own words, rather than attempt a verbatim account, for on this occasion, as on so many others in those days, she missed no opportunity to digress, diverting her own attention, as well as that of her listeners, to unimportant details and parenthetical events.

But now to her story: Clarissa was wakened in the middle of the night by Lady Fielding, who told her that she was needed by Sir John to accompany him to the residence of Lord Hillsborough where a burglary had taken place. Dressing hurriedly, Clarissa was ready to depart with him, and following the manner he suggested, she led the way down the stairs and out into the street with his hand placed upon her shoulder. Outside, in Bow Street, a hackney coach awaited them. Benjamin Bailey, the first of the Bow Street Runners, stood by and threw open the door to the hackney. He whisked them inside and jumped in after them.

As the coach moved them on toward their destination, Sir John did carefully explain to her the part she would play in the action that lay ahead. (Here I quote him, as she conveyed his words to us there at the table.) "Clarissa," said he, "as you know, I am blind. I manage to do the work of one with sight only with help, which is customarily provided by Jeremy. In his absence, I shall depend upon you to provide that help. In short, I ask you to serve as my eyes. When we arrive, I shall require you to describe to me all that you see at the scene of the crime. I shall prompt you and ask you questions. I shall ask you to be by my side when I interrogate any and all who may have information to give. I am capable of sniffing out all but the visible signs of lying. The smell of fear, the unsteady voice, the sound of the throat that must consistently be cleared, shortness of breath—all of these I can readily detect. But I shall depend upon you to tell me if there is overmuch sweating, or if there is an unconscious refusal to focus direct upon me whilst I ask the questions. Is all of that clear, Clarissa?"

Indeed it was. She must have done a remarkably good job of describing the place to Sir John, for she did a proper job of describing it to us—until she lost her way in a digression which took us to Bloomsbury Square for purposes of comparing its imposing facades with that of Lord Hillsborough's grand house in—or just outside— Whitehall.

(Clarissa said that she believed Lord Hillsborough's residence to be one of those by Inigo Jones. Molly wished to know who then was Inigo Jones and why he had such an odd name. It took me a bit of pleading to get matters back on track.)

The reason why she did concern herself with such matters was that the burglars had actually managed to enter by way of the front door. One of them (there were apparently only two in all) had been most adept with a picklock. As the night watchman made his rounds, timed roughly at five-minute intervals, the burglar worked upon the lock. It could not have taken long to gain entry, for there was no evidence of them having taken cover behind the shrubbery in the front of the house. Probably they were inside the house within five minutes—and probably a good deal less than that. Sir John had commented that such a bold entry by the front door was quite unusual. Oddly, none of the house dogs had barked.

Once inside, they did not have to roam about, looking for the right room. One of the two, no telling which, had acquired a bit of mud on the bottoms of his shoes, and it was possible for Clarissa to follow his track from the front door to their goal, Lord Hillsborough's study. It seemed certain that the burglars either knew the house well, or else had a detailed diagram of it.

It immediately became clear that while the burglars knew their way through the house, they had no notion of where to look for what they sought—nor perhaps did they even know exactly what they sought. Papers littered the floor; files were emptied; drawers were thrown about. All this could not have been done silently. Noise enough was made by them to bring one of the servants, a footman, from his station in the house. Though called a footman, he seemed also to have the responsibilities of a guard within the house, for he was well-armed. He was found upon the floor of the study with a pistol in his hand and another tucked into his belt. The back of his head was crushed. Sir John commented that he must have died instantly. He added that this, too, was highly unusual for burglars: They much prefer to enter and leave, their presence undetected and, if at all possible, their theft unnoticed. These were men in a hurry, so reckless in their haste that they were forced to kill in order to continue their search. And yet Sir John declared that he thought them experienced in their trade. "If nothing more," said he, "their entry through the front door proved that they were daring and resourceful—but desperate."

What could have been worth so much that they would dare to be so incautious? It was to the answer of that question that he had sought out Lord Hillsborough. But the nobleman was of no help at all. He appeared before Sir John in the study, wearing a dressing gown of lustrous black silk and an icy look of contempt. That expression turned to disgust as he stood in the middle of the room and surveyed the chaos upon the floor round his desk. Though he had been forced to step over the body of the footman in order to gain the center of the room, he gave the poor fellow little attention and no sympathy: What was left of him was now simply in the way.

"What will you, Sir John?" he asked. "There is but little of the night left, and I should like to use it to sleep."

"This should not take long," said the magistrate.

"Well, let's get on with it."

Nevertheless, Sir John was not to be rushed. Yet finally did he speak up: "This room has been described to me as being in a great state of confusion. Have you any notion who might have visited this upon you?"

"None at all. But then I have not many burglars or suchlike criminals in my circle of acquaintances."

"I suppose you do not. But you might have one or two who were so eager to have something of yours that they would hire men of that sort to get it for them. Now, I realize that it will take you quite some time to go through the contents of this desk—which, as I am told, are littered over the floor. Nevertheless, you may be aware of something in your keeping which is important to keep secret. You may have gone immediately to the place where it was hid just to see if it were still there."

"There was no such secret document or documents," said Lord Hillsborough, "and therefore no hiding place."

"Nothing of a personal nature?"

"No, nothing."

"Nothing that might be used to embarrass you? Or extort money from you?"

"Nothing at all, I tell you!"

"Well and good, well and good," said Sir John in the manner of a peacemaker.

"There is another matter, however. I know that you are a member of His Majesty's government."

"That is correct."

"I fear, however, that I know not which position you hold. Could you perhaps inform me in that matter?"

"I am secretary of state for the American colonies."

"Is that it indeed? Why, you must be kept busy these days, what with all of the trouble caused by the more quarrelsome of those colonists."

"That is so," said Lord Hillsborough.

"Could you then have had something in your possession to do with these colonial matters? Something, that is, which might invite a burglary such as this?"

"For the last time, I know of nothing that is missing. If, in making my inventory of the contents of the desk, I discover something missing, I shall notify you immediately."

"Please do. And Lord Hillsborough?"

A deep sigh, then: "Yes? What is it?"

"One last question: How did you learn of the burglary? I take it you were asleep?"

"Yes, I was. The butler, Carruthers, woke me to tell me."

"And how did he learn of it?"

"That you will have to ask him."

"Thank-you. That will be all I require of you for the time being."

And at that, Lord Hillsborough stamped out the door of the study, making no effort to disguise his annoyance at Sir John's rather direct interrogation.

Mr. Benjamin Bailey, as chief constable, had visited many such scenes as this one in the company of Sir John. And, having made his own investigations and asked a few questions, was ready and waiting with the butler, Carruthers, who had admitted the party from Bow Street; there was also another man, big and burly, who looked to be a footman, as well as he on the floor in the study.

Sir John and Clarissa went into the hall to talk with these men, and at that time the magistrate requested that the study be closed until the body therein could be delivered to the medical examiner for the City of Westminster (i.e., Gabriel Donnelly). The butler told them that he had learned of the burglary and the murder from the second footman, whose name was Will Lambert, waiting to be interviewed. It was the butler who sent word to Number 4 Bow Street to report the matter to Sir John. But that was about all that the butler told them. He had behaved well in an emergency, and he had done what needed to be done.

Mr. Lambert, however, had a good deal of significance to tell. It was he, after all, who had discovered the body of Albert Calder on the floor of the study and noted the chaos left behind by the burglars. It seems that Calder and Lambert had been charged with guarding the interior of the house each night for the past month; they were to be specially watchful round the master's study. When Calder had failed to wake up Lambert, the latter woke of his own accord and, noting the late hour (near three in the morning), believed something was amiss. He armed himself and—

That, as it happened, reader, was as far as Clarissa got with her narrative of the night before, for just then we heard heavy steps upon the stairs which led up to the kitchen where we were sat round the table. They were unmistakably those of Sir John. He reached the door, and without a pause threw it open. He marched into the kitchen. We all sat dumb before him. Thinking it only proper to offer some greeting, I rose from my chair.

"Good evening to you, Sir John," said I. "Mr. Donnelly and I have just—"

"Good evening?" he interrupted me. "Good, you say? I see nothing good in this evening. I'll be damned if I do." And so saying, he marched on past us, up the stairs and into the bedroom which he shared with Lady Fielding.

TWO

*In which Sir John
is forbidden access
to a state secret*

Within minutes, Mr. Donnelly had departed, and Molly had banked the fire. It was time for us in the kitchen to climb the stairs and proceed to our beds. I had seldom, if ever, seen Sir John in a mood so foul. It would not do for him to hear us buzzing and whispering there in the kitchen.

Weary in spite of the long nap I had had in the coach, I lay in bed in my small attic room high above them all. From the floor below, I could hear the voices of Sir John and Lady Fielding — his deep and rumbling in anger, and hers lighter, higher, and in a sort of pleading tone. I could hear the voices but not the words that were spoken. What might they be saying?

Next day, the three of us met once again in the kitchen. I was, as usual, the first to arrive. With shoes in hand, that I might not disturb Sir John and Lady F., I came quiet and knelt down to kindle a blaze in the fireplace; such had been my task as long as I had been there at Number 4 Bow Street. Having done thus much, I put on the water for a pot of tea. At about that time, Molly and Clarissa appeared, still groggy with sleep.

Tea was brewed. The loaf of soda bread baked for dinner, still fresh and light, was put out by Molly with a crock of butter. We ate and drank our fill and gradually came full awake as we whispered round the table.

"What do you s'pose has gotten into him?" asked Molly.

"Oh, it's to do with Black Jack Bilbo," said I, "of that I'm sure."

"Undoubtedly," said Clarissa.

"And it's all because of that woman, isn't it? I've little use for her myself. It's not personal, mind you now—simply because she took away my livelihood and turned me out of a place which had been my home for a good five years or more. Ah, no, for had she not brought her cook from France and sent me packing, I would not have met and married Albert Sarton. We were not together but a year—not even that—yet it was the best time of my life, so it was. So no, I don't see that I can blame her for personal reasons."

"What then?" said I.

"'Twas the way she set her hat for Mr. Bilbo there on the boat. She saw him as one who might rescue her from the god-awful situation which she found herself in. I've seldom seen a more bold and barefaced attempt to ensnare a man for reasons of personal salvation."

At that, Clarissa and I exchanged quick looks but said naught. From what we had seen there on shipboard on our return from Deal to London, the attraction between Bilbo and Mârie-Helene had been both real and mutual.

Molly caught the glances that passed between us and would not let that moment go unnoted.

"Ah, you two," said she to us. "I know, indeed I do, that she's won you over, as well. She's a charmer, she is, and no getting around it. But just remember what I've said, will you?"

I nodded soberly, but Clarissa simply said, "I will."

Then did we, all three, fall silent, and in that silence I heard stirring in that room at the top of the stairs wherein Sir John and his Lady slept. I wondered, would they emerge in the next moment or two and save us from this awkward moment.

But then Clarissa did rouse herself and announce—to me, in particular:

"I did not have the opportunity to finish my story last night."

"Ah," said I, "so you did not. What more have you to tell?"

"Simply this," said she. "I told Sir John when we left the grand residence in Whitehall that, in my judgment, Lord Hillsborough had not said a single word of truth all the time we had him before us."

"And how did Sir John react to that statement?" asked I.

"Oh, he jested with me. 'Not a single word?' said he. 'Surely something. Not even—oh, what do they call them?—the articles and the conjunctions?' Yet I stuck by what I said, even though I was forced to admit that Lord Hillsborough had neither sweated nor gone shifty-eyed."

"What then did you tell Sir John made you so sure?"

"It was his arrogance," said Clarissa. "He is that rare sort of liar who is so well-practiced at it that he tells lies as readily as the rest of us tell the truth. He feels neither worry nor guilt as we might. Yet, I must confess, I base this on naught but my feminine intuition. So I told him."

"And what was Sir John's reaction to that?" I asked her.

"Oh, again he jested, yet more in earnest than before, I believe. 'Tells lies readily? Feels neither worry nor guilt?' said Sir John, 'why, I believe you've found him out for what he is—a *politician!*' And at that he laughed in quite the most jolly manner."

By then I, too, was laughing—though a bit loud and lusty, I fear.

Next we knew, a knock came upon the door, hard and insistent, like that of one of the constables—and so it turned out to be. The laughter all of a sudden died in my throat, and I jumped up from my place at the table to open the door. It was none but Mr. Baker, jailer and armorer of the Bow Street Runners.

"Ah, Jeremy," said he. "The Lord Chief Justice, so I am told, requested the presence of Sir John and does so most urgently—so urgently that he's sent his coach-and-four to get him there quick."

"When will it be here?" I asked. "I'm not certain that he's yet awake."

"When? Well, it's down there in Bow Street right this minute, so you'd better get him up and let him know."

Having delivered his message, he gave me a wave and descended the stairs. I eased the door shut and called out, "Better make another pot of tea." Then did I rush up the stairs and pound upon the door to Sir John's bedroom.

The Lord Chief Justice was William Murray, Lord Mansfield. As such, he was nominally in charge of the administration of justice throughout the realm. This often put him in direct contact with Sir John, who as the magistrate of the Bow Street Court, settled disputes, sat in judgment upon lesser crimes and misdemeanors, and, after weighing evidence, bound over for trial in the higher court those charged with high crimes and felonies. Sir John's abilities and his reputation did exceed his office, and therefore Lord Mansfield often sought him out for advice and counsel and to undertake special missions for the Court. Thus had I traveled hither and thither throughout England in his company, visiting cities as far afield as Bath. Though naturally I said nothing of it, it was my hope that this sudden summons from Lord Mansfield would entail a trip of some sort to distant parts; for, reader, I must confess that I did greatly enjoy travel.

I wore my best. Once I had made Sir John presentable, I hied up quickly to my room and changed into the breeches and coat which Lady Fielding had just bought for me (complaining that if I would just stop growing, I would not need my store of clothes to be constantly replenished). Why did I feel it necessary to dress my best when I would more likely than not be given no notice whatever by Lord Mansfield? Well, there were sometimes men of distinction there — and one of them might sometime give me notice. I hoped to find employment as a law clerk eventually.

And then, of course, there was that nasty butler of Lord Mansfield's. He had been quite the bane of my life since the time I first arrived at Number 4 Bow Street and began delivering letters and messages to the Lord Chief Justice at his residence in Bloomsbury Square. I would never be denied entrance in the company of Sir John Fielding, but, at least, there would be no question that I properly belonged if I wore my best. In later years, I realized that the butler whom I so disliked had taught me the importance of proper dress.

Upon this occasion, I received not so much as a frown from Lord Mansfield's butler. Indeed it was quite the contrary. When he threw open the door and stepped back that we might enter, he gave an appraising look to my attire (which he had not seen before) and nodded his approval. Then did he lead us down the great hall to a door which I knew did open into the study of the Lord Chief Justice. He opened it. We stepped inside.

"Ah, there you are, Sir John. Do sit down. I've something to discuss with you."

"I'm gratified to hear it. I had hoped that we would not be pulled from our beds thus early only to sit here in silence."

I helped Sir John into his seat and then sat down in the chair beside him.

"Sorry about that," said Lord Mansfield. "But I must off to court in a short time, and this was best talked about in the morning, for there is a meeting in a short time that I wish you to attend."

"Oh? What sort of meeting?"

"I'll get to that in due course."

"That also is gratifying—but do continue."

"Night before last," Lord Mansfield began, as if about to tell a long story, "you visited the residence of Lord Hillsborough to investigate a burglary which had taken place there that very night."

"Indeed, I did. It was a rather extraordinary burglary in a number of ways. First of all, the burglars made their entry by way of the front door. Secondly, when they were detected inside the house by a footman, they were surprised by him in the act of searching through his master's desk. Or, rather, one of them was surprised, while the other dealt the footman such a blow upon the back of his head that he was knocked senseless—and dead. And, finally, it was an even more unusual burglary in that the victim, Lord Hillsborough, seemed not to know, nor even care what might have been stolen. He was, in any case, very reluctant to say, or even to guess, what was missing."

"I take it," said Lord Mansfield, "that you wish to solve this case?"

"Of course I do. Such a question."

"Well, I can help you in that, I believe, for I have persuaded Lord Hillsborough that if he truly desires to have restored to him that which was stolen, that he must give greater cooperation to you. You and your—what is it you call that force of constables you keep?"

"The Bow Street Runners."

"Yes. Well, I told him that you and they represent the only real chance he has of getting it back, whatever it is."

"Indeed I am pleased that you think so," said Sir John. "But I have a question for you, Lord Mansfield."

"And what is that?"

"You referred to the stolen object as 'whatever it is.' Don't *you* know what it is?"

"No," said he. "After all, I have no need to know."

"Is that how Lord Hillsborough put it to you?"

"Yes, dammit, but he's right. Tell too many and you'll hear all of London buzzing about it like so many bees round the honeycomb. Look here, Sir John, I've persuaded him to talk to you about this, and he has promised to be more forthcoming than before."

"Does that mean he'll tell me what's missing?"

"I don't know—probably it does, but you'll have to work all that out with him. There are, so I understand, certain restrictions."

"And what are they?"

"Again, I'm unsure of that. They are of the kind that anyone might use in handling secret matters of state."

"A state secret, is it? Well, this should be interesting."

"Interesting or no, Lord Hillsborough has agreed to meet with you . . . let's see . . ." from his waistcoat pocket he drew a round, fat timepiece, sprang it open, and studied its face somewhat myopically, "in approximately half an hour. You'll have no difficulty getting there, will you? If you like, I can send you in my coach."

"No," said Sir John, levering himself out of his chair. "It would not do to arrive early, and a bit of a walk might help me to recover from this dreadfully early rising hour." He turned toward me. "Jeremy? Shall we go?" He groped for my arm and found it. Together we started for the door.

"Oh, Sir John," the Lord Chief Justice called after us, "there is one more thing."

"And what is that?"

"That Frenchwoman."

Sir John's face seemed to darken as he turned back. "What about her?" His jaw set as he awaited the answer to his question.

"I shall try her on Friday, so you had best bind her over soon—though you may put it off till the next Thursday, if you like."

It took Sir John a few moments to respond. "I believe I shall put if off till then," said he at last.

"Your choice, of course. Good-bye then."

Sir John said no good-bye and wished no farewell. He simply urged me on. We raced the butler for the door. He barely managed to get it open before we arrived at it. We passed through without a word.

For more than half of our journey southward, I waited, trying
to suppose what might be going on within that mighty brain of his.
And though he gave no outward sign, I was fair certain that it was
Márie-Helene's day in court which had so sobered him; he was now
in the state we had seen him last night at evening's end. He must, I
told myself, feel a great sense of powerlessness. What a burden it is
for a man to carry when friendship does contend with duty. What
could Mr. Bilbo have said to Sir John? What could he have asked?
Did Lord Mansfield not know of the sense of loyalty and liking that
the two men felt one for the other? Did he even care?

Then, as if reading my thoughts, Sir John spoke up as one
might in offering excuses for another.

"Think not too badly of the Lord Chief Justice," said he, "for,
after all, he saved Mârie-Helene from the Maritime Court."

"Oh? How was that?" I asked.

"They wished to try her."

"On what charge?"

"Piracy. She would have been found guilty and hanged."

"A woman hanged for piracy? Has that ever happened before?"

"I believe so—sometime in the last century."

"Yet what proof was there of it?"

"Piracy has been defined as illicit trade—and that, they said,
was what she was engaged in."

"But . . . but smuggling isn't piracy."

"Of course not. What vexed them so was her barrage upon English soil—or English sand, as it happened. That was all the proof of
piracy they needed."

"Yet Lord Mansfield kept her from them?"

"He did, yes. And he's to be praised for it. But Mr. Bilbo would
give him no credit whatever. The man is impossible to argue with.
He kept saying over and over again, 'She shouldn't be tried at all. A
woman ain't got guilt the same as a man!' I know what he means,
and I must say that in some ways he's right. Women, in this society—perhaps in all societies—have what you might call 'diminished
capacity.'"

"We shall talk about that sometime," I urged.

"Oh, I'm sure we shall," said he, and then he fell silent once again.

By that time we were in St. Martin's Lane, just past the notorious Seven Dials, home to half the cutpurses and pickpockets of
London. Sir John walked safely there as few could, and I walked
safely beside him; his reputation saved us both.

Yet I was curious still regarding the coming trial. I put a few
questions to him. He answered them direct. Somehow that seemed
to steady him.

"On what charge will she be tried?"

"On whatever charge I put to her."

"Have you given some consideration to that?"

"Some. Perhaps not yet enough. But I suppose the charge will
be contrabanding, the same as her husband. That's what Lord
Mansfield expects."

"There were no victims, of course."

"Victims of that notorious cannonade, you mean? No, she did
naught with it but kick up some sand — thank God."

Again, silence. I had no more questions, and there seemed little
point to put to him frivolous interrogatives of the sort that are used
at dinner parties to keep conversation flowing. And so we simply
walked on, he grasping my arm at the elbow with one hand, and
with the other, exploring the territory ahead with wild swings of his
walking stick. Those along the way made room for him, as they had
to do. Still, he had something more to say on the matter.

"You must know the worst of it," said he to me.

"And what is that, sir?"

"The worst of it is that Mr. Bilbo will probably be called as a
witness for the prosecution."

"Against Márie-Helene?"

"Yes, of course. I told him this last night, and the man simply
went wild. Said he, 'You expect me to bear witness against the
woman I love?' And I said nothing. Indeed, what could I say? The
answer to his question is no, I don't expect him to bear witness
against the woman he loves. Yet if he fails to appear, or even if he
appears and refuses to answer certain questions, then he will be in
contempt of court. What then? What other course might he follow?
I tremble even to guess." We walked on. Sir John let forth a great
sigh. Then, did he remark: "Who would have thought that within

the breast of that old pirate, Jack Bilbo, beats the heart of a romantic?"

In this manner, we came to the residence of Lord Hillsborough. I had not viewed it before, yet there was no difficulty in finding the place, for it was the only house within Craig's Court. To the north was Charing Cross Road and to the south was Whitehall, that collection of grand buildings which housed the offices of the nation's government. I took us to the door, and thereon did I beat a sharp tattoo. A butler appeared, one who could have been brother—or at least cousin—to Lord Mansfield's gatekeeper: the same suspicious eyes, the same downturned mouth. I announced to him that Sir John Fielding of the Bow Street Court had arrived to fulfill an appointment made for him by the Lord Chief Justice.

"Of course," said he, stepping aside and opening the door to us. "I recognize Sir John from the unfortunate events of two nights past. If you will come this way, please." And then did he actually smile.

(All right, perhaps I had misjudged him. It sometimes happened that my dislike of a certain class of people—butlers being the best example—blinded me to the virtues of individuals within that class.)

He bowed politely at the door to a room which had the appearance of a study. There were books lining shelves that filled two of the room's walls, and there was a desk of large proportions—the same desk perhaps whose contents were spilled across the floor night before last. The man who sat behind it I took to be Lord Hillsborough; he had a long, narrow face which wore an expression of the sort that seemed to say he had just detected an unpleasant odor. Yet once inside, I was surprised to see another, younger man sitting to the left of the desk; he, it seemed, was more relaxed, more confident than the man behind the desk, in spite of his youth.

Both men rose at Sir John's entrance.

"Thank-you for coming," said the man behind the desk. "I hope I may be of greater help to you today than I was the other night."

"I hope so, too, Lord Hillsborough. But am I mistaken, or do I sense another here in this room?"

"You amaze me, Sir John. Indeed you do sense another present. He is Sir Thomas Dexter."

"Ah, the solicitor general. He must be here to ensure that you are not *too* helpful."

The two men laughed politely and in chorus at that; Sir John bowed in their general direction.

"It is a pleasure to meet you at last," said he who had been identified as Sir Thomas. "You were much discussed when I read law."

"That could not have been so very long ago, judging from the sound of your voice. May I ask, sir, what is your age?"

"I have attained twenty-five years, sir."

"Only that? Why sir, you seem a fair infant prodigy of the law. I believe I knew your father whilst I was in the Navy. He is Lord of the Admiralty, is he not?"

"Just so."

"Remember me to him, if you please." Then, after I had positioned him carefully so that the chair provided was directly beneath his backside, he took a seat. The other two returned to their chairs, and I, having nowhere else to go, took a post behind Sir John.

At a nod from the solicitor general, Lord Hillsborough cleared his throat and began: "As you may have gleaned from my welcoming remark, Sir John, I am prepared to be more cooperative than I was at our last meeting."

"That, at least, is a start."

"I must confess that on that occasion I was not altogether forthcoming."

"You knew, in other words, what the burglars were after?"

"Well . . . yes."

"Because you had already found that it was missing?"

"That's right."

"Was it something of value to you? Of course it was. But was it of value to the burglars? Monetary value? Not money, evidently, nor something that could have been sold immediately?"

"No, no, no," said Lord Hillsborough, "not money, nor something that could be easily sold. I believe I can make things considerably easier for you if I tell you that what was stolen could only have value to a very few men here in London. I would hazard that the burglars were, so to speak, hired to accomplish the theft."

"And who do you suppose would have ordered this done?"

Before Lord Hillsborough could respond, Sir Thomas cleared his throat sharply that he might catch the attention of the nobleman.

Once he had it, he rose from his chair and stepped across the short space which separated them, raised his hand to shield his lips, and whispered in his ear.

"That I cannot answer *at this time*," said Hillsborough, emphasizing the temporary nature of the stricture which had been placed upon him.

"But at another time soon?" queried Sir John.

"Perhaps."

"You seem determined to make this more difficult than it need be, my Lord. Why not now?"

"Because, sir," said the young solicitor general, "to answer that question we need the permission of one who is not at this moment readily available to us."

Oddly, Sir Thomas Dexter had not left Hillsborough's side. He stood by his chair so that he might be more immediately available to give advice.

"I appreciate your frankness, if not your lack of response," said the magistrate. "But perhaps now, since you've made clear to me your limitations, we can move through this a bit more quickly."

"I hope so," said Sir Thomas.

"Lord Hillsborough, you've made it rather clear what the stolen object was *not*, so perhaps now you can tell me what it was."

"It was a packet of letters."

"Indeed? Then I must repeat one of the questions I put to you the other night, and that is, to wit, whether these letters are of a private and personal nature, the sort that might be used to embarrass you?"

"No," said Hillsborough, dismissing the notion out of hand, "nothing of that kind—certainly not."

"Were you then the sender or recipient of these letters?"

"Neither."

Sir John seemed truly puzzled. "These letters must then have come into your possession in your capacity as secretary of state for the American colonies. Is that true?"

Lord Hillsborough was plainly annoyed at the question. He turned to Sir Thomas for advice—and received it. The two men huddled behind their upraised hands, buzzing away in whispers, first one and then the other. At last, fully informed, he turned back to Sir John.

"I must decline to answer that question direct," said he. "I can only say to you, Sir John Fielding, that His Majesty's government attaches great importance to the letters and to their recovery and wishes them returned to me at once. That, I believe, is all I care to say at this meeting."

"Well," said Sir John, rising from his chair, "since I was brought here specifically to hear what you had to say, and now you propose to stop talking, there is no point in remaining. I must say, though, that in spite of what I was led to expect from you by the Lord Chief Justice, I have gotten very little more from you than I did at my first visit here. Now I know what I did not know before, that I am to look for a packet of letters. How nice." Then, after no more than a pause for breath, he turned round in my general direction and said, "Come along, Jeremy, let's away from here."

I managed to push the chair aside and offered him my elbow. He felt the nudge I gave him and fastened onto me. But as we proceeded to the door, of a sudden he stopped, turned back to the two men, and spoke up once again.

"I shall put another question to you, Lord Hillsborough. You needn't answer it, for I believe I know the answer already. The question is this: Were you authorized to serve as custodian for these letters? Are there not rules against taking such important documents into your residence and keeping them there?"

"I . . . Well . . . I . . ."

"Just as I thought." And so did we set out again upon our path to the study door. It opened magically before us, and I knew then that the butler had heard all, as butlers will. Yes, there he was, bowing solemnly before us, closing the door behind us, then reappearing just ahead to lead the way. Not only had he sharp ears, he was also fleet of foot for one of advanced years.

'Twas at the door which led to Craig's Court that the butler paused and spoke out in a low, confidential tone.

"Sir John," said he, "there was a detail to the burglary which I failed to pass on to you. I don't know why I neglected to do so. Perhaps I was so upset that I —"

"Quite understandable," said Sir John, interrupting. "Events such as these have a way of disturbing one's equilibrium, so to speak, so that matters go forgotten and important details are overlooked. I've experienced it myself."

"Well, I'm not at all sure that this would be what one would call an *important* detail, but I could not help but note that the locks to this front door had been secured open with a stout strip of cotton. I discovered it thus unlocked."

"Hmmm, I know not if that be an important detail, but it certainly is an interesting one. And I thank you for passing it on to me, Mr. . . . Mr. . . . ."

"Carruthers."

"Yes, I thank you, sir."

So saying, Sir John bobbed his head in a proper little bow, which Carruthers returned as he threw open the front door and bade us good day.

I knew not the worth of that bit of information passed on to us by the butler, but it was plain that Sir John valued it highly. He bounced along beside me like a schoolboy off to holidays. I wondered at this and put the question to him. He responded with little more than a laugh at first.

"Really, Jeremy!"

"No, truly, sir, I'd like to know just why that oddment from the butler has excited you so."

"Well, how may I put this?" said Sir John. "First of all, it's physical evidence, and physical evidence is worth something—well, a good deal more than all those evasions and suspicions put forward by Lord Hillsborough. What did he tell us, after all? Only that a packet of letters was stolen—not who wrote them, who received them, nor what they concerned—simply a packet of letters."

Proceeding, he lowered his voice. As it happened, we were just entering the Strand from Charing Cross Road and were now part of a great crowd. Sir John must have felt that great gang of people milling about, and hoped to keep the matter quite between us.

"Yet consider," said he, "what we have just learned from that man, Carruthers. It *could* mean that the burglary was accomplished with the help of a confederate inside the house—that this ally had prepared the door in the manner described by the butler, in effect, leaving it unlocked for the burglars to enter whenever they might choose."

"But you do not think that, do you, Sir John?"

"I think it *may* be so, and it may well be worth explaining, but if it is not true, there remains the likelihood that the burglars themselves did this, either for a reason we do not yet understand, or as a sort of signature. I shall try to find if that signature has been left elsewhere on other occasions. And if we know that, we may know who they are. Now, let us make haste to Bow Street, for when we arrive, I have an onerous task to assign you. I dislike putting it upon you, but it is far too much for me."

He would say no more than that then, no matter how I plagued him to tell.

There were lesser tasks to perform before I came round to Sir John.

And when I did, he was in the company of his clerk, Mr. Marsden, going over the docket in preparation for the noon session of his Bow Street Court. I waited till he was done.

"You said you had a task for me, sir."

"Indeed I do. Take me to a quiet corner."

I did as he bade me, guiding him to a place secluded from the noise and unruly behavior of the prisoners in the strong room.

"Yes, this is much better, thank-you, Jeremy," said he. "I should like you to go cross the town to St. James's Street and deliver the news we received from the Lord Chief Justice this morn. You recall it, of course."

"Oh yes, certainly. Márie-Helene is to be tried upon Friday in Old Bailey, which means she must appear before you on Thursday."

"That is correct," said he. "But do not, I caution you, deliver this news in a manner so—well . . . so offhand."

"Oh no, indeed no, sir."

"And while you are about it, offer my apologies and my regrets that I was unable to deliver the information myself. Tell him . . . oh, tell him that I received the word from Lord Mansfield only this morning, that I had to attend at my court session, and so I sent you that he might have the news without delay. Do you have that, Jeremy?"

I assured him that I did.

"Well then, on your way— Oh, but there is this, too. Deliver the message only to Mr. Bilbo—not to your friend Bunkins, and certainly not to Márie-Helene."

"But only to Black Jack," said I.

"Only to him."

I bade him good-bye and slipped out of the door as a great many from the street poured past me and through the opposite door into Sir John's courtroom.

Reader, if l have left you somewhat in the dark with this discussion of smuggling, Márie-Helene, Black Jack Bilbo, and Sir John, then let me take a moment to explain.

It all dates back to a time a couple of months earlier that same year of 1773. Sir John had been dispatched by the Lord Chief Justice to the coastal town of Deal to look into sensitive matters of the magistracy, but he had soon become involved there in action against the local smugglers. Digging a bit, he had discovered that our host in Deal, Sir Simon Grenville, was himself deeply involved in the trade in contraband. Sir Simon had made an alliance with a family on the French side with a long tradition of what was known in Deal as the "owling trade." The alliance with Sir Simon was sealed by them with the marriage of Márie-Helene to Sir Simon.

Now, there can be no doubt that Márie-Helene, the Lady Grenville, participated most willingly in her husband's smuggling enterprise. After all, her father had been a smuggler, as had her grandfather and great-grandfather before him, all the way back to Roman times, no doubt. And, significantly, her four brothers were also in the trade. She, a tomboy from the time she escaped the cradle, took enthusiastically to their instruction. By the time she was offered to Sir Simon in marriage, she could handle a cutter, or a brig, or a sloop, as well as any of her brothers; she could heave a cutlass better than most; all she lacked was the size and strength of a full-grown man in the best physical condition.

All this came to a climax that night at Goodwin Sands, where Sir John trapped Sir Simon and his gang as they began to unload the brig which Márie-Helene had sailed over, filled with goods from France. She joined in the battle that ensued, ordering the brig's small-bore cannon fired in support of the smugglers on the beach. But then Black Jack Bilbo's armed sloop appeared, outgunning her two to one. The crew of the sloop boarded the brig. Only Márie-Helene offered any resistance, but she was soon overcome by Mr. Bilbo. On the voyage back to London, he fell in love as he had never before—according to my old chum, Jimmie Bunkins; and notwithstanding Molly Sarton's opinion to the contrary, Márie-Helene was quite as enamored of our friend Black Jack.

To spare her the horrors of Newgate Gaol, Black Jack persuaded Sir John to put Márie-Helene in his charge, giving his notice. The crew of her brig was returned to France, where the investigating judge dismissed one and all for "lack of evidence." Sir Simon Grenville was tried on a charge of smuggling and sentenced to three years in prison.

Now, time had come for Márie-Helene's trial. Since there was little doubt that she, no less than her husband, had engaged in contraband trade, she was sure to draw a term of no less than three years. Yet she had also ordered the discharge of cannon at English targets on English soil with lethal intent. There was no telling what punishment might be meted out for such an offense.

Thus did I consider all this and more in the course of my journey to Mr. Bilbo's residence in St. James Street. As I neared it, I found myself fair trudging along under the burden of my thoughts. I arrived and ascended the three low steps to the door, and I raised my hand to knock upon the door. But then, of a sudden, was I unable to follow through. My hand hung in the air as if struck by palsy. Did I really wish to deliver such a message? Those inside were my friends, no less than Sir John's. Yet a few days' notice had been promised them, and if I failed to tell them, they would be deprived opportunity to prepare for the ordeal, however one might manage that. No, indeed I had to tell them.

No sooner had I come to that decision, when the door opened wide, revealing my chum, Jimmie Bunkins. He looked at me queerly.

"What you doin' with your daddle up in the air like so?"

Embarrassed, I lowered my hand. "I was about to knock upon the door," said I.

"How long does it take you to decide? When I first spotted you through the window you was like that."

"Well, I've got a message from the Beak to your cove. I'm not sure I want to deliver it, but I've no choice."

"Oh," said he most glum, "I think I knows what it is, but I s'pose it must be delivered, no matter what. Come on in, and we can talk about it."

With a sigh, I stepped over the threshold and into the great hall. Bunkins eased the door to St. James Street shut behind him. He gave me a long look. It seemed that he, who was always quite loquacious, knew not what to say.

"I can't talk," said I. "I must deliver the message to Mr. Bilbo, and to no other. Is he here?"

"He's here, right enough, and I'll take you to him, but just say how many days we got. Or don't even tell me. Just hold up your crooks, and I'll count 'em."

I considered his request. That would not be telling, would it? As, for instance, if Sir John were to ask me, had I told anyone but Mr. Bilbo, I could honestly say, no, I hadn't.

"You won't tell anyone?"

He shook his head in a negative response.

I held up four fingers.

He gave a long, low whistle. "Only that?"

I nodded. "Keep your dubber mum'd," said I.

"Well, come along," said he. "I'll take you to the cove."

We walked together down the long hall. The house seemed strangely empty. It was the ordinary thing to hear voices from upstairs or down, doors opening or closing, all the little, insignificant noises that make a home of a house. I thought that strange, but stranger still was it to find Bunkins idle at this time of day. He should be at his studies with his tutor.

"Where's Mr. Burnham?" I asked.

"Ah, well, he's movin' on. That's as he puts it."

"Oh? He's pronounced you 'educated,' has he?"

Bunkins chuckled at that. "No, that ain't his way, as you well know. He says you can always learn more, and he trusts I will keep right on a-tryin' to do so. But he says it's time he ventured out into the world. The short of it is, Samuel Johnson put in a word for Mr.

Burnham and got him a job teaching at a school run by Monsieur Desmoulins—that's the one Johnson's man Frank Barber went to. It's somewhat out of London, so that's where he's gone off to."

By then we had reached the last door on the left, where I had expected to find Mr. Bilbo. Bunkins confirmed he was inside.

"Let me go and tell him you're here with a message—get him ready for the news."

Naturally, I gave my assent. He knocked softly upon the door and waited for the invitation to enter. When it came, he signaled that I was to remain.

"I'll tell him it's you with a message from the Beak," he whispered to me. Then did he slip into the room, closing the door after him.

Not only were things quieter here in this grand house, they were also altogether more formal. Or was it precisely that? Perhaps not. It may have been that a pall of secrecy had fallen over the house. It was as if, unknowingly, I had entered an area of signs and countersigns, passwords and paroles. It seemed I hardly knew this place I had once known so well. I wondered if Bunkins had divulged the content of my message.

But when he reappeared, I felt assured he had not. He held the door for me, and just as I entered the room, he whispered to me: "I got to watch the door. I'll see you when you leave."

Was he butler or guard?

When I spied Mr. Bilbo, so surprised was I that I halted for a moment, unable quite to believe what I saw before me. It was not that he had changed; his appearance was what it had always been— black beard, sharp eyes, balding head. No, it was not how he looked, but what he was about that took my attention.

He sat at the great desk amid many piles of banknotes and gold sovereigns. There were thousands of pounds piled upon the desk-top—tens of thousands, perhaps more than a hundred thousand. And there, among the stacks, half-hidden from sight, were those big-bored pistols which he ordinarily kept sequestered in his desk. He was counting his fortune, which was considerable, all of it laid out before him. When I approached and may have looked as if I were about to speak, he held me off by raising a finger and continued his silent counting.

As I waited, my eyes roamed round the room and stopped

suddenly when they met those of Márie-Helene. She stood at one of the windows which looked out upon the rear garden—yet she stared at me. She was beautifully dressed in a frock of French design, her hair perfectly set and combed. Having caught my eye, she nodded solemnly at me. It was a gesture, so it seemed to me, of great dignity. Then did she turn away and fix her gaze at the window. And so she remained through my brief interview with Mr. Bilbo, right up to the moment of my departure.

"Bunkins says you've a message for me. From Sir John," said Black Jack.

"Yes, I have, sir."

He looked me up and down, almost—but not quite—coldly. "Well then, Jeremy," said he, "let's have it."

I had thought it out beforehand, and so I managed to present it in good order—or so I supposed.

"Sir John was summoned by the Lord Chief Justice this morning, and among the matters they discussed was the trial date for Márie-Helene, Lady Grenville. The Lord Chief Justice has fixed it for Friday, the sixteenth of this month."

"Next Friday? We have but five days."

"Well no, not precisely."

"Say what you mean."

"There must take place beforehand an action in magistrate's court whereby she is bound over for the trial in criminal court. Sir John has fixed that for the day before the trial at Old Bailey."

"And so four days it is."

"Four days, yes sir." Then I remembered that I was to offer apologies and excuses. "Sir John wished to deliver this information to you in his own person, but he had to preside at his court. Because he did not wish to delay the news, he sent me in his stead."

Mr. Bilbo stared and nodded but said nothing.

I wanted to add something, something more personal. "Mr. Bilbo, sir, and Lady Grenville, I want you to know how sad I am to be the bearer of such tidings as these I have delivered."

"I know that, Jeremy," said Black Jack. "We blame none of you there in Bow Street."

Márie-Helene, who through all of this had stared steadfastly through the window at the brown and faded autumn garden, did turn to me at last, fixed me with her dark, glistening eyes, and spoke to me thus:

"Jeremy, will you bring here your friend Clarissa? I wish to see her before I go away. I feel she is my friend, too. Can you do this?"

"I can try. When do you wish to see her? It would have to be in the evening."

"Would tomorrow be possible?"

"I can send the coach for you," said Mr. Bilbo. "Say, tomorrow at eight."

"I'll see what can be done," said I. Then, with a bow to them both, I departed the room.

Bunkins awaited me halfway down the hall. He clapped me on the shoulder, turned, and accompanied me in silence to the door. Only there did we speak.

"How did they take it?" he asked.

"Well enough," said I. "Márie-Helene asked me to bring Clarissa here tomorrow evening. Black Jack offered to send the coach for us."

"That's good. So I'll see you again soon, won't I?"

"Surest thing ever."

"Good. I got some things I want to say to you, and now don't seem quite the right time."

Hearing that, I wondered what those things might be, yet I asked not and went upon my way. That house I thought I knew so well had changed. Those within it shared a secret. Though I suspected well what it might be, I thought it best to say nothing, for fear the whole truth might be told me, and like it or not, I should become part of their plan.

After dinner, with evening going swiftly to night, I sat with Sir John in the little room below my own, which he called his study. He reviewed the meeting with Lord Mansfield and our disappointing visit to the residence of Lord Hillsborough. And then, most surprisingly, he put a question to me.

"What do you suppose is in those letters, Jeremy?"

"In truth, Sir John, I have no idea," said I.

"Oh, come now, you must have some notion. Let us go over what little we know, and perhaps between us we can work out some sort of hypothesis on the nature of their contents. What did he tell us about them—about what they were, and what they weren't?"

I thought about that for a moment. "Well," said I, "he said they were not of monetary value."

"Yes, he declared that they would only be of value to a very few men in London. Notice that—'in London.' What does that suggest to you?"

"Why, the implication might be that the letters would be of value elsewhere, perhaps to many, in some other place."

"Exactly."

"Nor did they contain anything of a personal nature—according to him—the sort of material that would reflect badly upon him. He claimed there was nothing that could be used to extort money from him. He was very emphatic about that. And you, I noticed, accepted that without hesitation." I frowned at him. "Why was that, Sir John? Is he known to be of such exemplary character that such was quite out of the question?"

He laughed at that. "No, quite the contrary. He is of such notoriously *bad* character that there is naught that would be put past him. He has, so they say, left no commandment unbroken, and cares not who knows. But now, Jeremy, what more do we know about those letters?"

"That Lord Hillsborough was neither the sender nor receiver of them."

"Excellent. So what justification would he have to hold letters that were not his?"

"Well, as you pointed out to him, sir, the letter could only have been in his possession by reason of his position as secretary of state for the American colonies. And he said himself that the government attaches great importance to the letters and to their recovery."

"And so we find we have actually learned more about this packet of letters than I was at first willing to admit, do we not?"

"Yes, Sir John."

"Then in the light of all this, let me put to you again the question which started us out: What do you suppose is in those letters? Who do you think sent them and to whom? What are they about?"

"Just as an hypothesis? There is no right or wrong response to be made?"

"Just as an hypothesis," he agreed. "There could be no right or wrong to it. There can be only what is reasonable or unreasonable."

"Indeed now," said I, "let me consider."

And consider I did. I know not how long I took, for, after all, there was much to consider. For his part, Sir John kept silent. There was no impatient throat-clearing, no prompting, and certainly no call to get on with it.

He gave me time enough to form my hypothesis, and at last I came out with it.

"I would say that the key element, of course, is Lord Hillsborough's position as secretary of state. They may be of value to only a few in London, but could be of profound interest and therefore valuable to those in the American colonies. To say that the government attaches great importance to the letters and to their recovery is to say that the letters contain material that would be embarrassing to the government."

At that point, I halted briefly that I might think through what must come next. Then did I continue: "All who follow the news from those American colonies know that there has been much turmoil in that part of the world of late. There have been riots, and British soldiers have fired upon the rioters. The colonists have gone so far as to call one of these incidents 'the Boston Massacre.' Feelings, as I have read, run strong on both sides. Members of Parliament frequently accuse colonials of sedition and even treason. Nothing has been done to try any individual so far on such charges. But perhaps these letters, which Lord Hillsborough neither sent nor received, have to do with that."

"Oh, dear God, I hope not!" cried Sir John. It was as if the words had leaped from his mouth of their own volition. I had not even considered that possibility.

"But go on, Jeremy. Do go on, please."

"All right, to conclude then," said I, "let me offer this as an hypothesis. The stolen packet of letters are from some member of Parliament or, more probably, from a member of the cabinet, *not* Lord Hillsborough, to the Lord Chief Justice, asking him what might be done within the law to silence those loudest voices of rebellion in the colonies. There may have been a reply from Lord Mansfield, further inquiry on details raised by the reply—and so on. Three or four letters would constitute a 'packet,' wouldn't you say so, sir?"

"At this point, young Jeremy, all I can say is that you have frightened me quite to death, for who but I —"

Sir John was then interrupted by a knock upon the door below. He seemed almost relieved at the interruption.

"You get that, will you?" said he to me. "I shall sit here and consider the awful implications of what you have just suggested."

"But Sir John, 'tis just an hypothesis."

"Never mind. Go and answer the door."

The knocking had ceased soon as it began, which meant to me that either Molly or Clarissa had answered and were now considering whether or not the visitor were important enough, or the matter he brought urgent enough, to merit disturbing Sir John. The women of the house tended to be quite protective of him, his time, and his attention.

When I arrived in the kitchen, I saw that it was as I had supposed. Constable Perkins had penetrated no farther than just inside the door. There, Molly stood her ground, preventing him from going beyond that point by force of her considerable will. Clarissa was there behind her, fussing fruitlessly, offering to carry whatever news he had up to Sir John.

"'Course I remember you," Molly declared to Mr. Perkins as he attempted to push past. "You're the one-armed gentleman sat at my own table in Deal and celebrated with us all the downfall of that villainous baronet. And of course I'll let you up to see him soon as he says it's proper."

"I'll go!" declared Clarissa. "I'll go right up and tell him now what your news is."

"That won't be necessary," said I, as loudly and confidently as I was able. "Mr. Perkins is expected. Sir John sent me to fetch him up and save you the trouble — isn't that so, Mr. Perkins?"

"Oh, indeed so, Jeremy."

"And have you the answer to that puzzle we put before you earlier?"

"Yes, I have it right here." And, so saying, Mr. Perkins tapped his head with a great show of certainty.

Reluctantly, Molly stepped aside and left the way clear for him to join me. Clarissa, knowing me better, followed him suspiciously with her eyes as he crossed the kitchen and made his way to me at the foot of the stairs. The last I saw of her, she was looking dubiously directly at me.

I whispered to Mr. Perkins once we were out of sight and earshot: "There are times when a good lie, well told, serves better than the truth."

"It can save a good deal of time," said he.

Sir John who, I believe, had the keenest sense of hearing of any man alive, was chuckling with great delight when we entered his darkened study, as if to say to us that he had heard all. Yet he made no comment upon it.

"Jeremy, light a candle for Mr. Perkins, will you? You're the only one who'll abide my habit of sitting in the dark. I'm sure he'd rather a bit of light."

I reached for the tinderbox but was restrained by Mr. Perkins's hand upon my wrist.

"Don't bother," said he. "This should not take long and besides, I like sitting in the dark. It's restful is what it is."

"As you will then," said Sir John. "What have you for us, Mr. Perkins?"

"Well, it's this way, sir. When you gave us that little talk about that burglary in Whitehall, I got to thinking about it whilst I was out, and some of the details you described sounded pretty familiar."

"Which details?" asked Sir John.

"Why, the fact the dogs didn't bark and the tape that was left upon the locks. But I couldn't put it together myself, so I went to my favorite snitch, and put it all before her, and she says without so much as a blink-your-eye, 'No question of it, has to be Ned Ferguson and Tommy Skinner.' I've a question for you, Sir John. Did they go in the front door?"

"They did indeed."

"Well, that's Ferguson for you. My snitch says there ain't a better picklock in London, maybe in all the world, than Ferguson. He wants into a place, he gets into it in a minute or less. He's so proud of his work he leaves the locks taped just as a kind of calling card."

"A signature?"

"Right you are, sir. And while Ferguson is busy with the

locks, Skinner feeds the dogs with real meat—beef or mutton, whatever it is, whatever might keep them quiet. Tommy Skinner is also ready to provide muscle, as it's needed. Something must have gone wrong there in Whitehall, for he ain't killed nobody before. Too bad about that."

"Indeed it is," said Sir John. "What you've brought us is most welcome, let me assure you. All I can say, sir, is, bring in these two burglars, and I shall question them—the sooner the better."

THREE

In which Sir John seeks
Mr. Johnson's help in
planning a dinner party

The next day began in a manner quite like the one before it. Very early in the morning, even before I had had my morning cup of tea, Mr. Baker climbed the stairs to notify us that the Lord Chief Justice had once more sent his coach-and-four to bring Sir John to an early morning conference at his residence in Bloomsbury Square. The conveyance awaited him below, in Bow Street.

It fell to me to inform Sir John of this unexpected summons. I tried tapping upon his door, knocking, and finally pounding, before I managed to get some response. And then did it come from Lady Fielding, rather than from Sir John himself. Calling through the door, she promised to get him out of bed and into his clothes.

"It may take a bit, though," she warned. "He's still sleeping sound."

And, indeed, it did take a bit. It was near half an hour before he was up, dressed, and downstairs, slurping his tea and cramming buttered soda bread into his mouth.

At best he was a greedy eater; when he felt hurried, as he did that morning, he was like a poorhouse boy at Christmas, determined to eat his fill and more before it be taken from him. Yet I managed to separate him from the table at last with a reminder that Mr. Perkins might be returned with a bit of news of the two burglars.

Rising, brushing the crumbs from his waistcoat, he consented to go—but only if Molly would cut and butter another piece that he might take it with him in the coach. So it was—and though Mr.

Perkins was nowhere about, nor were Ferguson and Skinner in the strongroom, Sir John was satisfied that the constable would do all that need be done and permitted me to usher him out the door and into the waiting coach.

Once we were under way, he turned to me and asked, did I have some idea why this second early-morning invitation had been extended. When I told him I had none, he laughed somewhat bitterly.

"I put that to you," said he, "for you seem to have a talent for divining the worst possibilities, and I wanted to steel myself against the worst that could happen."

"What do you mean?"

"That hypothesis of yours kept me sleepless half the night. It is, if you will pardon me for saying so, all too reasonable. I ask myself how it could be that I, who knows these slippery blackguards who constitute His Majesty's government far better than you, could have neglected such a possibility as you have suggested."

"But sir, 'tis only an hypothesis, though as you say, a reasonable one."

"More than reasonable. I call it real."

I felt quite ambiguously about all of this. While I liked it not that I had given Sir John such a bad night of it, I was nevertheless secretly pleased that I had thought of something he had not. Was this wrong of me? I believed that, after all, what we had been involved in the night before was another of his exercises to teach me to think in the manner of a lawyer.

We finished our journey in silence. It was not such a long one, nor did our silence signify anger or hurt feelings. In truth, I thought that it was most likely that Sir John, having finished his morsel of buttered bread, had settled down for a brief doze. The black silk band which he wore round his head, covering his eyes, often made it impossible to tell if he were awake or sleeping.

Whether it was one or the other made little difference, for the moment we came to the residence of the Lord Chief Justice, and the wheels of the coach stopped turning, he was alert and upright.

The door to the coach was thrown open by the footman, and we descended to the pavement. And a minute later, we were in the house, following the detested butler to Lord Mansfield's study.

"Please sit down, Sir John," said the Chief Justice. "I've not much time, and I wish to get this done as quickly as possible."

I arranged the chair beneath the magistrate and tapped him to indicate that he might seat himself.

"That will suit me well," said Sir John.

"I have heard once again from Lord Hillsborough and from the solicitor general, whom I believe you met during your visit to Lord Hillsborough yesterday."

"It was a singularly unfruitful visit."

"Well, you'll not have to repeat it—not today, anyway."

"You know not how happy I am to hear that."

"No, I have been asked by them to urge you to continue your investigation and to suggest to you—and I quote—'in the strongest terms possible' to question Benjamin Franklin regarding the matter of the burglary."

"Benjamin Franklin?" echoed Sir John in a loud tone of exasperation, "what has he to do with this?"

"Quite a bit, if I'm to believe them."

"And do you?"

"That's neither here nor there, unless he appears before me and I hear the evidence against him."

"Evidence which I'm expected to assemble."

"Well . . . yes."

"Don't you think it rather an odd way to go about an investigation: to pick out the culprit first and then search about for the evidence to convict him? Who is conducting this investigation, may I ask? Is it you, Lord Mansfield? Is it the solicitor general? Is it Lord Hillsborough himself? Or someone higher—the prime minister, perhaps? Or—"

"All I can say to that, Sir John, is that I am not the one conducting the investigation. As for the others you mentioned, I can tell you that Dexter and Lord Hillsborough hinted broadly that they were simply passing on to me the wishes of another, obviously of one with greater authority than either one of them have. You mentioned the Prime Minister—yes, it could be he."

"Or another member of the Privy Council."

"That, too, is possible."

"In short, you don't know." At that Sir John paused. Then, in a more accommodating tone: "I don't mean to belabor this, Lord Mansfield, but you must understand my position. If I'm to be the cat's paw for another, I would like to know who that other is."

"I understand," said the Chief Justice. "I only regret that I cannot satisfy you in this regard. But do give me your assurance, sir, that you will question this man, Franklin."

"Well and good, I shall question this distinguished personage, but it will be at my own time and in my own way."

"Yes, yes, do it your own way, by all means. Do it any way you choose."

From the sly expression that lingered upon Sir John's face following this concession, I was fair certain that he had something planned. Yet what that something would be, I could not possibly, at this point, have divined.

"And now, Sir John, since I have twice routed you from your bed at an ungodly hour, let me at least see you back to Bow Street in my coach—unless you'd prefer to go afoot . . ."

"By no means," said Sir John. "Certainly I accept your offer. There remains something I should like to discuss with you. We could do so along the way."

"Excellent," said Lord Mansfield, rising from his chair. "Shall we then be off?"

Thus we went, Sir John at my elbow and Lord Mansfield leading the way. The butler was nowhere in sight until we arrived at the door to the street, and then did he pop out from a large closet and offer his master a cloak to wear against the morning chill. He assisted him in donning the garment, and then opened the door for us all. As I passed him, our eyes met, and he seemed to look upon me with a sort of benevolent amusement. I knew not if this were preferable to his unusual air of cold, aloof superiority. I decided that I should have to consider the matter.

Then up and into the coach, assisted by the footman. To be rich, I decided, was to be thought incapable of performing such mundane acts without help. Perhaps that was why so many of the wealthy behaved as children: They were treated as such.

We were well on our way when Lord Mansfield, who had been

running his hand idly over the upholstery of his seat, did suddenly sit erect and take notice of what he had encountered there.

"Good God," said he, "what is this stuff?"

He raised his finger with bits of white upon the tip, for closer inspection. "They look like . . ." He carefully tasted a few of the white bits. "Why, they are! They're bread crumbs. Now, who would be eating here in the coach? I'll wager it's that slovenly driver, Carling. That fellow is ever eating — ever and anywhere! Well, he shall hear from me about this. Indeed."

I was sorely embarrassed on behalf of Sir John. He, it was, who had spread the crumbs of soda bread where Lord Mansfield now sat. That I knew full well. What could I do or say to cover his crude misstep? Yet a glance in his direction told me there was no hope of covering up anything. He was just beginning to snicker, and well did I know that he would now progress from snicker to chuckle, and from chuckle to guffaw. And so it went precisely. In less than a minute, he was laughing so loudly and boisterously that the small space within the coach wherein we sat could scarce contain the noise of it.

"Whatever is the matter with you, Sir John?" said Lord Mansfield in alarm. Then did there pass a full minute in which the customarily dignified magistrate sought to bring himself under control. He did his best. Yet even so, there were a few times in which he lost himself utterly to laughter, and was forced to begin anew.

"I would only say to you, my lord" — and here he halted briefly, one last time lest he be overcome again with laughter — "I would say to you that your man Carling is not the culprit, but rather 'twas I, the slovenly magistrate, who spread crumbs all over the seat. So rushed was I to attend your meeting that I fear it was necessary for me to breakfast in your coach. I think, however, that I did no permanent damage."

Lord Mansfield, somewhat at a loss, cleared his throat, hemmed and hawed a bit, than said at last, "Yes . . . well . . . I'm sure no damage was done, none at all. Sorry to have made such demands upon you, but I've a long day in court today, and the sooner I get to it . . ."

"The sooner you'll be done, of course," said Sir John.

An uneasy silence fell inside the coach. Oddly, it was Lord

Mansfield, rather than Sir John, who showed signs of embarrassment. Perhaps a change of subject was in order.

"You said, Sir John, that there was something more you wished
to discuss."

"What? Oh yes, there is. I was wondering if you yourself are at
all familiar with the contents of these missing letters."

"Only in a general way."

"Meaning . . . what?"

"Well, meaning that they have to do with the American colonies
and naught to do with Lord Hillsborough's nasty pursuits."

"It has been suggested to me that since the letters no doubt
concern the talk of rebellion in the American colonies, and His
Majesty's government is so eager to have them back, they might
well have to do with a plan to silence the talk of rebellion by resort
to legal means."

"By what plan is that?" asked the Lord Chief Justice.

"By trying a few of the leaders on charges of sedition, or even
treason. Have you heard of any such plan? Perhaps been consulted
on how such might be made to work?"

Lord Mansfield gave that a bit of thought before replying in a
well-considered manner. "Nooo," said he, "I can't say that I have
been consulted on any plan of that sort. I must say, however, that it
is rather a good idea. There'd be nothing like a good treason trial
followed by a public execution to still those voices of contention."

"The reason I ask," Sir John persisted, "is that the suggestion
'in the strongest terms possible' that I focus my investigation upon
this man, Franklin, would seem to fit nicely into such a plan."

"Yes, wouldn't it."

"Benjamin Franklin may not be as noisy as Samuel Adams and
his faction in that place—what is it called?"

"Massachusetts," said I quickly.

"Yes," said Sir John. "Thank-you, Jeremy. Franklin may not be
as noisy as some, but he's right here in London—most of the time.
Ever so handy."

Alas, his irony was lost upon the Lord Chief Justice, who continued to appraise the hypothesis in muttered comments to himself.
At last, he looked to Sir John and spoke out in a manner most eager.

"Tell me, sir, who was it made the suggestion to you? I should like to tell him what I think of his plan."

"You already have."

"Already have? What do you mean?"

"Jeremy here offered it simply as an hypothesis—a mere guess—as to what the letters might contain. And in so doing, he gave me a most unpleasant fright."

"Fright? I don't understand you, Sir John. But in truth, I often don't."

"Now you have frightened me even more."

"But how?"

"By taking it all with the utmost seriousness, by thinking it rather a good idea."

At that, Lord Mansfield simply growled and said no more. The rest of our journey passed in silence. When it ended in Bow Street, he offered no more than a curt good-bye.

Once inside, Sir John swept down the long hall, as I trailed in his wake. He called out a loud hello to Mr. Marsden and asked how the docket looked that day.

"Barring a riot between now and noon," said the court clerk, "it looks to be a light day."

"Excellent, Mr. Marsden, excellent. I've a few things to attend to before court time." And, over his shoulder, to me: "Come along, Jeremy. I must dictate a couple of letters, and then you must deliver them."

Between the writing of the letters and their delivery, the rest of the morning was consumed—and a bit of the afternoon, as well. The letter to Samuel Johnson required special pains, for, in effect, Sir John asked in it that the great man cancel any and all plans that he may have made for tomorrow evening and come instead to a small dinner party that he was giving for Benjamin Franklin. Did Franklin know of this? No, he did not. In fact, Sir John was depending upon Mr. Johnson to persuade Franklin to come along to the party. He might tell him that "something special" had been planned for him, and indeed it had been. Sir John asked for Mr. Johnson's support in this, and his trust, as well. He concluded the letter: "I would not presume upon our acquaintance in this manner if I felt there were any other way of assembling the players at this rather serious game. You know Franklin, I do not; therefore I must depend upon you. For your part, you may depend upon this: though Franklin may have some uneasy moments during our table talk, he would find it far more uncomfortable if I were to handle this in any other way." This was then followed by the usual florid close.

A letter of invitation of a simpler and more direct sort was also dictated to Benjamin Franklin. It was to be given to Samuel Johnson that he might deliver it in person and use his justly famed powers of persuasion to induce the colonial gentleman to attend this occasion.

"Can you think of any other, Jeremy, whom we might invite? I'd say we have room for one more."

"Someone, perhaps, with an interest in science, and even some knowledge of Mr. Franklin's experiments?" I suggested.

"Exactly right."

"And yet with enough wit and gift for phrases that might acquit himself well in such company?"

"Perfect," said Sir John. "Do we know anyone who would meet that description?"

"Indeed we do. Our own Gabriel Donnelly is himself a man of science. He quite surprised me with his knowledge of Franklin's earlier work whilst on our recent trip to Portsmouth. And do we know another with his gift of the gab?"

So it was settled. Sir John hurriedly spoke forth a third invitation, this one to Mr. Donnelly. I copied it down, then hastily prepared all three for distribution to their intended recipients.

"See to Mr. Johnson first," said the magistrate, "and if he is in the least encouraging, leave with him the letter of invitation to Mr. Franklin. Visit Mr. Donnelly afterward, and you may be able to get from him the report on that poor chap who was murdered in the course of that burglary of Lord Hillsborough's residence. He promised it for today."

"He's usually quite dependable."

"He is indeed."

With the letters tucked into my pocket, I set off for Johnson's Court (which in no wise was named after its most celebrated resident), determined to do all that I could to persuade the great lexicographer to collaborate with Sir John in this endeavor.

I've no idea at what precise hour I arrived at the house in Johnson's Court. It was, in any case, near noon, and I found, much to my consternation, that the head of the house had only some minutes before awakened and would not be available for some minutes more when he took breakfast. Frank Barber was away on an errand, and so was not about to keep me company. I had no choice but to sit and wait. And as the minutes ticked by on the large, standing clock in the hall, my mind went back to the theft of the letters. The more I thought upon it, the more certain it seemed to me that they would not be recovered unless we were given to know what those letters contained. I could come up with further hypothesis regarding them, yet what good would it be unless we knew what actually was in them? Still, I entertained myself by considering possibilities other than the one with which I had frightened Sir John, each one more daft than the last. The only possibility which seemed in the least practical was that the letters in question may have been from Lord Hillsborough's predecessor to the Prime Minister, advising him to take certain actions which, if they were known to the colonists, would certainly not make them happy. Unless Ferguson and Skinner were located, and a case could be made against them, there would be no telling who had contracted to have the burglary done. Obviously, there were people in the government (how many? who were they?) who believed that Benjamin Franklin had put the two professional burglars up to it, and perhaps had made a map of the Hillsborough residence and had given a description of the letters to be taken. Yet save for a hearty dislike of the man, what reason had Franklin's enemies for thinking so? Who knows? If they had such a reason why had they not confided it in Sir John? And what contacts had—

"You're waiting to speak with Mr. Johnson, are you?" The woman who had let me in had returned from the interior of the house.

"I am, yes. I have a letter to deliver, also."

"Well, come along. He'll see you now."

She led me down a short hall to the breakfast room, which I had visited before, though not often nor recently. It seemed I met Mr. Johnson only on occasions when he was eating. This may seem stranger to you, reader, than in truth it was, for there were so many occasions during the day on which Samuel Johnson had before him a plate of something at which to nibble or snack, or a full meal. Thus did he appear always to be eating.

And, as a result, he was quite the largest man I knew. And by this I do not mean that he was merely stout or fat, for he was taller than most and had, in his own way, quite a powerful bodily structure. Yet he was in no wise physically attractive. The skin of his face was of a rubicund hue, roughened and pitted as a result of a childhood bout of scrofula, which had also left him blind in one eye. Still, he was a man who had to him a great sense of presence. Those who knew him not would pass him on the street, turn, and look back at him, knowing they had passed one of some importance. Even those who read no books at all knew him as "Dictionary Johnson," as a salute to the great work he had done years before in assembling his great lexicon of the English language.

And though, in the beginning, he took little notice of me, he had manifested greater interest when he learned from Sir John that I was reading law with him. On one occasion, he had taken me aside and informed me that it had been his first and dearest ambition to be a lawyer and that therefore he wished me the greatest success in my chosen field. Ever after he had spoken more freely to me and addressed me by name.

"Ah, Jeremy," said he, "it's you, is it? Poll Carmichael said there was a lad with a letter for me. She didn't say it was you, however. Perhaps she doesn't know you by name."

"Perhaps not, for I cannot say that I know her."

"I'll introduce you. But here," said he, "would you like a bit of this?"—indicating the great pile of johnnycakes and hen's eggs before him. "I can't possibly eat it all."

I declined and then watched him consume all on his plate with ease. However, I did accept his invitation to sit down.

"Well, you have a letter for me, do you?"

I withdrew the letter from my pocket and handed it across the table to him. He took it, broke the seal, and brought it up close to what I have heard him refer to as his "good eye." Then did he scan it quickly and lay it aside.

"Now you must tell me, just between us two, what is this all about?"

What indeed? I blurted out something, unconsciously using some of the same phrases Sir John has used in the letter.

"No indeed sir, that will not do at all. You need not rehearse the letter's contents for me. Tell me what is behind it."

I sighed. Sir John had not told me what might be said and what might not. Therefore, he had left it to my discretion, had he not? Secure in that, I told Mr. Johnson quite all—from the burglary of a few nights past to what had transpired that morning during our meeting with the Lord Chief Justice. I left out nothing of consequence. My listener had paid me the compliment of attending closely to every word I said—even though he continued to bite, chew, and swallow through it all. At last I finished, nodded to indicate as much, and waited for him to speak—waited, that is, till he had gulped down the last bite and might lay aside his knife and fork. "Bravo," said he, "an excellent summation of a deviously involved tale—well organized and well told, too. And now I understand better the reason for—nay, sir, the necessity of this hastily organized dinner party."

"Sir John merely wishes to put questions to Mr. Franklin in a more comfortable setting than the usual," said I. "It is out of respect for this distinguished gentleman that he wishes it so. After all, what might he think if a constable were to call at his residence and take him away without so much as a by-your-leave?"

"And wouldn't Mrs. Stevenson be dismayed!"

"Who is she?"

"Oh, never mind. Now, Jeremy, if I understand that letter properly, you've a letter of invitation with you for Franklin. Is that correct?"

"It is, sir."

I dove once again into my capacious pocket and pulled out the letter for Benjamin Franklin. That, too, I handed over to Mr. Johnson.

"Though I have little sympathy for those 'Sons of Liberty' and their cause, I like Franklin personally and would not have him punished for their sins. Furthermore, he is rather a good writer, and such poor wretches are altogether rare and should be protected."

"A good writer, you say sir? In which publications do his writings appear?"

"Oh . . . in various newspapers and gazettes," said he. "Yet he follows the custom of signing his letters and short essays with various noms de plume to do with his associations — 'a New England Gentleman,' 'an American,' — that sort of thing."

"An American?" said I. "I do not believe I have heard that as applied to . . . people. Do they no longer name themselves Englishmen?"

"Some do not. It's the influence of that Sam Adams, I've no doubt."

"Hmmm," said I, considering. Though interested as ever in matters pertaining to the colonies, I often did not fully understand such news, especially lately.

"But I believe," said Mr. Johnson, "that I may be able to win Franklin's cooperation with Sir John's plan. He has been dropping hints that he would like to be invited to the Thrales', so I shall drop a hint of my own that attendance at Sir John's might win him a place at Hester's table. She is doubtlessly the most popular hostess in London and I daresay it's all because of me."

"Well," said I, "the matter is left in your hands then."

"I shall do all any man can, but shall send word later today of my success or failure."

"I'll inform Sir John of that."

I rose and, after a proper bow, prepared to depart.

"Oh, and Jeremy, let me say again that I thought that quite an excellent summation. I've no doubt you'll make a fine lawyer."

Having knocked loudly and often upon the door to Mr. Donnelly's surgery, I had about decided that I should have to return to Bow Street and make another attempt to deliver his invitation later in the day. Yet just as I was about to leave, I heard a noise from deep within his chambers, which sounded ever so much like something shouted. What was shouted I could not possibly say, but I thought it best to wait a bit longer and see what might occur. And having thus decided, I knocked no more and did bide my time till at last I heard footsteps cross the rooms beyond. The key turned in the lock, and the door swung open, exposing Mr. Donnelly to view. He raised his hand in greeting, and I could not but notice that it was generously stained with blood, as was its fellow. If he were to appear below, in Drury Lane, just as he was at that moment, he would most certainly have been set upon by a host of right-minded Londoners and accused of bloody murder ere he walked ten steps.

"You have not, I hope, been busy amputating the limb of some poor soul," said I.

For a moment, he appeared quite puzzled by my remark. But then his eyes brightened with understanding, and he held up both bloody hands, and he laughed.

"No, the patient is dead and has been for a couple of days, I fear," said he. "Even starting to smell a little."

"Is he indeed? Well, perhaps I'd best come back another time."

"Oh no, I've a lesson in anatomy prepared for you, and you came at just the right moment to take it in. Come along."

He led the way through the anteroom, in which his patients awaited his attentions. (It was, or course, deserted at that moment.) Then on into the treatment room, where the body of the footman was laid out upon a table, face-down. I thought that strange for the moment—until I noted the gaping hole of near two inches in diameter at the base of his skull.

"Now, tell me, Jeremy, how many brains have you? Indeed, how many has anyone?"

"Why, one, of course—only that."

"Not so," said Mr. Donnelly. "There are actually no less than three."

"Three? But where are they kept?"

"Well, the large brain, which they call the cerebrum, is the one we think with. It's that which we consider our one and only brain. But under here—can you see that?—this is what they call the cerebellum."

"And what does it do that the other does not?"

"Well, I believe, though there are not many with me in this, that it handles all manner of bodily movements. If you decide to run, it allows you to do that. It manages your muscles so that your legs and feet don't become hopelessly tangled. There are all sorts of simple and complex motions that it manages for you."

"Doesn't that cover it all?" I asked. "Thinking, moving about . . . what more would there be?"

"A good deal more. Do you see this long, pulpy section here? It's a bit messed about, I fear, for two bone chips from the skull were driven into it by the blow that killed this poor fellow."

"And what do you call it?"

"The medulla oblongata."

I laughed in spite of myself. "Forgive me," said I. "The sound of it struck me as funny."

"Hmmm. Never quite thought of it that way."

"And what does it do?"

"In a way, it has the most important functions of all: those which take place inside the body and must proceed without our willing them to continue."

"I don't understand," said I. "What would they be?"

"Well, if you had to think your way through each heartbeat and every breath you took, you'd soon be dead, wouldn't you? As soon as you fell asleep, you'd lose your ability to keep concentrating on breathing, on keeping your heart pumping, on all those other necessities—and when you did that, you'd be dead."

I paused, giving all that he had told me due consideration. "I am curious about something," said I at last. "You said, when you were talking about the . . . ce-re-bel-lum, that there were not many who would agree with you? All that you've said seems perfectly logical to me. The separate parts of the brain have separate functions. Others believe—what?"

"That the brain functions as a single unit."

"But you've proven them wrong."

At that he smiled. "No, not exactly *proven* them wrong. It is naught but a theory. But I believe I *could* prove them wrong."

"And how would you do that?"

"I'm thinking of writing a paper and submitting it to the Royal Society of London."

"What a grand idea," said I.

"Yes, well, I've been persuaded by the example of Benjamin Franklin. He has no noble patrons, no university connections, and yet using his native intelligence and powers of observation, he has made some valuable scientific discoveries and conducted valuable experiments."

"Well, I suppose, by and large you are right, though I can't say that one down in Portsmouth proved of much value."

"We have not yet heard the end of it," said he. "Something may yet come of that oil-on-water theory."

"Perhaps," said I. "But tell me of the paper you wish to write."

"Well, you've heard the theory. And I have quite a marvelous anecdote, but as yet I have not thought how an actual proof of the theory might be managed."

"You say you have a marvelous anecdote? Tell it to me, by all means."

"Well, it was quite the most interesting thing I'd seen during my years as a Navy surgeon. I'm surprised I hadn't told you of it before. I haven't, have I? The fellow who had the top of his head blown off?"

"Sounds like a grisly tale if ever I heard one. Let me hear it please."

"Well, the frigate wherein I served, the *Advance*, was not in many battles, as such, but we did take part in one during the blockade of the St. Lawrence River. We were there, just north of Nova Scotia one spring, taking our turn with another frigate, the *Fortune*, when quite early of a spring morn a whole flotilla of the French came at us from the east. They'd just crossed the great ocean and had a fair wind in their favor, and they were determined not to allow a pair of frigates block their way. As I was told, the French had three frigates of their own in that convoy, as well as a ship of the line that mounted seventy guns, at least, and all the cargo ships were well-armed, too. They came at us out of the fog, just as the fog was burning off—and that put our gunners at a great disadvantage, for they had the early morning sun in their eyes.

"Not to make too long a story of it," Mr. Donnelly continued, "for there's not much glory to tell, the plain truth of it was that they were too much for us. We sank one of their frigates, set another burning so badly that it had to be abandoned, and one of the cargo ships was put out of commission. But that ship of the line, it played holy hell with us. There was little we could do against all those cannon. We were outmanned and outgunned. The *Fortune* went down swift and took half her crew with her. And while the *Advance* stayed in the fight longer, what with our decks being raked, our masts coming down, and our rudder damaged, we were forced to retire and fortunate to get away.

"Well, little of this did I see with my own eyes, for by the time the shooting started, I was down in the cockpit with my surgeon's mates, none of whom knew much, amputating legs, feet, arms, and hands, as the wounded were brought down to me. Amputation, you see, Jeremy, is the one sure treatment in battle; you may be doing too much, but at least you're doing something for the poor, bleeding wretches. I do recall that among the last brought to me—pulled off the deck he was, with little hope for him—was one who was wounded so badly I could scarcely believe that he still breathed. I daresay you can hardly picture this, but the top of his head had been taken off as neatly as if the fellow had been trepanned—skull, skin, hair, and a good bit of his brain, as well. It was possible to reach into the top of his head, what was left of it, and touch what was left of his brain, and in fact I did so as I tried to clean out the bits of skull and what-all, which littered the bloody, pulpy mass which was inside. But the medulla oblongata, which is deepest beneath all the rest, had gone uninjured and untouched. I saw that he breathed quite regularly. I put my ear to his chest and heard a strong heartbeat. The fellow was physically well, except that he had only half a head left."

"What could you do for him?"

"Very little. I bandaged up the great, gaping hole, and we laid him aside. It was as if he were asleep—and sleeping rather peacefully, too."

"But what about his—how do you say it?—his cere-bellum? Could he move?"

"It seemed to me that he could not initiate movement. He could not get up and walk away, for the part of him which could decide to do that had been destroyed, even though he was probably physically capable of doing so. But when I was given a minute or two alone with him, I took it upon myself to move him a bit, one way or another, and each time he moved himself back to the position he had originally held. It was as if he were sleeping."

"Were his eyes open?"

"Yes, but there was no light in them, no sign of consciousness.

It seemed to bother some that his eyes stared out in that unseeing way, and so eventually I closed them."

I had never heard such a story, nothing in the least like it. Yet there was more to know, questions I had to ask.

"What happened to him? Does he live yet?"

"I went to the captain with the problem. At first he wanted to hear nothing of the wounded, for, after all, it was his responsibility to bring a badly damaged ship back to port. That occupied him completely. But when I told him *how* the man was wounded, he was fascinated and asked to know what would happen to him if he were kept just so. How long would he survive? Not long, I told him, for I had already considered the matter—about as long as it would take him to starve to death or die of thirst. 'That's all he can look forward to?' I assured him that that was so. 'Then dump him over the side with the rest of the dead, after the chaplain has said his prayers over them.' Those were the captain's exact words—'with the rest of the dead'—they expressed the situation perfectly, for though the man without a cerebrum breathed well and had a strong heartbeat, he was nevertheless by all other measure a dead man. He was buried at sea."

I thought long upon the tale I had been told. There were moral implications, as well as medical, to this strange story. To me it seemed apparent that with it, he had proven his theory of the separate functions of the separate sections of the brain. Yet when I declared as much, he shook his head almost sadly.

"Ah, if it were only so easy, Jeremy," said he. "In truth, I have no idea how one would go about proving the theory, save for destroying, piecemeal, the brains of a number of poor fellows. If I could only get to Benjamin Franklin and talk with him at some length about it. Perhaps he would have—"

"Mr. Donnelly," I said, interrupting, waving his invitation under his nose, "I may have the answer to that problem."

"What then? What have you there?"

When I explained, Mr. Donnelly rejoiced. He accepted the invitation with pleasure and seemed not in the least dismayed when I told him that all depended upon Samuel Johnson's powers of persuasion.

"I have not the slightest doubt that Mr. Johnson will be able to bring the guest of honor round to your table. Mr. Franklin likes a good meal as well as the next man—or so I hear—and since that new cook of yours cooks as well as she looks, he'll be well fed. Oh, and by the bye, as I recall, Sir John has a very democratical table, does he not?"

"He does indeed. We all sit together, the cook along with the guests."

"Yes, well, do what you can to get me seated next to her. I should like to have gotten to know her far better that night we met."

"I'll do what I can."

A knock came upon the door in the next room.

"I must be rid of you, Jeremy. The report to Sir John is there on the cabinet. If you would let in the men from the mortician as you go, I would be greatly obliged to you."

"Ah, then the body's not bound for a potter's-field grave."

"No, Lord Hillsborough bought him a proper funeral."

"That's the first good I've heard of the man yet."

Clarissa and I were both surprised when Sir John gave his permission that we might accept Black Jack Bilbo's invitation to visit him and Márie-Helene that night. What surprised us was that he had given it with such alacrity. His only concerns were two: that we travel there by some safe means of conveyance; and that we not tell Lady Fielding of our visit. He was reassured when he learned that Mr. Bilbo was sending his coach for us, and he gladly took our word that we would tell neither Lady Fielding, nor Molly Sarton, nor anyone else.

"Why do you not tell them," said he, "that I have sent you two off to the Drury Lane Theatre to see David's production . . . of . . . what *is* he now doing?"

"I believe 'tis *The Merchant of Venice*," said I.

"You've both read it, have you not?"

Clarissa and I agreed that we had.

"Well then," said he, "you should be able to answer any questions put to you about the story—how it ends, that sort of thing."

Again, we agreed.

"Tell them, if you've a need, that it was in the nature of a reward for some specially commendable work you've done for me — oh, on this burglary, the missing letters, et cetera."

"What sort of commendable work?" Clarissa asked.

"Oh, I don't know. You'll think of something. You've a good imagination, and so has Jeremy."

And thus it was arranged. We descended the stairs promptly at eight and found Mr. Bilbo's coach waiting for us below in Bow Street. The footman hailed me by name, for we had met often and under all manner of circumstances. Then he did hop down from his perch and open the door for us with a bit of a flourish. As I passed him, accepting a boost at the elbow, he offered me a wink and a smirk. Why did people always seem to find it necessary to leer, smirk, wink, roll their eyes, and otherwise make strange facial contortions whenever they spied a lad my age in the company of a girl Clarissa's age?

We settled in side by side, and she put round her wrap to keep her bare arms warm. I wondered why she had not dressed warmer. She should have worn a scarf, as well, for, after all, even wearing the wrap, her bosom, of late a bit more prominent, was left half-exposed. Women were like that, were they not? They never seemed to wear sufficient clothing, nor did they think sufficiently ahead to bring along what they might need for warmth later on in the evening. Instead, they preferred to snuggle and complain of the cold — just as she was doing at that instance. As we got under way, I thought it best to involve her in conversation, do whatever must be done to keep her at bay.

"Why do you suppose Sir John wanted us to withhold from Lady Fielding our intentions to visit Mr. Bilbo and Márie-Helene?" I asked, finding it needful to clear my throat a time or two as I spoke thus.

She leaned forward and looked at me direct. (Truth to tell, she was a bit shortsighted even then.)

"You know, Jeremy, she's been behaving a bit strange lately. I would put it to her worries about her mother's condition. She came back from York declaring that her mother was past the crisis, and she thought it time to return to Sir John and her family — meaning us, which I thought quite nice of her to say. But no, I don't believe her mother is well. She has a tumor, and they are not got rid of so easily."

"Indeed not," said I, remembering the long suffering of the first Lady Fielding. "She seems to go up to bed earlier each evening. She says she reads."

"I've heard her voice at night. She's either talking to herself . . . or praying."

"But to address that question with which we began, I really can't say *why* she should object to our visiting Black Jack Bilbo. She seems to like him quite well, thinks he's rather a rogue, a scoundrel, nevertheless a lovable one."

"Ah, but Márie-Helene—that's another matter, entirely."

"I wonder what Lady Fielding has against her—not to mention what Molly might."

"With Molly, no matter what she may say to the contrary, I feel certain her anger at the woman is all personal."

"Not that she hasn't reason."

"Oh no, certainly not."

"It's just . . ."

"Right. It does no good."

We fell silent. There was little more to say on the matter. Clarissa leaned back again and nestled against me. She was most aggressive. She went so far as to incline her head upon my shoulder, which made me most uncomfortable. Not physically, of course. Yet when we went from the Strand to Charing Cross, the road went bumpy, and she was forced to lift her head from its place.

"My goodness but you do have a bony shoulder, Jeremy!"

"I can scarcely help that now, can I?"

If I could only think of something to say, this would be the time to introduce some new topic of conversation, anything to divert her from her foolishness.

"Well, I suppose not. You eat enough for two as it is."

Then came a sudden inspiration, a question which might engage her attention for the length of the trip.

"What do you think Márie-Helene wishes to discuss with you?" I asked her.

At that she laughed, which surprised me greatly.

"Have you not supposed what this is about?" she asked.

"No," said I, "I have no notion of it." Not strictly true, but anything to deflect her.

"Did not your friend Bunkins say that he would have some things to say to you?"

"He did."

"And do you not also suppose that Mr. Bilbo, too, would wish to talk with you?"

"I had that feeling, yes."

"Well, dear Jeremy, it is my certain conviction that we have been summoned that they may say their good-byes."

"Yes, certainly Márie-Helene wishes to say her good-bye to you—perhaps to me, as well, I suppose—for she will be gone some three years or more. But Mr. Bilbo? Bunkins?"

"Have you not the sense that God gave you? Do you not see that they are planning on *escape?*"

The word, which she had actually whispered, seemed to sound like a shout in the close quarters of the coach. I heard it, and heard it well, yet I refused to acknowledge it. I simply stared at her.

"Let me make it plain," said she, continuing. "If the woman you loved were about to be sent away to serve a term in prison, perhaps even to be condemned to death—and you had the means to take her any place in the world, would you not steal her away and take her out of danger? Jeremy, he has riding at anchor out there in the river a fine seagoing vessel. You told me yourself that when last you saw him, Mr. Bilbo was counting his cash, and there were so many banknotes and sovereigns that you could not see the top of the desk. We know that he has sold his gaming den—for cash—and he has probably sold that grand house in St. James's Street, as well. He has great wealth that can be spent anywhere. If you cannot see where all this is pointing, then you are not near as clever as I think you are."

She, who was but sixteen, appeared much older as she expounded upon my blindness to the obvious. Her eyes shone steady and sharp. There could be no doubt of the intensity of her feeling as she made her argument. It seemed altogether impossible that this was the girl who had but a short time before rested her head upon my shoulder. She seemed to contain within her some several females of various ages. Which must I now address?

"Listen to me please, if you will," said I, "and don't interrupt. I

have not heard what you have said, and for that matter, we have not
had this conversation. If I *had* heard, and if this conversation *had*
taken place, then I should have to go to Sir John and give it as our
suspicion that Mr. Bilbo was preparing to aid and abet the escape of
Márie-Helene, Lady Grenville. Naturally," said I (a bit sarcasti-
cally), "I would give you credit and declare that you had convinced
me. Now if—"

"But *why?*" she demanded, interrupting in spite of my request.
"Why would you have to bring this to Sir John?"

"Because I hope to be an officer of the court someday not so far
in the future, and I want no stain upon my record. And if you are
still as talkative as you have been in the past, you would not be able
to resist spreading your thoughts and observations about and boast-
ing you had convinced me. In other words, that I knew in advance
of their plans."

"I would *not!*" she declared. "I would do no such thing!"

"Perhaps indeed you would not. Perhaps you would get past
that temptation and all would be well. Nevertheless there is this
matter I should like to clear up between us. I should like to tell you,
Clarissa, that I *am* as clever as you think I am. By the time I left Mr.
Bilbo's residence yesterday, I thought that there was much amiss,
yet I would not allow myself to pursue such thoughts and draw the
sort of conclusions that you have drawn, for the reasons I have just
stated. I would have to be a dunce to thus overlook the obvious.
And if you want suspicions, here is one of mine you may not have
considered: I believe that Sir John himself is fearful that Black
Jack and his lady will try something of the sort you've suggested.
Do you recall how he came home from Bilbo's the other night? So
angry and out-of-sorts? I believe he sensed it then taking shape. He
sent me with that dreaded message, because he did not want to know
more about it, for if he did, he would have to prevent it—perhaps
report it himself to the Lord Chief Justice."

There I stopped, panting and quite out of breath. It seemed we
were both left with nothing more to say, for we were silent for a
considerable while.

"And so," said Clarissa, "what shall we do?"

"Nothing out of the ordinary, I should think."

"But it's all so plain," she protested. "Do we cover our eyes and stuff our ears with cotton wool?"

"If we must, I suppose. Yet I do not think it will pose a problem. Black Jack is much too canny a fellow to ignore the limitations put upon us all. He will have explained to the others, I'm sure."

As with so many things in life, the problems were greater in anticipation than they proved to be in actuality. It was a surprisingly happy occasion. Surmising correctly that we would have had our evening meal, Mr. Bilbo served us dessert rather than dinner—or, indeed, it was Márie-Helene who had proven so dangerous to Clarissa when last we had imbibed. The dessert was a tart in the French style—a variety of berries and other fruits in a base of sweet custard, and all of it baked in a pie of the finest, flakiest crust. I had had no such treat since our days in Deal. It was, in fact, so like what we had eaten during our first days there that I began to wonder.

"Tell me," said I, "was this delectable dessert baked by the famed Jacques?"

"It was," said Márie-Helene. "And do you remember him so well?"

"In truth, I never met the man. Yet I believe I would know him anywhere by his works, which are quite the finest of their kind."

"Put like a true gallant!" said she, punctuating her declaration with a bit of impromptu applause.

"Might I meet him?"

At my question, Márie-Helene and Mr. Bilbo exchanged glances; hers was of an inquiring sort, and his response came back in the negative.

"Ah, but no, Jeremy. That is not possible. He has begun his journey back to France, and left this tart which we eat as his final gift to us."

And Jimmie Bunkins merely smiled.

So it went through the evening as we recalled old times and other occasions.

Clarissa reminded Mr. Bilbo of our chance meeting with him in Bath, where he had come of a purpose to lose his money. I asked Márie-Helene if she knew how Black Jack and Bunkins had met;

then did I tell her the whole story before she could say yea or nay. Then did Bunkins stand and toast our host declaring that he was "the best cove a lad could want and to be equaled only by one who ain't with us at the moment."

It was thus a true valedictory moment with toasts raised and drunk; there was laughter, yet through it all a sense of underlying seriousness, as well. More stories were told, another bottle of wine opened, and then at last we divided; I went with Bunkins at his suggestion to the front of the great house, as Mr. Bilbo excused himself and said that there were matters which begged his attention in his study. Thus were Clarissa and Márie-Helene left alone to talk, as the latter had requested.

Bunkins and I walked down the long hall to the street door, which he threw open in an invitation to step outside. He followed me and left the door ajar.

"Let's sit right here on the steps," said he. "It ain't too cold for you here, is it?"

I assured him that it was not.

"I like to sit out here and do my thinking sometimes, and I decided, maybe I'd tell you what I been thinking about. I mean, if you don't mind listening."

"Go ahead," said I. "We've not talked so in quite some time."

"You was remembering for the lady how it was that me and the cove got together. Jeremy, do you remember how it was you and me met?"

"Well, I remember you took me to the Raker's to show me the body of the old barrow-woman."

"That's right, Moll Caulfield. We did that, but that ain't how we met. You remember? We fell to tussling one day right there in the middle of Berry Lane. And when the Blind Beak hisself come out to pull us apart, I knew him right off and took off running, fast as ever I could."

"Which was pretty fast back then."

"Still is." He laughed. "Anyways, that's how we came to know each other—by rolling around in the dust in Berry Lane. And I been thinking about that, so I have. And you know *what* I been thinking? That all the good things that came to me since then— meeting Mr. Bilbo, getting the little bit of learning I do have, all of it, came from meeting you and that fight we had some years back. You changed things for me. Never had much luck till I met you, and since then, it's all been good luck, and I want to thank you for that."

We talked on together for many minutes more, perhaps an hour in all. Yet what was said further was in no wise so seriously said as that eulogy that Bunkins had offered me. We ceased only when the coach was brought round. Then was it quite obviously time to think about leaving. Bunkins returned me to the dining room where all awaited us, and he did announce that the coach was out there in St. James's Street. Once again then at the door to the street Clarissa and I stood awkwardly wondering what was now to be said.

"*Au revoir,*" Márie-Helene offered. "That means, 'till I see you again.' It is a promise that we will."

"*Au revoir,*" said we all.

In the coach, Clarissa and I found we had tears to be wiped. I passed to her my clean kerchief, clearing my throat quite earnestly yet still sensing a certain huskiness in my voice as I attempted to speak.

"What did you think?" I asked Clarissa.

"Oh, many things," said she, "but let's not talk about it just now."

I took her hand and held it—loosely, so that she might take it back from me whenever she wished. Yet she did not withdraw it. "You may put your head on my shoulder, if you like."

That she did, and we rode thus half the distance to Bow Street. But then, without moving her head from its station on my shoulder, she spoke in a quiet voice.

"I can tell you one of the things that I think."

"And what is that?"

"Molly Sarton is wrong."

"Wrong about what?"

"About Márie-Helene seeking to trap Black Jack into saving her. She, in all truth, loves the man dearly."

"You're sure of that?"

Only then did she move her head from my shoulder and look me square in the face.

"Aren't you?" she asked.

I thought hard upon it for a long moment. "Yes," said I, "I'm just as sure as you are."

She put her head back on my shoulder.

"I heard no good-byes and no talk of escape," said I to her. "Let us not say a word of what was or was not said this evening. Let us speak only of *The Merchant of Venice*."

"What? *The Mer*—oh yes, yes indeed. Not a word . . . only . . . only, dear God, I hope I see them all again."

Having uttered that distressed cry, she did once again return her head to the spot where it had previously rested. I was content with that, in truth, I liked it very well indeed. I thought, as thus we kept our silence, of the many conversations we two had had over the past few years—conversations which more often than not had ended in debate. I had enjoyed such play, for play was what it was. Nevertheless, this silence between us was something new, something more serious, something vaguely profound. I rather liked it.

FOUR

In which Sir John
interrogates Ben
Franklin

"Tell me a little about your doctor friend, Jeremy."

It was Molly Sarton's first inquiry as we set off for our great buying trip to Covent Garden for the Franklin dinner. I was sure that there would be more questions to follow.

"You mean Mr. Donnelly, of course," said I. "What do you wish to know?"

"Well, there's something right there. You say he's a doctor, but you call him plain old mister. Now, how does that happen?"

I explained to her that Mr. Donnelly, the son of a prosperous Dublin draper, had been sent to the University of Vienna for his medical education.

"Ah, Vienna is it?" said she to me. "He must be properly educated then."

"And indeed he is," I agreed. "The medical faculty there has on it skilled surgeons—and none of them graduates of barbering school—so that a graduate in medicine of the University of Vienna may be skilled both in medicine *and* surgery, as Mr. Donnelly is. And a good thing, too, for when he graduated, the only place open to him was as a ship's surgeon in the Royal Navy."

"Which made him a plain mister, him being Irish and all."

"Just so."

"He and Sir John are good friends, are they?"

"Oh yes."

"They work together?"

"In a way they do," said I. "Sir John secured a position for him as medical examiner for the City of Westminster."

"Is that near London?"

"It's part of London. We're in Westminster now, as it happens."

"Well, pardon my ignorance, I've only just arrived," said she with a hearty laugh. "But what's medical examining got to do with judging?"

"Ah well," said I, "in matters of murder much is often revealed by the condition of the body—all sorts of details, perhaps even who committed it."

That did indeed impress her. "And he does that? Why, it's more than you could even suppose."

"And he does it all in addition to his regular practice."

"His patients are mostly women, as I understand?" She allowed that to hang in the air, as a question.

"Oh, I wouldn't know about that."

She looked at me curiously, as if she didn't know quite how to take what I had just said. In fact, I knew little about his patients. The few times I had been in his waiting room during his surgery hours, those sitting in attendance seemed about equally divided between male and female. Who would put such an idea into her head? Clarissa? I thought not. No, more likely that suggestion had come from Lady Fielding herself.

We were now in Russell Street, and the great crowd-filled expanse of Covent Garden lay just ahead. What must Molly think of all this—the huge, pressing throng of this great city? I remember when I first arrived in London some four years before, I could not, for the life of me, believe that there could be so many people in a single place.

"And what's this I hear about him following some noble widow out to Lancashire, hoping to win her hand? I suppose she was Lancashire Catholic . . . ?"

"Again you're asking me about something that I know nothing of." (Reader, I confess that in so saying I told a lie. Indeed I did know a good deal of that sad episode, for I heard if from his own lips. I recall sitting with Sir John and Lady Fielding and Annie as Mr. Donnelly had told his disastrous tales—no, Clarissa had not yet joined us then. This meant that Lady Fielding was again the source of her information.)

"Well, he *is* Catholic, isn't he?"

"So far as I know."

"Well, I'm sure he is. He's Irish and from Dublin, and he even *looks* Catholic."

What an odd thing to say! "What does a Catholic look like?" I asked her, all in confusion.

"Like me, for a sample. I'm Catholic—or would be if there'd been any priests in the part of Kent where I grew up. But that's what my mother said, and that's how she raised me. She even took me up to London and found a priest to baptize me."

I could not but laugh at what she had just declared. "If you look Catholic," said I, "then you must be wrong about Mr. Donnelly, for he doesn't look a bit like you. You're much prettier."

"Nice of you to say so," said she, "but for an Irishman he's not too bad, that one, not bad at all."

Ah, these complicated matters of human attraction. How good it was at least that each seemed drawn to the other. What sadness might result if only one felt attracted to the other! Poor Clarissa.

But it seemed to me that Molly and I had come to Covent Garden for a purpose, had we not? Was it my place to tell her that? Reluctantly, I began to frame my reminder as she spoke up again.

"I know you've a bit of influence with Lady F—" said she.

"I have?" I must have sounded astonished, for indeed I was.

"Any fool could see it," said she. "But that's neither here nor there. I was just buttering you up to ask a favor of you. Would you see what you could do to get me and the doctor seated together? It's not the place of the cook to dictate seating to the hostess, don't you agree?"

"Oh, I do. Most emphatically."

"All right, that's enough of that. We came here to buy the makings of a grand dinner, did we not?"

"We did—but where to first? The greengrocer or the butcher?"

"To the butcher, by all means," said she. "Buy your cut of meat, then build the rest of the meal round it. That's how it's done."

"As you say, Molly. Let's get through this mob then. Stay close behind me, and I'll lead the way."

As the day passed, Lady Fielding became more excited and flustered as she prepared for her role in staging dinner. At one point, according to Clarissa, she threw her hands into the air and shouted in a desperate manner, as one crying out to be saved from drowning.

"Dear God, help me! I have nothing to wear this evening."

Clarissa assured her that was not so, and took her up to the big bedroom shared by the Fieldings; from out of the wardrobe she began pulling gowns and laying them upon the bed, until there was not bed to be spied beneath them. Then did it become a matter of choosing rather than finding, and Lady Fielding discovered that to be nearly as difficult. Yet somehow they brought it down to a choice of three, and then was it a matter of trying them on, for Lady F. had put on a bit of weight, and what appeared well when held up by Clarissa might be altogether unsuitable when worn. By this wearying process a gown was chosen, one which was a favorite of one and all, certainly of Clarissa's and mine, and we had always supposed it to be a favorite of our mistress, as well, for she seemed to wear it at every opportunity.

Next came bathing, the fixing of the hair just so, dressing, perfuming, et cetera—all of which had Clarissa running about, back and forth through the bedroom door. Thus, at last relieved from such duties and requests, she was mightily surprised when Lady Fielding asked her to attend, as well, to the details of seating.

"I haven't given a thought to it," said Lady F., "and I'm much too tired to give any thought to it now, so Clarissa, will you please, please do it for me now? I do need some time to relax before dinner."

It was then, reader, that I happened along. I had caught Clarissa taking a moment's rest in a corner of the kitchen. She, near to tears from the effort she had already expended, confessed to me that she had no idea how to go about such a task as charting the arrangements of seating. Who was most important? Where should he sit in relation to Sir John?

Then did I do the decent thing and offer to attend to the matter for her. She gladly consented, kissed me on the cheek, and gave to me the place cards, each of which bore upon it the name of one who would sit at the table. Thanking me once again, she went off to attend to her own preparations — only to run back with a request.

"I wish to sit next to you," said she, "yet only if you, too, want it so."

With a sigh, I agreed. "I'll see if I can arrange it," said I, knowing that now that I had the place cards, such was well within my powers.

It was not truly what one could call a promise, yet giving some consideration to the matter, I decided it would be easy to honor it. After all, it worked out best that way. On Sir John's right would sit Benjamin Franklin, and down the table, Molly Sarton and Mr. Donnelly (as both had requested). On Sir John's left would be Samuel Johnson, Clarissa, and myself.

Lady Fielding would, of course, sit at the foot. It was thus easily done.

When I returned to Sir John's chambers below, I found, to my surprise, that Mr. Gabriel Donnelly had dropped in on the magistrate. I heard his voice and entered the room quietly, giving a wave of greeting to him. His visit, as I soon understood, had to do with an addendum to his postmortem report upon the corpus of the footman who had been murdered in the course of the burglary of Lord Hillsborough's residence. Mr. Donnelly had not preceded me by much. He had evidently only begun to explain to Sir John why he had come when l returned to ask the magistrate what more he might require.

"And how did you manage to miss something — or perhaps I should say *anything* — in your report?" asked Sir John. "You are usually so very thorough."

"But not faultless," put in Mr. Donnelly.

"None of us is, sir," said Sir John.

"But you ask how it was I happened to miss the obvious. In truth, sir, it was because I became so fascinated with the wound and what it revealed of the human brain that I gave insufficient thought to the sort of instrument that might have caused it."

"Why, I assumed it was a club of some sort."

"If by a club you mean one of wood, then I would have to say that no such club could have caused the wound that I saw. What, I began to ask myself, could so thoroughly smash through skin, the bone of the skull, and so damage the brain stem that all involuntary action—heartbeat, breathing, et cetera—would then stop?"

"And what answer did you give yourself?"

"None at first, for I had allowed the body to be taken away for burial. I fretted over it no end, wondering if it were a matter of sufficient import to merit exhumation. But then I thought that I had some bits of the body that might tell me all that I needed to know."

"Bits of the body?" said Sir John, clearly puzzled. "What bits were they?"

"The pieces of skull which I had picked from round and inside the wound. I did assemble them and noted two things. First, that there were too many bits, too many pieces, to form a wound of the proper size and shape. And second, the surplus pieces were, it seemed, of a different composition and, oddest of all, they seemed to be crumbling."

"What were they?"

"I could only be sure when I took down my microscope, for indeed the microscope cannot lie. Looked at so, these bits and pieces were revealed as naught but . . . cement."

"Cement?" echoed Sir John, "the stuff that binds building stone together?"

"Just so. The pieces—hardly more than crumbs were they— were the right color, yet of the wrong consistency."

"Well, I be damned! And you could tell this by looking at them under the microscope, could you? True enough, this is a great age of science, is it not?" Then did Sir John fall silent of a sudden, ruminating with a great, long hmmm. At last did he speak: "Yet now we are left with a problem: Leaving aside the possibility that the poor fellow who was killed in the course of that burglary was hit with the side of a house, what weapon could possibly have been used to cause such destruction to his skull and brain and leave behind little crumbs of cement?"

Again, silence did reign. I waited a proper interval as they gave consideration to the matter. Only then did I speak up.

"If I may, Sir John, Mr. Donnelly?"

"By all means, Jeremy," said Sir John, "if you have any answer to this puzzle, let us hear it now."

"I second that absolutely," said Mr. Donnelly.

"It was not terribly long ago," said I, "perhaps a six-month past that I happened to be talking to Mr. Baker of an evening, and he said to me, 'Jeremy, you'd not believe what lately I've been taking off prisoners before I lock them up in the strong room.' Then did he proceed to show me, pulling out a particular drawer among the files and reaching far to the back of it. It was an impressive array of weaponry—everything from a pistol which shot nails, to a long sort of pin which Mr. Baker said was the most deadly weapon of all in the hands of a desperate woman, and in among them was just such a one as you've described. It was of leather, short and blunt, less than a foot long. The bottom half was all handle, while the upper part, which was flexible, was about three inches round, heavier than you can imagine, and hard as a rock. I asked Mr. Baker, in fact, if there were a rock inside, and he said no, that it was filled with cement. Then did I ask what they called such a thing, and he said, 'They call it a cosh, and it will smash a skull as easy as you or I might break an egg for breakfast.'"

"But how then did those bits of the stuff leak out?" asked Mr. Donnelly.

"Well, they would, of course, because the leather round that chunk of cement had been stitched closed. And what is stitched can come unstitched, and what is unstitched could leak its contents."

At that Sir John laughed rather abruptly. "The lad sounds like something of a scientist himself, does he not?"

"He does for fair," said Mr. Donnelly with a great Irish grin upon his face. I must have matched him grin for grin, so pleased with myself was I that I had identified the murder weapon for them.

"Well, Sir John," said he, rising from his chair, "now that Jeremy has explained it all, I've no need to stay. I must, in any case, ready myself for the dinner. I take it that Dr. Johnson arranged everything, as you asked?"

"Oh yes, he sent his man Frank Barber by yesterday to inform us that all was set with Mr. Franklin. He will arrive with Dr. Johnson. Dinner will begin at eight. If you care to come a little earlier, I'll have a tot of rum with you."

Sir John stood and offered his hand. Mr. Donnelly grasped it
and gave it a good, manly shake.

"I wonder if you would allow me to borrow Jeremy for a few
minutes? There was a matter I wished to question him about."

"By all means, keep him as long as you like."

Thus was I lent out and borrowed like some garden tool—a
hoe, a rake, whatever—and only a moment before they hailed me as
a nascent scientist. Such, I told myself, is the lot of one still a lad and
not yet a man.

Together, Mr. Donnelly and I walked down the long hall to the
door to Bow Street. Though not a word passed between us, I could
tell he was quite burning to say something to me.

And so he was—yet there was naught that he wished to tell me;
rather was it something he wished to ask me.

"What are the seating arrangements?"

With that, he caught me off-guard. I know not why, but at that
moment my mind was quite elsewhere. All I could do was blink
stupidly.

"Pardon?" said I.

"Good God, Jeremy! Have you no memory at all? The *seating
arrangements*—don't you recall?"

"Oh yes, of course, you wished to be seated next to Molly
Sarton."

"And you said you would do what you could. Well, did you?"

"Certainly," said I. "It's all arranged." And, having said so, I
summarized the chart for him.

(I thought it worthy of note that his interest in her had not
waned in the slightest, but contrariwise, seemed to have waxed considerably since yesterday. He must, I reasoned, have been thinking
oft upon her in the interim.)

Mr. Donnelly was much impressed by what I had accomplished, yet not, as he considered it, completely satisfied.

"Hmmm, yes, well . . . too bad you couldn't have put me *between*
Mr. Franklin and Molly."

"And put Lady Fielding next to her cook?"

"Oh, I see your point. That would never do, of course. But
you've done well, Jeremy, and I commend your efforts in my be-

half—and thank you for them." So saying, he gathered himself together and prepared to depart. But something yet held him: "There
was one matter that I . . . oh yes, now I remember. The most remarkable thing happened this morning."

"And what was that?"

"You recall our traveling companion to Portsmouth, Arthur Lee?"

"How could I forget him—and all of the discomfort he
caused you?"

"Well, Mr. Lee—"

"*Dr.* Lee," I corrected him.

"I accept your amendment, Jeremy," said he with a sly smile,
then began again: "Our friend *Mr.* Lee called upon me quite early. I
was not even properly dressed and had half my face covered with
shaving lather. Thus was I in no state to greet a guest. Yet he
pleaded so to be admitted, I could do naught but open the door to
him—and so I did. Perhaps I thought perversely that this might be
my opportunity to tell the fellow what I thought of him."

"And did you?"

"Nothing of the kind, for the moment we were face-to-face he
began apologizing in the most abject manner for what he called his
'unforgivable gaffe' in forcing us to find our way home by ourselves."

"Is that how he put it?"

"More or less. I know not if I quote him exact. Yet he seemed to
be implying that his great sin was depriving us of his company—
and that did not sit well with me."

"Naturally not," said I.

"Yet he did then pull out his purse and ask what the experience
had cost me out of pocket, and I—well, by God, I told him—and he
paid up. He counted it out right there on the spot, full amount, right
down to the last farthing, so to speak. Then did he explain that what
had left him temporarily embarrassed was the failure of a new letter
of credit to arrive from his bank in Virginia. Of a sudden, he was left
penniless, or the next thing to it, and he was forced to resort to sub-
terfuge. He continued to beg my pardon all the way down the stairs
and out to the street—or so it seemed."

"That is indeed quite a story."

"It was indeed quite an event. He may not have behaved as a gentleman," said Mr. Donnelly, "what colonial does, after all? Nevertheless I, who have endured straitened circumstances myself, can certainly understand his predicament. Which of us has not had such problems, eh Jeremy?"

And with that and a wave to me, he was off down Bow Street in the direction of Drury Lane. I watched him go, and then, remembering our conversation with Sir John, I called out and whistled shrilly to catch his attention. He heard, stopped, and turned round to me.

"Come early," I shouted, "and I'll ask Mr. Baker to show you the cosh."

He laughed then, waved again and continued on his way.

When, an hour or two later, Sir John and I left his chambers to make our own preparations for the dinner, we were hailed by Mr. Perkins who, it seemed, had reported for duty a bit early that he might have a word with us.

"What will you, Mr. Perkins?" said the magistrate. "We've a bit of nonsense we must attend to, so . . ."

"I'll make it fast, sir. It's these two who I think might've done that burglary you've been working on."

"Yes, what about them?"

"They've both just disappeared, nowhere in sight, not a word heard about them since the burglary."

"Your snitch is no help?"

"None at all, but I remembered what you said about this being likely one of those for-hire jobs, and I was wondering would you like me to bring in one who's been seen keeping company with the two of them right up to the night of the burglary. He looked out of place down there in the dives of Bedford Street. I feel like he's involved in some way. He's too much the gentleman, if you know what I mean."

"Indeed I do, but I see no charge to be put against him—unless it be 'associating with known criminals'—which is no charge at all, really."

"That's what I was afraid of. But what I was thinking, sir, was that Jeremy here might be of some help in this."

"Oh? How is that?"

"Jeremy's been going out with you on all of your investigations, hasn't he?"

"All except the first of them. I had to rely on Clarissa on that occasion, for Jeremy was out of town. I don't know how many we've talked to, however, who would be likely to appear in Bedford Street."

"Well, like I say, Sir John, the one I'm talking about isn't *likely* to be found there, either. That's why he stands out so."

"All right, Mr. Perkins, you've made your point. What do you suggest with regard to Jeremy?"

"That he come with me and take a look. Maybe this cod who plays the gent will be there and maybe he won't, but this way I'll at least have satisfied my curiosity."

Sir John turned in my direction. "What about it, Jeremy? Are you willing to leave the dinner table a little early?" Somewhat reluctantly, I said I would, and it was agreed that Mr. Perkins would come for me at eleven and have me back by midnight. Ordinarily, I would have been delighted at a chance to explore Bedford Street in the company of the constable. On this evening, however, our table might prove even more lively than the lowly dives of Bedford.

We were ranged round the table in exactly the order I had devised. Yet what had seemed a perfect plan for seating just a few hours before seemed much less so now. None of the opportunities for conversation which I had anticipated (one might even say planned) seemed to be working out at all. Mr. Donnelly and Molly, each of whom had requested to sit by the other, found themselves altogether monopolized by the table partner next to them on the opposite side.

Lady Fielding talked quite incessantly to Mr. Donnelly, and she seemed to end nearly every sentence with "is it not?" or "wouldn't you say so?" So, he had no choice but to respond; simply nodding and smiling would not do. When she began to discuss her mother's tumor, I knew that she would be holding him prisoner for quite some time.

Molly Sarton was surprised to find herself the object of Benjamin Franklin's profound concentration and scrutiny. Afterward, she confessed to me that she had no clear idea who he was, yet she had heard his name often enough to know that he was famous. Just as with Lady Fielding and Mr. Donnelly, he did nearly all the talking. It consisted, for the most part, of the most outrageous flattery and questions of the sort which could be answered with a word or two, perhaps three or four.

As an example, I can only offer the following, since what was said by him between them vanished ever so quickly from my mind. I recall Franklin leaning close yet speaking loud enough to make me wonder if he were not perhaps a bit deaf.

"But surely you are not *just* a cook?"

"Well, I . . ."

"Mind you, I mean that as no reflection upon this superb dinner. But you—you not only planned it, but actually cooked it with your two beautiful little hands?"

"Oh yes."

"You seem so delicate for such work. Yet this beef chop, it's quite the best I've ever eaten."

"You're very kind."

"Whence came you?"

"To here? From Deal."

"Down in Kent? I know it a little, a charming place."

"I hated it."

"Goodness! Such strong language. What is it makes you hate it so?"

"My husband's death."

"You a widow? And so young! Such a pity. And how did your husband die, pray tell?"

"He was murdered."

"Oh dear! Oh my! Murdered, you say? One hears of that sort of thing here in London. But in Deal, of all places! It would seem there is no safe haven, would it not? But tell me, do please, what were the circumstances of his murder?"

To that she gave her longest response, yet with it, she did not more than beg off: "I fear I cannot oblige you, sir, for even to think of them vexes me so that I know I could not bear to tell them. I believe you would be far better advised to ask Sir John to relate them to you. Now, if you will excuse me, I have a kitchen matter to attend to." And with that she rose from her chair and disappeared through the door.

If you were then to suppose that Benjamin Franklin took Molly's advice and consulted Sir John regarding the details of Albert Sarton's death, then you would suppose wrongly, reader, for no sooner had she left than he began glancing round the table, eagerly searching for a promising object for his attentions. His eyes shifted to Lady Fielding, who was at that moment still in deep discussion with Mr. Donnelly, and so had gone across the table to Clarissa, of all people, who had been asking questions of Samuel Johnson. Just then, however, Sir John made some remark to Mr. Johnson, and I saw, from the gleam in his eyes, that Mr. Franklin was about to pounce upon the sixteen-year-old Clarissa. Yet before he could do that, Mr. Donnelly realized the situation and fought his way from Lady Fielding's grasp (speaking figuratively, of course). He then called to Mr. Franklin across the empty space where, until moments before, Molly Sarton had sat.

"Mr. Franklin," said he, "did you achieve any satisfactory results from your experiment in Portsmouth?"

Franklin seemed mildly annoyed at the interruption—and perhaps at the nature of the question, as well. He looked sharply at Mr. Donnelly.

"Not as yet, sir," said he. "Still, I am hopeful."

"Jeremy here"—Mr. Donnelly gestured to me—"and I, as well, were present at your initial attempt. Was there a second attempt that day?"

"Ah, so you were there in Portsmouth, were you? No, there was no second attempt on that day, but it is more than likely that there will be another soon."

"I wonder, sir, if you would explain the nature of the experiment to those here at the table who were not there. Your theory seems altogether ingenious."

"But surely it would only bore the ladies."

"Oh, not so, not so," said Lady Fielding, "we should be honored to hear of your theory and your experiment, sir. And if not I, then certainly Clarissa will be well able to understand it."

He smiled across the table at Clarissa. "And are you specially interested in matters scientific?"

"I am interested in all learning," said she fearlessly (and falsely).

Lady Fielding frowned at what must have seemed to her an unnecessarily bold response.

"How, then, can I hold out longer? Lady Fielding, I accede to your wishes. I shall tell you how, over a number of years, I developed the theory, which I tested in the experiment at Portsmouth."

"And have you given a name to your theory?" she asked.

"Not till this moment, no, but if you feel that it should have a name, let it be called 'stilling troubled waters by pouring oil upon them.'" Then did he turn to Clarissa. "What think you of that, young lady?"

"I think it sounds a bit too simple to work in any practical sense," said she.

"Ah, but I have found that most things in nature do work far more simply than we may at first realize."

Then did he tell the history of the theory, beginning with his discovery, while a schoolboy, of the passage in Pliny the Elder, which related the practice of sailors in ancient times of pouring oil upon the sea during a storm in order to still the waves. This much, of course, we had heard from Arthur Lee. Yet, as it developed, there was much more to the story. He told of an experience at sea in convoy of vessels in which he had noticed that at certain times the wake of some of the ships was "remarkably smooth" whereas those of the others were at the same time "ruffled by the wind."

"Puzzled by this, I went to the captain and asked him about it," said Franklin. "'I suppose,' said he, 'that the cooks have just been emptying their greasy water through the scuppers, and that has greased the sides of the ship a little.' That's what he said, and he said it as one would to a child or an ignoramus—one, in any case, who did not know what was well known to everyone else."

At that there was a bit of tittering from those round the table, as if they were amused that anyone would dare to speak in such a way to one as wise as Franklin.

He went on to tell of indications passed on to him by others. As an instance, a captain who had spent time in Bermuda told him that spear fishermen there would pour a bit of oil upon the surface of the sea when it was rough. The oil would calm the surface, so that they might strike at the fish when they spied them near the boat. Et cetera, et cetera, on and on, with example following example until it seemed to me that he was in danger of losing his audience.

He said he had tried out his theory at a pond in Clapham. On a day on which the wind roiled the pond surface into proper waves, he emptied a cruet of oil on the leeward side, where the waves were strongest, without much effect. But when he went to the windward side, it took little more than a spoonful to spread across a surface of about half an acre and turn it into one "smooth as a looking glass."

That much having been accomplished, it remained for the theory to be tested on the sea. That was made possible by Captain Bentinck who offered a longboat and a barge from his own vessel that oil might be spread upon the surface — yet here 'twas more than half an acre to be covered, rather a pair of miles was to be spread o'er. I have detailed at the beginning of this work how badly and in what way the experiment failed, yet Franklin would say only that results were "unsatisfactory." There was an air of general disappointment at the table at his pronouncement.

"But surely," said Lady Fielding, "you proved your theory already there in Clapham at that pond."

"Ah, but you see," said he, "calming the rough waters of a pond is of little practical importance. To be truly of value, it must be made to work upon the sea."

"Mr. Franklin," said Gabriel Donnelly, "you indicated that it was likely that you will attempt the experiment once again."

"That is correct, sir."

"What things, if any, will you change when and if you do make a second attempt?"

"I would have the vessels stay farther from shore and perhaps change the sort of oil that would be used."

"Oh?" said Mr. Donnelly. "What sort of oil was used in Portsmouth?"

"Whale oil. I have a notion to use petroleum."

"Petroleum?" echoed Samuel Johnson. "What is that? What good is it?"

"Not good for much at all, sir, yet it is heavy, thick, and viscous. The weight of it alone may serve to smooth the waves."

"Well, it will take a very weighty substance indeed to still the surface of Portsmouth Harbor," growled Sir John from the head of the table. "But in the course of flattening them out, you may make the waters of the harbor unusable for any other ship traffic. Would that be part of your plan? Surely not."

"*Certainly* not," said Franklin, all indignant at Sir John's warning.

"Then you would be well advised to put petroleum aside and attempt your experiment with whale oil again in some quiet, well-protected inlet. It may not succeed, but at least it will do no damage."

Benjamin Franklin had been properly stung, and it appeared that he meant to sting back.

"May I ask, sir, on what authority you, as a magistrate, speak to such matters? That is to say, do you have some special knowledge of the properties of petroleum? Have you a maritime background?"

"As to petroleum, or 'rock oil,' as I have heard it called," said Sir John, "I have no special knowledge of it, but I do know that it has been used in street lamps because it burns slow and steadily. A link-man of my acquaintance did once invite me to test the stuff by touch, and I found it as you said, thick, viscous, and sticky—altogether unsuitable for spreading upon harbor waters. And yes, though it is many years in the past, I do have a maritime background. I served as a midshipman in the Royal Navy. I lost my sight in the siege of Cartagena, near forty years past, during the war with the Spanish and the French."

Franklin seemed so totally defeated by Sir John's sharp response to his challenge that in truth he seemed to shrink before our eyes. The table went silent for a long moment until the silence was broken by a single "Ha!" It came from none but Molly Sarton, who had quietly resumed her place whilst the guest was grandly discoursing upon the long development of his oil-upon-water theory. He turned and threw her a withering look. Then did he shift in his seat in such a manner that I, for one, thought he was preparing to leap to his feet and leave. But no, he simply sat up straight in his chair, faced Sir John and asked his forgiveness.

"Nothing to forgive," said the magistrate.

"I meant to give no offense by doubting your authority to challenge mine. I shall bear in mind what you have said regarding petroleum."

"I took no offense, Mr. Franklin, yet it is I who may be begging your forgiveness before the evening is done, sir."

"Oh? How is that?"

"Let us finish our dinner before getting into it, shall we?"

"If you say so, of course, but I shall be on pins and needles till then."

And that was what we did. We waited through two more courses and another bottle of wine. Franklin was not the only one who was left on pins and needles. All were noticeably quieter. Each—even the best-informed of us—seemed to wonder what would come at the end of the meal. Sir John had certainly sent his guest of honor into a state of confusion. All the bravado and swagger had been taken out of him by the time the last dishes were cleared from the table.

"Jeremy," said Sir John, "why don't you break out that bottle of French brandy that Mr. Bilbo gave to us and offer it to the gentlemen at the table. Now the ladies may stay or leave, as is their wish." They stayed, of course, and all but Clarissa imbibed the brandy.

Benjamin Franklin remarked as I poured the brandy into his glass that it was not his custom to take strong drink. "But perhaps," he added in a voice loud enough for all to hear, "it's best that I take a glass to fortify myself for what lies ahead." Thus did he indicate, at least to me, that he had begun to regain a bit of his former confidence.

Yet once all were served, Sir John wasted no time in getting to the matter at hand.

"Mr. Franklin?"

"Uh, yes, Sir John, but may I ask a favor?"

"Certainly."

"Would you mind addressing me as Dr. Franklin? It is a petty thing, perhaps, for the doctorate I was awarded was but an honorary one. Still, I am entitled to it, and I do prefer it."

Even before Franklin had quite finished his explanation, Samuel

Johnson fell into a fit of coughing. So severe was it that Clarissa bounced up from her chair and belabored him upon his back with her open hand. (Sir John and I were probably the only two others who knew the cause of Johnson's upset: He, too, had an honorary doctorate—his from Oxford University—but would allow none to address him so.) I daresay Franklin had indeed regained his self-assurance.

"Then, *Dr.* Franklin, if you will, what do you know of the burglary at Lord Hillsborough's residence in Whitehall?"

"What do I know? Only what I have read of it in the *Public Advertiser.* But why? Am I in some sense suspect in that matter? I can assure you that I—"

"Allow me to ask the questions, please."

"Yes, of course."

"But since you asked if you were suspect, I shall tell you that I have in no wise come to any conclusion in the matter, but there are evidently some who have. I have been urged 'in the strongest terms possible' to question you with regard to the burglary. I do not like being told how to conduct an investigation, and so I chose this way to go about it."

"This way? I don't quite understand."

"I thought to conduct it here at dinner—or afterward—when we had both eaten our fill and had a bit to drink. Far better, don't you think, than having brought you in for questioning as would be done with any common criminal."

"It was either one or the other?"

"So it seemed to me."

"Then I much prefer the way that you have chosen."

"Very well then. Let us continue. You were, I take it, in Portsmouth on the night the burglary of Lord Hillsborough took place?"

"That was the night before the experiment in Portsmouth Harbor? Oh yes, indeed I was, and I remained there a second night, as well."

"What is your relationship with Lord Hillsborough, sir?"

"Well, professional, I suppose. He, as secretary of state for the American colonies, has been the man with whom I dealt in all matters which pertained to the colonies I represent."

"Do you represent *all* the American colonies?"

"Oh no, nothing of the kind—only four: Pennsylvania, Massachusetts, Georgia, and New Jersey."

"I see. And what has been the tenor of your relations with Lord Hillsborough?"

"Well, it is no secret that we have not gotten on well. He makes no effort to understand the position of the colonies on many issues I put before him. He even attempted to have me silenced as regards my work as agent for the State of Massachusetts. He claimed the Massachusetts House of Representatives had no right to appoint me as its agent, for, as he claimed, such appointment was invalid unless assented to by the governor of Massachusetts, Thomas Hutchinson, who was himself appointed by the king. I insisted that I was not the governor's appointment but the appointment of the *people* of Massachusetts, acting through the Massachusetts House. Lord Hillsborough did not like that well, and since then we have had little to say, one to the other."

Reader, during that last response of Mr. Franklin's I noticed a change come over him. He had, up to then, seemed lascivious, pompous, and petty by turns—and above all, was he foolish. He had not, in any of these previous modes, impressed me favorably. But I noted that as he talked of his conflict with Lord Hillsborough, the tone of his voice rose to a pitch of passion and conviction. The disagreement between the two was, after all, a philosophical one, was it not? It was a question of who carried the greater authority: the governor, with the power of the King behind him, or the House of Representatives, whose power was granted them by the people of Massachusetts? Either side, it seemed to me, could be argued, yet it was with near religious fervor that he declared himself; and when he spoke the word "people," he made a sort of climax of it, so that as he sang it forth, his rather thin, reedy voice took on unexpected strength. I doubted not that, given the proper cause, he could show himself a most gifted debater.

Nor was I the only one at the table who noticed the change in Benjamin Franklin. Clarissa turned to me and raised her eyebrows right at the climactic word. And just as Franklin concluded, Mr. Donnelly caught my eye, pouted his lower lip, and nodded—a positive appraisal.

Sir John, too, must have noticed, for he paused for some several moments in his interrogation of Franklin, waiting—for what? For his subject to recover himself? That was not the magistrate's usual way, certainly. Yet it was not long before he resumed.

"Tell me," said Sir John, "have you any idea what was taken from Lord Hillsborough's residence?"

For an instant, Dr. Franklin could do naught but gape in surprise. "Don't *you* know?"

"I could simply caution you once again that I am the one who asks the questions. But I shall not. I shall confess instead that I do not know *what* was stolen. It has not been revealed to me, and that I find to be the most annoying aspect of this most irritating case. And so, I pray you, accept my question in the spirit in which it was asked. Do you know what was taken from the Hillsborough residence?"

"In a word, sir, no. I do not know what was taken. I would hazard that only those who committed the theft know that."

"No, not likely, not *only*. We've a good notion who it was—and if they are who we think, they would have no use for what has most likely been taken. This was almost certainly a case of burglary committed for hire. We may rest assured then that those who ordered it done also know what was taken. The limited information I have from Lord Hillsborough indicates that what was taken was not to do with him personally; that it would have been of value only to a few people in London; and finally that it was, in fact, a packet of letters. Now you, Dr. Franklin, know as much as I do, but you are far better able to *guess* what might be the content of those letters than I ever could. So I invite you, sir: guess, suppose, conjecture!"

With that, both men sat silent for near a minute. There was perceptible tension amongst the rest at the table. Looks were exchanged. Two or three found it necessary to clear their throats. Samuel Johnson fidgeted.

Franklin began: "Clearly, the letters have to do with his position as secretary for American colonies."

"Yes, go on."

"Well, since you were directed—urgently—to give attention to me in your investigation, those letters must have to do with at least one of the four colonies which I represent. It also means that I am one—perhaps, in Lord Hillsborough's opinion, the first—of those few men in London to whom the letters would have value. The question, I suppose, is which of the four colonies do they deal with?"

"That should be easy," said Sir John.

"Why do you say that?" Suddenly Franklin seemed a bit tetchy—or sensitive at the very least.

"Well, because it is commonly held that Massachusetts is the most fractious of the colonies. The Adams brothers have achieved a certain notoriety even here in England, for their unruliness. Both of them are, I believe, members of that body which appointed you."

"But what has that to do with—"

"They—or one of them—may have been singled out for trial in these missing letters."

"Trial? On what charge?"

"Treason."

At that Benjamin Franklin forced a laugh. "That, Sir John, is ridiculous. They are as loyal to the Crown as I."

"None of this should be cause for laughter. First of all, keep in mind that this is not only a burglary investigation, but a search for a murderer as well."

"Oh well . . . I meant no . . . that is to say . . ."

"Furthermore, 'twas just yesterday I heard Lord Mansfield declare that what was needed to solve our problems with the American colonies was a good, old-fashioned treason trial followed by a public execution."

"The Lord Chief Justice said that?"

"I believe your name was mentioned in that conversation, Dr. Franklin."

"My name?" The color seemed to drain from his face. "Oh, dear God." (Indeed, it was mentioned by Sir John to lead Lord Mansfield on.)

Just then, I heard a knock upon the kitchen door, and for a moment I wondered who it might be. Then did I realize that more likely than not 'twas Mr. Perkins come for me. Had it got round so quickly to eleven? I rose and ran to the kitchen. Opening the door, I found the constable waiting, quite as I had expected.

"Can it be so late so soon?" I asked him.

"Well, soon enough," said he. "I'd a prisoner to bring in. And I thought, since I was here . . ." He pulled his watch from his pocket. "Time's about half past ten, give or take a minute or two."

"That'll do," said I. "Just let me tell Sir John that I'm leaving."

"As you wish. I'll wait downstairs by the door."

With that, he started down the dark staircase, and I hied myself back to the dining room. There I found Sir John and Dr. (if I must) Franklin hard at it once more.

"But what you say makes no sense at all," Sir John was saying. "Not even such a one as Lord Hillsborough would make pretense of a robbery, simply to blame it upon the colonials."

"No, you don't know him as I do," said Dr. Franklin. "The man is utterly without principle. Are you at all acquainted with his private life?"

I leaned forward and tapped Clarissa upon the shoulder. Reluctantly, she turned away, and I whispered in her ear.

"Tell Sir John, when you have a chance, that I left with Mr. Perkins. He knows of this."

She gave me a quick nod, then turned back to the fray. Well, I told myself, if they missed me, she would remember to tell Sir John. That much I could be sure of. I left, grabbed my hat off the hook at the door, and ran down the stairs to meet Mr. Perkins just at the door to Bow Street, where he had promised to wait.

It was inconceivable to me that I should prefer to remain at table and listen to Sir John and Franklin battle it out rather than set off with Mr. Perkins upon his rounds there in the vicinity of Bedford Street. There in Bedford was the beat, the very pulse of London. Still, I should have liked to wait. In truth, as I saw it, there was little good could be done by me in Bedford Street. Who might I see there and thus identify? Carruthers the butler? Ridiculous. Lord Hillsborough? Ah, but wait — Hillsborough — that was at least an interesting thought. His bad character had been remarked upon by many, and he would certainly look out of place in Bedford Street. In fact, Dr. Franklin had just suggested him as the culprit, had he not? But would Hillsborough arrange for the death of one of his own servants? Not likely, but indeed such violence could have been unintended and unplanned. No, I was forced to admit that in this instance Benjamin Franklin was no fool—far from it. His intelligence was indeed beyond question. He must have had reason to put Hillsborough forward as suspect.

As Mr. Perkins and I strode together down Bow Street and began our circle round Covent Garden, I thought hard upon Franklin. Was there ever a man of so many and such disparate parts? Unwittingly, he played the motley fool as he presented himself to Molly as a leering seducer. Then did he turn professional as he lectured us upon his oil-and-water theory, and then became all dewy-eyed speaking of the "people." Who were these people, anyway? Colonists— Englishmen like the rest of us, were they not? And all this from a man well past his prime in life, short-sighted, stout, wrinkled, balding, and gray-haired—anything but impressive in appearance. And yet he was no fool. What was most lacking in the man was any true sense of dignity.

"Who was at that dinner Sir John had tonight?" asked Mr. Perkins. "Anybody important?"

"Oh, a couple who were important—Samuel Johnson and Benjamin Franklin—and then there were the rest of us."

He snickered at that. "That's *Dictionary* Johnson, ain't it?"

"That's right."

"And that man, Franklin—ain't he the one who invented electricity?"

Now was it my time to snicker. "Well, he didn't exactly *invent* it," said I. "But I believe he's convinced the world that he did."

"He's a sort of imposter, is he?"

"No, not really," said I, hesitating, trying to put what I felt about him in just a few words. "He's done a lot of scientific work that's of real importance. Though he can be foolish, he's no fool. Yet I believe I have never met a man quite so full of himself."

"Interesting," said the constable. "I knew some in the Army like that. All of them was officers. The worst were the ones with titles."

Yet Dr. Franklin had not even a title to hide behind, thought I. We walked along in silence for the length of Charles Street, then turned down Tavistock. Harking back to my earlier thoughts on Lord Hillsborough, I thought to ask a bit about this mystery man I had come out to view.

"You've no name for this fellow, the gentleman sort who's been about with Skinner and Ferguson?"

"That was what I was hoping you could give me."

"Well, I will if I can, of course, but what does he look like? Could you describe him to me?"

"Well, like I said, he seems like a gentleman."

"In what way? That is, is it the clothes he wears, the way he talks, or what?"

"All of that. He dresses like a gent, talks like a gent, has his hair combed like one, and he's got the cleanest hands you ever saw."

"Hmmm. How tall is he?"

"Oh, I don't know. You and me, we're about the same height ain't we?"

"Just about."

"Well, he'd go a couple of inches taller, though just a couple."

Lord Hillsborough was a good deal taller than I — perhaps four inches. But come to think of it, Mr. Perkins was probably not quite so tall as he believed himself to be. (I, for one, thought him to be at least an inch shorter than I.) Perhaps it was wrong to ask for such an estimate. I would reserve my judgment until I saw the man in question.

When we arrived in Bedford Street, we began the search from inn to tavern to dive. But before we entered the first, the constable had a word of caution for me.

"Now, Jeremy," said he, "the place I believe him to be is down from this one about four or five — just this side the alley. But it's best we don't go there direct, like we was looking for him. If we was going to bring him in, it wouldn't matter. But we'll just do a walk through these places, like it was all just a part of the routine. That'll suit you, won't it?"

"Certainly, it will."

"All right then, here we go."

The first of the places, right at the corner of Maiden Lane, was a dram shop of the name the Duck and Drake. We walked through at a leisurely pace. And, as we did, Mr. Perkins nodded at a few along the way who recognized him for what he was — a constable, a Beak Runner. In and out, just so, then on to the next, and the next one after that, and the next. Until at last we came to the King's Pleasure, so advertised by a great hanging sign which was positioned right above the door. A coach waited outside the door.

"That is the place he usually comes," said he to me. "Now if you'll just give me a moment . . ." He whistled low and was answered in kind from someplace ahead. We walked to the door of the place and then beyond to the mouth of the alley, whence the answering whistle had come. Mr. Perkins led and I followed. As we arrived, a figure stepped forward but remained in the shadows.

"Jeremy," said Mr. Perkins, "this is Bess. 'Twas her pointed out to me this cod I wish you to view. And 'twas her tied him to Skinner and Ferguson."

So Perkins's snitch was a woman. Somehow, I hadn't quite expected that. I offered my hand. She took a step closer and grasped it strongly. Thus did I see her close for the first time. I smiled and said merely that I was happy to make her acquaintance.

"Glad to meet you, too," said she. "Oliver speaks well of you."

Oliver? Who was Oliver? I wondered. Then did I remember that such was Mr. Perkins's Christian name. What she said and how she said it did not quite fit the physical presence of the woman. She was a person of stature, as tall as either one of us. Yet it was her face that was most arresting: not that she was a great beauty—for she was not—but because of the look of hard-won wisdom that was writ upon it. Her green eyes, while not cold, seemed to have deep within them the kind of wariness seen in animals just come in from the wild. Though undoubtedly a whore, she seemed to be meant for grander things.

"Is he in there now?" Mr. Perkins asked her.

"He is," said she. "His nickname is 'Duke' or 'the Duke.' He's with one came in about a week ago, then dropped out of sight—at least dropped out of *my* sight,"

"And of course no sign of Skinner and Ferguson."

"No, and not likely to be by the talk on the street."

The constable sighed, gave me a wave, and said, "Well, let's go inside, Jeremy. Just follow me and be easy. Don't let him know you came to give him a look."

I nodded my understanding, turned back to bid farewell to

Bess, and found she had already retired noiselessly into the shadows. Already I had slipped a bit behind Constable Perkins. I hurried to catch him up at the door.

Inside the King's Pleasure, it was dark, crowded, and murky with tobacco smoke. Though the poor lighting made it difficult to see into the far corners of the place, the smoke was even worse for my purposes: I was no more than a few steps inside when I fell into a violent coughing fit. Thus did I find it impossible to search out Mr. Perkins's "gent," because of the tears that flooded my eyes, and at the same time was I brought to the attention of the entire tavern. There was harsh laughter; fingers were pointed; a few nearby blew smoke up into my face just for the sport of it.

Yet somehow I managed to survive the fit. Clearing my throat, wiping my eyes dry of tears, I looked round the room and blinked as I caught sight of a man at the far end of the room running for the side door to the alley, the same alley where we had talked to Bess.

He was dressed in black, as were half the men round me, and in a way there was naught to call my attention to him, except that there was something familiar in his movements. Even from behind I seemed to recognize a certain awkwardness in his hurried stride. But then, just as he grabbed at the doorknob to make his exit, he turned his head slightly, for an instant enough to give me a view of his profile, or most of it—and again he looked even more familiar. Who was he?

"Come along, Jeremy. Let's sit at a table," Mr. Perkins whispered. "An ale will clear your throat."

Reluctantly, I assented, my mind still laboring to put a name to that profile. The constable took me to a table just emptied nearby. As if by magic, two tankards of ale appeared upon the table before us. Mr. Perkins put a few pence into the serving girl's outstretched hand, then leaned across the table and said again in a whisper:

"Now Jeremy, the one sitting alone at the table behind me, he's the one I want you to take a look at. See if you know him."

I sighed, and did as he told me. I let my eyes sweep around the room a bit until they came to rest upon the man called to my attention by Mr. Perkins. They did not linger upon him long but continued their traverse of the room. He was certainly not Lord Hillsborough, nor was he even my idea of a gentleman. True enough, he was expensively outfitted, and he was clean-shaven and may well have had the cleanest hands in Christendom (though I should have to have been much closer than I was to tell that). Still, he had the features, and wore the expression, of a villain. I would ever keep a watchful eye round such a fellow and never turn my back upon him.

"No," said I to Mr. Perkins. "I've never seen him before."

"Well, drink up and we'll go."

It was a challenge to which I was unequal. Had I the practice Mr. Perkins had I might well have taken the ale down in a single long gulp, as he managed to do. As it was, it took me near two minutes with frequent belching to empty my tankard. He smiled indulgently and rose from his chair.

"Let's be gone," said he.

Outside, we were met by Bess, who was standing out on the walk at the mouth of the alley.

"How did you fare?" she asked. She seemed eager to know.

"Not well," said the constable. "Jeremy said he'd never seen him before."

"But tell me," said I to her, "did you notice someone coming out the alley door?"

"Notice him? I was near knocked over by him. He came out running like the devil was after him."

"Where did he go? Did you see?"

"Indeed I did see. He ran right over there and jumped into the hackney which was waiting for him right there at the front door."

"That was his coach?"

"That's the one brought him here." She hesitated, then added: "He's the one was sitting with the gent when I took my stroll through the King's Pleasure."

Things now were becoming a bit clearer. "And the 'gent,' as Mr. Perkins names him, has been seen with Skinner and Ferguson?"

"Yes," said she, "often."

I pulled out a shilling piece and offered it to her. "Here, take this," said I. "You've helped us out a great deal."

"Oh, I can't do that. Oliver here, he pays me regular."

"Take it, Bess," said Mr. Perkins. "Jeremy wouldn't offer it if he didn't feel what you told him was worth it."

And I did feel it was so, for what she had said suggested to me that the man I had seen leaving the King's Pleasure in such a great hurry was none but Arthur Lee. Still, I could not be sure. I had seen him only in profile and then only for the briefest moment. How *could* I be sure?

FIVE

In which I wrestle
with my doubts
and am overcome

"Arthur Lee? Are you serious, Jeremy?"

"Indeed I am. I would not be here to discuss this with you if I were not."

I had come to Mr. Donnelly to present my case against Arthur Lee, complete with all my doubts and ambiguities. He was in his dressing gown when he greeted me at the door. He said that he was just preparing to shave when I knocked upon his door and asked if I might speak with him at some length on a certain matter. He was most willing to hear me but asked if we might talk as he shaved.

I told him of our suspicion that the Hillsborough burglary had been done for hire, and that, of course, had been the reason for bringing Benjamin Franklin to dinner the night before. Then did I tell Mr. Donnelly of where I had gone with Mr. Perkins and why, which led in turn to the figure I saw running for the alley door at the King's Pleasure, the glimpse I had of him in profile, and his hasty departure in the waiting coach. It was then that I told him that though I could not be sure, I believed that the man who, upon my entrance, was so eager to leave was Arthur Lee. And that was when and why Mr. Donnelly yelped in such surprise and brushed aside my declaration of utter seriousness in the matter.

"But my dear fellow," said he, "much as I respect your sharp eyes, I must say that I simply cannot believe that a man such as Lee would involve himself in the theft of letters of state. He may have behaved in an ungentlemanly fashion in the matter of our return from Portsmouth, but he explained the matter and made restitution. I have forgiven him, and you should, too."

"There is nothing for me to forgive," said I. "He did me no direct harm."

"True! And that's all the more reason for you to harbor no such resentment against him. Look at it this way, Jeremy; there are those who are able to move with ease in that dark world of spies and conspiracies, and there are those of us who cannot. Arthur Lee almost certainly belongs to that far more numerous, latter group."

"You said 'almost,'" I pointed out to him.

"Well, I know I did. After all, I am not God. I have not the ability to see all and know all. I cannot say with absolute certainty what sort of man he is, on such brief acquaintance. I've known him but a year or so."

"Would Arthur Lee do it if he were directed to by Benjamin Franklin?"

At that, Mr. Donnelly wiped his face dry and peered at me for what seemed to me a considerable length of time. "Why are you so determined to condemn Lee?" he asked at last.

"I'm not!" I protested. "I have made it most clear that I saw that man at the door of the King's Pleasure for but an instant—and then only in profile. It is because of my uncertainty in this that I came to see you and discuss this with you. But your defense of him is as weak as my accusation. You seem to be saying that Arthur Lee couldn't have been involved in any such matter as this because he's not that sort of fellow."

Mr. Donnelly, who had listened to me carefully through it all, allowed a smile to spread slowly across his face. "You know, you're getting more like a lawyer every day," said he. "I'm not entirely sure that's a good thing, but I know it's true."

Hearing that, I relaxed a bit. "Someone else said something of the sort to me just the other day."

"About that question you raised as to whether Lee would allow himself to be involved if Dr. Franklin had put him up to it, I have to admit that mentioning Franklin does put a different complexion on the matter. Lee is, near as I can tell, completely devoted to Franklin. And I must admit that he would probably do whatever he was told to do by him."

"So the question becomes, would Franklin take part in it *through* Lee?" I posed it thusly to Gabriel Donnelly. "And in so doing, he would keep his hands clean, would he not?"

Mr. Donnelly thought about that for a moment. "He would, you're right," said he, "*if* Benjamin Franklin were the chief plotter, but I don't believe he is—no, not for an instant."

"Why not?"

"Why indeed? You heard him last evening. It was such a treat listening to him and Sir John going each at the other. Two of the best minds in London. It was a joy to hear them. They were perfectly matched."

"If by that," said I, "you mean they had dueled to a draw, I must disagree. Dr. Franklin showed himself on a number of occasions to be rather foolish."

"Well, you have me there. Not least among those occasions was his prolonged conversation with Molly. You may as well know, Jeremy, he has quite a reputation as a libertine."

"I'm not surprised to hear it."

"Molly was made quite uncomfortable by his attentions—so she said to me after he had left." Then, remembering, he added: "I must thank you for putting me next to her and very cleverly done it was, too. It did me little good till after the dinner had ended, however. I helped clear the table and lingered in the kitchen and had a bit of a chat with her."

"And what did you discover?"

"Only enough to tell me I should know more. I did not learn, for instance, how a woman so thoroughly Irish came to be in Kent. Do you know, Jeremy?"

"Well, I believe she grew up there and that she considers herself Catholic, more or less. But in truth, I do not know the details of her story, nor even her name before she married."

"I'd like to see her again," said he. "How might we arrange that?"

"That might be difficult."

"Why? Does Sir John keep her cloistered?"

"Not exactly that," said I, "but I believe he does feel responsible for her safety."

"Physical or moral?"

"Both."

"I could meet her more or less by chance—with your aid, that is. For instance, when does she usually go buying in Covent Garden? What route does she take? Which stalls does she visit?"

"I usually do the buying for the house. She prepares the list."

"Oh," said he, sounding disappointed.

"Yet she does upon occasion do the buying by herself, or with me. I could let you know when I know in advance—*if* I know in advance."

"Well, that might be all right for a time or two, but I can't keep on popping up every time she leaves Number 4 Bow Street, now can I?"

"It might seem a bit suspicious," I allowed. Then did there dawn upon me a solution to the problem. "Look," said I, "why don't you simply go to Sir John with it?"

"Oh, I don't like the sound of that. It seems a bit like going to her father and asking his permission to court his daughter."

"No, no, nothing of the sort. It would be more in the nature of getting to know her well enough to tell whether it might be worth your while to court her."

"Hmmm . . . well, perhaps. You mean, just talk it through with him in manly fashion."

"Yes, that's just what I mean."

"It might be worth a trial. I would want nothing of this sort to come between me and Sir John."

"It won't, so long as you approach him properly."

"I suppose not," said he, continuing to think upon the matter. By then, of a sudden, he did rouse himself. "What sort of host am I? May I brew you a pot of tea?"

"No," said I, "nothing of the sort. I must be back to Bow Street. Sir John will have errands and tasks for me, I'm sure." I weighed the possibility of one last effort with him; it seemed worth a try. "You still think there is little chance that it was Arthur Lee that I spied leaving that den of criminals on Bedford Street in such a hurry?"

"That is still my opinion. And have I convinced you of my position?"

"That Lee would not involve himself in a crime such as that burglary because Lee is not that sort of fellow?"

I started out of the room.

"Ah, Jeremy, you are incorrigible. Allow me to accompany you to the door and let you out before I do truly become annoyed at you."

Though I should have in no wise wished him to know it, Mr. Donnelly had managed to shake further my already weak conviction that it was Arthur Lee whom I had seen the night before. Before visiting him that morning I had been undecided as to whether I should bring my suspicions to Sir John. But having left his surgery, I found myself turning the matter round in my mind as one might a mathematical problem. Looked at thusly, whereas I had been half in favor of turning the matter over to Sir John, I was now half against it. Mr. Donnelly had argued better than he knew. Essentially he said what none but Black Jack Bilbo had said before him: that if you know a man well, you know what he is capable of, and what he is not. Yet the proper response to that had already occurred to me: The operative word in the phrase "know a man well," is *well*. Perhaps knowing Arthur Lee over a year meant that Mr. Donnelly had not known him well enough; Mr. Donnelly was, after all, quite astonished when he learned in Portsmouth that he would have to pay his way (and mine) back to London; he hadn't known Lee well enough to be prepared for that, had he? So was it that I turned the matter over and over again in my mind, and still did it come out to half and half, in spite of all.

I was right in assuming that Sir John would have work for me upon my return to Bow Street. There were letters to be dictated and then delivered—"but not just yet," as he put it to me. "Come back in the half of an hour, and Mr. Marsden and I should have this mess cleared up by then."

"May I ask just what sort of mess it is, Sir John?" said I.

"Scheduling—it's always scheduling."

And so did I return down the long hall from Sir John's chambers and then climbed the steep flight of stairs to the door leading to our kitchen. Expecting to find Molly in her domain, I was a bit surprised to find Clarissa instead, sitting at the table, as always with a book before her.

"Where have you been?" she asked, ever serious regarding my comings and goings. "You just disappeared after breakfast."

"I was off on a visit to Mr. Donnelly."

"Are you ailing?"

"No, nothing of the kind. I simply had a personal matter to discuss with him."

"Not clap, I hope."

"*Clarissa!*" I exclaimed, quite aghast. "I said, it was a personal matter."

"Don't you consider clap personal? It's about as personal as can be, it seems to me."

"Well, it was *nothing* of the sort."

"Just asking," said she, somewhat mollified. "You will tell me if you have any of that . . . sort of trouble, won't you? I believe I deserve to know."

At such times she puzzled me—nay, she more than puzzled me; she sent me into a despair of confusion. *Why* did she believe she deserved to know? So that she—no, I refused even to speculate upon such bizarre matters.

"Now that we have that settled," said I rather frostily, "I believe I shall go and change my attire." But I paused at the stairs and turned to ask her how she happened to be here so late in the morn.

"Oh, it's Lady F," said she, lowering her voice to a whisper. "She went back to bed for another hour's sleep after breakfast. The party exhausted her. Exhausted Molly, too."

"But not you."

"How could I be exhausted with Samuel Johnson at my elbow? We had such a good talk. He was much more receptive to me than the first time we met, and I was better behaved. The conversation we had energized me greatly. I believe I shall begin my first romance this very evening—or at the very least I shall write a poem, a sonnet perhaps."

At that I excused myself and started up the stairs. What a strange girl she was. She would indulge herself in these grand flights of fancy—writing a romance, composing a sonnet—yet she might look at me straight on and ask if I had caught the clap. How that thought had come to her I had no idea. Had Molly Sarton made the suggestion? That seemed unlikely. Lady Fielding? That seemed even less likely. Yet as I pondered upon the matter, it seemed not in the least remarkable that she had such knowledge of the sordid side of the life round us. After all, had she not escaped from the Lichfield workhouse, only to take up residence in a "rookery," in which whores walked the halls in a state of near-undress? And did she not work daily with Lady Fielding at the Magdalene Home for Penitent Prostitutes? There she would hear tales of the clap, I'd no doubt, and of the pox, too.

Sighing, I took down the clothes from the hook where they hung opposite my bed. Yet, even as I changed, I thought of her and of the strange mixture within her which set romantic fantasy jostling with brutal reality. Still, within me was a mix of parts even more numerous and diverse — as I well knew — and in others of my acquaintance, as well. To myself I confessed that I had thought ill of her because she embarrassed me only moments ago. Now I determined to cheer her when I saw her again in the kitchen. But as luck would have it, she and Lady Fielding had left by the time I returned.

The letters which Sir John would dictate were two. The first, to the Lord Chief Justice, was no more than a routine report upon the interrogation of Benjamin Franklin. It was actually little more than a summary, for it included few of the details and almost no direct quotation. It was simply a report — and nothing more. The second, which was addressed to Dr. Franklin, was remarkable only in that he both apologized for the trickery involved in bringing him to Bow Street and thanked him for submitting to it so generously. It was, to my way of thinking, far more polite in its tone than was necessary, and in that way was quite distinctive, if not unique, among the letters he had dictated to me.

"And now," said Sir John, "if you will but deliver the two letters, we shall be done with Franklin and be able to get on with the true business of investigating."

It was true then that I came closest to telling Sir John of what had occurred during the night past at the King's Pleasure. Yet I did not, and I came to regret that. I had some daft notion that I would investigate the activities of Arthur Lee myself.

"Have we an address for Dr. Franklin?" I asked.

"Ah yes, Mr. Johnson delivered the invitation, did he not? Nevertheless, I believe Mr. Marsden has searched it out. Check with him."

With that, I left with the two letters in my pocket and found, to my relief, that Mr. Marsden, court clerk and general factotum, did indeed have Benjamin Franklin's proper address, so it was unnecessary for me to go seeking it out for myself. First, however, I headed north to Bloomsbury Square and the residence of William Murray, Earl of Mansfield, the Lord Chief Justice.

There was no need for me to wait for an answer. Thus was I able to hand the letter over to my old antagonist, the butler, and inform him of that. I was just turning to leave when a hand reached round the butler's shoulder and grabbed from the latter's hand the letter which I had just handed over. It was Lord Mansfield, of course, none but he would have the courage to do such a thing.

"Here you!" said he to me in a tone betwixt loud speech and a shout. "Wait whilst I read this." He elbowed the butler out of the doorway.

"Will there be a response, my lord?"

"How do I know till I read it?"

His eyes hastily scanned the page. Was it possible that anyone could read so fast? Perhaps—yet I knew how little content there was to be found in the text of that letter. When he had done, he threw it down at my feet. I stooped to pick it up.

"Yes," said Lord Mansfield, "there *will* be a response."

"Would you care to pen it at the bottom of this report?"

"No, you tell him what I have to say."

"And what is that, my lord?"

"BAH! That is my reply, and be sure to shout it loud at him, as I have shouted it to you."

With that, he slammed the door shut, leaving me blinking in astonishment at his doorstep. Well, I consoled myself, at least he had omitted the boot in the arse, which usually puts final punctuation to such messages as this one. With a sigh, I dropped the letter in my pocket and started off to deliver the one to Dr. Franklin.

Taking St. Andrews Street through the notorious Seven Dials, I found my way to St. Martin's Lane and thence to the Strand. It was then just a few steps to Craven Street, which opened off the

Thames side of the Strand. I had no idea it was quite so close to Covent Garden and Bow Street.

I knocked upon the door of Number 10, which was not by any means a grand house. My knock was answered by a pleasant woman, a little older than I had expected, who I later learned was Mrs. Stevenson.

"I have a letter here from Sir John Fielding to Dr. Franklin," said I to her. "There is no reply expected, so I should be happy to leave it with you."

With that, I offered it to her, yet she did not immediately accept it.

"Ah well," said she, "I'll take it for him, if you like. But he is here in the sitting room and not presently engaged. Why don't you step inside and let me announce you to him?"

"Well . . . I . . . certainly, thank-you." It would have been churlish to decline.

As I took my place by the door, after closing it behind me, Mrs. Stevenson bustled off into the interior of the house.

"Dr. Franklin had such a fine time at Sir John's yestereve," she declared, calling back to me. "He thought it a great joke that he had been summoned in that manner for interrogation."

"No ill will then?"

"Not a bit."

Then did she disappear through a door (which led, presumably, to the sitting room), and I took the opportunity to survey my surroundings. It was a pleasant little house, surely no more than two floors in height, but comfortable in a way few houses were — except for our own. No wonder if Franklin had liked his visit to us so much as this good woman had said. He felt at home.

I heard the door to the sitting room open. Mrs. Stevenson emerged first, followed by Benjamin Franklin. She gestured rather grandly toward me as he came forward to give me welcome. He offered his hand and gripped my own very firmly, which, I recalled, was his wont.

"We met last night," said he, "though I can't for the life of me recall your name."

"Jeremy Proctor, sir."

"Ah yes, you sat at the far end of the table, next to that charming young girl."

"Clarissa is her name," said I. "Clarissa Roundtree."

"Ah yes, I shall have to remember that, eh?" Then did he wink rather rudely.

Mrs. Stevenson giggled.

"You, as I recall, had little to say, but you listened very carefully." Then did he clear his throat and say, as one might speaking before an audience: "A good listener hath twice the value of a glib talker."

"Do you think so?"

"Oh, I know so. But I understand you have a letter for me."

"Yes sir." I produced it and offered it to him. He accepted it, but gestured toward the sitting room where the door now stood open. "Why not come inside? I shall read the letter and give any comments to you I think suitable. And then perhaps we may have a chat."

Having little true choice in the matter, I did as he suggested and followed him through the door into a small, snug room altogether perfect for conversation. There were but two chairs, though facing them was a sofa of goodly proportions. Between them was a low table, and off to one side, a fireplace where a low fire burned steadily, providing sufficient warmth for comfort. Dr. Franklin offered me a place at one end of the sofa, and as I settled myself, he sat down at the other. He brought out a pair of spectacles, opened the letter, and, with a nod to me, began reading. He smiled a few times, as if amused, before removing his spectacles and laying the letter aside.

"I take it you took down the letter, and so you know its contents," said he to me.

"Oh yes. The words are his alone, however. I am simply his amanuensis."

"I've no doubt of that. He is the ablest blind man I have ever seen—or even heard of. Is it true, as I have heard tell, that there are thousands whom he can identify by the sound of their voice alone?"

"I know not the number, nor do I think he does. Nevertheless, it is a great many, certainly over a thousand."

"Amazing, quite amazing." Then did he pause for a moment, his eyes roaming the room, as if searching the place for the right words to express himself. Then did he speak. "As for what I might say in reply to Sir John's generous letter, all I can think of telling you is this: Please give him my deepest thanks for the most unusual evening I have had in London in quite some time. I found it both entertaining and intellectually stimulating. The food and the company were quite beyond compare. I look forward to repeating it sometime soon." Again, he paused, then leaning toward me, he smiled a smile of keen interest, and urged, "And now, Jeremy, do tell me something about yourself."

There is one invitation that I, like the most of mankind, could not at that age decline, and that is the one just extended to me by Benjamin Franklin. Once I began talking of myself—how I was orphaned, how I came to London, how I was brought before Sir John's magistrate court on a false charge by a pair of villains—there was simply no stopping me.

Not, in any case, until Mrs. Stevenson came through the door bearing a tray well loaded with cups, a teapot, and a plate of scones. I rose from the sofa and made to help her with the tray.

"Oh, no, no," said she, "I can do quite nicely by myself. I was just about to make some tea when you came along, young sir. I'm sure you'll join us, will you not? Do sit down."

And having no excuse for hovering about, I resumed my place upon the sofa. She set the contents of the tea tray on the low table, poured tea for all, and handed the plate of scones about.

"I was struck," said Dr. Franklin, "by certain similarities in our personal histories. For instance, we did both begin in the printing trade. Thus did I become engaged in writing. And I do believe that my attitude was much like yours is now."

"How do you mean, sir?"

"Well, when I was your age and attended such occasions as last evening's, I would have been every bit as silent as you were then. I listened and learned, as I believe you do now."

"Yes sir."

He had by that time quite overcome my resistance. Let none be deceived in this matter: Benjamin Franklin had a good deal of personal charm. It was, I believe, a matter of his power of concentration, for he had a manner of giving his listener his attention so completely that it quite flattered me. I was not used to such attention from one so renowned.

"Oh," said he, "and I had great ambitions, just as you do—or so

I believe." He waited for me to confirm that. But I, with a mouthful of scone, could do naught but nod. He continued: "Mr. Johnson told me that it is your ambition to become a lawyer."

I swallowed. "Yes sir. It is, sir."

"And toward that end, you are now reading law with Sir John?"

"That is true, sir."

"Well then, you are well along for one of your years. Do you intend to be, as he is, a magistrate?"

"I would follow a somewhat different path," said I. "I have it in mind to be a barrister."

"A barrister, is it?" He let loose an indulgent cackle. "Well, you have your work cut out for you then, haven't you? You must not only learn the law, but also learn to think as a lawyer."

"So says Sir John oft to me."

"And to think quickly."

"Yes, that also does he tell me."

"Mrs. Stevenson," said he to her, "have you some notion where the almanacs might be? After the move I fear I have little idea of the location of anything."

She jumped immediately to her feet. (She was quite spry for a woman of her years.) "Why, I know exactly where they are," said she. "Shall I bring them down?"

"Not all, no. One or two should do."

With that, she went off to another part of the house—to the rear, certainly, perhaps to the cellar. But what was that? A voice from someplace deep in the house? What sort? Male? Female? Yet Franklin did not notice, nor did he wait for her return. He simply continued questioning me, more or less along the same line.

"I noted that you were called away from the table early. Are you learning the duties of a constable, along with all else?"

"Oh no, not really. I fill in for a constable now and again. Occasionally I accompany one of them on some special errand—an arrest or some special undertaking."

"And last night? Was that something of the latter sort?"

Why was he asking me such questions? Though his tone and manner of speech were relaxed, almost casual, he leaned forward in a manner most tense and uncomfortable. His eyes, too, had an anxious look to them.

"Oh no, nothing of the sort," said I, lying with a facility which, frankly, shocked me. "The constable who called for me is taking a leave of absence, and I shall be filling in for him. He wished to acquaint me with his territory."

"Ah, I see. So they really do keep you busy, don't they?" He relaxed a bit with that, settling back at his end of the sofa.

As I cast about for a proper response, there were the sounds of steps and of a second door opening. Mrs. Stevenson entered, waving two small booklets of about the size and shape of the pamphlets which were printed in Grub Street and hawked all over London.

"Here they are," said she. "They're a bit dusty, but no worse for it." She picked up a napkin from the tea tray and gave them a quick brushing off, then handed them over to Franklin.

"Ah, very well," said he to her, and then to me: "This was a project that occupied me for over twenty years and brought me a good deal of money. You've seen these almanacs, have you not, Jeremy?"

"Oh yes, my father printed one or two, as I recall. They were assembled by a local man in Lichfield."

"Yes, assembled, rather than written. That's fair enough. Still, they are useful. They predict the weather with fair accuracy, which is useful for farmers, offer facts and advice, and give bits of wisdom for one and all. The last I took particular delight in writing. Such bits are as difficult to write as poetry, and, in fact, achieve a kind of poetry in their brevity and pithiness. Let me show you."

He opened one of the two almanacs and rustled through the pages.

"Here's one from 1737: 'A Penny saved is Twopence clear. A Pin a day is a Groat a Year. Save and have. Every little makes a mickle.'" He looked at me with a smile. "What think you of that?"

"'Tis a good argument for thriftiness."

"Well said. And what about this from 1739? 'Prithee isn't Miss Cloe's a comical Case? She lends out her Tail, and she borrows her Face.'" Then did he offer the same sort of rude wink he'd given me earlier.

"Dr. Franklin," scolded Mrs. Stevenson, "shame on you."

"Heh-heh"—a mirthless laugh—"perhaps you're a bit young for that one. Heh-heh."

He offered the two almanacs to me. "Would you like these?"

"Why, certainly." Yet, as I reached for them, he pulled them back. "Or perhaps you would wish me to sign them?"

"Even better, sir."

He rose from the sofa and went to a small writing desk, whereon a few loose sheets of paper sat, perhaps a letter he had been writing when I arrived. Taking a quill, he dipped it and then, with practiced authority, signed his name to both almanacs. He blotted the ink on both, turned, and offered them to me again.

I, sensing that my visit had come to an end, rose to my feet and accepted them with thanks. I then said my good-bye and, with a bow, took my leave of him. Mrs. Stevenson took me to the door.

"So nice of you to come," said she. "Dr. Franklin so enjoys talking with young people. He says it keeps him young, too."

Then did she open the door for me. I bowed to her, as well, as I left.

Outside, in Craven Street, I turned toward the Strand. Upon reaching it, I sought a place away from the crowd, secluded from sight, where I might wait and watch. I found quite the perfect spot in an alley which led to St. Martin in the Fields. There were various goods boxes piled high near the entrance. I slipped behind the pile and saw that I had a good command of Craven Street from this point. And anyone leaving Number 10 Craven would turn up here, in the direction of the Strand, for to turn in the opposite direction would take him straight to the river, with no other exit.

I became suspicious only gradually after Franklin began asking me about my duties there at the Bow Street Court: whether I had some authority as a constable, or any duties of that nature. This, of course, led to the question of why I had been called away from the table, which I answered by improvising a leave of absence for Constable Perkins. Dr. Franklin seemed to accept that. At any rate, he asked no more questions. There was also the matter of the voice heard when Mrs. Stevenson went off to fetch the almanacs. Was it a voice—or my imagination? And what if it were a voice? There might indeed be other residents in the house—servants of Dr. Franklin or Mrs. Stevenson, her sons or daughters. So, all in all, I was less concerned about the unidentified voice than I was regarding Franklin's curiosity in the matter of my early departure.

What good it would do to wait here I knew not, nor was I prepared to remain long at the mouth of this smelly alley. I heard the pattering of rats' feet all round me, and yet I was determined to watch Craven Street for ten minutes, give or take a bit, just to see who, if anyone, would emerge, and what, if anything, they might do. There are times, after all, when one does something for no better reason than it feels like the proper thing to do.

It did not take nearly so long as I had prepared to wait. There could not have been more than five minutes passed when Arthur Lee came hurrying up Craven Street in that same ungainly manner I had seen him run for the door last night at the King's Pleasure. Clearly, he was a man with a mission, though what it might be I could not say.

He turned onto the Strand heading east. Mr. Perkins had taught me a good deal about trailing people in the street, though I had not, until that moment, had occasion to put what I had learned from him to use. The constable had told me that it was best done when there was a bit of a crowd about, so that he who did the trailing might hide in the crowd. "Don't stay close behind," he would caution me. "Just stay close enough so that you have him in sight, but always try to keep at least two or three people between you and your target."

Yes, I remembered all that Mr. Perkins had said, and that day I was fortunate in that all the conditions were right. I stayed behind Arthur Lee for a good many streets. There was, however, one worrisome matter: Lee turned round a number of times. At first I thought he had spied me and was looking back a second time and a third simply to confirm his fears. But no, it became evident that he was looking beyond me and into the street. It was not until we came to Half Moon Passage, a favorite spot for hackney coaches to wait for fares, that I understood. He had been looking all the while for a hackney open for hire. Of a sudden he broke into an awkward jog-trot, leaving me behind in a quandary. Should I run after him, thereby showing myself as his pursuer, or risk losing him by—And then I saw him stop and take a moment to bargain with the driver. They came to an agreement, and he jumped inside. My heart sank as the hackney coach pulled away. Yet just then another pulled up to take the place of the first. I ran to it, giving the driver no time to climb down from his perch.

"Hi, up there, do you see that hackney just pulled away?"

"'Course I sees it," said the driver. "I ain't blind."

"Well, follow it, wherever it goes. Let it keep a space ahead, though."

"You want to come up here and drive my team?"

"No, I'll trust you to do that much."

With which I opened the door, hopped up the step, and into the coach. I had not quite managed to get the door shut before we were off.

Only then did I think to explore my pockets to see if I had money enough to take us the distance. The question was, of course, just how far would Arthur Lee travel? If it were to Deptford or beyond, then I was altogether lost. I should have to give the driver whatever I had in my pockets—no more than a shilling—and hope that I might impress him with my association with the Bow Street Court. Well, I told myself, I shall worry about that when the time comes.

In the meantime, we traveled a familiar route, moving roughly alongside the river, past London Bridge and along Thames Street. There, at no particular place, we stopped. I had no idea why we had done so—whether Lee's coach had also stopped, or whether he had escaped us. I threw open the coach and prepared to descend.

"Best stay inside a bit longer if you don't want to be seen," said the driver.

"All right," said I, "and thank-you."

He climbed down and rapped on the coach door, when he judged the moment suitable. When he did, I exited and saw that we were close to the Tower, which meant I had enough to pay the fare and a bit more.

"Here," said I, offering him a penny over and above what he asked, "have an ale and think of me."

Pleased at that, he explained that he was sure we had not been observed trailing the hackney in which Arthur Lee rode.

"There's a lot of goods wagons along here in Thames Street. The driver was too busy dodging them to look over his shoulder at us. Anyway, your man, the passenger, crossed the street in a great rush and went down the Bear Key Stairs. That's a great gathering place for the watermen hereabouts, and so my guess is that he is headed out to one of those ships anchored out there in the river. Good luck to you, young sir, no matter what this is all about."

Having said that, he climbed up to his place atop the coach, cracked his whip above his horses, and pulled out into the stream of wagons and coaches which plied the waterfront.

It was no easy matter getting to the other side of Thames Street, but with a bit of dodging and a dash I made it to the stairs. Before beginning my descent, I looked close at the watermen round the little pier below. I saw that one of their number had just pulled away with a passenger aboard. Undoubtedly it was Lee.

And so, wisely, I took my time going down to the river. I had no wish to call Lee's attention to me, nor did I think it wise to excite the interest of the watermen by seeming overly concerned. By the time I reached the pier and had declined offers from four to take me "up, down, or across the Thames," I saw that Arthur Lee had reached the ship anchored farthest out. A rope ladder had been tossed down the side to him. There could be no doubt that this was his destination.

"What is that ship out there?" I asked the waterman nearest me, "the one with the ladder down the side?"

"That one?" said he, "with the boat pulled alongside? That's the *Rose of Sharon* out of Boston, Massachusetts Colony. They got pious names for their ships in Boston."

He was a tough and wizened old cod and looked to have been a waterman for fifty years or more.

"So I hear," said I. "Has it been here long?"

"Long enough. It took on a cargo of tea and coffee over there at the wharf. It finished loading this morn. It'll leave on the morning tide."

"Is he the last passenger?" I asked, pointing at Lee, who was now ascending the ladder with no little difficulty.

"Him? Oh no. He's just someone had a package that he said had to get to Boston right away."

"How big was it? He doesn't seem to have anything with him."

"Oh, it was small—fitted in his pocket. Said it was important, though." He paused and began filling a small pipe with strong black tobacco. "But if it was so damn important why wouldn't he pay a fair price? I quoted him the usual, and he wouldn't hear of it.

Finally, the boy of us agreed to haul him over to the ship and back for tuppence. *Tuppence!* Can you suppose it?"

I had no choice but to walk back to Bow Street, which took an hour or so from the Bear Key Stairs. I was well aware that I had used up far more time than would have been thought necessary to deliver two letters. So it was likely that I should be given a proper reprimand upon my return. Yet not, I hoped, before I was given a chance to tell all that I had learned to Sir John. No doubt I should have told him earlier what I had seen — or thought I had seen at the King's Pleasure — but to be able to tell him now where he might look for that packet of letters, that was worth the delay, was it not?

Arriving in Bow Street, I made for Number 4, half-expecting to find Sir John's court still in session, yet I found nothing of the sort. Alas, it was later than I had even thought.

I threw open the door to enter the part called "backstage" by Sir John and as I did, collided with Mr. Donnelly, yet without injury to either of us.

"Ah, Jeremy, it's you, is it? I confess I was not attentive to my direction. I didn't see you until we bumped."

"Nor did I see you. Sorry." I moved to go round him.

"Oh, but don't rush off. I've something to tell."

"But I —"

"And it concerns you direct."

"Oh?" He had my interest.

"Yes, I went to Sir John just as you suggested. I addressed him in manly fashion and told him of my interest in Molly and that I should like to get to know her better. He asked if I meant to court her. And I told him that though my intentions were honorable, I wished to know her well enough to see if she were *worth* courting. He thought that most amusing. He did laugh loudly but recovered himself sufficiently to say that I might call it as I liked but that it sounded like courting to him. And therefore, if I wish to get to know Molly better in the manner I had described, then it would be best to do so in public places and in the company of friends."

"Well," said I, "that's courting then — as I understand it."

"Of course it is," he laughed, "and he well knows it. But the upshot of all this mutual deceit is that Molly and I are to go to the Covent Garden Theatre tomorrow evening, and that you and Clarissa are to accompany us."

"Why, that's . . . that's fine, that's excellent." So said I, yet I could tell something troubled him. "But is anything wrong?"

"Not really," said he. " 'Tis simply that you and Clarissa are to be my guests, and if it is to continue so, I shall soon have to give up this before-courting arrangement and get on to the real thing."

Having said that, he began to muse silently upon it. And I, not knowing quite what he meant, kept my silence, as well.

But then, rousing himself: "Good to bump into you, Jeremy. I shall be by for you and the ladies at seven, if that suits all."

With a distracted wave, he left me at the door.

My interview with Sir John, though it had a somewhat disappointing conclusion, went rather better for me than I had expected. He cared little that I had come back late from delivering the two letters, and only slightly more that I was tardy in reporting to him the events at the King's Pleasure the night before.

With a severe look, he said to me: "You should know better, Jeremy. If ever this situation or another like it should arise, you must tell me at your earliest opportunity."

I hung my head appropriately enough and vowed that I should always do so in the future.

But then did he lean forward eagerly. "But go on," said he. "You've obviously got more to tell."

And indeed I did. I told him all. From Mrs. Stevenson's invitation to come into the sitting room to meet Benjamin Franklin, to my wild pursuit of Arthur Lee along the Strand, into a hackney and on to Bear Key Stairs. I concluded with what the old waterman had told me.

"I asked him if Lee were a passenger come late to board the ship for Boston," said I to Sir John. "The old codger told me, no, Lee simply had a small package that had to be delivered to Boston as quick as ever could be. So all that need be done is to prevent the *Rose of Sharon* from departing, go through the mail they carry, and pull from it the package containing the packet of letters."

Evidently, Sir John thought little of the course of action that I suggested, for the face that he showed me as I ended my tale was a sad one — or, perhaps better put, one that expressed frustration and dismay.

"What you suggest is not so easily done. The Royal Post is not, except in extreme cases, to be tampered with. It takes a special warrant that is to be issued by a judge at the Old Bailey. And in that warrant, the package and its contents are to be described in precise detail. Are we able to do that? No. We know not to whom the package is addressed. We know not its exact contents — for Lord Hillsborough may have lied about that, just as he did lie to us about other things. But let us say he did not. Let us say there is a packet of letters inside the package. Do we know how many? No. Do we know to whom the letters are addressed? No. Do we know who wrote them? No. Do we know, in detail or in general, what they contain? Certainly we do not. They have kept that from us right from the start. Now, Jeremy, do you see what we are up against?"

"Yes sir, I do." Had I then wasted the better part of a morning and an afternoon? Probably.

"Yet perhaps," he continued, "it is best that these difficulties are placed before us."

"Why do you say that, Sir John?"

"In answer, let me tell you first of all that if I were to make application to Lord Mansfield for that warrant to halt the *Rose of Sharon* and dig into the Royal Post in search of that packet, I believe we would receive it from him, so eager is he to please those in the government. That's right; knowing as little as we do of the package and its contents, he would have given us a free hand to rifle the mails, working against the very laws he is sworn to uphold. And if he were to do so, it would only be typical of the way the rest of this investigation has been carried out. This matter of Franklin is the worst. In effect, they have given me the name of him they have chosen as the culprit and told me to build a case against him. This is unheard of! It is against all rules of proper investigative procedure."

"But what if the name that has been given you is indeed the name of the true culprit?" I asked.

"You mean Franklin, of course?"

"Yes sir."

"Well, I should prefer to lose Franklin than to conduct an improper investigation."

"Truly so?"

"Yes, truly."

"So there will be no arrest, no questioning of Dr. Franklin?"

"Not until we have more to go on."

"And what about Arthur Lee? Will he not be detained? Questioned? Arrested? I'm now certain I saw him in that dive in Bedford Street."

"On what charge should he be arrested? Consorting with one who consorts with known criminals?"

SIX

*In which a friend
leaves for parts
unknown*

Next morning Sir John announced to me in his chambers that we should now turn, in our investigation, to Albert Calder. I was delighted to know that the investigation would continue, yet couldn't, for the life of me, remember who he might be.

"Who is Albert Calder?" I asked in all innocence.

"So quickly forgotten is he?"

"I fear he has been by me."

"Well then," said Sir John, "just as a reminder, Albert Calder was the poor fellow stretched out upon Lord Hillsborough's floor with the back of his head bashed in."

"Oh, certainly I do remember him," said I, "but what more can he tell us? He's dead, after all. We know how he was killed and have a good idea of why."

"Ah, but do we know why? There is, after all, a possibility that he did *not* surprise the burglars, that he was in league with them."

"Their man on the inside? Is that it?"

"Why yes, let us bear in mind that Skinner and Ferguson knew exactly where to go. They went into the correct room and began ransacking the desk. They must have had an exact map, or been led there."

"Sir John," said I, "it could be just as you say, but would it not be reasonable to suppose that Dr. Franklin had oft been inside the study doing business there with Lord Hillsborough?"

"Perhaps . . . yes, I would call that reasonable."

"Then why not question Dr. Franklin in that matter?"

"Because I have done with him for the time being. Had they not set me like some hound upon Franklin, I would have begun to find out all I could about Albert Calder. I simply look at this as resuming our investigation at the point where it was interrupted. Do I make that clear, Jeremy?"

"Perfectly clear, Sir John."

"Good, because I wish you now to pursue that part of the investigation. Go to the residence of Lord Hillsborough and talk first of all to Carruthers, the butler, and then to Will Lambert, as well."

"Will Lambert?" I echoed. "He was the other footman, was he not? It was he who found the body in the study."

"Correct. And find out what they know about Albert Calder. Carruthers must have hired him, so he, no doubt, knows something. And as for Lambert, he and Calder worked together, so presumably he would have been as close to him as any. If they have any suggestions as to others on the staff you might talk with, then talk with them, too. You can attend to all of that in a morning, can't you?"

"Well, perhaps, why?"

"I'd like you back here for my court session."

"I understand," said I—but, of course, I did not. I simply perceived from the tone of his voice and the little he said that he wished not to be questioned further. "Good-bye then."

By the time I reached the door to the long hall, he had something more to add:

"Try to find out what the footmen were guarding there. It strikes me as odd to have armed guards walking about in the night. When did it start? What was it about?"

"As you will, Sir John."

As I hurried down the Strand toward Craig's Court, I passed Craven Street, of course, and noted with interest how close was Benjamin Franklin's residence to Lord Hillsborough's. Could he have chosen that location so as to be nearest to the man in government with whom he dealt most frequently? They were practically near neighbors.

Then did my mind go from Franklin to Sir John. It seemed to me that the magistrate was behaving both oddly and obstinately in this matter of Franklin. I could scarce believe my ears when he had said to me that he would rather lose Franklin as a suspect than conduct an improper investigation. Was that not putting the form of law over its intent? Sir John was forever telling me that I must learn to think as a lawyer. I asked myself if he, in this case, was thinking as a lawyer. That usually meant—to me, at least—thinking more realistically, even perhaps cold-bloodedly. Was he now exalting principle at the expense of all else?

Luckily, Lord Hillsborough had left for the day by the time I arrived. As for Lady Hillsborough, I never saw her once during this entire episode and later discovered she was ever in their castle in Ireland with their three children.

Naturally, it was Carruthers, the butler, who opened to my knock, and it was to him that I talked first. He was a tall man of rather advanced years, self-contained in the manner of some who work in service to the very rich. Though he never, I'm sure, put it into words, his attitude seemed to be: "I may be a servant, nevertheless I am my own man." I admired him for it. He recognized me and invited me in.

"What may I do for you, young sir?"

"Sir John has sent me here that I might ask a few more questions of you and Will Lambert, and perhaps of any others whose answers you would deem likely to be pertinent."

"Very well," said he most agreeably. "Why don't we go sit in the drawing room? It's much more comfortable there."

He led me a bit down the long hall and into a room, which, though dark, was restfully so. The curtains were pulled, yet sufficient daylight sifted in round them to brighten the room a bit. A small fire burned in the fireplace, adding more light. He poked at the fire and managed to get it to burn a bit better.

"I find that as I get older, I prefer darkened rooms." He gestured at a chair opposite the fireplace and, as I sat down, seated himself in one near it. "I hope you don't mind the dark."

I assured him I did not.

"Such a nice room," said Carruthers, looking about. "It gets little use by Lord Hillsborough." He paused. "Well now, what can I tell you that you and Sir John don't already know?"

"As much as possible about Albert Calder. For instance, you are the head of the household staff, I assume?"

"Yes, oh yes."

"Then I take it you are in charge of hiring and firing," said I. "When did you hire Mr. Calder? How long, in other words, had he worked here?"

"Nearly five years, I should say. I have been with Lord Hillsborough for a bit more than that, and Albert was one of the first I hired—if not *the* first."

"You called him by his Christian name, I note. Was he so well known to you? Was he a friend?"

"Oh," said Carruthers, "I'm not sure what that means in a large staff as we have here. A friend? Possibly. He was certainly a fine fellow. He kept everyone round the kitchen table well-entertained. There was that about him which begged familiarity. You could not think of him as any sort of Mister." Yet having said what he had said, the butler fell silent, as if for a moment reconsidering. "But I must say," he resumed, "it was not quite so with him during the past few weeks."

"Would you say that he changed?"

"I would say so, yes—but in a rather subtle way. He still joked and jollied with us, but it was as if he just tried to keep up appearances, as if he weren't really behind it. I remember I caught him alone—why, in this very room!—and though he sat in its darkest corner, I perceived that he had been weeping. Now, it ain't usual for a man to weep, especially one such as Calder."

"What do you mean by that? One such as Calder?"

"Well, as I said, he was, in his way, a jolly sort, but more than that, he seemed ever the sort who could take care of himself. A great hulking fellow, he was. He feared none—or seemed not to till I found him so here in the drawing room."

"Did he account for this? Did he say what burdened him so?"

"No," said he with a judicious shake of his head. "He said naught but that it was money troubles."

"Money troubles?"

"Yes, and no more than that. I sought to relieve him, cheer him a bit, saying that we all had those. But I did say that if ever he wanted to be more specific, I was there to listen, and maybe I could help. But he never did come to me. We never talked further of it."

He ended with a gesture—open hands raised into the air—as if to signify that he had told all there was to tell. Yet I was not to be put off quite so easily.

"Why was it necessary for Lord Hillsborough to put the footmen on duty as guards? What was it of such value that it required that sort of protection?"

"That," said Carruthers, "I fear I cannot answer. Perhaps only Lord Hillsborough can."

"Or possibly Will Lambert?"

"Possibly. But you would have to pose such questions direct to him."

"And may I do that now?"

"Unfortunately not. He is not here, nor is he likely to be for some time yet. It is the duty of driver and coachman to wait with the coach until such time as it may be required by Lord Hillsborough."

"And where would they be waiting?" I asked.

"Well, if you wish to seek him out," said he, "you would best look among the coaches in line at Middle Scotland Yard, for that is where Lord Hillsborough keeps his office."

With that I rose and returned with him to the door which led to Craig's Court without. There he paused and gave me more detailed instructions.

"I can tell you this," said the butler to me, "if he is there at all awaiting the master, the coach will be in the second space in line."

"How can you be certain?" I asked.

"There is a distinct order of rank maintained there. Nothing is done by chance, nor will it ever be."

I bowed my thanks and took my leave of him.

He had given most explicit directions, sending me to Charing Cross Road and to its end, where it widened considerably into Whitehall. Middle Scotland Yard, I was to remember, would be the second building on my left. I was grateful for all this, for in truth I was not well acquainted with these grand buildings of government and could easily have lost my way.

What went on there in Whitehall I had no exact idea, though had I been asked, I should have replied quickly enough that all matters pertaining to Britain and her colonies were handled there, in its many offices. Yes, but handled in what way? Could the price of bread be dictated from Whitehall? Were men such as Lord Hillsborough to preside over spaces and places which they had never even seen? It seemed to me that Sir John ruled his piece of London more truly and fairly than any such "secretary" or administrator who might happen to preside over this territory or that island. And he did so by virtue of his residence there in the heart of Covent Garden.

Ah, but there was no denying that the buildings which comprised this seat of governance were indeed impressive. Tall they were and of great dimension. Yet, in a way, the spaces between were just as impressive, for they were of such size that they might accommodate whole troops of men and regiments of soldiers. The rest of London — or the most of it, in any case — seemed narrow, dark, and constricted by contrast. Here, in Whitehall, a man could see the sky and feel the sun.

When I turned through the gate and into the great cobbled court of Middle Scotland Yard, I found all to be just as Carruthers the butler had described. To the right, just beyond the carriage entrance, was a line of coaches that seemed to stretch half the length of the great hall. There were more empty spaces in it, and so I assumed that the second coach in line must be that of Lord Hillsborough. I satisfied myself in that by approaching the two men who had taken places beside it and asking them which of them was Will Lambert.

"That would be me," said the younger of the two. "What can I do for you, young sir?"

I explained who I was, where I had come from, and on whose authority I had been sent.

"I have some questions for you," said I to him.

Lambert, who seemed increasingly concerned as I identified myself, wore a rather long face by the time I had done. He exchanged significant looks with the short, squat man whom I took to be the driver of the coach. In other words, reader, he took some time to respond.

"What say you," said he to me, "if we take a little walk that we might talk a little easier and in private?"

I assented and saw most immediate that it was not away from his companion, the driver, that he wished to take me, but rather out of earshot of those coachmen and drivers round us who had moved perceptively closer to hear what might be said. Perhaps I had been a bit loud in pronouncing the Bow Street Court and the name of Sir John. I vowed to watch my tone.

"I have come," said I, "to learn more of Albert Calder."

"Well, what is there to learn?" said he in little more than a whisper. "He was a footman, same as me. Not much to tell there."

"But he was also a house guard—just as you are."

"That's right—but that hadn't gone on long."

"How long?"

"Oh . . . I don't know, maybe a month."

"And what was it you were guarding?"

"What were we guarding?" He became agitated. His voice rose. "Why, just like you said, we were guarding the house."

"Come now," said I, "you were both going on short sleep. There must have been some special reason, something special you were guarding."

He hesitated, then blurted forth: "No, there wasn't, least not what we were told about. All I can say is, we were to keep special watch on that one room."

"What room?"

"You know what room, the one I found him in, the one where he met his end."

"Lord Hillsborough's study?"

"That's right."

"But you were never told what it was in that room you were guarding that was so important that you were to do without sleep to protect it from theft?"

"No, we were never told that. All I can say is, whoever killed poor Albert must've got what he came for."

"Why do you say that?" I asked.

"Because there's no more of that house guarding. I got a fair night's sleep the last few nights."

"What were your instructions regarding the use of your weapons?"

"Try to capture the thief, if possible, and if not, shoot to kill. What I think happened was, Albert come upon the robber and pulled out his pistol and told him to cease and desist, not knowing there was another robber just behind him. He got whacked from behind, as anyone could plainly see. It must've been one hell of a blow put him down."

"It could've been you."

"Ain't I told myself that a hundred times?"

I waited then, allowing him to make it one hundred and one. He roused himself then and gave me an expectant look. It was as though he had something to tell, yet would offer me nothing gratis. He depended upon me to ask the right question. I perceived this, yet knew not what that question might be.

"What sort of man was he?" I asked lamely.

"What sort is any man? He was a fine fellow, was Albert. There's little could be said against him, the way he could get everyone laughing and carrying on."

"Yes, I've heard he was quite a dinner-table entertainer."

"And so he was."

"But I've also heard that in the last few months he seemed secretly to be worried."

"You must have heard that from Carruthers," said he, yet waited for no confirmation from me before plunging on: "About a month past he come to me and asked what was it wrong with poor Albert. I told him there was nothing wrong with him — just that he ran into a spot of trouble, as we all do from time to time."

"I was told that Albert Calder's problems were money problems."

"Ain't they always? By God, with money enough a man could solve all the problems life puts before him. Now, ain't that true?"

"It may well be," said I, "but I would like to know what *sort* of money problems Calder was having."

He, who had become quite forthcoming, did all of a sudden fall silent. Taking a step back, he gave me a hard, assessing look, as if to satisfy himself that I was worthy of the information he might or might not offer me.

"What did you say it was you had to do with Bow Street?" he asked.

"I am Sir John Fielding's assistant."

"You look pretty young for that."

"That's as may be," said I. "Nevertheless, that is who I am and what I am."

"You got any piece of paper says so?"

"Could you read it if I did? Listen, you have something to tell. I want to hear it. You can either tell me now, so that I may pass it on to Sir John, or wait until tonight when one of the Bow Street Runners comes and hauls you out of bed and brings you to Sir John that he may hear it direct from you. Of course by then he may be asleep, in which case you shall have to wait in our strong room until morning when he wakes and has breakfasted. And, of course, by this time Lord Hillsborough will have missed you, at least to the extent that he will have noticed that there are not two up top his coach but only one. And having noticed that—"

"Awright, awright," said he, "you made your point right enough. What do you want from me?"

"What you have to tell me. I asked you what sort of money problems Albert Calder was having. Answer that, and we'll have made a good beginning."

He sighed and then nodded his assent. "Albert Calder was a gambler. He would as soon bet upon the fall of a penny as drink the ale the penny could buy. He'd bet upon anything, whether it be two mice made to race, or the time it would take for the shadow of the Admiralty to reach the Middle Yard. And if he'd stuck to those farthing and tuppence wagers and suchlike, he'd have been alright, but he didn't. The worst thing that could happen to any gambling man happened to him."

"And what was that?" I asked.

"He got lucky."

"How could that be bad?"

"Oh, you know how it is. You win a bit, and then a bit more, and pretty soon, you've got a few pounds and maybe a sovereign or two, and with them you get the itch to try your luck at the games where winning would mean winning big—like dicing and twenty-one. Oh, and he used to visit the terrier pits, the big one down in Bedford Street. The funny thing is, his luck held up—for a while—and he was bringing five or ten pounds of an evening. Albert was getting rich, or would have been if he'd had the good sense to quit whilst he was ahead—but he never. He just looked at all the pounds, shillings, and pence he won as just so much to gamble with to get more.

"Well, you know what happened. Just as quick as the luck had come to him, it went even quicker. It couldn't have taken more than two or three nights to clean him out. And if that wasn't bad enough, that last day of losing and maybe a day or two after, he played on credit at this one place. The man who ran the game took his notes and chits, and Albert woke up one morning to find himself in debt near a hundred pounds."

"And that, I suppose, was just about a month ago."

"So it was," he said, "so it was."

"Just about the same time you two started house-guarding."

"Well now, you got that right. Why didn't I ever think of that?" And just in case I had not caught his attempt at irony, Will Lambert delivered to me a great wink of his eye.

"I have but one question more for you, sir," said I.

"And what is that?"

"What was the name of that fellow who ran the last game, the one wherein Albert Calder was allowed to play on credit?"

"Can't help you much there. Y'see he don't have a name so much as he has a sort of nickname — and that is 'Duke.'"

"Duke? Is he a duke? One of nobility?"

"No, not by much, he isn't. It's for the way he dresses, which, as I've heard, is in the manner of a gentleman."

"Ah," said I, "then perhaps you can tell me where it is that he runs his game of chance and what sort of a game it be."

"You said there'd be no more questions after the last."

"Oh, did I, didn't I? But then, that answer you gave wasn't much, now, was it? No name but a nickname?"

"Ah well, perhaps you're right. No, I can't tell you where the game might be, but I think it must surely be in or around Bedford Street, for 'tis there that the Duke spends most of his time. And as for what sort of game it is, I don't really know that, either, for I ain't never been there. I've no doubt, though, that it is played with cards and could even make a poor man of the king."

I learned soon enough why Sir John had requested that I return to Bow Street for his court session. There was little time to discuss the matter beforehand, for he was on his way into the courtroom when I arrived.

"It's you, is it, Jeremy?"

"Yes sir, and I've found out some things about Albert Calder that you'll be interested in."

"I'll be glad to hear them—but not now. I must get on with it, I fear. I've a full docket today."

"As you will, Sir John."

Mr. Marsden threw open the door to the courtroom and assisted the magistrate in his entrance. I held back, thinking it best to seat myself at the rear of the room. But Sir John would have none of that.

"Come along, Jeremy," said he. "I want you in the front row, for you've a role to play in this drama."

What role? What drama? Truly, at that moment I had no idea, yet as I was then as always Sir John's faithful servant, I followed him in and, following the "all rise" intoned by Mr. Marsden, took a place in the front row that had been held for me by Mr. Fuller, the day jailer.

Sessions of the Bow Street Court are usually well attended by the denizens of Covent Garden. And on this day it seemed that an especially large assembly of layabouts, whores, and pimps had come for their midday entertainment. They came to laugh at the predicaments of those who came before Sir John on such petty charges as public drunkenness and disturbing the peace; to jeer and cheer at those who brought their disputes to be settled in magistrate's court; and, finally, to thrill to the tales told in their own defense by those charged with felonies, who would in a day or two face trial at Old Bailey. Whatever was brought before them, the crowd found diversion and even some excitement in these daily sessions. But lately, as Sir John oft complained, they had grown a bit unruly; and the boldest of them seemed to wish to influence him in his decisions with their catcalls and shouts.

At that moment, there was a loud hum of anticipation, so loud, in fact, that Sir John found it necessary to beat upon the scarred table before him with his gavel, and call for order. They responded properly, and soon all had quieted down.

"Mr. Marsden, call the first case."

"We summon Lady Márie-Helene Grenville before the bar."

There was an immediate response from the crowd, more in the

nature of a roar than a hum. Any criminal charge to a member of the aristocracy or the nobility was of keen interest to those of the lower classes. Yet this one had been talked of for weeks for a number of reasons. First of all, Márie-Helene was (it was rumored, for none had seen her) a beautiful Frenchwoman. She was bold and brave and had undertaken to fight when challenged in the course of a smuggling expedition. And, finally, she was under the protection of Black Jack Bilbo, gambler and previously a privateer. Mr. Bilbo, long a favorite with the mob, was said also to be her lover.

I turned and looked behind me, half-expecting to see them marching down the aisle in answer to Mr. Marsden's loud summons. Yet only half, for well I recalled Clarissa's clear-eyed prediction of their defection. Sir John, too, must have been of a like opinion.

Nor was I the only one who turned to look for them. All round the courtroom people turned and stretched their necks that they might catch a glimpse of Márie-Helene or Mr. Bilbo. Where were they? The roar of the crowd rose to a hubbub. Sir John beat down savagely upon the table with his gavel.

"Order!" said he. "I will have order here, or I shall clear this courtroom, if I must."

That was in no wise necessary, for immediately he had spoken a hush fell over the crowd. It seemed to me it had come to most that neither Márie-Helene nor Mr. Bilbo were present, nor would they be arriving late.

"What is the difficulty, Mr. Marsden?" he shouted out to the man who sat next him. "You summoned the woman. Where is she?"

"She does not appear to be anywhere in this room," said Mr. Marsden.

"Oh, she does not, eh? Well, we shall see about that, so we shall. If she will not come to the law, as she has been ordered to do, then the law will come to her." He paused but an instant before bellowing out my name.

I jumped to my feet, not quite knowing what lay ahead. "I am here, sir. What is it you wish?"

"I wish Lady Grenville to be here in this courtroom, as was solemnly promised to me by her and by another party, whom I take also to be absent. Now, Jeremy Proctor, I do hereby deputize you as constable and direct you to arm yourself and proceed to the house in St. James's Street, which is known to you, and bring back Lady Grenville to stand before me. Use all means necessary. Do you understand?"

"I do indeed, sir."

"Then on your way."

As I slipped out of the courtroom, I heard Sir John ask Mr. Marsden to call forth the next case on the docket.

Strange it was to perambulate the rooms of the house in St. James's Street which I knew so well. They were empty—emptier than empty, for only a few remnants of furniture were left; and they, it seemed, belonged to another era, another time and place. I wandered about, looking into this room and that, so I might report to Sir John that I had searched every room. Nevertheless, it was evident from the way my footsteps echoed through the entire house that it was quite useless to expect to find any other living soul present.

I had entered by the front door, for it was unlocked. As I made my inspection of the rooms, I looked forward to viewing the last there on the ground floor. And just as I expected, in that room, the entrance to the tunnel I had discovered a few years ago had been left open, revealing the final exit taken by Black Jack, Márie-Helene, and Jimmie Bunkins. They would have emerged in the mews out beyond the back hedges. There, Black Jack's coach-and-four would have awaited them and taken them away to Black Jack's *Island Princess*, which he had kept moored somewhere in Wapping. And from there, you could be certain, they would have sailed on the morning tide.

Then, interrupting my ruminations, came the sound of voices from the front of the house. The door slammed. I heard footsteps echoing hollowly in the hall, just as mine had done only a few minutes before. By the sound of them there were but two men. If they were burglars or looters I resolved that I would chase them away. As the footsteps approached, I moved swiftly into the hall and, with pistol drawn, challenged them to identify themselves.

One of them, well-dressed and properly bewigged, stepped forward and announced himself as William Slade. He looked familiar, and the name, too, struck a certain chord in my memory. Who was he?

"I am the owner of this house," said he. "And who, may I ask, are you?"

I gave him my name and explained my errand. As I did so, I took note of the man beside Mr. Slade. He, too, looked familiar, and it did not take me more than a moment to identify him. He was the one I had seen in the King's Pleasure in company with Arthur Lee. And Slade? Still I was unsure of his exact identity, yet ever so certain that our paths had crossed previously.

I tucked the pistol away in its holster, which seemed to ease matters considerably between us.

"I should have known that Mr. Bilbo would sell this house rather than simply desert it," said I. "They have gone then?"

"On the morning tide. He could be anyplace within a hundred miles by now."

"So he could," said I. "I believe that we have met before, sir." At last it had come to me.

"Oh? That could be, I suppose."

"Weeks past you were alone in Mr. Bilbo's gaming house one afternoon and were kind enough to help me find him."

"Ah, so it was," said he. "Now I recall." I was not at all sure that he really did.

"Since then, as I understand, you bought the gaming club from him. And now I find that you are the new owner of this house, as well."

"So I did, and so I am." He seemed to be growing impatient with me.

"And you, sir," said I to him I had seen in the King's Pleasure, "are you not the one they call the 'Duke'?"

The two exchanged glances of an uneasy sort. And did I perhaps detect a slight negative shake of the head from Mr. Slade?

"Aw, I don't know," said he in a thick London accent. "A body gets called one thing and another. I've no notion what name I might be given from one day to the next."

"And you are properly named . . . ?"

Another signal from Slade: an all but unnoticeable affirmative nod.

"Isaac Kidd."

"I've heard it said, sir, that you run a game of chance in one of
the cellars along Bedford Street," said I. "I've been known to try my
luck now and again. Perhaps I might do so at your table."

"Aw no, young sir. I fear you're mistaken, so I do. I run no such
games, nor would I ever wish to in such surroundings."

"I can certainly understand that," said I, "but—"

"Mr. Kidd is a business associate of mine," said Slade. "We have
worked together for many a year. I can vouch for him."

"Oh, there be no need for any to vouch. I simply thought that—"

Again he interrupted: "As I said I have bought this house and
am now in the process of taking possession of it, which is to say, I
must do a walk-through and take note of any and all items left or
out of proper order. Much as we would like to talk further with you,
Mr. Proctor, we must get on with it. Now if you will excuse us?"

"Certainly, sir, and I thank you for putting up with my questions and satisfying my curiosity."

With that I bowed low and allowed them to pass.

Upon my return to Number 4 Bow Street, I sought out Sir John to
tell him what I had heard and seen in the course of my travels back
and forth through London. Having thought through my presentation as I made my return, I offered it all to Sir John more or less in
a single telling, tying that which I had learned regarding Albert
Calder to my chance meeting with Isaac Kidd and Mr. Slade in the
house in St. James's Street.

The magistrate sat, considering all that I had said. Then, of a
sudden, he sat up and slapped the top of his desk.

"Well, there, you see?" said he. "We have our mapmaker."

"Our . . . mapmaker, sir?"

"Why yes, we agreed, didn't we, that our burglars would have
required a map of some sort in order to go direct to the study? Who
knows what greater support he may have given them?"

"But if Albert Calder were one of them, why was he then
killed?"

"Surely that should be obvious to you, Jeremy. Perhaps they feared he would snitch on them. It is always an advantage to burglars to have a man on the inside. Yet, as is so often said, dead men tell no tales."

"Admittedly," said I, "Calder had the motive and the opportunity to pass on to Skinner and Ferguson—through Isaac Kidd—a plan of the house and other details that would have been necessary or merely helpful in the commission."

"Indeed," said Sir John, "your man Kidd, the 'Duke' as he is called, no doubt put it to Calder that his debt—which must have been considerable, would be forgiven if only he would cooperate in the burglary."

"That's as I myself supposed. But really, did he have any better motive or opportunity than Dr. Franklin?"

"Ah, back with him again, are we?"

"Indeed! Don't forget that when Albert Calder was dealt that death-blow, he had a pistol in hand, and it seemed to be pointed directly at the one behind the desk—which is to say, at the burglar, or one of them."

"Don't forget, you say? What do you take me for?"

"What do I take you for?" said I, boldly. "Well, I must confess that 'stubborn' is the word that leaps to mind."

"'Stubborn,' is it? 'Stubborn,' indeed! How come you to such a conclusion?"

"How can I avoid it? You refuse to pursue the possibility of Dr. Franklin's involvement in the burglary. And now, for some reason quite incomprehensible to me, you seem also reluctant to pursue the matter of the late Mr. Calder's guilt."

"Well, Jeremy," said he, "the reason which you find so incomprehensible is, in fact, the same in both cases."

"It is? How do you mean?"

"Well, I take it you have decided that I should charge or bring in for questioning this fellow Isaac Kidd as well as Arthur Lee—Kidd to establish the connection between the burglars and Albert Calder, and Arthur Lee to establish the link between the burglars and Franklin. Is that correct?"

I gave that but a moment's thought and agreed. But then did I add: "Truly, they all fit together, do they not? 'Tis only a question of which provided the plan to the house and other information helpful to Skinner and Ferguson, is it not?"

"We are not there yet," said he, cautioning me. "The point is that none of them can be charged on the basis of what we now know—not even Skinner and Ferguson. What you have constructed, Jeremy, is a theory of the crime, and a rather good one it is. In other words, it all may have happened just as you suggest. But as for questioning any of them about it, why tip our hand? We don't wish them to know what we suspect but can't prove, do we?"

"I suppose not."

"Rather than bring it to a boil, we would do better to let the pot simmer for a bit, don't you think so?"

Reluctantly, I conceded the point to him.

This spirited conversation took place in Sir John's chambers upon my return from the fool's errand on which I had been sent. I told him all I had learned whilst supposedly searching for Black Jack and Márie-Helene. Sir John knew, of course, even more certainly than I, that the two would not be present when I went to fetch them from that grand house in St. James's Street, though it was news to us both that in addition to Mr. Bilbo's gaming club William Slade had also purchased the former's residence. And it was, indeed, news in which Sir John took considerable interest.

"What was your estimate of this man Slade?" he asked me as I made ready to leave.

"I was not favorably impressed," said I. "He seems rather a slippery sort to me, but I daresay he seems also to have limitless money."

"Indeed he does. I fear we'll be hearing more from him in the future."

"And I fear you're right."

"Jeremy, I have one more task for you, and a rather onerous one it is. Still, if I'm to report this properly to the Lord Chief Justice, we must cover every possibility."

"Have I neglected something?"

"The *Island Princess*," said he. "I think you should go down to Wapping and confirm that Black Jack's sloop did actually depart early today."

Sighing, I said, "All right." Perhaps I even let out a bit of a groan.

"It's a bother, I know, but it must be done. Take a hackney to and from. Try to get the name of a witness and an estimated time of departure for the vessel." He paused. "I'll not need you further after your return, which is just as well, for you'll no doubt need the rest of the day to prepare for your evening."

"What evening is that?" I knew not quite what he had in mind.

"Why, your trip to the theatre. Don't you recall? I've engaged you and Clarissa to chaperone Molly and Mr. Donnelly. Are you up to it?"

To make quick of it, my journey to Wapping established that the *Island Princess* was no longer moored at the slip that had previously been her London home. And I managed to draw from one Ebenezer Tarkenton, wharfmaster, testimony to the effect that the sloop had sailed at 7:06 in the morning. He was able to be quite exact in this by consulting the wharfmaster's log. Destination? Timbuktu — or so said his log. That seemed no more than a thumb of Mr. Bilbo's nose at all who might think to pursue him.

I returned with this information for Sir John, and, having delivered it, made straightaway upstairs to prepare for the evening's entertainment. Only Molly was there in the kitchen, running about this way and that, doing her valiant best to cook an evening meal for Sir John and Lady Fielding before the rest of us left for the theatre. I greeted her and made an attempt at conversation but was properly rebuffed.

"Oh, Jeremy," said she, sounding a bit desperate, "I'd like to talk, but I can't. Lady F. will soon be here, and I must have all ready for them before I can even think about readying myself." And so it was brought home to me that I must also hurry — if only to get into the proper spirit of the evening. I washed well, shaved, and daubed myself here and there with rosewater, so that I was at that moment quite the cleanest and sweetest-smelling I had ever been in my life. As I was pulling on my cleanest shirt, I heard Clarissa arrive with Lady Fielding. She immediately ran for the room she shared with Molly that she might also make ready. The long and short of it is that we three were all ready and waiting some time before seven whilst there was still light enough to walk cross the Piazza to the

Covent Garden Theatre in complete safety—or so Mr. Donnelly declared as he started us on our way.

We arrived in time for curtain and were seated most immediately in seats provided for us, we were informed, by the playwright,
Mr. Goldsmith. He, Mr. Donnelly's fast friend, had put at our disposal an entire box and left word that he would join us after the performance. Molly was much impressed.

For our part, Clarissa and I were more impressed by the play
Mr. Goldsmith had written. We agreed later that *She Stoops to Conquer; or, The Mistakes of a Night* was quite the funniest comedy we had
ever seen or ever read. The very walls of the theatre (larger than
Garrick's Drury Lane, though not so well-designed) did shake with
laughter only minutes after the performance had begun, and they
did continue to shake until it was done. Clarissa and I walked about
the lobby during the two intermissions, at first discussing the matter of the play in a manner most sober and in suitably serious tones.
Yet twice did we conclude this exercise by reminding each other of
the funniest lines and silliest situations in what we had just seen—
and then how we would laugh!

We came back giggling from the second of these outings, only to
find our two companions staring silently and deeply one into the
other's eyes. He held her hand between his own. They appeared to
have been discussing the very deepest questions, yet as we made
our noisy entrance we saw and noted how they pulled away most
quickly and how guiltily they did welcome us back to the box.

After the final curtain, just as the cast was bowing to the enthu-
siastic applause of the audience, Mr. Goldsmith made his appearance in our box. Yet he barely paused to say hello, so rushed was he.
He went straight to the railing, where he stood for a moment, tall
and proud. I glanced down at the stage and only then did I begin to
understand: The actor who had played Tony Lumpkin (and had
made us laugh most) stepped forward and, with a broad, sweeping
gesture, pointed up to our box, where Mr. Goldsmith waited. The
audience, which had applauded the cast so generously, now turned
to our box and clapped ceaselessly for the playwright, standing and
cheering. The members of the cast upon the stage applauded him—
and so, of course, did we in the box. Oliver Goldsmith waved to

all, accepting the tribute gracefully, if perhaps not humbly. The happy racket ended, and the honored playwright seated himself in our midst. He heaved a great sigh. During introductions, I noticed that he sweated profusely, either from extreme exertion or the drinking of spirits. His face shone red in the candlelight. I could see that what Mr. Donnelly said of him was true: He was not a well man. Nevertheless, he was one of the most entertaining of all in London.

"Almost didn't make it this time," said he. "A fellow tried to rob me on my way over from Bedford Street. I brushed him aside. 'Haven't got time to be robbed,' says I, 'sorry.' 'Oh, that's all right,' says he, 'I'll catch you on the way back.'"

That won a proper laugh from us—but Mr. Donnelly was curious.

"Nolly, you say you almost didn't make it *this* time. Do you get such applause at each performance?"

"I have so far," said Mr. Goldsmith. "Isn't it marvelous? I only wish David Garrick were present to hear it."

"Can he not come?" I asked. "Is he ill?"

"No, he *would* not come—for I have proven him wrong in rejecting my first play, *The Good Natur'd Man*. Oh, it was not near as good as this one you've just seen, but it was good *enough* for him. Turning it down was one thing, but to say, or at least imply, that I would never be a playwright! No need for that."

"No need indeed!" said Mr. Donnelly.

"Ah, but I'll not dwell upon it. No need for that." He then looked round at us and tapped his head knowingly. "I've an idea," said he. "Let's all of us be off for a meal of turtle soup."

"Turtle soup?" echoed Molly. "Can you make a meal of it?"

"You'll make a meal of John Twigg's turtle soup, for there's none can eat a bowl of it without wishing a second. It's thick enough to stand a spoon in it. And good? Good's not good enough for it, and delicious won't do. Why, I'll have to coin a new word for it. But come, why delay when such delights await us only steps away from this theatre? I have reserved a private dining room for us. You'll not be disappointed, I promise."

"What is the name of this most marvelous eating place?" asked Clarissa.

"Why, child," said Mr. Goldsmith, "it is Shakespeare's Head tavern and naught else."

Now, I had often heard the Shakespeare's Head discussed, but never in quite such glowing terms as Mr. Goldsmith's. I had been there once or twice and had eaten Twigg's turtle soup, and while it was all he claimed it to be, it was not primarily for turtle soup that the place was known. Shakespeare's Head was one of Covent Garden's notorious meeting places for prostitutes and their clients. True enough, it was not near so infamous as the places in Bedford Street, and that was because it was attended by a higher class of whore. Nevertheless, it did have quite a jolly reputation of the wrong sort.

There was one thing Mr. Goldsmith had neither exaggerated nor altered in his description of Shakespeare's Head, and that was its nearness to the theatre. It was literally down the colonnade but a bit from where we were at that moment. With Mr. Goldsmith leading us on, we started out. Somewhere along the way, I caught Mr. Donnelly's eye — or perhaps he caught mine. Our eyes met, in any case, and what I saw in his look was not so much fear as it was uneasiness. He, who lived so close by, must know the reputation of this place to which we were headed.

With a sort of flourish, Mr. Goldsmith gestured to the door of the tavern, opened it, and ushered us inside. He prevailed upon the first waiter he saw to take us to the private dining room, which he had reserved. The waiter passed us on to another who started us on our long walk through the narrow aisles and past the tables, toward a few closed doors at the rear of the place.

The place was relatively quiet — yet at the same time fairly dark, so that one wondered just what it was that went on in the quiet that could not be seen in the dark. I, who brought up the rear, received a signal from Clarissa just ahead: eyebrows high and eyes wide, as if to say, who could have expected this? What had she seen?

We came to a halt, and over her shoulder I spied the surprise. 'Twas a man seated between two women, an arm around each, and each hand cupping a breast. The women were broad and brawny; they busied themselves pleasuring the man between them with kisses and love pats; each whispered earnestly into his nearest ear. The man seemed foolishly drunk; his square spectacles had dropped down his nose and were attached only to his left ear. He seemed oblivious of his state but happy, more or less.

The name of this sorry fellow was Benjamin Franklin.

Molly, who had halted our little caravan, thrust her face at the three and asked loudly, "Dr. Franklin, is that you? What are you doing here?"

He had no proper answer for her.

SEVEN

*In which little
happens whilst much
history is made*

Next day, when I made my report on our outing to Sir John, I included something of our meeting with Benjamin Franklin in Shakespeare's Head, telling the story (I fear) as a bit of gossip. Yet Sir John was uninterested, dismissing the incident as of little or no importance.

"Such a silly fellow," said he. "I had heard it said by some that he was a libertine, but I never credited it till now. Still, what surprises me more than his commerce with bawds is that he should appear to you and the rest to be inebriated. He is one—or so I have heard—who keeps close watch upon his health."

"Strange, is it not, Sir John," said I, "that one so admirable in so many ways should seem foolish, even contemptible in others." (Yes, reader, I confess that I said this, or something quite like it, for in those days I was much given to such priggishness.)

"I find that not in the least strange. We are none of us complete human beings—neither completely good, nor completely bad. Why, you may find this difficult to credit, but even I may have a fault or two."

I let that pass without comment.

Sir John was pleased to hear of Mr. Goldsmith's triumph at the Covent Garden Theatre. He bridled up a bit, however, when I gave it as my opinion that *She Stoops to Conquer* was the best of all comedies.

"Of all comedies?" he echoed. "Frankly, Jeremy, I am surprised. Do you hold it higher than the *Midsummer Night's Dream*, or *Much Ado About Nothing*, or *The Comedy of Errors*, or . . . or . . ."

"Or any of Shakespeare's?"

"All right, it's you who've said it. Do you hold it higher than any of his?"

"Ah well, Sir John, 'tis a different sort of comedy from those others by Shakespeare."

"Different in what way?"

"Well, Mr. Goldsmith himself makes the distinction between Laughing and Sentimental Comedy."

"I hold no brief for the so-called sentimental stuff, but what has that to do with Shakespeare?"

"Mr. Goldsmith also would make the distinction between Laughing comedies, and comedies of character, comedies of wit, at which one may smile but seldom laugh aloud."

"And naturally," said Sir John, "his sort of comedy he finds superior."

"Not necessarily, but I would say that his audience at the Covent Garden certainly would find it superior."

"And so you vote with the many—is that it?"

With that final thrust, he felt he had won the argument. I held my tongue, allowing him to think so.

What I find odd as I think back to the occasion, and others that followed, is that never once did he question me regarding the behavior of Mr. Donnelly and Molly, which, presumably, was why he had sent us to accompany them. Nor, for that matter, did he ask me or Clarissa about our own conduct.

In fact, as it happened, the conduct of all four of us (or five, counting Mr. Goldsmith) was quite above reproach. 'Twas always a pleasure to hear Mr. Donnelly and Mr. Goldsmith trading witticisms. And Clarissa and I found, to our great enjoyment and amusement, that Molly Sarton could hold her own with them. She, by the bye, pronounced the turtle soup at Shakespeare's Head to be all that Mr. Goldsmith promised. Save for the embarrassing sighting of Benjamin Franklin in his state of disarray, which we never afterward discussed between us, we had a fine time that night. Clarissa pronounced it the best evening she had ever had, and I concurred, saying that I, too, knew of no better and could think of none to equal it.

·   ·   ·   ·

Thus it was that Benjamin Franklin passed out of our sight for weeks, even months. His name was not even mentioned. The investigation, so energetically undertaken, was allowed simply to come to a halt. There were no new developments, because those who might be questioned — chief among them, the burglars Skinner and Ferguson — were nowhere to be found. 'Twas as if the two had been quite erased from the population of London. Constable Perkins looked high and low for them, in and out of every dive in Bedford Street, and Bess, his snitch, made discreet inquiries of all her scarlet sisters. All to no avail.

Yet we remained not idle through that autumn of 1773. Sir John sat in judgment before the usual stream of miscreants, petty litigants, and the like. There were letters of all sorts for me to take in dictation and deliver. I put in a good deal of study upon the law, and even had occasion to put my studies to practice: Sir John's clerk, Mr. Marsden, fell ill with a severe catarrh, which Mr. Donnelly had taken to calling by its more exotic name, "influenza." Sir John appointed me to work in his stead. I could manage it easily, combining it with my other duties of correspondence, running errands of a miscellaneous sort, et cetera. My duties consisted of interviewing prisoners and witnesses, gathering statements of complainants and defendants in matters of dispute, and then, during the court session, prompting and advising Sir John at any extent necessary. I enjoyed the work whilst I did it and found it most instructive. Though it may seem cruel to say so, I was really rather sorry to see Mr. Marsden return. At last to be working in the law! And to hear from Sir John that I had performed my duties competently! That bode well for the future.

By far the most important event of the autumn was a long overdue visit from Tom Durham, Lady Fielding's son by her first marriage and now Sir John's stepson. He, now a lieutenant in the Royal Navy, owed his career and indeed, his very life, to the magistrate. When his father died, he and his mother, Katherine Durham (later Lady Fielding), immediately found themselves in reduced circumstances. Tom fell in with bad companions and took part in the robbery of a shopkeeper in the Covent Garden area. They were apprehended, and Sir John had no choice but to send the three boys to be tried for robbery at the Old Bailey. Found guilty, they were condemned to

be hanged—at age thirteen. Sir John petitioned for clemency and
put forward a proposal: that young boys be given the option of en-
listing in the Navy rather than be sent off to Tyburn Hill. When his
petition was granted, Tom Durham shipped out on the Royal Navy
frigate, *Adventure*. And when that proposal, which had appealed
greatly to Queen Charlotte, was made into law, John Fielding was
knighted by the king, and he became *Sir* John Fielding.

After he married Tom's mother, Sir John intervened a second
time in the boy's behalf, making it possible for him to become a midshipman, and thereby opening up to him the probability of becoming an officer and living his entire life before the mast, if such was
his desire. Being a bright lad, strong, and blessed with a good sense
of priority, he had little difficulty with his apprenticeship at sea. At
the earliest opportunity, he took and passed the lieutenant's test and
was commissioned an officer in the King's Navy. He was now reas-
signed to a ship of the line, the *Reliant*, with a full seventy guns and
a complement of over a thousand officers and men. But the *Reliant*
was to be reoutfitted before its voyage out to its next station in the
Caribbean. That left Tom Durham with three weeks leave which he
might spend as he chose. And he did choose to spend them in London with us.

From the first I sensed that much had changed in Tom Durham—
perhaps not many things but one big thing. What it was I could not
say for a considerable time. And when at last I came to recognize it
I was loath to accept it.

It fell to Clarissa to accompany Lady Fielding to the Post Coach
House to meet Tom, for as it happened, this was the first day on
which I was called upon to substitute for Mr. Marsden, and the time
of arrival of the Portsmouth coach coincided precisely with the beginning of Sir John's court session that day. So off went the two
women at some time near midday to welcome Tom to London.

Lady Fielding had not seen her son for over a year. While he did
write, 'twas not often enough to suit her. Yet considering that he
was most often on shipboard, I did not think he did badly. There
was little to write home about, one day being much the same as the
last. As a result, his letters, which she read aloud at table, seemed
lately to become more impersonal.

Clarissa, who had never met Tom Durham, gave her opinion to

me that he was rather a stiff sort of fellow—and rather boring, judging from his letters. When I insisted he was not like that at all, she shrugged.

"What then is he like?" she asked, putting the burden on me.

Well, reader, if you have ever been challenged to describe what another is "like," then you know what a bootless task it can be. I bumbled and blathered and started and stopped, and realized at last that there was little could be said.

"You'll find out soon enough when he comes for a visit."

And then, of course, he came for a visit.

My first day as acting clerk for Sir John went well enough—as so he assured me—though I was to remember to lower my voice whilst prompting cases, witnesses, et cetera. I took this modest criticism in good stead and counted the day a success. Then did I remind him that Lady Fielding and Clarissa had no doubt returned from the Post Coach House with Tom Durham in tow. And, seeming specially eager, he consented to look in on them and wish young Tom a happy homecoming.

All were present there in the kitchen. Molly had baked some scones and boiled up a pot of tea, which were set out upon a cloth of Irish lace. Yet none sat at the table. Lady Fielding stood talking to her son, as Molly and Clarissa looked on with interest. They fell silent and turned as we entered.

"Sir John!" called Tom as he dodged round his mother and moved quickly to his stepfather's side. Moving to embrace him, Sir John found instead a hand proferred to be shaken. He shook it right enough and gave a properly warm greeting to him. Then was there an awkward pause.

"Sit down, sit down, all of you," Molly called out. "This is an occasion for tea or something stronger. What will you, Sir John?"

"Tea will do."

"And you, Lieutenant?"

"Something stronger."

She produced a bottle of French brandy and filled a dram glass for him. Then did she pour tea all round for the rest of us. Sir John rose from his chair, tea glass in hand, and offered "a toast of welcome to Lieutenant Durham—and may he prosper in his chosen profession."

All drank as Tom raised his glass.

"I'll give you Sir John Fielding, knight of the realm, a man famed for his fairness, his generosity, and his love of justice."

To that I gave a "hear! hear!" as all joined in to raise glasses in tribute to the magistrate.

Thus was it that Tom's return was celebrated. The table fell into a single conversation in which Lady Fielding and her son participated and the rest did merely listen. But no, Molly also asked a question now and again ("Have you sailed round the world to get here?") as did Clarissa ("What is the most beautiful place you have seen?"). Sir John and I merely listened. And, in truth, I am not at all sure that he remained awake during that time at the table, so deep within himself was he. For my part, I simply looked and listened. And I concluded that of all those at the table, Clarissa behaved the most strangely. There was something altogether odd about the way that she looked there at the table, as she stared at Tom Durham. I could scarcely suppose what had got into the girl. It was not until the little party was done, and Clarissa and I were close together, doing the washing up, that I got some sense of what was troubling her.

"Jeremy," she whispered, "why did you not tell me about Tom Durham?"

"I thought I did."

"I asked you to tell me what he was like."

"Well, I tried."

"You did not tell me he was so *handsome!*"

Handsome? I turned that over and over again in my brain during the next few days, trying to determine just what she had meant by that. It's true, as I knew, that women (and girls most specially) set great store by handsomeness — but what, actually, did it mean? To be handsome, I supposed, had to do with a certain set of facial features. Height, too, would play a part, as would bearing. Yet, during the early days of Tom's visit, I would look at him and wonder what it was that made him handsome and another . . . well, ordinary looking. His nose was suitably placed; he was neither cross-eyed, nor wall-eyed. But so was it with the greatest number of men one might happen to meet whilst walking upon the streets of London. I, for instance — was I handsome? I found myself staring into the looking glass and asking myself that question. Frankly, I hoped I was, yet none had ever remarked upon it. My nose, too, was placed as well as Tom's, and the pupils of my eyes were also properly set, neither inward- nor outward-looking. Still, no one had ever named me handsome — not even Clarissa who, in most particulars, had seemed to find me quite satisfactory, at least in the past. Oh, what did it matter? I asked myself. I took solace and strength from the old proverb "Handsome is that handsome does." I would *do* handsomely and let the rest take care of itself.

Indeed, Clarissa's all-consuming interest in me seemed a thing of the past. She now opened no discussions of ethical or literary matters. She asked no questions regarding what Sir John might be up to. She plotted no romances, nor did she spin tales of histories past that had kept me fascinated, in spite of myself. Even less did she seem desirous of resting her head upon my shoulder, as she had done in Black Jack Bilbo's coach on our final visit with them there. No, none of that — and, in truth, I missed her.

What did she now with her time? Why, insofar as her duties to Lady Fielding permitted, she followed Tom Durham about, ogling him quite idiotically. I was greatly embarrassed for her. He gave her little encouragement. She attempted to start conversations with him, yet he responded only vaguely (though this would change). If anything, he showed even less interest in her than he did in me.

Yes, Tom was indeed different from the sixteen-year-old youth who had bade us a tearful good-bye and called me brother only a few years before. The habit of command had altered him permanently, no doubt. On shipboard, he may have been the most junior of the junior officers, yet each man jack of the crew was bound to hop to at his command, no matter in what peril it placed them. Such circumstances were bound to make an impression upon a fellow, particularly one as young and malleable as he was. There were obvious changes. He talked less than the lad I remembered, and kept his own counsel until such time as he was ready to give an opinion — or make a demand.

I first glimpsed this new Tom Durham after our first night's sleep together in my little attic room. Admittedly, my narrow bed made things a bit tight, but I, for one, had a fair night's rest. Yet, next morn at breakfast, when Tom was asked how he had slept, he answered with a groan.

"As badly as that?" asked Sir John. "I recall that when you visited us last, you two managed well enough in Jeremy's bed."

"Well, it would seem that we've both grown a bit since then. I slept better in a hammock back when I was a midshipman."

"What shall we do about it?" said Sir John, opening the question to the table.

"I should be happy to share a bed with Clarissa or Molly," said he.

"Tom!" said Lady Fielding most sharp. She meant to make it clear there would be none of that.

"Just a joke, Mother. Perhaps it would be better," he added, "if I were to put up at a hostelry. Oh, I've plenty of money after all those years at sea."

"No doubt you have," said Sir John, "but surely we can accommodate you."

He was accommodated, of course, by me. I'd given up my bed once previously, when Clarissa, half dead with pneumonia, was too ill to be moved, and mine became her sickroom. The memory of her pale face above the blanket as she struggled to breathe properly came to me unbidden in the way of a dream, and with it an odd feeling that I can only describe as . . . well, tenderness. I slept on a pallet in the kitchen before the fireplace. Not my best nights, certainly, but I survived—just as I survived once again when pillow and pallet were laid down for me before the fire. I had volunteered, of course.

Having mentioned his heavy pockets, Tom must have felt obliged to lighten them somewhat. If that were the case, he could not have chosen a better and surer way to accomplish this than a visit to the Tyburn Gaming Club, formerly Black Jack Bilbo's. Already the new proprietor had sent rumors flying that his tables were not governed wholly by the laws of chance.

Sir John passed these rumors on to him, yet Tom paid them little heed. This occasioned a remark from the magistrate, which has stayed with me always. "When a man is determined to throw his money away, there is simply no dissuading him," said he to me in private. "To do so gives some a feeling of power, though why this should be I cannot understand." In any case, Tom lost a considerable amount in a single evening—perhaps half his fortune—so he must have felt very powerful indeed.

After a time, it became clear to me that Tom's guiding purpose whilst in our midst was to displease his mother. I believe I do not exaggerate in this, for he not only took every opportunity to make remarks in a joking manner that would be sure to vex her, but he also created occasions that were sure to cause conflict. I have mentioned his visit to the Tyburn Gaming Club; that caused conflict aplenty. There was also an absence of most of a day and half of a night from which he returned over the shoulder of Benjamin Bailey, chief of the Bow Street Runners, who had collected him from the Bedford Street gutter. When, before all the rest of us, Lady Fielding had demanded an explanation from him, he at first declined to give any. But when she insisted, he said that he had "found an appealing little whore and got drunk with her." Which may or may not have been true, but distressed his mother no end. There were other such events.

Yet, to a remarkable degree, she seemed to bring it upon herself. She was forever telling him how to conduct himself, what to say and do. He would make no comment, nor pay any attention to her whatever. She insisted, as an instance, upon accompanying him when he went out to search for a new coat to take the place of the one which had been befouled in the Bedford Street gutter. I know not what happened, nor what was said between them, yet I do know that afterward neither of them spoke to the other for a full day.

Sir John bore up well. To me he confided that he felt that both were wrong.

"Kate seems to believe," said he, "that she has still the right to assert the parent's authority. She refuses to recognize that her boy is now a man. And Tom, for his part, sees no way to declare his manhood than by making himself as offensive in his behavior and speech as possible. He is simply playing the bad boy, which in a sense is just what she wishes."

"Hmmm," said I, "why then do you not speak to them that they may adopt more reasonable ways, each with the other?"

He considered that for a moment, then did he shake his head in the negative. "No, Jeremy," said he. "I fear they must find their own way. She must allow him to be a man, and he must find better ways to demonstrate to her that he has become one, than he has so far discovered. Yet perhaps I can do something that may give the two of them a bit of a rest from these emotionally exhausting pursuits."

"What had you in mind?"

"A trip to the theatre. David Garrick stopped by whilst you were away on your afternoon errands, and he told me that his new production would be of considerable interest."

"Shakespeare, of course."

"Of course," said he. "*Romeo and Juliet.* He has offered us his box for tomorrow night, should we wish it."

"Oh, I wish it," said I with great enthusiasm.

"And I also," said he. "Consider it done then. Between us we shall overcome any reluctance on Tom's part, or Kate's."

So we did. I could not imagine Lady Fielding declining an invitation to the theatre, yet I knew naught of Tom's interest—in Shakespeare, particularly—indeed whether he had any at all. Yet for all of his ill-tempered behavior, he had managed to be quite civil to Sir John. Perhaps he had somehow been made newly aware of Sir John's reputation—or perhaps he merely liked and respected him.

In any case, there was neither resistance nor reluctance when Sir John announced at the dinner table that he would be taking all to the Drury Lane next evening.

"And what is the play?" Tom asked.

"What indeed but *Romeo and Juliet?*" I responded.

"Ah well," said he, "not my favorite, but doubtless a work of considerable worth."

"You've seen another production, have you?" asked Sir John.

"No, but I read it long ago while in school."

"It is unquestionably the greatest of all Shakespeare's plays," said Clarissa with great authority, raising her eyes heavenward. "To me, there is no more beautiful and tragic theme than young love . . . thwarted."

Following that announcement, there was a good deal of coughing and shuffling of feet round the table.

When we settled into our seats there in the box which Mr. Garrick had provided, we found it a bit tight. There were, after all, six of us, and the box, which was located closest stage left, was smaller than the rest—or so it seemed to me. Still, snug or loose, we fitted it in separate rows—Sir John and Lady Fielding, together with Tom Durham, sat in front of Clarissa, Molly, and me.

There were some minutes before first curtain, and so, while the others buzzed in anticipation, I opened the program and glanced at the cast list. Of a sudden did I understand Sir John's hidden purpose in organizing his expedition to Drury Lane Theatre. I looked round me—at Tom, feigning boredom, at Clarissa and Molly beside me, deep in whispered conversation, and Lady Fielding, straining back to listen in—and saw that none of them had even so much as opened their copies of the program. I decided to say nothing of my discovery. Let them find out in the manner that Sir John had intended.

A few minutes later the curtain came up on that street in Verona and on the two male servants of the Capulets, and soon the air was filled with scurrilous ambiguities. In the next scene, the Montagues arrived, and we saw the two feuding houses clash for the first time. I waited impatiently for the third scene of the first act, for I knew that, in the course of it, Juliet would make her first appearance. Yes, here it was, and here she came: Miss Anne Oakum, as announced in the program, in the role of Juliet. 'Twas our Annie, our former cook, in her first leading role at the Drury Lane—thus the visit by Mr. Garrick to Sir John to put him on notice that she would be appearing as Juliet. He was certain that we would all wish to attend.

Though Clarissa and I had seen Annie in some of her appearances as she served her apprenticeship with Mr. Garrick's company, we had not seen all. We had not been aware of her swift progress from supernumerary roles as a lady-in-waiting to the role of Juliet, one of the most demanding of Shakespeare's female parts.

I watched closely to see which of our party would be first to recognize her. I expected that it would be Tom—for hadn't he and Annie been lovers, in their fashion?—but indeed it was not Tom. I saw him frowning down at her, as if asking himself who this Juliet could be who looked so familiar. He continued looking until Clarissa leaned forward and provided the answer. At about that same moment, Lady Fielding clapped her hand to her mouth that she might trap the exclamation of surprise which leaped to her lips; something of it escaped, a kind of muffled gasp, which seemed to amuse Sir John sitting close beside her.

The acts went by. Dear Annie proved more than equal to the part. To some extent, I would have to say that she was only held back a little by the performance of her Romeo. David Garrick had cast himself in the role, and she could hardly have asked that another be given a chance, for after all it was his company, was it not? The voice and the sense of the poetry in the lines were all very well, of course, but it was painful to see a man into his fifties attempt to play a boy forty years younger. He lacked the swiftness of youth, the sense of impetuous passion of a much younger man. He should not have attempted it.

If anything, Mr. Garrick's performance seemed to heighten Annie's and reveal the energy and spirit behind it. Only once did she falter, and that was during the famous balcony scene. In the course of one of her longest speeches, she did raise her eyes and, for the first time, spy Tom Durham hanging over the railing, consuming her with his own eyes. I'm certain that she recognized him immediately, for she grew flustered and repeated a line, yet did so in such a way that she seemed carried away by the excitement of the moment—just as Juliet might have done. A graceful recovery.

During intermissions, the women buzzed about Annie—how well she was doing, how beautiful she looked in costume and makeup—while the males in our party (each for a different reason) kept silent. Sir John, I believe, said not a word till the play was done. Only after the thunderous applause had subsided and the final curtain rung down, did he speak.

"Well," said he, "I think we must all go down now and congratulate Annie upon that magnificent performance. What say you all to that?"

All were eager, right enough, and so with Clarissa and me leading the way (since we knew it best), we journeyed through the lower depths of the theatre to the row of dressing rooms at the far end. After knocking on a few wrong doors, we came upon the right one. Something was called out from inside in answer to my knock, and I boldly threw open the door—only to find the room crowded with those, like us, who had come to congratulate her upon her triumph (for triumph was what they called it). There were members of the cast—including Mr. Garrick himself and the actress who had played the Nurse—and a few of the audience who were themselves costumed so elegantly that they must be nobles. And in the midst of this array of talent and riches was our Annie, dressed still as Juliet, recognizable as such beneath her makeup. Clarissa dove through the crowd and was at her side in no time at all, hugging the very life from her. The rest of us hung back somewhat timidly. Sir John, and I with him, were taken aside by David Garrick, who was smiling broadly, looking happier than I had ever before seen him.

"What think you now of your little cook, Sir John?"

"I am as pleased as I can be," said he. "I blush to think how close one can be to such talent and never recognize it as such."

"Talent is one thing," said the actor, "but ability another. True, she had a good deal of talent when she joined the troupe, yet I have never had an apprentice who took so well to teaching, nor a young actress who responded so well to coaching. Talent is more common than most would suppose, but ability on the stage such as hers is rarer than any would guess."

"Indeed," said Sir John, "that, coming from you—"

"Must never be repeated to her," said Mr. Garrick, interrupting. "It would not do for her to know how good she really is."

Sir John threw back his head and laughed at that. "You might lose your hold upon her, eh?"

"Actresses can be very difficult."

With that he gave a polite little bow to the magistrate and a wave to me. He whispered good-bye and left for his own dressing room. Little by little the room emptied. The other cast members were the first to go. Then, almost reluctantly, the more gaudily dressed of the nobles drew away and, bidding good-bye, departed the room. Only then, cautiously, did Lady Fielding and Molly Sarton move forward. Tom Durham held back still.

I had an opportunity to study him. He was off in one corner of what was really a rather small room, and though I had an opportunity to study him, I may as well have been completely invisible to him, for he looked neither to the right nor left, but rather did he concentrate with all his energy upon Annie.

He was quite overwhelmed by her success—that much was evident. As the noblemen and a few of their ladies left the room, he followed them with his eyes, the look in his eyes expressing something of awe, something of longing and envy. I understood for the first time how removed Tom must feel from the great world of London. All he knew how to do was order men about on shipboard. I believe that following that realization I never again envied the fellow. It was only when the last of Annie's legion of well-wishers had left her that he came forward hesitantly, hoping shyly to be recognized by her.

"Hello, Annie," said he, "do you remember me?"

"I know I should," said she, taking a step back that she might better study him. "Oh, I know! Your mother is Lady Fielding, is she not? And I believe — correct me if I'm wrong in this — that you're in the Navy, are you not? Or was it the Army? I confess I have a good deal of difficulty keeping the two apart."

She was acting, of course, improvising her lines. Of that I was certain, for I had seen the momentary shock in her face when she saw and recognized Tom from the stage. For years he had studiously ignored her, sending no greeting to her in his letters to the rest of us, enclosing no notes to her. This was the punishment she had meted out to him. Had she planned it so? I doubted it, though perhaps in a daydream or two she had enjoyed just such a revenge.

As for Tom, no such possibility as this had ever occurred to him, I am sure. It was simply beyond the laws of chance that one that he had known as a cook would become not just an actress but overnight the toast of London. Yet here she was, his first conquest, apparently unable to recall him clearly, even less did she seem to remember the circumstances and details that he must have known so well. As he had snubbed her for years, she now snubbed him most cruelly and with great effect. He seemed to shrink before our very eyes.

Annie had placed her knife well. She was now to give it a final twist.

A knock came upon the door. In response, Annie called out an invitation to enter. Into the room came a young man of about twenty-five, handsome of countenance and graceful of manner. He was extremely well dressed, yet in a manner more conservative than those who had left but minutes before. He removed his hat, smiled a greeting to Annie, and offered all a little bow.

"Ah, Harry," said she, "let me introduce you to all here." She proceeded to do just that, presenting him to us as Harold, Earl of Bardwell.

With that done, he informed her that he had had the coach brought round to the stagedoor.

"Ah then, I take it we must hurry."

"I fear so. The party is, after all, given in your honor."

"Then it would be a sin to keep them waiting, would it not?"

He nodded shyly.

"Alas," said Annie, "I must ask all to leave whilst I change out of my costume." She gestured to a stern-faced woman who, through it all, had remained at her post beside the dressing screen in the corner.

"This is Mrs. Biggs. She is my dresser, and I fear that in another minute she will take up her whip and drive you all out of the room." Mrs. Biggs showed no sign of amusement at Annie's little joke, and she said not a word, so that I half-believed she might do as Annie had said.

There followed a swift round of good-byes, and, in no more than a moment or two, we were all out in the corridor, taking our leave of the Earl of Bardwell.

"Anne speaks so well of you all," said Lord Bardwell. "And let me say, Sir John, what a pleasure it is to meet you at last after having heard so much about you."

"Not all of it bad, I hope."

"Oh, not at all. On the contrary," said the other most earnestly. "As I grew up, you were held up to me often as an example of just how a public man ought to conduct himself."

"Well then, I shall return your compliment, for I have heard you discussed, and in the most favorable terms. I believe my informant, who might indeed be known to you, referred to you as 'the most intelligent *young* man in the House of Lords.'" Sir John smiled and raised his hand in salute.

"But it is past time that we should be going," he added. "It was most pleasant to make your acquaintance, Lord Bardwell, specially under such happy circumstances."

Sir John offered his hand, and the younger man shook it eagerly. With a farewell chorus, we departed down the long hall.

Just outside the theatre we encountered Constable Bailey, whom

Sir John had requested to accompany us back to Number 4 Bow
Street.

"Been to the theatre, have you, Sir John?"

"We have indeed, Mr. Bailey."

"And was it a good play?"

"One of the best, truly one of the best."

"I must try it sometime — going to the theatre, I mean."

"You've never been?"

"No, never. It always seemed to me from what I heard that the
stories told in those plays was too far-fetched to really enjoy — just
fairy tales, really."

"Ah, not so," said the magistrate. "There is little cannot be put
forth in whole or in part as possible — from Cinderella to Sinbad the
Sailor."

"Well," said Mr. Bailey, "I ain't too familiar with that Sinbad
fella, but I know my Cinderella, and it never did seem real to me.
Lives don't change in a night. Not to mention mice into horses."

Sir John considered this as we walked on. Then, at last, he
cleared his throat, and I, expecting a lengthy and well-reasoned
pronouncement, was somewhat disappointed when all he said was,
"Some lives do."

The experience of this night worked a great change in Tom Durham. He had little to say of it the next day, and it was only from
Lady Fielding that we learned that he had agreed to accompany her
on another of her trips north to see her mother. She had, it seemed,
been urging him since his arrival to take such a trip with her, yet he
had held out until that very day. As she told it, Tom had always been
a special favorite of his grandmother, and he had come to the realization that he owed her a visit, since it seemed unlikely she would
live long enough to see him at some later date.

All of which may have been so, yet there seemed to be other,
more immediate factors which may have brought him round. It appeared to me that he had been driven so low by his meeting with
Annie that he needed a few days to recover his self-confidence.
Such a trip provided him with just the sort of respite he needed.

Well do I recall the morning of their departure. Not only was I called upon to see them off at the Post Coach House; but, more important, upon my return, the mystery of the missing letters began at last to unravel. Thus it is sometimes so that we recall events of great consequence by their nearness in time to others of comparative insignificance.

It was Sir John's custom to have the day's newspaper read to him first thing in the morning. I was frequently the reader, though more often it fell to Mr. Marsden to perform the task. Since Mr. Marsden himself was absent, his "influenza" (as he now called it) still troubling him, I brought with me the day's copy of the *London Chronicle* from my trip to the Post Coach House, and sought out the magistrate. I found him in his chambers, and, at his invitation, I sat down before him, opened up the newspaper, and began searching it for items, announcements, and stories in which he might be interested. A word should be said about that, perhaps: Sir John had little interest in those that had naught to do with the law and its enforcement, the judicial process, or its legislation in Parliament. Comment upon these subjects absorbed him only insofar as the commentator did. If his views agreed with Sir John's preconceptions, then the magistrate would give him his attention; if not, I would be instructed to move on quickly to something else. I know not how it was with Mr. Marsden, but when I read the day's newspapers to him, Sir John was ever accusing me of fastening upon those items which interested me alone and not him, and "wasting" his time with them.

There was just such a story in the *Chronicle* that morning, and I half-expected him to stop me as I began to read it aloud. Since I no longer have a copy of the text that I might insert it here, I shall be forced merely to describe the contents of the piece.

It was a report from the *Chronicle*'s Boston correspondent upon a remarkable meeting of the Massachusetts assembly, at which excerpts from a packet of letters were read out to the members of the body. The letters, which numbered about fifteen, were an exchange between Thomas Hutchinson, now governor of the colony (appointed by the king himself), Andrew Oliver, the lieutenant governor (and Hutchinson's brother-in-law), and the late Thomas Whately, a member of Parliament and an author of the Stamp Act so hated by the colonists. Though the letters were written between 1767 and

1769, they were as relevant and alarming to the colonists as they would have been had they been written but a day before.

What frightened the citizens of Massachusetts was the cavalier manner in which all three of the correspondents were so willing to dispose of the rights the colonists enjoyed as free-born Englishmen — should they continue to behave in a manner as fractious as in the past. In the most frequently quoted letter, that which was written and sent by Governor Hutchinson to Thomas Whately, it was said by him: "I never think of the measure necessary for the peace and good order of the colonies without pain. *There must be an abridgement of what are called English liberties.*" No matter how much pain this would have caused the governor, it would have caused the colonists a good deal more.

I read to the end of the item, expecting to be cut off by Sir John. Yet not to the very end, for when I was near it, I looked up to catch his reaction to what I had read thus far. I saw him leaning forward and eagerly taking in each word I said. Was he truly so excited? Yes, I believe he was, for in a few moments more I finished my reading, and he did indeed jump up from his chair in his excitement.

"That's it!" He fairly shouted it out. "That's *it!*"

"What do you mean, sir?"

"Do you truly not see? Those are the very letters that were stolen from Lord Hillsborough."

"But . . . but are you certain? How can you be sure?"

"Of course I can't be certain — not as you mean it, yet I would wager any amount of money that I am right in this."

"How can we confirm it?"

"Why, I don't know," said he. "I can't imagine how one would go about it."

"Can no one be charged?"

"You mean Franklin? No, not on such grounds as these."

"What about Arthur Lee?"

"Because he was rowed out to a ship sailing for Boston to deliver a package? No, I fear not."

"So we are no farther along than we were weeks before."

"No, we're a bit farther along. Now, at least, we understand what it was had been stolen."

"Well," I said after thinking upon it for a time, "can we not bring in Dr. Franklin that you might interrogate him for a bit?"

"No, still it would be unwise to tip our hand. It is best to wait."

Events moved swiftly. Following a good deal of impassioned rhetoric in the newspapers ("we shall not countenance," etc.), a shocking bit of news came to light. William Whately, brother to the late Thomas who was one of Hutchinson's correspondents, took it upon himself to defend his brother's reputation, for there were some who believed Thomas Whately to be the source of the letters. In doing so, William accused John Temple, a minor government official, of stealing the letters. True, Temple had been granted access to Thomas Whately's papers and had examined them, yet he insisted that no such letters were among those he had gone through. Nevertheless, William Whately continued to point his finger at Temple and accuse him publicly of theft. John Temple saw no solution but to challenge him to a duel.

It was fought in early December in Hyde Park, and was fought in deadly earnest by both men. They hacked away with swords, one at the other, till Whately fell, too badly wounded to continue He was carried from the field, vowing to continue the fight as soon as he was physically able.

All this was reported in most, if not all, of London's newspapers and became widely known. What became even better known was a short notice that appeared in one newspaper alone—and that was the *London Chronicle*. Well do I recall returning from Covent Garden with the copy of the *Chronicle* I had purchased from the news vendor there. Once settled in Sir John's chambers, I commenced reading the notice to him before ever I had noted its author. This, then, is what I read, under the heading "Public Statement on the Hutchinson Letters."

"Finding that two Gentlemen have been unfortunately engaged in a Duel, about a transaction and its circumstances of which both of them are totally ignorant and innocent, I think it incumbent on me to declare (for the prevention of farther mischief, as far as such a declaration may contribute to prevent it) that I alone am the person who obtained and transmitted to Boston the letters in question. — Mr. W[hately] could not communicate them, because they were never in his possession; and for the same reason, they could not be taken from him by Mr. T[emple]. — They were not of the nature of *"private letters between friends."* They were written by public officers to persons in public station, on public affairs, and intended to procure public measures. Their tendency was to incense the Mother Country against her Colonies, and, by the steps recommended, to widen the breach which they affected. The chief caution with regard to Privacy, was, to keep their contents from the *Colony Agents,* who the writers apprehended might return them, or copies of them, to America. That apprehension was, it seems, well founded; for the first Agent who laid his hands on them, thought it his duty to transmit them to his constituents.

[signed] B. Franklin, Agent for the House of Representatives of the Massachusetts — Bay.

PART TWO

EIGHT

In which Sir John
questions Dr. *Franklin*
for a second time

"Bring him in, Jeremy," cried Sir John, beating upon his desk with the flat of his hand. "Bring Benjamin Franklin to me, and I shall have at him again."

Never, I think, had I heard him so full of purpose as at that moment. I, who had for weeks been clamoring for Ben Franklin to be brought in for another, less accommodating interrogation, found myself actually pitying the poor fellow as I anticipated the ordeal he soon would endure.

I jumped to my feet, ready to depart. Yet he had not done with me.

"If this were later in the day," said he, "I would send one of the Beak Runners to bring him in. Since Mr. Fuller must be responsible for the rowdy prisoners in the strongroom, a particularly nasty bunch this morning, I ask you to play the role of the runner once again. But show Franklin no sympathy. He is not a prisoner, but he is to suppose himself such. Wear a brace of pistols and look like you would be pleased to use them. Is that clear?"

"Most clear, sir."

By the time I left Number 4 Bow Street, I not only had round me the brace of pistols Sir John had told me to put on, but I had also in my coat pocket the cosh which Mr. Baker had taken from one of our overnight guests. For some reason, it came to mind that it might be useful—and so it did prove. Weighted down as I was with pistols and such paraphernalia, there was no possibility for me of going there at a run, or even jog-trotting the distance. Yet I felt a sense of urgency that seemed to call for such haste. After all, I had been pushing for this, had I not? To be ordered at last to bring in Dr. Franklin, even at this late date, seemed to me a vindication. And so I walked as swiftly as I was able down the Strand, and there, across from St. Martin in the Fields, was Craven Street.

Yet when I turned down it, I found that a considerable crowd, more than a dozen though less than twenty—had gathered before Number 10, which I knew to be Benjamin Franklin's address. They shouted, and the gentlemen waved their walking sticks in a most threatening manner. It seemed that Dr. Franklin's notice in the *Chronicle* had angered quite a few.

What, I wondered, was I to do to get him out of this situation? It appeared to me that it would not be long till certain of the crowd began throwing stones or paving bricks through Mrs. Stevenson's windows. I could not allow that to happen, could I? I studied the situation for a moment and came up with a plan. Taking a place to the rear of the crowd, I shouted out at them.

"ORDER! Let there be *order!*"

There was none. One or two turned round and regarded me briefly, yet, if anything, the uproar increased following my cry for silence. Just as I expected.

From its holster upon my right hip, I drew the pistol which Mr. Fuller had reluctantly supplied. I cocked it and fired it into the air. Then did the crowd fall silent as swiftly as they might if the king himself had called for it. Mouths were left open in midyell. Shock and astonishment were written upon their faces. I had their attention.

"I am come," said I loudly, "upon the orders of Sir John Fielding, magistrate of the Bow Street Court, to collect Benjamin Franklin and bring him to Number 4 Bow Street. I would now have you make way and give me access to the door. If you do not, I shall take it as an insult to the Bow Street Court and to Sir John himself and I shall deal with it accordingly."

I looked round the gathering as I tucked away the pistol I had just discharged.

"How do you plan to deal with it?" asked one of the braver of the bunch. "You only got one bullet in that other pistol. You can't arrest us all."

"That may be," said I, reaching into my pocket, "but I have this to use on those who block my way."

Wherewith I produced the cosh and held it up for all to see. They were impressed. No longer silent, they began mumbling and whispering, one to the other, yet they fell back and allowed me passage to the door. I made my way through them and mounted the two or three stairs to the stoop. Each step of the way I allowed the cosh to bounce in the palm of my left hand, so that all might note the weight of the thing. Having reached my destination, I turned and addressed them once again.

"Gentlemen," said I, "my advice to you all now is to go about your business. In other words, *be gone.*"

I did not wait to assure myself that my order was obeyed. Rather, I turned and, with the cosh, beat upon the door of Number 10 Craven Street thrice, loud and hard. The sound made was like unto the very strokes of destiny.

The door came open in a most timid manner: slowly and no more than a foot. It was just enough to recognize the face of Mrs. Stevenson. She sighed, more or less in relief.

"Oh," she said, "it's you."

"I am here to conduct Dr. Franklin to Sir John Fielding."

Then another voice, a whisper. "It's all right, Margaret. Let him in."

That she did, throwing the door open wider, grasping me by the arm, and pulling me inside in a swift movement. She was much stronger than I had suspected. Then did she push the door shut behind me.

Benjamin Franklin cowered in a corner of the entryway. He seemed less in every sense—even physically—than he had been. Had he shrunk? It seemed so. His cheeks had hollowed somewhat since last I saw him. And he now stooped, perhaps trying to make himself smaller, less visible to his enemies, who must now number a great many. I addressed him direct.

"You heard what I said to Mrs. Stevenson, did you? I'm to convey you to Sir John."

"Yes, yes," said he, "and I'm greatly relieved to hear it. I count Sir John Fielding as a friend."

I gave him as hard a look as I could. "I should not count over-much on Sir John's good will, if I were you."

He looked as if he were taken somewhat aback at that. "Oh, I . . . I . . . oh." His lower lip trembled. "I'll get my hat."

So saying, he disappeared into the depths of the darkened house.

Mrs. Stevenson watched him go, then turned to me fretfully. "Are they still out there?" she asked.

"I've no idea, but they'll cause us no trouble." I managed to sound more confident than I felt. "How long have they been there?"

"Well . . . we began to hear them shouting just a few minutes before you came."

"And what did they shout?"

"Oh, terrible things, some of them I would not repeat. They were too . . . too crude. But Dr. Franklin was called 'traitor' and 'thief' and I know not what more. It's so unfair!"

"Unfair? Do you think so?"

She looked at me in surprise. "Well, don't *you?*"

Before I could answer that, I heard the rush of feet upon the stairs. He then appeared, properly hatted, with his walking stick in hand. Pausing for a moment, he set his jaw and cleared his throat.

"I'm ready," said he.

I threw open the door and found — nothing. All who had threat-ened Dr. Franklin but minutes past had disappeared from the front of the house. Then did I step out the door and look Craven Street up and down. I caught sight of what might well have been the last of them, turning into the Strand.

"Come along," said I. "Sir John is eager to have at you there in Bow Street."

"What do you mean by that?"

"You'll find out soon enough."

By the time I arrived with my charge, it was late enough so that I knew that I must get on with my duties as clerk to the magistrate's court. And so it was that when I had delivered Dr. Franklin up to Sir John, I went off to interview the prisoners and prepare the docket. Sir John was correct in calling them a nasty bunch; they were fractious and uncooperative, and so what ordinarily took no more than the half of an hour, lasted well over a full hour. As a result, I had no chance to listen in to the first half of Sir John's interrogation of Franklin. I called the magistrate out to impart to him the substance of my interviews that he might ask pertinent questions of the prisoners—this was my usual—and he asked me, when I was done, if there were time to resume with Franklin before commencing his court session. I told him that there was not.

"Well then," said he, "we shall have to keep him here through the session, I fear, for I am not through with him. Where shall we do that?"

"Not in your chambers?"

"No, I fear not. I want him to feel less at liberty than he would feel in such circumstances."

"If that is your wish, then why not have Mr. Fuller lock him up in the strong room? It will be empty of prisoners when Fuller has brought them out to sit in the courtroom till they be called."

"Quite impossible, Jeremy, as you must know. Dr. Franklin cannot be locked up till he be arrested, and I am not yet ready to charge him."

"Yes, I understand you."

"I have it," said Sir John. "Why not install him in the front row, directly in your view. You can give him hostile stares, and I shall be even more stern than is my wont. That should do quite nicely, don't you think?"

"It should, certainly, but tell me, sir, have you got anything from him yet?"

"Yes, a great deal of annoyance is what I have from him thus far. He maintains doggedly and monotonously that he did *not* lie to me when I questioned him earlier, for at that time he knew naught of the theft of the letters but what he had read in the newspapers, and that the letters fell into his hands—charming figure of speech, eh?—only after we had our talk. He claims, in fact, that it was the very next day."

"How convenient," said I. "Has he named the individual who put the packet of letters in his eager hands?"

"That he refuses to do so far. It was, if I'm not mistaken, also omitted from the statement in today's *Chronicle*."

"So it was. I believe I can supply that name."

"Yes, of course—your man, Arthur Lee. He is a key, connecting element in your theory of the crime. Perhaps we should try it on Dr. Franklin after our court session. And this, for that matter, may be the time to question Lee."

"Ah, well," said I, "I'm happy to hear you say it."

All was done as Sir John had suggested. We two sat at the table, as was customary. Opposite me, sitting in the first row, was Benjamin Franklin. During the court session our eyes often met, yet not happily for either of us. Franklin seemed altogether miserable. I could tell that he had been often flustered by Sir John's questions and by his badgering manner. His eyes were red-rimmed, and it seemed to me that his hands shook slightly. Just to intimidate him further, I had laid the cosh on the table just off to one side of my right hand. His eyes had widened when I put it there. He knew what it was. I thought that interesting.

Most of the prisoners had been taken by Constables Bailey and Patley in the course of breaking up a great battle in Bedford Street. The two sides in conflict, it seemed, were members of rival robber gangs. Such melees were common enough, and most often had to do with who might have the opportunity to rob whom in which part of town. There were a great many who were chained together and marched into the courtroom by Mr. Fuller. I had interviewed them all and read the arrest reports left by Constables Bailey and Patley, so that I knew in advance that none had been killed in the affray, nor had any received grievous bodily harm. There were a few bloodied heads, a broken arm or two, some missing teeth—that sort of thing. A certain restraint had been exercised: clubs had been used, neither pistols nor knives. I knew, too, that all meant to plead guilty and pay the fine of a pound that they might get out and get on with more serious matters of larceny. All this I passed on to Sir John. He said he would handle that case first.

Seventeen had been arrested, and seventeen it was who hobbled in with Mr. Fuller, the day jailer, at their head. There was little room to seat so many, and so he herded them before us as I called the case and charged them to give their names. This they did, I following carefully to make certain that the names given in Sir John's court matched those given me in the course of my interviews. That was the last of my duties with regard to the prisoners; the rest was now up to the magistrate of the Bow Street Court.

"Have you elected one among you to speak for all?" asked Sir John. "I should be greatly disappointed if I must try each of you separately."

Not one, but two shuffled forward a step or two. One of them spoke up immediately.

"There's two of us will speak for the rest," said he. "There was two sides of the fight, after all, so it's best we do it so."

"What is your name, then? Is it Falker? So I remember it."

"Yes sir, Daniel Falker, at your service."

"And who speaks for the other side?" asked Sir John.

"Henry Tinker," said the other—his name and no more.

"Very well, are all the rest of you in agreement with this? These two may speak for all?"

There was an affirmative chorus in which all of the remaining fifteen seemed to sing forth.

"And none opposed?"

Silence.

"In the report of the arresting officers, it was told that half of you were quite willing to give up the fight, but the rest were not. What was the course of this? Which side was the more pacific, and which the aggressor?"

"We was peaceable," said Tinker. "We did just like the two Beak Runners said."

"That's 'cause they was losin'," Falker blurted forth. "There was more of them, but we was better fighters."

"No such thing. We was just obeyin'—"

The tumult of laughter and shouting from the courtroom audience blotted out the last few words of Tinker's sentence. Sir John beat so mightily upon the table with his gavel that I felt certain that he would break one or the other—yet he did not. He yelled for order. It was some minutes, however, before it was restored. When at last some semblance of silence was restored to the room, he leaned over to me.

"They get worse and worse, do they not, Jeremy? If it continues so, I shall have to close these sessions to all but witnesses, litigants, and prisoners."

Secretly, I suspicioned he would never do such a thing. I believed that though he would be unlikely to admit it, he did truly enjoy these shouting matches with the riffraff of Covent Garden. Well did he know that his courtroom was notorious for its rowdiness and disorder. He cared naught that the lords and ladies who visited Number 4 Bow Street for their idle entertainment were oft-times shocked. Let them be. He had a certain affection for the rabble who came each noon. More often than they angered him, they amused him. Yet he gave no hint of this as he moved on with the proceeding. Remembering that Dr. Franklin sat just opposite us, he remained outwardly cold and severe in his manner.

"Now that you can hear me, let me proceed with a few more questions," said he. "The arresting officers did also say in their report that it was difficult to learn from either side just what this battle between you was all about. Can you say, Mr. Tinker?"

"Well, sir," said Henry Tinker, "It's one of those things that just . . . just . . . well, it just started."

"Yes, but *how* did it start? Can you be somewhat more helpful on that, Mr. Falker?"

"Perhaps I can. I would say it started because we was all drunk. And you know how it is, sir. When you've had a bit too much to drink, you sometimes takes offense at things you might not if you wasn't under the influence, so to speak."

"It does sometimes happen so," Sir John admitted. "Some statement may be made, a boast, a bit of braggadocio, then a challenge thrown out, and before you know it, or even might have wanted it, you've a fight on your hands. Was that how it went?"

"Ain't that so, sir!" said Falker.

"It's almost like you was there!" said Tinker.

"And by next morning, you can't even recall what it was all about. Is that it, gentlemen?"

"Certainly, sir."

"No question of it."

"But, Mr. Tinker, yours is a voice very familiar to me, and it is widely known that I never forget a voice," said Sir John. "You've appeared before me here in the Bow Street Court, have you not?"

Mr. Tinker looked left and right, as if hoping to find some way out of this predicament in one direction or another. But finding none, he returned his gaze to Sir John.

"That's right, sir, 'twas about a sixmonth past."

"And it was on this very charge, was it not? Brawling? Simple assault?"

Tinker sighed. "It was, sir."

"And what about you, Mr. Falker? Did you and some of these friends of yours put in an appearance here at that same occasion?"

"Yes sir."

"And was it not the same set of charges that brought you here today?"

He hung his head. "It was."

"Tell me, both of you, what sort of punishment do you feel I should dole out to you and your fellows?"

"Why indeed, sir, as I recollect, that earlier time we was all assessed a pound each," said Falker. "Now, a pound is a lot to poor workin' men like us, but considerin' the serious charge and all, 'twas just—oh, more than just, 'twas merciful. P'rhaps you could see your way clear to finin' us each a pound once again."

"Hmmm, interesting. And what about you, Mr. Tinker?"

"I'm of the same mind. A pound apiece seems about right to me."

"It does, does it? Well, gentlemen, I am of a different mind, for as you can see, the fine you paid taught you nothing at all. Here you are, back again on the same charge. And so I think it time you served a sentence in jail—let us say sixty days for each, shall we?"

They took that bravely enough. Yet Sir John was not finished.

"And since," he continued, "by your own admission, drunkenness was the cause of this riotous melee, I sentence each of you to thirty days for public drunkenness, the sentence to run consecutive to the sixty-day term for brawling and assault. In other words, each of you will serve ninety days in Newgate Gaol."

"Newgate!" Henry Tinker groaned as the others joined in.

"But Sir John, sir, it's a well-known fact that you send them off to the Fleet," shouted Falker above the chorus of complaint. "That ain't fair to send some one place and us to Newgate."

I happened at that moment to glance in the direction of Dr.

Franklin. The look of consternation upon his face seemed equal unto that of any of the prisoners.

"Oh, it is fair enough. I am free to fix your lodging in whichever jail or prison I like. Besides, in sending you off in such a way, I am conducting an experiment. I have reason to believe that I shall see the number of robberies in London decline quite remarkably." He paused, then shouted them all down.

"Mr. Fuller, take them away."

I accompanied Benjamin Franklin to Sir John's chambers once again. But just at the door I found, to my surprise, that Clarissa awaited me. She carried a basket and was dressed for an outing. She stepped back, somewhat in awe, as I sent him inside and told him bluntly to wait for Sir John. I shut the door behind him and took her aside.

"We're all ready," said she. "How long will you be?"

How long indeed? I was confused. "All ready for what?"

"Don't you remember? You said that you'd be free right after Sir John's court session."

"I . . . I don't . . ." And only then did I remember. "Our trip to Vauxhall Gardens, of course!"

"Well, how long will it take you? Mr. Donnelly has rented a wagon—and thank goodness, he really does know how to drive it. Molly is sitting there beside him, and Tom, you, and I will be in back. It's a perfect day for it, Jeremy—more like autumn than December. Come along. We've only a few hours of daylight left."

"But—I can't. I just can't. You saw who I sent into Sir John's chambers—Benjamin Franklin!"

"Yes, and I must say you did not treat him with the courtesy he deserves. You'll never get anywhere in this world, Jeremy, if you don't learn better manners."

"You don't understand. Didn't you read Dr. Franklin's statement in this morning's *London Chronicle?*" I looked at her dubiously. "No, of course you didn't. You never read newspapers, do you?"

"You know I don't. I've always maintained that they concentrate too much on public events at the neglect of true human drama, which is ever so much more important."

"So you say. I'll not argue the point with you now."

Far down the long hall I saw Sir John turn away from Mr. Fuller and the prisoners and start toward us.

"Clarissa, I have been urging Sir John for weeks to question Benjamin Franklin a second time, and now he will do so. I simply *must* remain here for the interrogation. I am needed here. Can't you understand that?"

"Oh yes, I understand," said she, chin in the air. "What puzzles me merely is why you must always disappoint me so."

She turned then and flounced away with a great rustling of her skirts and clicking of heels. Yet she moved not so fast that I would have failed to see tears glistening in her eyes. They were there, in truth, for all to see.

For all, that is, except Sir John.

"Good day to you, Clarissa," said he to her with a smile.

After clearing her throat, she managed a proper greeting.

A few steps beyond, he reached me and asked after her health. "Has she a catarrh, or perhaps just a case of the sniffles?"

"The latter, I think, sir."

"Well, she must be careful—and you, too. This is the season for such, you know. I wouldn't want any of you infected with this 'influenza' that has Mr. Marsden down. He's evidently far more ill than we supposed."

I was greatly frustrated at having missed the trip to the Vauxhall Gardens. Oh, I had been there once or twice before, but I had heard that the autumn leaves decorated it still, and there was much beauty yet to be seen there—even now, so late in the year. Yet I supposed that Tom Durham would do as well as I for Clarissa's escort. Quite honestly, I feared that he would do all too well. He had only returned from York two days past after an absence of a week. During that time I felt I had won her back from Tom. True, when he first arrived, I had ridiculed her behavior somewhat. Yet she no longer followed him about and stared at him, for the excellent reason that he was no longer present to be followed and stared at. Nevertheless, during the time he was absent I made a great effort to win back her attention, even her affection, because in all truth I had come to miss her and, indeed, to miss her terribly. Was I jealous?

Surely not. Yet I was certain that if I had observed those same changes in another, I would have named that person jealous. But now Tom was back, much changed from the cocky and rather repugnant fellow who had left. Was the change due to his visit to his dying grandmother? Or because of the shock he had felt in seeing Annie's swift rise? Whatever the reason, he came back from York a changed young man—quieter, more considerate and sensible. Nevertheless, just as handsome as before—at least, perhaps, in Clarissa's eyes.

In spite of all this, I had chosen to remain in order to witness Dr. Franklin's interrogation. I was convinced for the time being that I had chosen wisely and properly, and would probably remain so for the next few hours. After that, I was not near so certain.

Though not much pleased by it, Dr. Franklin had been deeply impressed by the rough justice that Sir John had administered. Before he was even addressed, much less asked a question, he put forth a comment which said far more than he may have intended.

"I have heard," said he, "that ninety days in Newgate will kill some men."

"These I have sent there will survive."

"Perhaps, but all the same, it does seem a particularly severe sentence for brawling in the streets."

"It would, were it not for the fact that these two gangs were fighting over territories which they might have as their own to pillage and plunder."

"Pillage and plunder?"

"They are thieves, Dr. Franklin. They would as soon take you down a dark alley, knock you over the head, and strip you of your clothing as they would greet you in the street. They prey upon prostitutes, poor shopkeepers, and the like. Falker's gang left an old couple bleeding in their home because they were at first unwilling to surrender their life savings. They are bad men, all of them."

"If you know this to be true, then why do you not pass them on for trial at Old Bailey?"

"Why, because I have no evidence against them and I have found no witness who is willing to testify against them. And so I have decided to make do by getting them off the streets whenever possible. This battle in Bedford Street afforded me just such an opportunity. Do you wish to know what it was about?"

"Indeed I would like to know."

"The Tinkers, who have always operated in and around Seven Dials, took off on a bit of a robbing spree in the environs of Bedford Street, which has always been the territory of the Falkers. The line was drawn and the Tinkers stepped over it. A battle royal ensued, and both sides lost because both will spend the next three months in Newgate."

"And why did you merely fine them when last they appeared before you?"

"Why, because we were trying to put an informer in their midst. Unfortunately, the informer himself was betrayed and murdered."

"Oh."

"Now you, Dr. Franklin, would not get off with a fine, I can assure you."

"What do you mean?"

"Why, if I choose, I may now put you under arrest and send you off to Newgate for a term of three months. That would be about right. I'd have to check the books on that to be absolutely certain."

"And what would the charge be?" Franklin demanded. "Surely you have no proof that I was in any wise involved in the actual theft of the letters from Lord Hillsborough."

"No, I have none, but I need none."

"How can that be, sir? Or have the protections of English law already been put aside here in England?"

"You have asked what the charge would be, and I shall tell you," said Sir John in his deepest, gravest court voice. "The charge would be 'Giving a false statement to a magistrate.'"

"But I told you that at the time you questioned me, I knew nothing of the letters, nor of their theft."

"You said, as I recall, that you only knew of it what you had read in the newspapers."

"That's right. It was not until the following day that I learned more."

"So you say," said Sir John. "If I choose not to believe you, then

you have given a false statement to a magistrate. And frankly, Dr.
Franklin, I *don't* believe you."

"But I have told you how it was!" Franklin cried out in exasperation.

"A simple denial of the charge is no defense."

"What, then, would be a defense?"

"Well, if you were to give me the name of him who passed on to
you the packet of these famous letters, he might back up your version of the events."

"What if I were to give you my word?"

"What good would that do, for it is, after all, your veracity that
I am calling to question. As I see it, your statement in today's *London
Chronicle* casts doubt effectively upon all that you said at my table."

"But could you, as the magistrate, try the case?"

"I don't know why not. First of all, who better than a magistrate
knows when he is being lied to? Secondly, are you sure you would
prefer this to being tried in Old Bailey? I doubt that you would."

"Why? Why are you so sure?"

"Well, because Old Bailey is a felony court. Perhaps you're unaware of the distinction, but giving a false statement to a magistrate
is naught but a misdemeanor, and misdemeanors are not tried in
felony court—unless, of course, the false statement charge were tied
to another."

"Such as?"

"Oh, such as conspiracy to commit treason, or outright treason.
I recall telling you at our earlier meeting that Lord Mansfield was
eager to conduct a treason trial. Jeremy here was present when it
was discussed. He will confirm it, I think."

"Not necessary," said Dr. Franklin before I could frame the sort
of response that Sir John had called for. "You were quite right to
assume that I would not wish to be tried in felony court. But is there
no other magistrate in London who could try it?"

"There is Saunders Welch, of course. He could, I suppose, but
I'm not sure that he *would*, if you follow me."

"Why is that? Why shouldn't he be willing?"

"He might fear that if he were to find in your favor—though
in the case of Mr. Welch that seems unlikely—I might, in some
way, seek to get back at him. And it has long been bandied about

London that not all his practices could stand close scrutiny. No, I believe you would do better taking your chance with me. After all, you can speak for yourself in my court, and you know from our earlier discussion that there is naught I like better than hearing a good argument. You may have my word, sir, that if you can present justification for your behavior, I will discharge you without a moment's hesitation."

"And if my argument does *not* convince you?"

"Well, then it's off to Newgate with you."

"For three months?"

"Perhaps I was a bit hasty there. It may prove to be that I have some choice in sentencing—perhaps only sixty days then. That is not a great piece from a lifetime, you know—and it would be an altogether new experience, finding yourself surrounded by such as Falker and Tinker. Might be interesting, eh? Something to tell your grandchildren."

"Interesting!" Dr. Franklin shuddered. "But look," said he, "what if I could convince you that I was justified in taking the action I did?"

"Do you mean right here and now?"

"Yes."

"Well, you may try to convince me. Let's hear what you have to say."

That Benjamin Franklin attempted to do. He contended that relations with the North American colonies had gotten into such a bad state because the personalities involved had become so set in their positions that they could not, or would no longer seek to compromise. Among these "personalities" he numbered Thomas Hutchinson, Andrew Oliver, and Thomas Whately, who were the three correspondents in the letters under discussion. And to these three he added Lord Hillsborough, until recently the secretary of state for the colonies.

"Yet at the time the letters were written," said Sir John, "Hutchinson was not governor of Massachusetts, nor was Oliver lieutenant governor."

"How do you think they got their royal appointments?" countered Dr. Franklin.

"You're suggesting then that these Tory sentiments were part of a campaign to win their present positions?"

"I could not say that in court, for I have no proof of it, but that is my belief—yes."

"Continue," said Sir John.

Franklin declared that when the packet of letters was brought to him, he saw them as an instrument by which Hutchinson and Oliver might be revealed for what they are.

"And what do you say they are?" asked Sir John.

"Why, they are betrayers of the very people they have been appointed to govern. After all, 'There must be an abridgment of what are called English liberties,'" said Franklin, quoting from one of the letters written by Governor Hutchinson. "What would you do, sir, if the prime minister spoke such words in Parliament?"

"I should do all I could to get him out of office."

"So, too, have certain members of the Massachusetts legislature."

"But I would do so—by democratic means," protested Sir John.

"So, too, would the members of that representative body. A petition was being prepared requesting the king to remove Governor Hutchinson from his office. It was never my intention to discredit the writers of those letters publicly."

"What then?"

"I wished to give those preparing the petition what they needed to get the majority of the Massachusetts House to vote for it. Therefore I sent the letters in question to the House Speaker, Thomas Cushing, with a strong request that the letters not be widely circulated or printed, but be shown individually to 'men of worth.' I asked for the letters to be returned after a few months. I intended, in other words, to see that they got back to their former possessor."

"Yet in spite of your cautions and your best intentions—"

"The letters were read out in the House by Samuel Adams. They were printed in a newspaper, the *Massachusetts Spy*, and were made available in a pamphlet to anyone with a few pence to buy it."

Dr. Franklin hung his head and slumped forward, the very picture of disconsolate dismay.

"Benjamin Franklin," said the magistrate, "if you will forgive me for saying so, I believe you to be a rather foolish and naive individual—that is, if you did truly believe that given such material as you gave them, those 'sons of liberty,' as they style themselves, would ever have exhibited any degree of restraint. Sam Adams, and the rest of his ilk, will have independence and accept nothing less."

"I know that now."

"Is that what you also want?"

He was silent for quite some time before responding. At last, he raised his head and spoke.

"No, in all truth," said he, "I would keep the relation between the mother country and her colonies as it is, except that I should like to see Parliament, the prime minister, and, may God grant him wisdom, the king, demonstrate greater intelligence in dealing with the colonies. We are all Englishmen, after all. It is just that some of us are also Americans."

"Dr. Franklin, for what it is worth, I believe you. I believe your intentions were as you present them, and I believe, too, that your feelings about mother country and colonies are also as you would have me believe. But good God, man, how can you expect me to treat this as some sort of misunderstanding when a burglary has been done, in the course of which a murder has been committed? You must tell me who brought the letters to you, and whatever else you may know about these felonies."

"But . . . but I cannot do that."

"And why not?"

"Because," said Franklin, "I gave my word to him who put the letters in my hands. I can tell you this, however. According to the man in question, he was approached by the burglars after the burglary had taken place. He did not seek them out. At the time he purchased the letters from them, he did not know that there had been a killing done."

"Or so he said to you," said Sir John, pronouncing each word with derisive sarcasm. (Overacting a bit, I fear.)

"Having said all that I have said to you, have I at least convinced you, Sir John, that I was justified in my actions?"

"I understand that you feel that you were, and I accept that you have told me the truth, as much of it as you judge necessary to explain yourself. But understand this, Franklin. I care naught for the politics of all this. I care only that a man was murdered in the course of a burglary. When you are prepared to give me the name of him who supplied you with those infamous letters, I will put away for good all thought of charging you with giving a false report."

"Until then," said Franklin, "it will hang over my head as a threat?"

"No, not *merely* that. I must consider the matter further. That will be all, sir. You may go now."

Without a word more, Benjamin Franklin rose, hat and stick in hand, and left the room. He did not look at me, nor would he have seen me if he had, for his eyes brimmed to overflowing with tears. The humiliation that he felt was plain upon his face. I, who had urged his interrogation so insistently, could not help but feel pity for the man. I wondered what Sir John felt for him. I started to ask him just that, but he silenced me with a finger to his lips and a softly whispered, "Shhh." We listened to Franklin's footsteps fade as he drew closer to the end of the hall and the door out to Bow Street. Sir John signaled for me to go and take a look. That I did, moving quietly on tiptoe to the hall just in time to see Dr. Franklin disappear through the door, which he closed quietly behind him.

"He's gone," said I.

"And good riddance," said Sir John.

"Why? Do you feel you were lied to? From where I sat, he seemed greatly moved and eager to convince you, yet not disposed to lie. There were tears in his eyes when you ordered him out. He seemed fearful, Sir John."

"Going soft on him, eh?"

"Not at all, but he did seem to be telling the truth."

"As much as he told us, I suppose."

"Do you truly intend to charge him with giving a false report to a magistrate? In all the years I have attended you here at Bow Street, I have never known you to charge any in such a manner."

Sir John scowled mightily. "Of course I do not intend to charge him so! What do you take me for? The reason you've not heard me charge any thus is not because none lie to me, but rather that *all* lie to me. It would be impossible to find a truth-teller amongst all those pickpockets, sneak thieves, killers, and robbers. They know that they must have a story ready to tell when they appear at the Old

Bailey. When it is told to me, it is given its first trial. They polish it as they wait for trial, and a few have actually gotten off before certain judges in felony court when they had a good tale to tell, or when it was told in a specially entertaining style."

Just as I was about to ask if Lord Mansfield had been one of those judges, we heard the door to Bow Street open once again. We listened, saying nothing, as a single set of footsteps approached. Had Benjamin Franklin returned? No, the footsteps were of a man much larger. Was it Mr. Fuller coming back from Newgate? No, it was too early; the papers to be filled out for seventeen men would keep him there for another hour, at least.

"See who that is, will you, Jeremy?" I jumped at his order.

The man coming down the long hall was at first barely visible. Not the time of the day, but the time of the year, made dusk come quite early; and if it was not quite so dark as that, 'twas well on its way by midafternoon. Still there were patches of light through which he must travel before reaching Sir John's chambers. At the first of them, I was able to get my first true look at the man. He was one of considerable size and weight. There was something vaguely (or perhaps more than vaguely) threatening about him. Instinctively, my left hand went to the pistol on my hip and my right hand to the cosh in the pocket of my coat.

"I am George Burkett," he bellowed forth in a voice big enough to fit his huge body. "I am come to make the acquaintance of Sir John Fielding, the Blind Beak of Bow Street."

"Come ahead," said Sir John.

Said I: "Give me but a moment, and I shall light a few candles."

"Not on my account," called George Burkett. "I likes the dark."

Close at hand he looked no different than I had first supposed—except larger and even more threatening.

Ignoring me, he stepped through the doorway and went straight to Sir John. He grasped his hand and gave it a punishing squeeze. Yet if he had inflicted pain, Sir John gave no sign of it.

"Now you have me, Mr. Burkett, what is the purpose of your mission?"

"I like a man what gets right to the point," said Burkett, "so I shall put it to you straight. I am hired by Lord Hillsborough to assist in finding them who burglarized his house and murdered his manservant."

From an interior pocket of his coat he fetched out a letter and placed it in Sir John's hand.

"I have delivered to you a letter of introduction from Lord Mansfield, the Lord Chief Justice. In it, he asks that you give unto me all aid which I may need in finding and capturing these villains. Now, what say you to that, sir?"

NINE

*In which I serve
as a guide for our
American visitor*

Something was amiss. That much was certain. There was quiet at
the dinner table; Sir John and Lady Fielding exchanged low mut-
terings; Molly looked left and right, first at one and then at the
other; Tom Durham kept his eyes upon the plate of food in front of
him. Clarissa was, as Lady Fielding said, "indisposed" and was not
even present at table. I estimated no more than a dozen words were
spoken during the meal. What was most annoying was that every-
body but me seemed to know what this great unmentionable was.

Perhaps if I had returned earlier for dinner I would not have
felt excluded. Sir John had sent me off with George Burkett for a
tour of the Covent Garden area. As we went round these points of
interest, so familiar to me, I learned a little about him—but only a
little. Mr. Burkett came, he said, from the province of Georgia in the
North American colonies (which accounted, perhaps, for his odd
manner of speech, so different from Dr. Franklin's). He had been
brought here to London by Lord Hillsborough expressly to help in
pursuit of the perpetrators of the evil deeds. I thought that a bit
strange. Was Mr. Burkett so well known as a thief-taker that Lord
Hillsborough had sought him out specially? I recall asking him how
he had come to know Hillsborough, and he responded, "Him and
me, we got a mutual friend." Which told me nothing at all, or at
most, very little.

He was most taken by Bedford Street with its taverns, dives,
and alehouses, particularly when I gave it as my opinion that the

entire burglary plot had been hatched right there in Bedford Street at the King's Pleasure.

"This very spot, eh?" said Burkett. "Now ain't that interestin'. I must spend a bit of time there."

"It would best be done later."

"So be it then."

I accompanied him to the Strand wherein his hostelry stood, and left him there at the entrance. We agreed to meet at that very spot at ten that night.

"One of the Bow Street Runners shall accompany us. They know these precincts far better than I."

All this had I communicated to Mr. Perkins, who seemed to know Bedford Street and its denizens far better than the rest of the Runners. He was willing to accompany us but wanted to know more about the fellow. I could tell him little, for I knew little myself.

"Don't we even know what it was he did back in—where was it? Georgia?"

"That's the place," said I. "He seems to have been some sort of thief-taker, as I understand it."

"Well, he must have been God's own gift to thief-taking if he was worth bringing over from America."

There I had to agree. "All I can say in his behalf is that he came bearing a letter from the Lord Chief Justice, instructing Sir John to give him any help that he may need."

"You saw the letter?"

"Indeed I did. It was in Lord Mansfield's own hand, signed by him, just as it should have been. I read it out loud to Sir John myself."

"All right," said Mr. Perkins. "Maybe we can get more out of him over a glass of ale."

And so we left it, agreeing to make the walk together from Bow Street to Burkett's hostelry in the Strand.

Having done so, I made my way up the stairs to the kitchen. I knew that was a bit late, and hearing naught of talk or laughter at table, I assumed that dinner was done. Thus was I somewhat taken aback when I opened the door and found all but Clarissa present at table. All looked up as I made my entrance, but not a word of greeting was spoken. True, Sir John nodded and spoke my name, and Molly hastened to the pot on the fire and dipped out a generous helping of mutton stew for me, but, otherwise, they took no notice of my arrival. I sat down at my place and tasted the stew.

"Ah, up to your usual high standard, Molly," said I. (Actually a lie: It wanted more time on the fire and was indifferently spiced.)

She mumbled her thanks and resumed eating.

"Where's Clarissa?" I asked innocently enough. "Not ill, I hope."

Lady Fielding looked at me sharply. What had I said?

"No, not sick," said she. "Clarissa is indisposed."

What could she mean by that? But I knew enough not to ask; rather, I would wait till the pall of silence had lifted, and people were once again acting sensible. How long, I wondered, would that take?

With naught to impede them, they sped through dinner like starvelings given their first meal in a month. When he had done, Sir John suggested all go upstairs and talk a bit more. What was it could be discussed there could not be talked of here?

With that, all at the table rose, including myself. 'Twas then that Lady Fielding turned to me, frowning, and said, "Not you, Jeremy. Do the washing up, as you usually do."

"And afterward," said Sir John, "I should like you to go on to Mr. Donnelly. He has prepared a letter for me."

All four did then depart, leaving me alone with the dinner dishes to be washed, the pots and pans to be cleaned. Time was not a problem: 'Twas near two hours before I was to meet Mr. Perkins that we might take George Burkett on his evening tour. And so I pitched in, and made all ready in the shortest time ever. Once I had done rattling pottery plates and eating utensils in the wash water, I listened at the bottom of the stairs. I thought I might overhear something, yet all I caught was the murmur of voices — no words at all. So was it. I sought out my cloak, which hung upon a hook on the door. Donning it, I wondered if perhaps Mr. Donnelly might not be able to explain to me just why the members of this household were acting so peculiarly.

Gabriel Donnelly came in immediate response to my knock upon his door. It was as if he had been waiting nearby, expecting me to come at any moment.

"Ah, Jeremy, come in, will you? I was hoping you would come by soon. I'm off again to another of their damned dinners."

"Whose damned dinners?"

"Who indeed? Oh, the beau monde's, I suppose. The better I become acquainted with them, the better I understand that no matter how I may have wished otherwise, I am indeed no more than a Dubliner, the son of a draper, nothing more nor less, and proud of it. It's why I've come to value Molly so highly."

"But she won't be there. Why are you going to this particular dinner?"

"Because Mr. Goldsmith will be there—dear old Nolly. I feel I must be on hand for each and every appearance he makes in society, lest he be struck down at table."

"Is he so ill? What ails him?"

"What does not? A heart stoppage could hit him at any moment of distress. I have seen him pant so for air that he is as some great bull charging cross the field. Apoplexy is also a likelihood. In argument, his face often turns a rosy hue, and one of the veins in his forehead throbs dangerously. I always ask to sit next to him and keep a bottle of vinegar and hartshorn handy that I may revive him, should he collapse."

"You had said he was ill. I'd no idea of how serious his illness."

"I wish it were not so—but it is." He fumbled into his coat pocket and produced a letter. "This, I believe, is what you came for," said he.

"I suppose it must be. Sir John said you had a letter I was to bring him."

"Yes, it concerns the illness of Mr. Marsden. I visited him just this morning."

"He has that new thing, influenza, hasn't he? How is he?"

"He is a very sick man."

"Truly? But I had heard that in its symptoms it was quite like a catarrh."

"Well, that is in some sense correct. But there are important differences. For one thing, it is highly contagious. For another, while the symptoms are *like* a catarrh, they are very much stronger. Influenza can kill."

"Oh my, I'd no idea," said I.

"Indeed," said he. "I wore a kerchief mask over my face and advised the woman caring for him to take the same precaution. I can do little for him, except to make sure that he takes plenty of water. He sweats so that he is in danger of drying out completely. I gave him a bit of cinchona bark to control the sweating." He sighed. "We shall see."

"Indeed, I shall hope for the best."

I tucked the letter away and made ready to go, but then a thought occurred to me, and I stopped.

"Mr. Donnelly, I've a question for you. When I returned from a task Sir John put me to, dinner had begun, and everyone at table was acting most peculiar. None spoke all through the meal, and it seemed that everyone there knew something I did not. Do you have any notion what that was all about?"

"Hmmm . . . well . . . yes, I suppose I do." He seemed reluctant to discuss it, made uncomfortable by the matter.

"Oh, and one more thing," said I. "Clarissa was not even there at dinner. I asked after her, and Lady Fielding told me that Clarissa was 'indisposed.' An odd sort of expression, don't you think — 'indisposed,'"

"Indeed, it's one that women often use to prevent further inquiries."

"What sort of inquiries?"

"The kind you're making of me right now." He frowned angrily. "Oh, bloody hell," said he, "why shouldn't you hear about it? Why should you be kept in the dark? And I daresay you'd be more likely to get an accurate version of what happened from me than from anyone else."

"What *did* happen? What *is* this all about?"

He heaved a sigh and raised his eyes to the ceiling, as if trying to think where he might best begin.

"Well," said he. "When Clarissa came out of Number 4 without you, I sensed that there might be trouble, though I've no idea why I should have had that feeling. Everyone was quite well-behaved on the way to Vauxhall Gardens."

"And afterward?"

"Well, yes, up to a point. Molly had brought a basket of dainties and cakes, which she had cooked that morning, and I contributed a bottle of claret. We had a grand time of it, eating and drinking in the fresh air beneath the trees, some of which had yet half their leaves. And right pretty they were, too—all particolored, brown and red, and in some corners there were remnants of the fall flowers, blooming still. There were not many besides us there in the gardens, and so we may not have carried on as we did in other circumstances . . ."

"You mean eating, drinking, and making merry?"

"Well . . . no . . . you see, Molly and I became carried away by the happy occasion, and fell to kissing and fondling. Not indecently, you understand, but I must say, a bit passionately. And I fear we offered Clarissa and Tom rather a bad example. You must understand, Jeremy, that the Irish lack the reserve of the English, and—"

"Do sir, please, get on with your story," said I, interrupting.

"What? Oh yes, sorry. Well, what then happened was that Clarissa and Tom went off to walk amongst the trees. That, in any case, is what she called to us as they left; I believe that she was somewhat embarrassed by our carrying-on, and wished to leave us to our amorous play. As for Tom Durham, it seems to me he must have had base motives in mind right from the start. Or perhaps Clarissa's intentions were not the highest either, for in truth she had been flirting rather shamelessly with Tom from the moment we left Number 4 Bow Street. So in that sense, you might say that she brought it upon herself." Mr. Donnelly let forth a great, deep sigh. Then, with a shake of his head, he added, "There you have it."

"There I have *what?* You have not told me what the *it* is that I now have. What *happened*, sir?"

He was driving me quite to distraction, circling round and round, and shying from any sort of direct statement. I believe I preferred the silence of the dinner table to this.

"In truth, Jeremy, I'm not quite sure what it was," said he. "All I can tell you is that some minutes after they had left our sight, we heard a cry for help. Molly identified the voice as that of Clarissa. We went running out to find them, and we did not need to go far before we did. They were just off the path, secluded somewhat in the grove of trees—though not actually hidden." And having said thus much, he stopped.

"Well, go on, won't you?"

"Of course I will. I've just taken a moment to find the right words. It is important, as you well know, to describe only what you have seen in such situations. What did I see, precisely? I saw Tom atop Clarissa, and she bellowing for all she was worth. I assure you that when I pulled him off her, he had not exposed himself, nor were his clothes in disarray. Yet clearly, his intentions were not honorable—or at least that was how Clarissa interpreted them. Hence, her cry for help. I believe it would be accurate to say that Tom Durham had made an improper advance."

"I daresay," said I. "At least that."

"No, no more than that, I can assure you. Tell me, Jeremy, how old is Tom?"

"No more than nineteen. He is but a year older than I."

"During my time in the Navy," said Mr. Donnelly, "I knew many such as he. Boys they were, and little more than that. In matters of maturity you are years older than he. You know how to conduct yourself in the great world. You have met men of importance which Tom will only hear of during his lifetime. More important, however, you have learned, partly by observation and partly—I should think—through Clarissa, just how to get along with women. Whereas, a fellow such as Tom, because he spends most of his life aboard ship and in the company of men, will no doubt ever be awkward with females. Because he suffers the same storms of passion that all boys do, he will be the prey of prostitutes and courtesans who will flatter him and cozen him till his head spins. Only much later, should he be lucky enough to advance in the Navy, as he probably will, and reap the rewards of command, he will find a wife who will bring with her a considerable dowry and very little else. He will, in other words, likely go through life, from beginning to end, never once guessing the great secret that all wise men must learn: that in most of the ways that matter, women are not much different from men."

I knew not quite what to say. I knew well that Gabriel Donnelly was given to philosophizing, but I had never got quite so much of it from him in a single dose. There was much there that I might disagree with, particularly that major conclusion of his (so I thought and still think). Yet I also felt that this was neither the time nor the place to do so. I would put but one more question to him.

"What happened afterward?"

"After what?"

"Why, after you had rescued Clarissa."

"We went back, of course. There was no resuming our carefree mood after that, now was there?"

"I suppose not."

"On our return, however, Tom rode beside me—not a word passed between us—and the ladies in the back of the wagon. I know not what was said between them, for I could not hear them, but the two of them buzzed and whispered all the way back to Bow Street."

That was truly the end of his story, for he did leave them there at Number 4, and then did he drive off and return the wagon and team to the stable in Half Moon Passage.

"One last question before I go, sir."

"Well, ask it quickly. I must be off to my dinner, Jeremy."

"Oh yes, sir. Could you give me the address of our Mr. Lee?"

"Arthur Lee?"

"Yes, with whom we traveled to Portsmouth."

"Hmmm, no, no I can't. I know the house, but not the number. You know the house, too, of course. It's that one just beyond my old surgery in Tavistock Street. I met him there—I forget quite how—and thought him an interesting fellow. And—well, you know it, I'm sure."

"Two stories, red brick with a flat roof?"

"That's the one. He's on the second floor."

"Thank-you, sir. Enjoy yourself, and give Mr. Goldsmith my best."

With that, I dashed down to the ground floor and out the door. My wish to make contact with Arthur Lee was an afterthought. Considering that, as I made my way back to Bow Street, I thought it perhaps odd that I had had afterthoughts of any sort after having heard Gabriel Donnelly's account of the disastrous outing in Vauxhall Gardens. I could tell myself that if I had been along, things would never have come to such a pass—and no doubt I would be right in that. Still, no real harm had been done to Clarissa, for which I thanked God and all the saints. And I suspected that I had chosen right in remaining to hear Sir John's interrogation of Dr. Franklin. All that had happened, in truth, was that Tom Durham had disgraced himself. And that he had done on at least two other occasions during this single stay. Had ever a visit gone so poorly?

Upon my return, I was given a bit of news that did not in the least surprise me.

"Tom will be leaving us," said Lady Fielding. "He'll be returning to Portsmouth a day early. We should like you to give us a hand with his baggage, Jeremy."

I had no choice but to agree. Considering that to be the case, I believe I acquiesced quite gracefully. I got from her his time of departure, and ascertained that he would be returning, as he had come, with naught but his sea chest.

"Then," said I to her, "there should be no need for me to take the barrow."

"That is entirely up to you, Jeremy."

"As you say, Lady Fielding."

Forcing a smile, she left me there in the kitchen and made for the parlor, where Tom no doubt awaited her. Then did I hasten to the little room on the floor above, which Sir John named his "study." He often sat in the dark there, dark and light being as one to him, but on this occasion the room was well lit, for near as I could tell, the meeting had just been adjourned. There I found him, in any case, alone in the room, a glum expression upon his face.

"Who is there? Is it you, Jeremy?"

"It is, Sir John, and I have that report on Mr. Marsden's condition which Mr. Donnelly prepared."

"Then read it me, will you?"

That I did, and I found it more pessimistic than I would have supposed from my conversation with the good doctor. In it, he stated his fear that the "influenza" might penetrate Mr. Marsden's lungs, leaving him with pneumonia. He promised to keep a close watch upon the clerk and inform Sir John regularly regarding his condition.

"Not a good report, eh?"

"I should not call it that, no sir."

"You'll not mind then carrying on as you are now?"

"Sir?"

"In Mr. Marsden's place."

"Oh no, Sir John, I rather like it."

"Good lad." He took a moment to rub his temple. That seemed to portend a headache; they did not often come to him, but when they did, they were most severe. "I suppose you heard an account of this matter to do with Tom from Mr. Donnelly."

"Uh . . . yes sir, I have."

"I've no doubt that the version you got was more accurate than the one I heard. What with Molly Sarton leveling accusations at Tom, and Kate defending him like the good mother she has tried to be, I'd no notion of just who I ought to believe—probably neither. Well, he's going back a day early. That will take care of the immediate problem."

"Yes," said I, "I heard of his leaving from Lady Fielding."

"Why did she tell you?" he asked sharply.

"She requested I accompany them to carry Tom's sea chest."

"Let him carry his own. He's caused naught but trouble since he came. Why should we give him comfort?"

Because I could think of no good answer to that, I held my peace.

"Surely you can think of something better to do with your time in the morning," said he.

"What I would like to do would involve you."

"In what way? What is it you wish me to do?"

"I should like you to interrogate Arthur Lee."

"Arthur Lee? Who . . . ? Ah yes, I remember now. He's the fellow you suspect of complicity with Franklin."

"I'm sure of it," said I. "He is the link between Franklin and the burglars. 'Twas he who brought the letters to Franklin."

"All right, bring him in then. But mind you, Jeremy, this will in no wise excuse you from your duties as Mr. Marsden's substitute."

"Agreed," said I.

Having met Mr. Perkins at the appointed hour, I set off with him for the Globe and Anchor hostelry at which George Burkett lodged. It was indeed one of the best in the city. Lord Hillsborough had not stinted in bringing this thief-taker extraordinaire to London.

As we made our way round Covent Garden and down Southampton Street to the Strand, Mr. Perkins questioned me intently regarding our visitor from America. It was, to say the least, most unusual for Sir John to have aid forced upon him by any member of the government, including the Lord Chief Justice. To my knowledge, it had never before happened so. It was plain to me, though not from any remark made by Sir John, that he was unhappy with this development. Yet Benjamin Franklin's public admission of his role in passing the letters back to his compatriots in the Massachusetts legislature had put the magistrate at such a disadvantage that he felt he could not, in spite of his feelings, strenuously object. Eventually, however, I felt certain he would take up the matter with Lord Mansfield.

Constable Perkins had also asked among the Bow Street Runners if there were any precedent for this and found that there was none. This disturbed him no little, and he brought it up to me early in our journey to the Globe and Anchor. He did so by putting a question to me.

"Who's been the longest in service of all the Runners?" he asked me of a sudden, quite apropos of nothing at all.

"That would no doubt be Mr. Bailey, would it not?" I responded.

"So I thought, as well," said he. "But it turns out 'twas Mr. Baker. He goes back to the days of Sir John's brother."

"Henry Fielding?"

"Was that his name? I guess it must have been. Anyway, he wasn't always the gaoler. He started out just like the rest of us, as a runner, but it was way back in '52. But when I found this out, I went to him, you see, and I asked him straight out if he ever heard of Sir John—or his brother, for that matter—accepting help from an independent thief-taker or any such. And Mr. Baker says to me, no, he never heard of it. He says it's been years since Sir John would even let a thief-taker into his courtroom, no matter how many witnesses he might have with him to back him up."

"That's right, as far as I can tell," said I.

"That's right as far as *anyone* can tell. So just answer me this, Jeremy. Why is it now he's started taking help from such as this fella Burkett? Has he changed his mind all of a sudden, or what? Have they cut the Bow Street budget so deep that he's going to let some of the constables go and throw open the door to these independent thief-takers? I don't mind telling you that some of us are a bit worked up about this."

I hastened to assure him that there was no reason to worry at all. No, the Bow Street budget had not been cut. No, Sir John had never expressed to me any desire to let thief-takers in the back door, as it were. He was, so far as I knew, opposed to these private operators and their practices, on both moral and legal grounds. He had only praise for the Bow Street Runners and had often said that he only wished he could hire more like those now in the force.

"In short," said I to Mr. Perkins, "neither you nor any of the rest have anything to worry about."

"You're sure of that, Jeremy?"

"Sure as I'm here walking beside you."

"Then what's this all about?"

With that, I began a hasty explanation of the matter of the Hutchinson letters, and their importance to the government; of the role played by Benjamin Franklin in it all; and the personal insult which their theft did constitute to Lord Hillsborough. I left out many important details, but I did manage to communicate to the constable the outline of the situation, and stress to him the awkward predicament in which Sir John now found himself.

"Ah well," said the constable, "he should have told us."

"No doubt he should," I said, "but he knows that he made a mistake with Franklin, and you know as well as I how he does hate to be caught in error."

"Well, none of us likes that."

Mr. Perkins fell silent then. We had thus reached the Strand. The Globe and Anchor lay just ahead by a street or two. Having walked with him oft through the city, I knew his pace, easy but steady; 'twas the sort one might use to walk the whole night long — and that he often did. I liked him well — and indeed I should have, for I owed him much. As Sir John had provided my intellectual development, Constable Perkins had contributed much to my manhood. He, it was, who had shown me how I might walk these dark streets of London and fear no man.

"What's he like?"

The constable asked it in a quiet voice, almost as if he feared he might be overheard. My mind was elsewhere. His question brought me back to the present.

"What's who like?" I asked.

"This fellow—what's his name? Burkett? The one who came all the way from America just to give us a hand."

His irony was not lost on me.

"He's big," said I. "Just a shade below giant size."

"Big, is he? In what way is he big? Is he seven feet in height? Is his chest thick as a fifty-gallon barrel? Does the ground tremble when he walks?"

"Well, he's over six feet. I fear he'll grow no taller than six and a half. His chest is more in the forty-gallon range. And whether or not he makes the ground tremble, I cannot say. But I did notice that he has a way of making people tremble wherever he goes."

Mr. Perkins chuckled appreciatively and gave me a wink.

"And this is the fellow I'm to show round Bedford Street."

"This is the fellow."

"Well, seems to me," said the constable, "that 'stead of showing Bedford Street to him, we'll be showing him to Bedford Street."

That proved to be the case, for when we met him just inside the entrance to the Globe and Anchor, we found him dressed, (or perhaps better said, overdressed) in popinjay fashion of the kind some from the country might wear in imitation of the city blades. He was all gaudy and garish. Between his neck and feet, I counted no less than five contending colors, each brighter than the last. If his size alone were not sufficient to attract attention, his outlandish attire certainly would. Mr. Perkins caught my eye and offered a look of surprise. I wondered for a moment if it might not be up to me to urge that he return to his room and don a costume a little less . . . colorful. Yet there was to be no such suggestion, for immediately we arrived, George Burkett began, in the most blatant and least subtle manner, to take command of our little expedition.

Introductions were handled quickly and without ceremony. It mattered little, however, for neither man made much use of the other's name. For his part, Constable Perkins addressed the man at his side direct, turning to him when he spoke that there might be no doubt for whom his words were intended. Mr. Burkett, on the few occasions he addressed me, called me naught but "lad." For Mr. Perkins, he had another form of address.

"So you be a Bow Street Runner, eh?" said Burkett to him.

"That's what they tell me."

"Well, Mr. Bow Street Runner, how far we got to walk? If it's more than a stroll, we can find us a hackney, for I've a pocket heavy with coin."

"It's not far, not far enough to ride the distance, anyway."

"One thing fair 'mazes me about this town of London."

"What's that?" I called out from behind, hopping to keep up with the two of them.

"Well, lad, I am just taken by surprise how pushed together it all is. Bein' from America, I am used to some space 'tween things. Ain't it terrible hard getting' used to all this crowdin'?"

And so on. His manner of addressing Mr. Perkins as "Mr. Bow Street Runner" was vaguely insulting, and it seemed that he intended it to be so. In any case, the constable took it as such, and our American visitor continued in that manner for the length of our walk.

"Tell me, Mr. Bow Street Runner, is it fair difficult to get to be one of your number? I'd always heard it was."

"Well, you got to read and write and know how to tell time, and it helps if you got a good record in the Army or Navy and can handle firearms and such. Sir John, with his background in the Navy and all, he just about requires that."

"Ah then, I fear I ain't got a chance, for though I can shoot with the best of them—and there's many a dead man will swear to that—I tell time by the sun, I can't read, and all the writin' I know is the 'X' it takes to write my name. No, Mr. Bow Street Runner, I fear I ain't got what it might take to be one of you all."

All this was said in a joking, teasing manner, as if to say that this was their loss and not his own.

And it prompted this response from Mr. Perkins: "That doesn't seem to bother you none . . ."

"No, it don't," said Mr. Burkett, "for in my part of the world, I am known far and wide as the best at my trade."

"And what is your trade? We been wondering about that. Sort of a thief-taker, are you?"

"In a way, I s'pose I am. I am what they call a slave-chaser. I reckon you know that in Georgia we got slavery. It's why the province is so rich. Well, any time you got slaves, you got runaways, and I'm the fella brings the runaways back. Y'see, it ain't so easy findin' them in a place like Georgia, 'cause we got swamp and mountains and Cherokees."

"Beg pardon, Mr. Burkett," said I, piping up from the rear, "but what's a Cherokee?"

"'Tis a brand of red nigger, lad," said he, tolerating the interruption. "But as I was sayin', it ain't easy findin' them and gettin' them back in that part of the country—too many places to hide, and too many Cherokees a-waitin' up in the mountains to make the runaways slaves of their own. But I'm a good tracker, even in swamp country, and I ain't afraid of riddin' the province of a few Cherokees to get my blacks back. Each one I bring I get paid—and get paid right handsome. So that's my trade, Mr. Bow Street Runner. What do you think of that?"

"What I think of that," said Constable Perkins, "is that you'll find it ever so much different chasing thieves in London than it was chasing blacks in Georgia. But that is just my personal opinion. You'll have to find out for yourself—and this is where you start."

"This Bedford Street?"

"It is," said Mr. Perkins. "I understand you're interested in visiting the King's Pleasure."

"If that's the place the lad here said the plot was hatched to rob Lord Hillsborough."

We had stopped. He looked to me for confirmation of this.

"That is the place," said I.

"Well and good. Now, tell me what put you in mind to say that."

And as briefly as possible, I did just that. Yet it was not told so briefly that I omitted a single name: Tommy Skinner and Ned Ferguson, the burglars; Isaac Kidd, "the Duke," who arranged it all; Arthur Lee, who purchased the fruits of their thievery, and presented them to Benjamin Franklin.

Having had it laid out before him, George Burkett was surprisingly slow to give response. He stood in silence for what seemed a great long while—so long indeed that Mr. Perkins glanced uneasily in my direction. Passersby directed uneasy looks at the large, ill-dressed fellow who stood at the corner, indifferently blocking their way; they walked round him. At last he did speak.

"You say this one they call the Duke runs a card game in the cellar of one of these places in Bedford Street. Which one?"

"It's not known for certain," said I, "but it seems likely that it is the King's Pleasure."

"Yes, it do, don't it?" He rubbed his chin and said, "I wish there was some way I could pick out this fella Kidd without you two bringin' me in and pointin' him out. They know you for what you are, Mr. Bow Street Runner, and they might know you, lad."

I thought back to my meeting with Isaac Kidd and William Slade in the house which had, until that day, belonged to Black Jack Bilbo. Yes, the Duke would know me for a certainty.

"Yes, he would recognize me."

"Don't you worry about that," said Mr. Perkins. "I believe I may be able to arrange something."

On the strength of this, Burkett nodded his assent, and we started off to the King's Pleasure, which lay in the middle of the long block. I was in no wise surprised when the constable led us beyond the door. A moment later an answering whistle came, and then a few steps were heard, and Bess appeared. She smiled at Mr. Perkins, nodded at me, and looked inquiringly at George Burkett (she did not appear to like what she saw).

The constable introduced her simply as "Bess" and explained that she kept an eye on things around Bedford Street for him.

"Did you make your rounds yet?" he asked her.

"I did early on," said she.

"Was the Duke about?"

She nodded. Her eyes kept returning to Burkett. It was evident he made her uneasy.

"Where was he sitting?"

"Where he usually does—in the back table under the window, best-dressed man in the place. Easy to pick out."

"That ain't good enough." It was Burkett, stepping closer to Bess looking down upon her in a manner which seemed frankly threatening.

"What do you mean?" She started upon him, refusing to be intimidated.

"I mean what I say. It ain't good enough. You're a whore, ain't
you? You take me in there and introduce me, and you tell this man
Kidd, who you call the Duke, that I'm your customer, and that I'm
looking for some action in a game of chance. Then you stay around
for as long as I want you to, just to make sure that everything's going right." He hesitated then but a moment, and he added, "Don't
worry yourself, my girl, I'll pay you well. It's worth a sovereign to
me."

"There's a few things wrong with what you just said," she declared. "First of all, I'm not a whore, not the way you mean. Second
thing is, that's not the way it's done. You don't invite yourself in, you
get invited. But I'll tell you, if you go in there dressed the way
you're dressed, have a drink at the bar, and pay with that sovereign
you offered me, they'll be falling all over themselves to get the cards
in your hand and the money from your pocket."

"What's wrong with the way I'm dressed?"

"Why, nothing at all, except you look quite like a clown from
the colonies with all those bright colors and little buttons that don't
button anything."

What then happened went so quickly that I scarcely could follow. Burkett reached round Bess, grasped her hair, and jerked her
head back, at which she let out a great "OW!"

"We'll do it my way, hear?" he shouted simultaneously.

Yet, just as quick, Mr. Perkins pulled his club from his belt and
brought it down sharply upon the big man's forearm. Such a blow
would have broken the arm of most men, and though it did not
break his, it caused him to release his grip on Bess's hair. She
jumped quickly a safe distance away from him.

"We'll leave you here," said Constable Perkins to him. "And for
your information, sir, all that Bess told you is correct, right down to
the little buttons that don't button anything." He turned to her then.
"Come along," said he. "We'll see you to your door."

George Burkett stalked off toward the entrance to the King's
Pleasure. But then, of a sudden, he halted and whirled about.

"Let me give you something to think about, Mister One-armed
Constable. If anything should happen to that arm you got left, you'd
be in one hell of a bad situation, wouldn't you?"

"Is that a threat?" Mr. Perkins called back.

"Naw, it's just something for you to think about."

And so saying, he threw open the door to the King's Pleasure and swaggered inside.

'Twas I who was escorted home by the other two. We had little to say, except to agree that we would do naught to help Burkett further. Inwardly, I knew well that I had done far too much in offering him the names of the five who, according to my theory, had seen the letters from Lord Hillsborough's residence into the hands of Benjamin Franklin. It was now public record what Dr. Franklin had done with them.

When the constable and Bess had seen me to the door to Number 4 Bow Street, it was not much beyond eleven on the clock, yet it was late enough, so that only Mr. Baker, of all the Runners, was present. I called a halloo to him as he stuck his head out to see who had entered. Then did I start up the stairs, thinking how good it would be to have my old bed back—tomorrow night. Tonight, it seemed, I would be back on the pallet, sleeping before the fireplace.

When I opened the door to the kitchen at the top of the stairs, I found Clarissa sitting alone at the table, a loaf of bread and a bowl of butter before her, as well as a small pot of tea.

"Ah," said she, "it's you. I'd been hoping you'd come along."

"Why? So you might tell me all about your lovely afternoon in Vauxhall Gardens?" I seemed to have decided to make things difficult for her.

"Ah, so you heard about that. Would you like some tea?"

"If there's any left. I heard something about Vauxhall, sketchy but reliable—from Mr. Donnelly."

I took down a cup and sat down at the table near her.

"There's plenty of tea," she said. "I just brewed a pot. And what about some bread and butter? I had no dinner, you know. I'm quite famished."

"I don't mind if I do have a piece, and yes, butter would be nice. Thanks."

And so she tended to the tea and all, and before we knew it we were having a proper little meal there in the kitchen.

"I knew you'd missed dinner," said I, chewing lustily on my

quarter-loaf. "I came in a few minutes late and sat down at the table and no one would say anything, and then, right after dinner, they went up to Sir John's little room . . ."

"The one he calls his study?"

"That's right. But I was not invited. They seemed determined to keep all from me."

"Oh, they would, wouldn't they!"

"What do you mean?" I was a bit alarmed at what she had just said.

"Well, it was all about you, of course."

Now I was more than a bit alarmed. "You *must* explain yourself. And please begin by assuring me that you're not laying the blame on me for staying to listen in on Sir John's interrogation of Benjamin Franklin."

She sighed a deep sigh. "No, I don't claim that. The fault—if fault there be—was mine, and perhaps a bit Molly's as well."

As Clarissa told it, upon Tom Durham's arrival weeks past she had been encouraged by Molly to use him in order to make me jealous. She played at it rather halfheartedly, commenting to me upon Tom's handsome appearance, following him about "like a lovesick puppy," just to see what it might be like to play such a role, and to see if indeed it might have some effect upon me. Yet so far as she could tell, her ruse worked not at all. I was the same—somewhat distant, absorbed in my studies of the law and by the work done with Sir John—in short, just being myself.

But if she had only known how greatly I was affected by the game she played, she would in no wise have thought me indifferent. Just when I had at last put proper value to her and learned to treat my feelings for her in earnest, it seemed that she was to be taken from me.

"I was *so* disappointed when you refused to come along to Vauxhall this afternoon," Clarissa said to me, "that I fear that I became spiteful and foolish. I flirted quite shamelessly with Tom on the way there. And once we had had the sweet cakes and goodies that Molly had prepared, and she and Mr. Donnelly had settled down to spark, 'twas I and not Tom, who suggested we leave them and go for a walk. Again I flirted rather dangerously, implying, I fear, that I was offering more than I wished Tom, in all truth, to take. Yet I was not so brazen that I was prepared, when we were out of sight of the others, for Tom's impetuous response. He threw me down in a pile of fallen leaves and jumped atop me. It was all I could do to get out a couple of healthy screams. They were quite effective, though. Not only did they bring Molly and Mr. Donnelly a-running, they quite paralyzed Tom, so that, let me assure you, I am still intact."

With that she ended her tale and looked up at me hopefully, expecting a comment, forgiveness—or something. Instead, I offered her a lawyerly sort of question.

"Do you intend to tell this in full to Sir John and Lady F.?"

"Do you think me mad? No, you heard the raw and unedited version. I've discussed all this with Molly so that our stories would match precisely, and she told me just what I dared say, and what I did not."

"That's good," said I. "Follow her advice. Tom can take care of himself."

"That's just what Molly told me," said Clarissa, subduing a smile. "But really, you know, he's quite safe from my vengeance. I shall tell them, 'It's all a misunderstanding.'"

"And am I safe from your vengeance?"

"What do you mean?"

"Well, you must have thought me terribly unresponsive. I believe you used the word 'distant.'"

"Yes, yes, I did."

"Is that how I seem?"

"Most of the time—or some of the time, anyway."

"But I am not near as unresponsive as you think," I declared. "Nor did Molly's plan for you go amiss."

"Again I must ask what you mean."

"She encouraged you to believe that if you paid attention to Tom, I would immediately become jealous. Well, indeed I did become jealous."

"Jeremy!"

"Yes, of course. Do you think me a blockhead? I am no crude, unfeeling fellow, no matter that I may appear so to you."

"But no!" said she. "I would never think such of one as fine and intelligent as you. There was never any but you."

"I feared the worst, Clarissa. It seemed likely to me that Tom would leave London engaged to you."

As that she pulled a most fearsome face.

"Truly I did," said I, "and I was terribly sad at the thought. Until Tom Durham came along, I supposed we might be engaged. I wanted you for my own, and I wanted you most awfully, yet . . ."

"Yet what? What should stop us?"

"Well, for one thing, I have no money, nor do I have prospects of earning any. And, well, there are other practical considerations."

"Oh, I can imagine what they are easily enough, but listen, I'll tell you a secret. You must promise not to tell *anyone*."

"I promise."

"All right, Molly and Mr. Donnelly have an understanding."

"An understanding? Of what sort?"

"They're not formally engaged. They're more or less engaged to be engaged. But Molly assures me that they'll be married before the coming year is out."

"Well, I'm pleased to hear it," said I, "though not truly surprised."

"But don't you see? We could get married, too, perhaps have a double wedding."

"I'm afraid not. They're Catholic and we . . . we're not."

"Oh, what does that matter? I'll be seventeen, and you'll be nineteen, and that's old enough to be married any way we wish, isn't it?"

"No, it's not," said I quite emphatically, "and let me give you some good reasons why it is not. First of all, if we were to marry next year, I could not support you, for I would have no profession, no job, nothing."

"Well, I could work, too. I could take over from Molly, for she has promised to teach me to cook."

"And when you become pregnant?"

"Well . . . I'll . . . I'll . . ."

"No, we must wait till I have reached my majority and may pass the bar."

"But that seems so far in the future." She hesitated but a moment, then did she blurt forth: "You said we would simply wait till then, did you not?"

"I did."

"Then we have an understanding! But Jeremy, this is wonderful! We're engaged to be engaged."

She jumped to her feet and flew round the table. I had barely time to stand upon my own two feet before she had her arms about me, quite covering my face with kisses. She squeezed me and I, having the hang of it, kissed her back.

To say that we enjoyed ourselves does little to describe our feelings at that moment. Clarissa's bosom heaved with excitement, as all the while we kissed and fondled. I held her so tight I wondered that I might hurt her. And indeed I thought I might have done, when of a sudden, she threw back her head in what I took to be a swoon.

"Clarissa," I whispered in fright, "are you all right?"

"Oh, Jeremy," said she, "I'm so happy."

TEN

In which Mr. Burkett
makes known the true
purpose of his visit

Tom Durham left more or less in disgrace, accompanied to the Post
Coach House only by his mother. He had engaged a barrow man to
haul his sea chest to the coach house. 'Twas only by chance that I
saw them leave, and it happened so because at the hour of their
early departure I was just setting off upon my first errand of the
day. The barrow man was just loading the sea chest. He was a big-
ger, and I may say, stronger man than I, and he had difficulty with
it; I wondered who would have supposed that I could simply throw
it up on my shoulder and trudge off to the coach house. Tom would
have been better able than I.

I considered the situation, as mother and son gave their attention to the travail of the barrow man, and I decided that I must offer some sort of good-bye. And so I stepped over to Tom, touched
him lightly upon the arm, and offered my hand.

"Tom," said I, "I wish you all the best in the pursuit of your
career."

He looked down at my outstretched hand so long that I thought
he would refuse it—yet he did not. Reluctantly, he took it with his
own and gave it an indifferent shake.

"Thank-you," said he, and that was indeed all he said to me.

Lady Fielding smiled a bit too brightly. "Remember, Tom?" said
she, chiming in, "Sir John had given Jeremy an important task and
therefore he could not accompany us."

"Yes, Mother, I remember." And then, to the barrow man:
"Ready? Then let us be off."

He, without a look back, and she, giving me an uncharacteristically timid wave of the fingers, did set off in the proper direction, with the wheelbarrow following behind.

True enough, Sir John had given me an early task to perform. He had urged me to bring in Arthur Lee if ever I wished to have him interrogated. "You do wish that, don't you?" he had said to me. "I can recall when there was naught you wanted more. Or are you no longer so certain that it was Lee gave Franklin those pestiferous letters?"

I assured him that I was just as certain as I had ever been.

"Well, you had better go out and get him. And do it now, else I be called a liar by my wife. I've already made your excuses to her. I told her you would be unavailable to serve as Tom's porter."

And so I had left, and just outside the door to Number 4, I encountered the two, mother and son. There followed the brief scene that I have just described. I've no idea why Tom acted so boorishly toward me. Perhaps he now thought of me as no more than a deckhand.

I remember well that all the way to Tavistock Street I fretted over a problem that was truly none of my own. I was worrying over whether or not to reveal to Sir John what sort this fellow Burkett was truly. He seemed to me to be naught but a villain, for he had treated Bess cruelly and made a fearful threat to Mr. Perkins. Yet in the end, of course, I came to the only possible decision: If anyone were to report this to Sir John, it would have to be Constable Oliver Perkins himself.

Mr. Donnelly was certainly correct in supposing that I would know the building in which Mr. Lee dwelled. I had a fair picture of it in my mind when it was first mentioned—two stories above the ground, red brick with a flat roof—and I spied it easily from a goodly distance away.

It was early, just past seven, and still dark but for the gray half-light of dawn. Still, candles burned in a window or two or three; the residents seemed now to be rising to meet the day.

I went up the two steps, tried the door, and found it locked, as I expected. Then did I begin beating upon it with such energy that I expected to rouse all in the building. Yet only one came, and he a man of sixty years or more. He had rheumy eyes and a bad case of the sniffles.

"What will you, you young wild man?"

"Naught but a bit of help from you," said I to him. "I am come from the Bow Street Court at the direction of Sir John Fielding to talk with one of those who lives here in this building."

"What is his name?"

"Arthur Lee, and he lives upon the floor above."

"Ah, Mr. Lee, is it? He was one of our best tenants."

"'Was,' you say? Where is he gone?"

"Back to America, as I understands it. I don't know to what part, for I ain't well-acquaint with that side of the world."

"When was this?" I asked. "Surely not so long ago."

"Oh no, not long ago at all. Just last Thursday, it was—day before yesterday."

That, I mused, would make it the day before Dr. Franklin's public notice in the *Chronicle:* He had but a day to get out of London.

"He was in a great hurry, he was. He said he had a ship to catch. There was much he left behind, so it took a lot of cleaning up after him, but I can't complain."

"Why not?"

"Always paid on time and in full, and because of the way he left it, he gave a bit extra to me to get the place clean. I ain't no fool. I cleaned the place up, and kep' it for myself. You can look at it if you want to but like I told the other fella, there's nothing up there now, so it don't—"

"Wait," said I. "What did you say about another fella?"

"Oh, didn't I tell you about him? No, I guess I didn't. Believe it or not, just as you choose, but you're the second come by this morning asking after Mr. Lee. And it's pretty early in the day yet. I wonder how many will come looking for him before the day is through."

"When was this?" I asked, becoming more excited by the moment.

"Very early indeed. I was still asleep. It must've been half-past five, or anyways earlier than six, but he woke me with all his banging and hollering. 'Course he would."

"And what do you mean by that?"

"Well, he was so big, and not just tall, either. He had legs like tree stumps, fists as big as your head."

Only one man in London would answer such a description.

"Did he ask to see the rooms?"

"No, when he heard I'd cleaned it up, he wasn't interested. He just asked more of the same kind of questions you did—when did he go? Where was he headed?"

"And then?"

"Nothing at all. He just left is all, and I went back to bed."

"Could I see the rooms?"

At that, he took a step back and squinted as he looked me up and down. "Hmmm," said he. "You sure you're here from the Bow Street Court? What kind of work you do there? You look too young to be a Runner."

"I'm Sir John's clerk." Which was true enough, if only temporarily.

"Well, you look like you could handle that."

He threw wide the door and stepped aside, inviting me in.

"If you'll just wait, I'll get the keys," said he. He stepped out of sight for a moment and returned with a ring of big brass keys, each one near the size of a carrot. He led me up the stairs to the apartment just above his own. There he inserted one of the keys, which looked like all the rest, turned it in the keyhole, and swung open the door. He nodded me into the room. It was fairly large, but there was sufficient furniture inside to give it a somewhat cluttered appearance: there was a sofa with a long table before it, padded chairs, and so on. Actually, it looked to be quite a comfortable room, and I surprised myself by picturing Clarissa and me taking our ease there. This and the smaller bedroom would seem to be just the right size for us two.

My eyes fell upon a small writing desk which folded compactly into a single unit. It was, indeed, folded up at that moment. I walked to it and swung back the lid, which extended the writing space of the desk by a good foot or more.

"You interested in buying any of these pieces?" the householder asked. "They're all for sale, except that little desk you're lookin' at. Mr. Lee, he made me promise to ship that to him within the week."

"To what address?" I asked.

"Someplace in Boston. I've got it writ down in my place."

"Then it must be there that he's headed."

"Hmmm. Must be. But he did say something about Virginia. Is that near Boston?"

"No."

"Can't help you then."

The writing desk had a fair number of little drawers and compartments secluded in and around the writing space. I began systematically to open them and search through them, finding oddments of paper in some, and in others nothing at all.

"Say," said the householder, "I don't know as I ought to let you do that. I'm sending that on to Mr. Lee. Some of those bits of paper might be important to him."

"If they were, he wouldn't have left them."

"Well," said he, rubbing the stubble on one cheek, "I s'pose not."

"I'll just go through them, and see if there's anything of importance. Then you can have them all."

"Is Mr. Lee in some kind of trouble?"

"He may be."

"Is that truly so? Why, I'm surprised to hear it—always paid right on time, he did—except once when he'd been out of town, and he . . ." As the householder rambled on, beginning an anecdote which proved what a fine fellow Arthur Lee was, I shuffled through the bits of paper in my hand until I came upon one which interested me—the *only* one, as I recall. It bore the name of a ship—"the *New Covenant*—Wharf 17, Wapping," and then the date and time of departure. It was last Thursday, the day before Benjamin Franklin's announcement. I palmed it and handed over the rest.

Thus I made another trip to Wapping and sought out my acquaintance Ebenezer Tarkenton, wharfmaster, who confirmed what was written upon the slip of paper. I asked him if he had in his office the passenger list for the *New Covenant*, and so he took me there and sought it out.

"Who you looking for, lad?"

"Does the name Arthur Lee appear on the list?"

"Oh, it does indeed—right at the bottom, last passenger aboard. I remember him well."

"Oh? How is that, sir?"

"He was so eager to get aboard, he tried to bribe me to get a cabin. I told him there was plenty of cabins, for the very good reason that people don't like to travel across the ocean in the winter season. I wished him well and added his name to the list."

"And the ship sailed on time?"

"Just as you have it there."

I hastened then to return to Bow Street. Too much of the day had been taken up by Mr. Arthur Lee. That he had escaped was perhaps no great matter, though Sir John might well have wrung a confession from him. Of far greater interest, and ultimately of greater importance was the fact that George Burkett had preceded me in inquiring after him. How had he learned so much in so short a time? What more could he tell us? Pondering such questions, I returned, just in time to perform my duties as Mr. Marsden's substitute.

Two days passed. On the first of them we were paid a visit by Mr. William Slade, the new proprietor of Black Jack Bilbo's gaming club. As it happened, he came by in the afternoon not long after Sir John had held the day's court session. Nevertheless, Mr. Fuller, the jailer, was away, conveying two prisoners to the Fleet Gaol. Thus I was alone, at Mr. Marsden's desk, completing the last bit of paperwork on the day's cases for our files, when a knock came upon the door. Thinking it best, I fetched the cosh out of the desk drawer and tucked it into my pocket. There was no telling who might seek admission from the street here in Covent Garden. We had had experiences in the past, which I need not relate here, that would caution any gatekeeper to beware.

I walked to the door, and as I did, the knock sounded a second time. It was neither measured nor hurried, but rather commanding and direct. The man who knocked in just such a way was used to being admitted at once. Few doors were closed to him. "Who is there?" I asked.

"William Slade," came the answer. I knew the name. That was good enough for me.

I threw open the door and recognized the man before me most immediately. He, too, seemed to recognize me.

"We have met before, have we not?"

"So we have," said I, "on two occasions."

"Ah yes, and the last was upon the day when I took possession of my new house." He paused, hesitating there at the door, as if coming to a decision. Then did he continue: "I should like to call upon Sir John Fielding—that is, if he be available."

I invited him inside and asked him to wait whilst I announced him to Sir John. Walking briskly, I traveled down the long hall to Sir John's chambers and informed him of William Slade's request for an interview.

"The fellow who bought Black Jack's gaming club? He's here now? Well, bring him to me by all means."

Returning to the hall, I waved Mr. Slade forward, then went to meet him. Except for his clothing, which was beautifully tailored and richly decorated, he was in no wise an impressive figure. He was short and squat in shape, and the appearance of his face was marred by the wealth of pockmarks upon his cheeks. He would not, in any case, win favorable attention from any, were it not for his possessions and obvious wealth; even his somewhat sardonic manner could be counted against him.

"Everything then is in order?" he asked as we marched forward together.

"Of course," said I. "Why should it not be so?"

"No reason."

I sped ahead the last few steps and announced him at the door. Sir John was standing, his hand outstretched in a welcoming gesture. Mr. Slade came forward quickly and grasped his hand warmly, pumping it for all he was worth.

"I'm very happy to meet you at last, Sir John. You're famous far and wide."

"Truly? And where was it you did hear of me?"

"Perhaps in Jamaica, Trinidad—or was it the Ivory Coast? All three, no doubt."

"My fame spans continents—good God! What a thing to consider! But please do sit down, Mr. Slade, and tell me what I can do for you."

"I thought it well that we meet, since I am new to London. I have heard that you and Mr. Bilbo, whose gaming establishment I now own, were on very good terms. I sincerely hope that we may be, too."

"I sincerely hope so, too."

Somewhat nonplussed by Sir John's brief and ambiguous reply, Mr. Slade eased himself down upon the chair I had provided him. I retreated to a place near the open door, where I might keep one eye upon the long hall and the other on Mr. Slade.

"There was, however, a particular reason that I'm calling upon you," said he.

"And what is that, sir?"

"A business associate of mine is missing."

"Oh? And how long has he been—as you say—missing?"

"Not long, a little over a day and a night."

"Well, that's hardly—"

"I know, I know," said Mr. Slade, interrupting Sir John, "yet I am worried for his safety, for he often carried great sums of money with him late at night and was perhaps a bit *too* confident in his ability to protect himself."

"I see," said Sir John. "Well, that does change things a bit, I suppose."

"He was more than a business associate. He and I have worked for years together in various ways. Indeed, we were to meet at noon to discuss changes that might be made at the gaming establishment. He failed to appear, and that was when I first missed him."

"Did you send someone to his residence to make certain he had not simply overslept?"

"There was no need. As I said, he was more than a business associate. He shared that large house with me and one or two others whom I trust completely. I simply went to his room and saw that his bed had not been slept in. Thus I knew that he had never arrived at home."

"What is the man's name?"

"Isaac Kidd."

I can't say that I was surprised, reader. Nevertheless, to hear the Duke named as William Slade's missing associate left me indeed fearful that I had unintentionally taken part in a crime of some sort—abduction at best and murder at worst. And having spent some time with George Burkett, I naturally feared the worst.

"Isaac Kidd? Did you get that, Jeremy? Do make a note of that, won't you?"

Though I had no need to do so as an aid to memory, I did as Sir John asked and wrote the name down on a small pad of paper, which I kept always with me.

"Now, Mr. Slade," said Sir John, "we shall initiate a search, but what can you tell us to help?"

"What do you mean by that?"

"Information, sir—information to help us in our search. Has he a lady friend? Has he enemies? What places does he frequent? Any sort of names, facts, et cetera, that may be of some aid."

"Ah yes, I see," said Mr. Slade. "Well, there is a place which he frequents. Indeed he is there most every night. And that is the King's Pleasure in Bedford Street. As for lady friends, he has none, for most of his lady friends are men—if you get my meaning. And I can't give you names there, for I myself do not travel in such circles. As for enemies, yes, Mr. Kidd had a few, for he is a gambler, as I am myself. Those who lose blame the dealer, or him who backs the game. And so each night someone, or two, or three are added to the list of enemies. I fear I can add little to that. Perhaps those at the King's Pleasure can provide more."

Having said that, he rose from the chair and prepared to depart. Sir John then did also rise.

"We shall do what we can with what you have provided us with, Mr. Slade. Who knows? Perhaps we shall prove lucky. Jeremy, will you see our visitor to the door?"

They shook hands once again, and I led William Slade out of Sir John's chambers and down the long hall.

"Your Sir John is a remarkable man," said he. "His blindness seems to bother him little. But . . . can he truly get by as a proper magistrate outside his courtroom?"

"If you mean by that, can he take an active role in investigations, the answer is emphatically yes."

"Yet can he see the details which I should think are so important to every criminal inquiry?"

"Indeed he can, for I, sir, am his eyes." That may have sounded a bit impertinent, but I wanted him to understand that Sir John was at no disadvantage.

He took it as no impertinence. He threw back his head and laughed as one might when told a most delicious joke.

"Well, I meant no disrespect," said he as we parted at Bow Street.

"Nor did I."

He waved and went on his way.

I then hurried back to Sir John and revealed to him my fears that I had myself unwittingly collaborated in the disappearance, or worse, the death of Isaac Kidd. I told him nearly all—from my sally to Burkett that the entire burglary plot had been hatched in the King's Pleasure; to naming the principals in that plot—Skinner and Ferguson, Isaac Kidd, and Arthur Lee. Yet I did withhold all mention of Burkett's angry threat against Mr. Perkins. That, it seemed to me, was the constable's to tell.

"And you told me, did you not, that this man Burkett had already been by Arthur Lee's place of residence to inquire after him."

"That's right, sir, and he found that Lee had already left for America."

"We may assume then that he will go after Skinner and Ferguson."

"Or Dr. Franklin."

Sir John heaved a deep, despairing sign.

"I blame myself," said I. "If I had not been quite so free with names and locations, then Kidd might . . ." I did not finish the sentence, for I was loath to pronounce Isaac Kidd dead.

"Well, Jeremy, you should not feel guilt in this, for the Lord Chief Justice himself did instruct us to give Burkett whatever help he might need in finding those who had burglarized Lord Hillsborough's house and murdered his manservant. No indeed, Jeremy, you are not at fault—nor in all likelihood is Lord Mansfield. He himself was no doubt duped."

"Lord Hillsborough then?"

"I fear so," Sir John observed a somber silence. "What could have led Lord Hillsborough to hire such a man? What sort of thief-taker could Burkett be?"

"Not a thief-taker at all," said I. "He revealed to Mr. Perkins and me that he is the leading slave-chaser of Georgia."

"A slave-chaser? Oh, my God, that damned institution raises its head once again. Well, we deserve it. We send our trash off to the colonies, and what do they send us in return? The likes of Burkett and—what is his name?—William Slade."

"Slade?" I echoed. "How does he figure into this?"

"Didn't you catch what he said? That I was famous across oceans and continents? Specifically he had heard my name in Jamaica and Trinidad and the Ivory Coast. What sort of merchant visits such places?"

Of a sudden, was it quite plain to me. "Why, a slaver!" said I.

"Precisely. When a man comes to London, suddenly wealthy, yet very mysterious about the sources of that wealth, you can bet that he was engaged in some unsavory trade; and in my mind, at least, there is no trade more unsavory than the slave trade."

"Do you suppose that Isaac Kidd is alive or dead, sir?" I asked.

"Oh, dead—unquestionably so."

"Where do you think the body has been hidden?"

"Too bad it is winter. If 'twere summer we should begin smelling him in a day or two. They're harder to hide in the summer."

Sir John sent me off to the Globe and Anchor to invite Mr. Burkett to visit us and tell us how he is faring in the task given him by Lord Hillsborough. I was to ask him if he had information to share. In general, he wished me to entice Burkett to visit. "It might then be possible to interrogate him properly," said Sir John.

And so did I dutifully tramp off to the Globe and Anchor, where I was told by the major-domo behind the desk that Mr. George Burkett was no longer a guest at the hostelry.

"He *was* here, was he not?" I asked.

"Oh, indeed he was, yet he left us quite suddenly yesterday morning."

"Did he say where he was going?"

"Not a word of it."

Then did I return to Number 4 Bow Street and report this to Sir John. He seemed not in the least surprised.

"No, on the contrary," said he, "I should have been surprised if he had been there."

"If that is so, sir, then why did you send me?"

"Because, Jeremy, it was a necessary step—a precaution."

"I see what you mean, sir. I suppose it was."

"You might tell Mr. Perkins, when he comes in, of these developments. And perhaps on his travels tonight, he could stop off at that place, the King's . . . what is it?"

"Pleasure, sir."

"That's it. Perhaps he could stop there and question the innkeeper and anyone else who might know something about Isaac Kidd's disappearance—and so on—that sort of thing. That is probably all that can be done for now."

"Would you consider informing the Lord Chief Justice, perhaps by letter, of what Burkett has been up to?"

"No, nothing can yet be proven."

Early on the second day following the disappearance of Isaac Kidd, his body was found by a waterman; it was submerged but trapped upon a stanchion supporting the Manchester Stairs. The waterman, a young fellow from Kent (by the sound of his words), had delivered the corpus in a wagon and asked if we wanted it. I had come out to Bow Street at his invitation and saw that the open wagon had a canvas thrown over what was doubtless a dead body.

"We'll take him only if he died violently."

"Oh, he did that," said the waterman with an emphatic nod. He seemed awfully sure of it.

"I think it best for you to take it direct to Gabriel Donnelly. He's the medical examiner for Westminster. He's right over in Drury Lane—Number 12."

"Well, don't I get a reward or something?"

"Not that I've heard of. I think this is the first time anybody ever delivered a body to our door."

"Well, what about the wagon? Can't you at least pay me what it cost to rent the wagon?"

It seemed a reasonable request. "How much was it?"

"A shilling for the morning."

I paid him the shilling, and gave him thruppence for his trouble.

But before he left for Mr. Donnelly's, I asked to see the face of the corpus. He threw back the canvas about a foot to show me.

"The face is in pretty fair shape," said he. "I doubt he's been in the water a terribly long time. Queer thing is, he was wrapped like this when I found him."

Indeed, the face was recognizable. I saw that it was Isaac Kidd. His eyes were closed, his mouth open, yet somehow the expression upon his features conveyed a sense of shock and horror.

"He don't look like he died happy, does he?"

"No, truly he does not."

With that, we parted. He climbed up on the wagon box and urged the team into motion. I called after him, repeating Mr. Donnelly's address. He waved his understanding and continued on his way.

I ran back to Sir John's chambers and informed him of what had just happened. He was most amused, laughing long and hard as one might if tickled by a feather.

"He just pulled up in front of our door, did he?" Sir John asked, once he had regained control.

"Oh, indeed sir, he did."

"I'll wager the passersby stared queerly when you took a look at his face, did they not?"

"Oh, yes sir," said I. "But Sir John?"

"Yes, Jeremy?"

"It was truly Isaac Kidd there in the wagon. I did see his face. Would you mind, sir, if I went to Mr. Donnelly's surgery to find out just how Kidd died? I promise to be back in plenty of time to attend to my duties as clerk of the magistrate's court."

"Oh, go if you must, but I'll expect you back an hour before court time."

With that, I left him, and running once again, I burst through the door and out into Bow Street. I did not stop running, in fact, until I spied the wagon with its grisly cargo pulled up just at Number 12 Drury Lane.

Mr. Donnelly and the waterman were wresting the body from the back of the wagon. The surgeon was tugging away at the canvas-wrapped feet, and already the legs had cleared the tailgate. Would the young fellow be able to jump down in time from the wagon to save the body from tumbling to the cobblestones? I sped cross

Drury Lane to help and arrived just in time to grasp Isaac Kidd at the shoulders at just the right moment.

"*Saved!*" shouted Mr. Donnelly; and then, to my surprise, I heard a round of applause and a cheer or two.

Looking round me, I saw that a small crowd had gathered beyond the wagon and the team of horses, which had obscured them at first from my vision.

"Well done, Jeremy!"

"He hooked on this nail, he did," said the waterman. "Then when we got him loose . . ."

"As long as we've got him, let's take him on up to my surgery, shall we?"

Calling a good-bye to the young fellow, and to those of the crowd still hanging about, we struggled inside with the corpus. I kicked the street door shut behind me, and then we took on the challenge of the stairway to the first floor. In the end we met that challenge, though not without a good deal of effort and the usual cautionary cries as we worked our way through tight corners. As we passed through waiting room, I was gratified to see that it was empty; except in extreme emergencies, Mr. Donnelly did not usually take patients before ten. His examination room came next, and that—thank God—was the end of our journey. We threw our burden up upon the table and took a moment to catch our breath.

"Where was this one?" asked Mr. Donnelly whilst panting.

"In the river," said I.

"Waterlogged, watersoaked, et cetera. I suppose Sir John wants a complete report in ten minutes?"

"Nothing so demanding," said I. "We know a good deal about him already. If you can just tell us how long he's been dead, and the probable cause of death, that should suffice."

"Well," said the medico, "let's get this package unwrapped, shall we?"

In truth, it was necessary to unwrap the body in much the same way (as I later discovered) that a baby is separated from its bunting. Near as I could tell, the canvas had been wound round the corpus two and a half, or perhaps three times. Then it was strapped with rope, top and bottom, perhaps three times. It took a bit of trouble and the right sort of concentration, so that when Isaac Kidd was at last free of his shroud we did not at that moment notice the horror that was revealed.

'Twas Mr. Donnelly spied it first. "Good God," said he, "just look at that, won't you?"

"At what?" said I, for I did not, even then, quite understand the reason for his alarm.

"At this," said he, grabbing Kidd's arm near the shoulder and bringing it up for me to see. "Now look at the one on your side."

I did as he said, and so shocked was I that I actually found it necessary to take a step back, feeling a pressure upon my chest as if I had been given a push.

The point of all this is that each arm had been cut off—nay, chopped off—at the elbow. Where forearm and hand should have been, there was naught but . . . sinew, stanched blood, and ligament. It was quite the most ghastly sight I had put my eyes upon in all of my years with Sir John Fielding.

"There's your cause of death," said Mr. Donnelly, pointing at the mutilated arm. "That alone would have killed him, no doubt."

"Truly so?"

"Certainly. The shock to the body, the loss of blood. In the Navy, I saw men who were so affected by the loss of a limb that they simply keeled over and within minutes did die. Think of it. How would you feel if you knew that the leg lying on the deck was *your* leg?"

"I should be greatly affrighted," said I.

"Oh, indeed you would—at *least* that. Tell me, was this man tortured for information? I see no other lethal wounds on his body."

"Yes, well, I suppose he was tortured."

"Well, what we see there would be sufficient to wring answers from even the most stubborn." He paused, then asked: "But why were *both* arms hacked off?"

"I believe I know the answer to that, but I must discuss this with Sir John before . . ."

"I understand,"

"Yet tell me, when would you place the time of death?"

"Oh, a day and a half to two days ago, I suppose. The skin, the face are still in good shape. If he had been in the water much longer, there would have been a general breakdown, a kind of melting of the flesh. Do you understand?"

"Oh yes, I understand. But now I must hasten to inform Sir John of all this."

He held up a hand. "Ah," said he, "wait, Jeremy. I must have your help in carrying this poor, armless creature into the backroom. What do you suppose my patients would think if they found this fellow on the table when they come in to tell me of their fainting spells?"

I told Sir John quite directly of what Mr. Donnelly and I had discovered upon unwrapping the body of Isaac Kidd. Even he, who seemed to take the most gruesome tales with equanimity, registered mild shock at this one. Yet when told of the angry threat directed by Burkett at Mr. Perkins, he seemed most deeply disturbed.

"You should have told me of this before," said he to me.

"Well, it was Mr. Perkins's matter—or so I told myself—and so I felt it was not up to me to tell you. I believe he would have resented it."

"No doubt he would have, but what's a little resentment if his life is in the balance?"

"Do you feel that it is?"

"I'm not sure, just as you were not when you failed to notify me," said Sir John. "But I mean to be on the safe side and protect him as well as I can. Just how I shall accomplish that is the question that I must now consider. But it is time for you to make preparations for my court session. Mr. Fuller has a number of prisoners— five, I think. Interview them. Get what you can from them for me. In the meantime, I shall consider what shall be done regarding Mr. Perkins. Oh, and it may be that a letter to the Lord Chief Justice is in order to let him know what sort of villain Burkett is, or perhaps something more than a letter, eh?"

And so it was, reader. The session of his court was handled without difficulty or complication. Though there were five prisoners, each was charged with a misdemeanor—and only that. There was a dispute to be settled between two greengrocers of Covent Garden, yet it was a dispute between two reasonable men, and it was settled by Sir John with a reasonable compromise. All left the courtroom fairly happy: Quite an ideal day in court it was, according to Sir John.

As for the letter, he dictated that to me as per usual. In it, he made plain his dismay that one hired by Lord Hillsborough should turn out to be naught but a hired killer. Care was taken, I noted, not to blame the Lord Chief Justice directly.

"We may need his help before this is done," said Sir John.

He also surprised me by declaring that he would accompany me to the home of Lord Mansfield.

"Do you feel the need for a bit of exercise?"

"I always feel the need. It is finding the will to act upon it where I fall down."

It is true that he had fallen down a bit, neglecting his usual habit of touring Covent Garden whenever he pleased. He now restricted himself to a morning walk of not much more than a mile. The truth was, as he confided to me once, that he was troubled by arthritis in his left hip, and he now leaned heavily upon the walking stick which he had heretofore used as little more than decoration. Nevertheless, once we were out and on the street, he seemed as quick as ever upon his feet. Though his hand rested upon my arm in such a way that I seemed to be helping him along, the truth was, I had to press myself and keep a fast pace in order to match his own.

Thus it seemed to take little time to reach Lord Mansfield's house in Bloomsbury Square. Along the way, he had explained that his reason for accompanying me was that he hoped to present himself, uninvited, and ask for an audience with Lord Mansfield. If the Lord Chief Justice were absent, or if he were conferring with another, or could not otherwise be disturbed, then we would leave the letter and return posthaste to Number 4 Bow Street. And so, inevitably, we came face-to-face with Lord Mansfield's butler, the keeper of the gate.

"Yes, what will you—oh, it is you, Sir John. How may I help you?" He was never so polite to me; and there was even a touch of unaccustomed warmth in his voice.

"Well," said Sir John, "something has come up, you see, and I wish to inform the Lord Chief Justice of it, and perhaps discuss it,

if need be. Is he in? Can he see me? Offer my apologies for disturbing him."

"Certainly. In the meantime, won't you and your assistant step
inside? Sit down on the bench, if you like."

Having said that, he threw the door wide, and we took our
places inside.

The butler then closed the door behind us, and, promising to be
no more than a minute, he set off to inform Lord Mansfield of our
unexpected visit. Neither of us showed any wish to sit down.

"Jeremy, I cannot suppose why you so frequently clash with
that butler of Lord Mansfield's. It's a thankless job at best, and he
seems to do it as well as any."

"Perhaps so, sir, but you should at least consider the possibility
that he shows one face to you and quite a different one to me."

"Oh, pish! Utter nonsense, say I. You perceive villainous intentions in all and sundry—as in this matter of the stolen letters."

"Not so, sir. I did in the beginning give some benefit of doubt to
Dr. Franklin—and to some extent, I still do. 'Twas Arthur Lee
whom I now see as the moving force in the theft of the letters—and
his flight to America proves it."

"And Benjamin Franklin his dupe? Come now, Jeremy, it
seems to me that you are shifting your position to accommodate the
latest developments. How can you do that? After all, his reason for
owning up he gives as his desire to prevent a second duel from being fought and more blood from being shed. How nice! Franklin,
the peacemaker. Yet will he confess any part in the actual burglary?
No indeed! Franklin, the pure in heart. Did he even see the letters
before I first interrogated him? Ah no, it was not till the day afterward that he was approached by one *he will not name* and was given
the letters in question. Is that not convenient? Shall we then call
him Franklin, the . . . what? Franklin, the fortunate, say I."

I wavered. There was a good deal of truth in what Sir John
said. Nevertheless—

"Do you two always argue in this manner?"

It was none other than Lord Mansfield, who looked neither
amused, nor disapproving, but rather puzzled. My back had been
turned to him as he approached, and I heard nothing. Sir John,

who usually hears all, had perhaps failed to hear on this occasion; or perhaps indeed he had heard but wished to have his say in spite of all.

"We often do, Lord Mansfield," said he. "I consider such arguments to be an important part of Jeremy's legal education."

"Ah yes, I seem to remember now: He is reading law with you, is he not?"

"Just as I read with my brother."

"Interesting. Well, come along, both of you." With that, Lord Mansfield gave me a critical look, as if judging me somehow. "I've sent the butler off to make some coffee—enough for all."

He led us down the hall to the library, a room of Lord Mansfield's in which I had been but once before. There was a book—one of hundreds in the room—out and open at Lord Mansfield's place at a long table He gestured to the chairs on either side of his own. I guided Sir John to the one at the right of the Lord Chief Justice, and I took the one just beyond.

"You have something to report, Sir John?"

"Yes," said the magistrate, "we do. But first may I ask *you* a question?"

"Of course. Proceed."

"How well do you know this fellow, George Burkett?"

"Burkett? Burkett? The name is familiar, but at the moment I cannot place him."

Sir John turned to me. "Are you sure it was Lord Mansfield's signature at the bottom of that letter of introduction?"

I was about to assure him that indeed I was certain of it, when Lord Mansfield cried out, "Oh, *that* fellow. Burkett was his name? Yes, yes of course it was. Now I have him in mind. What do you wish to hear of him?"

"How well do you know him?"

"Why, not at all. Lord Hillsborough brought him round to me and said that he wanted this rather large fellow with him to have a letter of introduction to you, Sir John. He wished him to have your help and the benefit of what you have thus far discovered in this matter of the Hutchinson letters. And so I dashed off a letter to that effect and gave it to them."

"You knew nothing of his background?"

"Well, I knew he was a colonial, I suppose. Thus much you could be told from his speech. But what more is there to know? I assume he was some sort of thief-taker."

"He was a slave-chaser," said Sir John.

"Ah well, not a very savory occupation, to be sure, but slavery is still a legal institution. And if slaves run from their masters, then they must be chased. Don't you agree?"

"Whether I do or I do not matters little. What Burkett has done is use the same despicable methods here in England that have become commonplace in America."

"Sir John, what has he done?"

"Tell him, Jeremy."

And tell him I did. I made what I judged to be an unusually strong presentation, one definitely prosecutorial in tone and worthy of comparison to any I had heard from the lips of the Lord Chief Justice himself. This time I did not omit the hostile incident which occurred between Burkett and Constable Perkins and had such dreadful consequences. On the contrary, I dramatized it a bit and pronounced Burkett's threat in a deep tone which mimicked Burkett's own. And, finally, when I described the condition of Isaac Kidd's body when Mr. Donnelly and I unwrapped it in his surgery, I did not hesitate to supply colorful details — sinew, bits of ligament and protruding bone, all of that.

Through it all Lord Mansfield gave me his full attention. His eyes widened at appropriate places along the way, and as I finished, he could not hold back a shudder. Then did he fall silent.

"*Both* his arms?" said he at last.

"Both arms indeed," said I, "which was surely meant as a message to Mr. Perkins."

"Good God," said Lord Mansfield, his voice cracking slightly. Then, recovering, he looked from me to Sir John and cleared his throat that he might address the matter at hand with greater authority. "Still, you know, bad as it sounds, what I have heard just now would not convict him. There are no witnesses and no material evidence."

"Come now," said Sir John, "I have heard you send men off to the gallows with far less against them."

"I'll not respond to that," said the Lord Chief Justice, "for it is not worthy of you."

"I withdraw it in any case. But you will admit, surely, that this monster, Burkett, must be stopped."

"Certainly I do."

"And that Lord Hillsborough is responsible and must call off this . . . this . . ."

"That we cannot say with certainty, for we know not what Lord Hillsborough's instructions were to this fellow, Burkett. I shall speak to him myself, for what he has done reflects upon me far worse than upon you."

Sir John jumped abruptly to his feet. "I can only ask that you do so quickly, for I should like to save Constable Perkins's remaining arm. Come along, Jeremy."

I had already risen to my feet and extended my own arm that he might grasp it. Thus we left the room. Lord Mansfield stared after us, yet he made no move, and uttered no cry, to halt us.

Moving swiftly as we were, we did nearly collide with the butler, who appeared from the direction of the kitchen. Yet I guided the magistrate round him with a certain skill, and we moved on.

"I have your coffee here, Sir John," said he—and indeed he carried a tray which supported an entire coffee service. It gave off a delicious odor. I should have dearly liked to carry a cup with me to Bow Street.

"We'll not be needing it," he replied.

"If you wait a moment, I'll see you out."

"We'll see ourselves out," I called out to the butler.

And so we did.

As we entered Number 4 Bow Street, opening the door to the backstage area, we passed two men sitting upon the bench. One of them rose, but Sir John was not stopping. He moved on, no longer in the least dependent upon me, as Mr. Fuller came forth to discuss a matter.

"Sir John," said he, "there's a man to see you. Some sort of lawyer, as I understand it."

"Where is he? In my chambers?"

"No sir, he's right behind you now."

Sir John whirled about to face the man who had sought him out.

"Good day to you, sir," said he. "What is it you wish?"

"To talk with you upon a private matter, sir."

I studied the fellow. He was of medium height and size, and in no wise remarkable. Of his face there was naught to say, except that his brown eyes (almost black) were of an unusual intensity. He seemed to stare at Sir John.

"Well, you may do so," said Sir John, "but you must admit my assistant, Jeremy Proctor, into your confidence, for I have no secrets from him."

"That is your sole condition?"

"It is, yes."

"Then I accept it."

Sir John nodded and pointed with his stick down the hall.

"This way," said he.

Once we were seated and settled in Sir John's chambers, the visitor leaned forward and without preamble said, "I am Jonas Hastings. I am a qualified solicitor, acting on behalf of my client, Mr. Thomas Skinner, whom I believe you seek."

"We have sought him, you are correct, Mr. Hastings. We also seek his partner, Mr. Edward Ferguson. Do you have dealings with him, as well?"

"Only through Mr. Skinner."

His reply struck me as rather ambiguous.

"What brings you here, sir?"

"Mr. Skinner would like to surrender to you."

"Well," said Sir John, "this is indeed a surprise. There is not yet a warrant out for his arrest, though he is suspicioned for the murder of Albert Calder, a footman in the household of Lord Hillsborough."

"There are conditions, however."

"I am not surprised to hear it."

"First of all, Mr. Skinner would like it understood that while he admits to killing Albert Calder, death was unintended. In effect, he is willing to plead guilty to manslaughter."

Sir John did not respond immediately. Clearly, he was giving the question some consideration. "Let us say, I am willing to accept the homicide as unintentional if he is able to convince me."

It was Jonas Hastings's turn to sit silent and consider. "I shall present that to him," said he at last. "There is another condition, however, though it is related to the first. It is that no matter the charge at Old Bailey, you will recommend transportation, rather than death by hanging."

"If he convinces me, and I send him on to the Central Criminal Court with a charge of manslaughter, he would naturally receive a sentence of transportation and penal servitude. Even if found guilty of murder, he might receive such a sentence. I sometimes recommend such, and until very recently my recommendations were always followed."

"And what happened then?"

"My recommendation on sentencing was ignored."

"How many times, over the years, were your recommendations followed?"

"Oh, perhaps a hundred."

"I shall take that to him, too."

Mr. Hastings rose, thanked Sir John, and turned to go.

"One more thing," said Sir John just then. "It will count greatly in his favor if he surrenders."

"That is understood," said Mr. Hastings.

And so saying, he left. As soon as he was out of the room, I posed the question of what more might be learned from Tommy Skinner once he had surrendered. That is to say, I started to pose such a question; but Sir John cut me off in midsentence with a finger to his lips and a shake of his head. Thereafter we sat in silence for a long space of time. I must have become notably restless, for at last Sir John spoke.

"It should not be long," he whispered. "Be patient."

Shortly afterward, we heard footsteps in the hall again. One could tell in an instant that there were two men, for besides Hastings's light, quick step, there was another, slower and heavier, which simply had to be Tommy Skinner.

The footsteps stopped just outside the door. Jonas Hastings stepped into the room. "May I present my client, Mr. Thomas Skinner," said he in a peculiarly dramatic manner.

When Skinner followed him in, he turned out to be near as big as George Burkett himself. He was the man who had shared the bench with Mr. Hastings.

"Tommy and I have already met, is that not so, Tommy?"

"I never thought you'd remember, no, I never."

"Let me see, it must be a good five years ago that you appeared before me for . . . what was it?"

"Drunkenness, I fear." He bowed his big head in shame.

"Ah, so it was, so it was. You were but a lad then, your great size notwithstanding. I remember fining you a half crown and urging you to use your strength in gainful employment."

"Yes sir, you was generous to me then, so I thought I'd try you once more."

"There's a bit of a gamble involved here, you know."

"I'll take my chances."

"Jeremy," said Sir John, turning in my direction. "Bring this Bible to Mr. Skinner, that he may take an oath upon it." Saying thus, he pushed the Bible across the desk toward me.

I took it and brought it over to Skinner. He placed his right hand upon it, and his left he held over his heart. Then did he swear, as God was his witness, that what he was about to tell was "the absolute and honest truth." And he added his wish to burn in hell if it wasn't. I took the Bible then and returned it to Sir John's desk. Skinner remained standing throughout his recitation, and his voice remained steady and calm.

The tale he told was essentially the one Sir John had put together from visits to the crime scene, my talks with witnesses, et cetera. He confirmed that Isaac Kidd had served as a kind of broker for the burglary, hiring Skinner and Ned Ferguson to do the burglary for a very high price indeed. He also arranged for them to be given a diagram of the ground floor of Lord Hillsborough's residence, which one of the footmen had drawn, showing the probable location of the letters they were to take. They were also warned that they must make their entry at a specific time, for the footmen were guarding the place against housebreakers, and Skinner and Ferguson were to wait to go in when the inside man was making his rounds. Now, to prevent him from getting blamed for the burglary, it had been arranged that the footman would lay down upon the floor, and Skinner would give him a tap with his cosh—not enough to do permanent damage, just enough to put him under and bloody his head.

"And the truth of it is," said he to Sir John, "I just hit him too hard. I popped him on the back of his head, and the blood just ran. He tried to lift himself up a bit, and then he fell back to the floor and stopped breathing."

Tears coursed down his cheeks. "I never killed nobody before, and I hope never to do it again. 'Scuse me now whilst I blow my nose." That he did, most thunderously loud.

I, for one, was convinced and hoped that Sir John was, as well. There was something childish about the big fellow, was there not? How could such an overgrown child be punished in the same way that a practiced killer might be—one such as, say, George Burkett?

"I have some questions for you," said Sir John, "though not many."

"Well and good. I'll do my best to answer them."

"What happened afterward?"

"Not much of anything. Ned had some trouble finding the letters we were supposed to take, but he located them at last. He said they had something to do with the North American colonies. I guess we left the place in kind of a mess."

"You did indeed. But tell me, is that all you remember of the aftermath?"

"Well, we were a day or two late getting our money, and we didn't like that, but we got paid in full eventually."

"Do you have the weapon with you, the cosh with which you dispatched Albert Calder?"

"Was that the fella's name? Yes, it's right here in my pocket."

"Surrender it to Mr. Proctor, please—that, and any other weapons you might have on your person."

He did as he was told, stepping over to me and handing over the leather-covered club. It weighed heavy in my hand. Indeed, it could have cracked Calder's skull, or mine, or any other. I dropped it in my pocket.

"Tell me, Tommy, what led you to surrender and confess your crime?"

"Well, sir, you treated me right before and gave me good advice I wish to God I'd taken. I committed a terrible sin, but to be honest with you, I don't want to get my arms chopped off for it."

"Ah, you've heard about that, have you?"

"I have," said Skinner, "and he's been following me all round London, asking after me."

"And what about your partner, Ned Ferguson?"

"For his own good, I think you better arrest him, sir. He bought himself a little farm just north of Robertsbridge in Sussex with his cut of the wack. I told you we got paid right rum for the job."

ELEVEN

*In which Burkett
strikes again as more
history is made*

The word was out in Bedford Street that the body of Isaac Kidd had
been horribly mangled. Whether before or after death seemed to
matter little to those who heard the story and passed it on. What
caught the fancy of the mob was the manner of mutilation. Jokes
were made about the missing forearms; bets were placed on where
they might turn up. There were those who insisted that such bizarre
brutality was doubtless the work of the Devil; and there were others who speculated that, considering Kidd's known background in
the slave trade, he was no doubt the victim of some revenge plot of
the blacks in London.

There were but a few of us who knew the truth and two of that
small number were riding in the post coach next morning, completing the journey to Robertsbridge. I was one, as was Mr. Perkins.
Because the town (hardly more than a village) had few visitors, we
had the coach to ourselves by the time we made the last leg of the
journey. That gave us an opportunity to talk freely of the matter
which concerned us both so deeply. I sought from him an answer to
a question that plagued me.

"What I, for one, cannot understand is how the grisly condition
of Isaac Kidd's body became general knowledge so quickly," said I.
"I know that I told nothing to anyone but Sir John. Mr. Donnelly
would not have divulged such matter. It must have been the waterman who discovered the body who spread the news."

"No, it was known before ever he found it," said the constable.

"But how?"

"Burkett, just as bold as brass, let it be known on the street that he had a body to be rid of, and that he'd pay well to them who attended to it."

"And he actually found someone to take care of it?"

"As a matter of fact, he found two someones. 'Twas the Colter brothers. It's said they'll do anything for money."

"It seems they would, and they did," said I.

"The Colter brothers wrapped the Duke in canvas, bound him at both ends, and tossed him in the Thames. Now, in preparing the body for burial they couldn't help but notice that the fellow's arms were a mite shorter than before, and his hands, which was so clever with the cards, were nowhere to be seen. They remarked upon this to their chums and fellow drinkers in Bedford Street, and you know how it is there, Jeremy—word just traveled like wildfire."

"Did you arrest them? Did they confess?"

"You mean the Colters? Oh, I talked to them right stern about it, and they made out to be plain shocked that such horrible stories could be told of them. The two shared the same doxy over in Southwark, and she swore she entertained the both of them a whole night and the better part of a day before the body was pulled from the river. So all we've got against them is hearsay, and Sir John says that ain't good enough."

"And you think, don't you, that this was done as a warning to you?"

"Oh I do, no question. But something more than a warning, Jeremy—more like a . . . well, a promise."

"No doubt it was also a most effective means of torturing information out of Isaac Kidd," said I, having given some thought to the matter.

"Just as you say," said he in agreement. "Kidd refuses to tell him what he wants to know, so Burkett just up and whacks off the Duke's arm. Then says Burkett: 'If you want to keep the other one, you better answer up.' So he gets all he wants from him, and he just chops off the other arm for cursedness."

"You think that's how it happened?"

"Well, your ideas are worth as much as mine on that partic'lar matter."

We fell silent. There was probably much to discuss regarding what lay ahead, yet we had both seemed to lose the taste for it. Each of us turned to the window on his side of the coach and idly studied the countryside as we watched it reel by. Sussex was farm country and, to my eye, little different from Kent. Fields and trees that would bloom green in spring were now dun brown in this mild early winter. Yet perhaps winter had not been near so mild here as in London for here and there I saw patches of snow, while in London there had been none, at least so far as I had seen.

We seemed to be entering the town of Robertsbridge, for the coach had slowed. Soon I saw houses crammed close on either side of the road, and then a shop or two, and down a side street I spied a church with some sort of activity outside it. Was it—yes, it had to be—a funeral? I slapped Constable Perkins upon the shoulder and pointed

"Look, look," said I excitedly, "the church! A funeral!"

He strained forward to look out of the window on my side of the coach. Perhaps he caught a glimpse of the church and the little crowd before it—but no more than that, for we were past it in a moment or two. He looked at me oddly.

"A church," said he, "a funeral? What's there to gawk at? See what . . . oh . . . oh yes, I do see." The light of understanding had kindled in his eyes. "You think that Ned Ferguson might . . . ?"

"I think we must find out," said I.

As soon as the coach pulled to a stop before the Robertsbridge Inn we jumped out, grabbed our bags, and ran back to find the side street wherein the church did stand. There was the undertaker's coach in front of the church. Still, the mourners I had seen before the church were now inside. The service had begun. I could hear the organ and voices raised in a hymn.

As luck would have it, the driver of the funeral coach was there still, preparing to turn the coach and team round, now that their part in the ceremony was ended. We approached in a friendly manner, not wishing to cause offense.

"Beg pardon, sir," said I most respectfully, "but could you tell us the name of the party whose funeral just now is taking place?"

"I could," said he. He was a tight-lipped, taciturn sort of man of about forty years of age. But he looked to be the sort who would not be above playing a trick or two on a recent arrival in town.

"Uh, would you then tell us the name?"

"I would." And that, of course, was said with a smirk.

"Well sir," said I, my patience at last wearing thin, "what *is* the name?"

"Ferguson," said he. "Edward Ferguson."

Unbeknownst to me, whilst I conducted this maddening conversation, a man emerged from the church, listening intently. According to Mr. Perkins, who observed the man descending the church steps, "he looked sharp at us and quite suspicious." Yet I remained unaware of his presence until I felt his hand upon my shoulder and heard his question to me.

"Why do you ask after Edward Ferguson?"

I turned round to find an elderly fellow whose eyes were magnified somewhat by a pair of thick spectacles, which were perched low upon the bridge of his nose. Viewed thusly, he seemed quite fierce. Nevertheless, I was determined not to be intimidated.

"And why do you wish to know?"

"Because, young sir," said he, sending his jowls and wattles aquiver, "I am the magistrate of Robertsbridge and its environs up to Tunbridge Wells. As such, it is my place to ask such questions, and it is your place to answer them."

"If you are the magistrate, then your name must be Peter Hollaby. Is that correct, sir?"

He was taken somewhat aback. "Why yes, yes it is."

"Then I have a letter for you."

I reached into my voluminous coat pocket and produced the letter Sir John had dictated to me the night before. Then did I hand it to him.

"For me?"

He said it timidly, as if he did not often receive mail of the official sort, and Sir John's seal upon it made it plain that this letter was indeed *very* official. He pushed his spectacles higher up on his nose and set about to read the communication.

Since I had taken it down, I knew its contents quite well. It was remarkably like the letter of introduction from the Lord Chief Jus-

tice, which began our troubles with George Burkett. It presented
Constable Perkins and me to Mr. Hollaby, and asked that we be
given aid and information to assist them in the capture of Edward
Ferguson and George Burkett. It also asked his permission that we
two be given the right to carry arms within his jurisdiction, and, if
necessary, to discharge them. And so, having served as Sir John's
amanuensis, and knowing what had been said, I anticipated each
blink and widening of the eyes by Mr. Hollaby, assured that the letter was having the desired effect. I believe he read it through twice.

He looked up at last. "Do you have arrest warrants?"

I nodded and pulled them from the same pocket from which I
had produced the letter. He took them and examined each one, then
returned them to me, appearing somewhat bewildered.

"Ned Ferguson was wanted for burglary?"

"That's right," said I. "His partner gave witness against him."

"And this George Burkett?"

"A murderer twice o'er," said I, "once in London and now, I assume, again here in Robertsbridge."

"You two are armed?"

His eyes went first to Mr. Perkins, who opened his coat to display two pistols, worn each on his right side, for it was the side of
his good arm. Then did he look at me, and I showed him the brace
of pistols, belted one on each hip.

"Since this is all being done proper, I'll make out a paper that
says you've got my permission to wear those things and shoot them
off if need be."

I had by this time noted that the driver of the undertaker's
coach had taken such a keen interest in our discussion that he had
interposed himself between Constable Perkins and Mr. Hollaby, so
that now we seemed to be a group of four, rather than three. I remember well, from my childhood, the curiosity of townsmen.
Where little happens, all must be known about that little.

Catching Mr. Hollaby's attention, I pointed to the intruder in
our group.

He nodded his agreement. "We must talk about this some
more," said he. "I've an idea. Why don't we go to the inn and have
us an ale? You two must be dry from all that traveling. I've got
questions for you, and I'm sure you'll want to hear a few things that

I have to tell." Then said he to the driver: "Henry, you can tell the widow that I'm sorry I couldn't stay for the rest of the funeral, but I got called away by something important. I'm sure you'll agree that *this* is important, won't you?"

"Oh, I certainly do, Mr. Hollaby. All the way from London, Bow Street Runners and all. I'm sure she'll want to hear all about that. It'll help ease her pain, I'm sure."

The story told by the magistrate of Robertsbridge was of the sort I might well have expected to hear. Still, the magistrate was correct in his surmise that we might welcome a pint of ale or two after our journey. And upon learning that it would be near two hours before the next coach for London came through, we were well satisfied to spend the time sipping ale, listening to Peter Hollaby's tale and telling our own.

The magistrate was much embarrassed to reveal that he had actually aided Burkett in finding Ferguson. The big man had stopped by Hollaby's office in the evening three days past and asked his way to Ferguson's farm. He presented himself as a friend from London come down to Robertsbridge at Ferguson's invitation.

"He said to me, 'I know he's just outside of town, but I don't know which road to take.' I pointed out the right one to him, and that just about wrote the end to Ned Ferguson."

I asked how long the magistrate had known Ned Ferguson, and when it was he had first made his appearance in the town, and I was surprised to learn that it was a good ten months past.

He courted a local girl—called her his "lass," as a Scotsman would, 'cause that's what he was—and was well liked in Robertsbridge. The parents of the girl thought him a good match for their daughter and offered a decent dowry. Though he was a bit tight-lipped about his business (he claimed to be a coffee merchant), which took him off to London with fair frequency, banns were posted in the church, and about a month and a half past Edward Ferguson and his lass were wed.

The magistrate of Robertsbridge was a bit vague about what had happened after that. It was known about town that the young bride was eager to go with her groom on his next trip to London, but following a visit from one of Ferguson's business associates

(Isaac Kidd, according to the description given by Peter Hollaby), he made no more trips to the city and stayed rather close to the house. A change had come over him, and she let it be known to her parents that Ned was acting in a rather disturbing manner.

Yet she was not near so disturbed then as she was early in the morn, two days past, when, finding her husband absent from their bed, she went looking for him about their place and found his body in the barn.

"What was the condition of the body?" asked Mr. Perkins, who had been unusually quiet all through the magistrate's recitation.

"Well you might ask," said Hollaby, nodding plainly at the constable's empty sleeve. "But may I inquire of you, sir, did you have an encounter of your own with this fiendish fellow?"

"Not the kind of encounter you mean," said Mr. Perkins. "Yet we have met, and ever after he has been trying to frighten me away by chopping off the arms of his victims."

"But you, I take it, are not frightened?"

"Oh, I'm frightened, right enough, yet I try not to let it bother me."

"And have you been successful in that?"

"In all truth, I cannot say that I have been."

"Well, I hope I didn't cause you any pain making inquiries where it ain't my business to do so, but I have to tell you, sir, that ever since I was summoned to that barn I have been frightened. I've had bad dreams, I have. I wake up nights in a proper sweat. The constable who went out there with me quit the next day. And the young widow—she's done naught but weep and carry on ever since that dreadful morning, and I can't say that I blame her any. The place was all bloody, blood on the straw, blood on the walls, and the milk cow was goin' crazy."

"What was judged to be the cause of death?" I asked.

"Well, besides having both arms chopped off at the elbows as you two have certainly guessed by now, he had a gash in his throat of a kind so deep it damned near took his head off."

"Yet he kept quiet through it all?" I asked.

"He was gagged, and Mrs. Ferguson was a sound sleeper. But that fellow—Burkett, was it?—he must have spent an hour or more with him, torturing him, trying to get him to tell something. There must be a lot of money involved in this."

"No," said Constable Perkins, "I think Burkett does it because he likes it. No other reason." Then did he ask if there might be any possibility that Burkett were still in the area of Robertsbridge.

"I'm certain that there's no chance of that. He was on horseback, and he left in the direction of London at a gallop. You could tell by the track he left." At that point, he paused. Then he came back to us with a demand. "Now," said he, "you've heard my story. You must tell me now what this was all about. And don't say that this man Burkett was a rival coffee trader. We may not have much experience of this kind of thing here in Robertsbridge, but we're all pretty much agreed that this wasn't about coffee. You say Ned Ferguson was a burglar . . . ?"

I had a difficult time offering him information enough to satisfy him, yet not so much that he would know the part played in it all by Lord Hillsborough and Lord Mansfield. In fact, I had decided that Mr. Hollaby should know as little as possible about the burglary and nothing at all about Benjamin Franklin, Tommy Skinner, and Arthur Lee. The result was a rather disconnected narrative, one hardly deserving at all to be called a narrative. The magistrate asked many questions, a few of which I could not answer. He looked skeptically at me a number of times and must have thought me a terrible dunce. Nevertheless, I managed to get through my so-called recital of the facts as Sir John would have preferred: divulging as little information as possible.

By contrast, however, Mr. Hollaby seemed to get on wonderfully well with Mr. Perkins. As time grew shorter before the departure of our London-bound coach, he seemed to direct more of his comments and questions to him.

Finally, as we two waited to board the coach, bags in hand, the magistrate turned to Mr. Perkins and asked if he were from Sussex.

"No," the constable replied, "but you're close. Just the next county over—in Kent."

"I thought so. You've got a certain way of speaking common to people down here."

"I grew up on a farm just outside Deal."

"You see? I wasn't far off at all." He hesitated, then came out with what I judged to be the reason for his remarks. "If ever you get tired of London and want to come back south, you just let me know. I need a good constable, always do."

Mr. Perkins chuckled at that. "You mean you're hiring one-armed fellas like me? You must be desperate."

"No, I reckon that if you're good enough for Sir John Fielding, you're good enough for me—one-armed, one-legged, or whatever."

Again, Mr. Perkins laughed in embarrassment.

"Tell you what I'll do," said the magistrate, persisting. "Whatever he's paying you in London, Mr. Perkins, I'll match—and you'll find your money will go a lot farther in Robertsbridge than it will in London."

"Well, I—"

"No, don't say a word. Just think about it, and look round you as you leave town. No place nicer than Robertsbridge."

Having had his say, Peter Hollaby bade us farewell and sent us on our way. All the way to Tunbridge Wells, I teased Constable Perkins intermittently regarding the job offer. He simply laughed and allowed me to have my fun, yet I could tell that he took the matter more seriously than I. Why should he not? He had an affinity for the south of England, for it was from here that he had come. Oddly, he had received the offer of a job in Deal but a few months past in much the same way as he had here. And again, why should he not? He was one of the most able—in my opinion, the best—of all the Bow Street Runners, worth more than any man with two arms, it seemed to me.

Passengers boarded the coach at Tunbridge Wells, and I ended my mischief. Mr. Perkins must have thought it high time that I should have done. He dozed then all the way to London.

We arrived in Bow Street after dark and made our report to Sir John in his chambers. Sir John was sobered by the news of Ned Ferguson's death, and he wished to hear all the details whilst they were still fresh in our minds.

"You wish to know if his arms was intact?" said the constable.

Sir John sighed. "Yes," he said, "I suppose I do."

"They were cut off at the elbows, just as it was with Isaac Kidd." Without hesitating, he added: "I want to go out and look for Burkett."

"No," said Sir John quite firmly. "You were out last night doing your job. You traveled all day today. You're tired and weak, and you must sleep the night."

"But I have a good idea of where I might find him."

"No. If I must threaten you to make it plain, I shall do so. Even if you find him, bring him in, and lock him up in the strong room, I shall discharge you forthwith. You will no longer be a constable. And you know me well enough to tell the difference between a mere threat and a promise. What I have just offered you is more promise than threat. Do you understand me?"

Evidently he did, for he nodded and took his leave. Sir John then rose and suggested we have our dinner.

"It awaits us above," said he. "A special treat is to be served us this evening, I am told."

"And what is that, sir?"

"Clarissa has cooked the entire meal herself, part of her culinary education. The girl seems quite determined to learn all that she can as quickly as she can."

"Under Molly's strict supervision, I assume."

"I assume so, too. Oh, I know. You're doubtful, are you not? Yet Kate assures me they know what they're doing."

If I seemed doubtful, it was not without reason, for I recalled that not so long ago, before Molly had joined our household, Clarissa had attempted a meal on her own (a beef stew, as I recall) which left us all a bit queasy. Sir John himself seemed to suffer most.

"And what has she prepared for this evening?"

"Beef stew, as I understand."

Sir John hastened to admonish me to give Clarissa a proper chance.

"A good lawyer must always keep an open mind," said he.

As it happened, no special consideration needed to be given. Dinner was as good as any Molly had made for us that week. I realized, as Clarissa later confessed, that she had served as little more than Molly's hands in preparing the meal. Nevertheless, I was also aware that with Clarissa's memory and eye for detail, she would probably be able to duplicate that same stew in appearance and, most important, in taste, a month or even a year hence. There were frequent comments round the table and all of them quite flattering to Clarissa. I joined in with the rest and praised the spicing of her stew. "You've made good use of Annie's paprika," said I, earning a frown from Molly. (I later learned that the red spice was the single original touch in Clarissa's stew; Molly had warned against it because of its exotic origin.) But by any measure, the evening was a great success for Clarissa—and she deserved it.

She remained in the kitchen after the others had left, savoring her triumph as I washed up the pots, the pans, and the dishes. I was oddly aware of her eyes following me round the kitchen as I went about my usual duties. What did she mean by watching me so closely? I was made a bit uncomfortable by such attention. I was relieved when at last she spoke.

"What did *you* think of the meal?"

"Why, like all the rest I thought it excellent—wonderful, really."

"Good," said she with a solemn smile, "for it's you I wish to please, more than anyone else in the world."

I was quite taken aback by what she said. I knew not what to say. None had ever addressed me in such a way.

"Please don't look so shocked, Jeremy," said she. "You'll be hearing more of such from me now."

"Now?" I echoed.

"Yes, of course—*now* that you and I have an understanding. Now that I've no need to watch my tongue, lest you think me too flattering, too forward, lest I frighten you with such words and have you run from me. Why do you suppose I was so often tart, so frequently critical of you?"

"I don't know; because it is your nature, I suppose."

"Well, that's partly true, but it was also true that I did not wish to frighten you."

That seemed a strange thing to say. Frighten me away? George Burkett frightened me, not Clarissa Roundtree. "I don't understand," said I—and I truly did not.

"Oh, never mind," said she, scowling, putting words to her sour expression. She was silent for a moment, then did she blurt out in a most ironically mundane tone, "And tell me, Jeremy, what did you do today?"

Not knowing how better to respond to that, I treated it as an honest inquiry. I shrugged. "Constable Perkins and I went down to Robertsbridge in Sussex to arrest two men and bring them back to London."

"And did you?" She was becoming interested.

"No," I sighed. "One of them was dead, and the other, who'd killed him, had already fled."

"Oh, Jeremy, you do such dangerous work for Sir John. Supposing the killer had *not* fled. Supposing he had tried to kill *you.* What then?"

"Why then, Mr. Perkins would have killed *him.*"

"But . . ."

I disliked the turn that this had taken. Just as with Sir John and Mr. Donnelly, I thought it unwise to discuss the nastier aspects of keeping the peace with the women of our household. I decided that it would be wise to change the subject.

"Something interesting happened there in Robertsbridge, however," said I.

"Oh? What was that?"

"Well, toward the end of our stay there—just before we boarded the return coach—the magistrate in Robertsbridge offered Mr. Perkins a job there as constable. He said he would match whatever he was paid here in Bow Street, and that his money would go much farther in Robertsbridge. I'm sure he's right about that, too."

"Did Mr. Perkins accept the offer, or not?" She seemed oddly disapproving.

"Neither one. The magistrate wouldn't let him turn it down. He told him just to think about it. And frankly, I believe he is doing so."

"Well, I cannot understand that," said she.

"You mean, why he should be considering it? You must remember that he grew up in that part of the country. And as for Roberts—"

"No, that is *not* what I meant," said she, interrupting sharply. "I care not if he be considering the matter. What distresses me is that this magistrate should be offering him the position and not you. Could he not see your worth? Your superiority?"

"Clarissa, Oliver Perkins is likely the most capable of *all* Sir John's force of constables. He is brave and intelligent . . . and . . ."

"You are far more intelligent. You have the law! When will you cease underestimating yourself?"

"First of all, I do *not* have the law — not yet. I have not been admitted to the bar. When I am and am looking about for a position, I shall not accept one as a constable. I shall aim higher."

Still she sulked. "Well, that's good to hear. Still, I think that the magistrate, whoever he may be, should have offered it first to you. Then at least you would have the chance to turn him down. You deserve recognition. If only you knew what I see in you!"

I was beginning to have some notion of that, and, quite frankly, I found it disquieting. I wondered if I could ever live up to her expectations. I wondered if anyone could. Love, marriage, and all the rest made great demands, did they not? I only hoped that I was equal to them.

Of a sudden we had little more to say, each to the other. I wondered if it might not be true that she, too, had suddenly been struck by the immensity of what lay ahead of us. Until now I had given little thought to anything beyond the completion of my studies and admission to the bar. But beyond that lay all of life. How was I to prepare for that?

Next day, as I went out to do a bit of buying for Molly in Covent Garden, I was halted by the cries of the newsmongers who ran about shouting the news and selling their papers. There were remarkable events in America. I snatched up a gazette from the nearest lad, and raced with it back to Bow Street, ran down the hall, and into Sir John's chambers.

"What? What is it?" said he to me. "What is worth such a disturbance?"

"News from Boston," said I.

"Of what sort?"

"Insurrection — or something close to it."

He groaned. "All right, let us hear what that wretched gang of rebels have gotten themselves into now."

With that, I set out to read him the entire article, which, I noted, had been reprinted from a Boston newspaper of four weeks past. (It was not always that news came so swiftly from America.) The story it told was bizarre in the extreme. Let me summarize briefly, reader, for the event is no doubt still well known and well remembered.

In protest against the tax levied by Parliament against the tea sold by the East India Company (chartered by the king), many of those in the colonies had simply refused to drink English tea. They instead drank tea smuggled in from Holland, or formed a new habit and took coffee as their morning drink.

Yet a plan was hatched to force the most recalcitrant of the colonies, Massachusetts, to accept English tea in spite of the tax. The price was lowered. The tea was sold in advance to American importers. Nevertheless, the Massachusetts patriots held firm and insisted they would not allow the tea to be unloaded in Boston.

Three ships sailed into Boston Harbor loaded with tea. A mob gathered at the wharf where they tied up, to make certain that they were not unloaded. Yet more was done. That night, three "raiding parties" of fifty men each appeared, made up of individuals with faces darkened with soot and decked out in feathers, who claimed to be Indians. Each of the raiding parties boarded a separate ship. They brought up the cargo and dumped the precious tea into the waters of Boston Harbor. No resistance was offered, and no force was necessary. It was all done in a matter of a few hours.

"Who was it?" said Sir John. "Sam Adams and his crew, I've no doubt."

"It doesn't say. I don't think they really know. But you have to admit, sir, that the entire business does have to it a certain comic element."

He scowled. "Oh, I suppose so. Whoever it was thought of masquerading them as Indians showed a bit of spirit and some imagination, yet I'm sure that the king and the prime minister will not be amused."

"Even so, sir, I think —"

"Hang it all, a mob is a mob, say I. Perhaps no force was used, but that was because the captain and the crew complied. If they had not, then there probably would have been shots fired and swords bloodied. They're a violent bunch, those colonials."

"You are generally hesitant to distinguish any one group or race as more violent or immoral than the rest. I've heard you say quite often that all are about the same in the proportion of good to bad. Do you feel that the Americans are an exception to that?"

"Well, the circumstances of their lives—Indian raids and so on—encourage a reliance upon firearms for protection, I suppose."

"In the hinterlands, perhaps," said I, "but Boston and Philadelphia are large cities. There are others—New York, Baltimore, and Char—"

"I know, dammit! I'm not entirely ignorant of geography. But just look at this fellow, Burkett. He's an absolute monster—murdering, mutilating. There's no end to the brutishness of the man."

"Aren't you generalizing rather recklessly? Near all of the Americans are English, are they not? A good many of them were even born here."

Sir John let forth a great sigh. "I shall not argue the matter further," said he, "for I admit that in the heat of the moment I have just now said a number of things that were intemperate and unconsidered. But you see? I admit it, now that I have cooled down a bit. Yet there are those of us true-born Englishmen of a more choleric and vengeful nature than mine, and some of them hold high positions in the government. Think of Lord North and Lord Hillsborough; think of their sovereign. Given such provocation, they will not forget, nor will they forgive. I fear that those in the North American colonies—Americans, as they call themselves—are in for a bad time of it, and—oh, my . . ."

There he broke off, as if a thought had just struck him. From the expression that appeared on his face I judged it to be a particularly distressing thought.

"What is it, sir?"

"They may be planning to strike at him who is nearest at hand."

"Sir? I don't quite understand."

"God help Benjamin Franklin."

Later that day, long after Sir John had concluded his court session, we were blessed with another of the infrequent visits of the Lord Chief Justice to Bow Street. He was as blustering and rude as ever. He, who could manage a certain style and grace within the four walls of his house in Bloomsbury Square, became ill-mannered the moment he ventured forth into the world outside. As it happened, he had been hearing cases all day at Old Bailey, which seemed to put him in a particularly foul mood. Wearing the black hat more than once in a day would sour anyone, I suppose.

Sir John and I were sitting in his chambers when, without overture, the drama of Lord Mansfield's entrance began. The door to the street slammed open. We heard Mr. Fuller come forward and ask how he might be of assistance.

"By getting out of my way," came the sharp reply.

The voice was immediately identifiable—loud, harsh, and rasping. Sir John mouthed the name "Mansfield" quite soundlessly, and I whispered my agreement. I rose and took a place near the door, that I might be out of his way when he entered. We heard the click of his heels and the tap of his walking stick upon the wooden floor growing louder as he came closer. Then, without troubling to knock, he came charging through the open door.

"Who is there?" Sir John asked, rising from behind his desk.

"'Tis I," said the Lord Chief Justice. "Who did you suppose?"

"Ah, Lord Mansfield, how good of you to drop by. You seem to be somewhat disturbed. Won't you sit down and tell me about it?"

"Yes, by God, I will."

With that, he began to squat precisely where he stood. I could do naught but tuck a chair swiftly beneath his backside and hope he came down properly upon it. Luckily, he did.

"Yes, Sir John, I am disturbed, though not directly because of you."

"Well, I'm glad of that, truly I am."

"It is Lord Hillsborough who has my dander up. I had little use for the man before I talked to him, as you urged, and now I have even less. You, better than most, know what it is to be lied to. When one sits upon a court of any degree, he develops a sure sense of discrimination between truth and untruth, a certain feeling of nausea."

"A bad taste in the mouth," suggested Sir John, "a bad smell in the nostrils. I told a fellow so not long ago."

"Exactly! Well, sir, I talked to Lord Hillsborough, and sure as I sit here before you now, that man lied to me in the most flagrant manner. He did not even make the effort to conceal his contempt for my questions.

"He told me that he was shocked at your report on his fellow, Burkett, and he had the audacity to call to question the information you gave me. And, by the bye, I am now willing to concede that indeed I have sent men to the gallows with less hard evidence against them—though not without compunction. Still, when one knows, then one knows—if you follow me."

"Perfectly well."

"Yet what annoyed me most—nay, angered me—was the manner in which he gave his answers. Throughout our interview, he wore a sly smile, something quite like a sneer, as if he were drawing me into complicity in the matter. At one point—well, I'll tell you exactly when it was. He insisted that of course he appointed Burkett only to help *you,* Sir John, and instructed him to stay in close contact with you, and share whatever information he might gather on the theft of the letters with you. He declared he had been very explicit in that. And in saying that, do you know what he then did?"

"No idea, none at all."

"He had the audacity to wink at me. He asked if Burkett had done as he was told and kept in contact with you. 'No,' said I, 'he has been too busy searching for victims and murdering one said to have some share in the burglary.' Then did I tell him of the murder of him who had brokered the crime, sparing none of the ugly details. Pretending shock, he reminded himself that he must speak to Burkett about that. 'That sort of thing should be discouraged,' said he, referring to the mutilation of the body, as if making a jest—certainly in bad taste. I asked him if he had indeed seen Burkett since the day he brought him to me, and he admitted he had not. 'But you know,' said he, 'that is the way I prefer it. When I give an order, I like it carried out without a lot of consulting and conferring. I may have said as much to him. But of course,' he did add, 'I said nothing about murder or mutilating.' And that, of course, was said with a smirk, as well as all else."

"I stand shocked but not surprised," said Sir John. "I fear I have long had a low opinion of him."

"It seems that that low opinion is now so widely held that he is losing his place in government."

"Oh? How is that?"

"Piecemeal," said Lord Mansfield, making a bit of a jest himself.

"They have relieved him of responsibility for the American colonies. He is being forced to resign over some silly land matter in Illinois, or Ohio, or one of those Indian parts of North America."

"Who is taking his place?"

"Lord Dartmouth."

"A good choice," said Sir John. "He is a reasonable man and has influence with the prime minister."

"Indeed he should. The two are stepbrothers."

"I'd forgotten." (This I doubted, reader; Sir John seemed to forget nothing.) "It may bring some relief to this fellow, Franklin."

"I doubt it," said Lord Mansfield. "You've heard about this new outrage, of course? All that tea dumped in Boston Harbor?"

"Yes, I've heard."

"I have heard that all in the government are now so powerfully set against this Massachusetts colony and its agent, Franklin, that they have set a trap for him."

"Oh? What sort?"

"Well, it seems that for some time he had withheld a petition put forward by the Massachusetts legislature for the removal of the governor—appointed by the king himself, of course—Thomas Hutchinson."

"He of that packet of letters?"

"Yes, yes of course. Franklin had held it back, waiting for a more favorable time to present it. The departure of Lord Hillsborough and the entry of Lord Dartmouth upon the scene must have seemed the best opportunity he was likely to have, and so he made application to present the petition. As was proved by the news from Boston, there are no opportune times in regard to such matters. He has been summoned before the Privy Council to defend it and himself."

"It *and* himself?" said Sir John. "I do not follow."

"He has been told that he must answer also for the packet of letters which he sent off to Boston, for they maintain that the letters prompted the petition calling for the governor's removal. And so Franklin is to appear with counsel to confess his sins. They are out, in short, to crucify him. I do truly believe that this is but prologue to a trial for treason—and in spite of myself I pity the poor fellow."

"A crucifixion, eh? And who is to drive in the nails?"

"Why, our new solicitor general — or had you not heard?"

"Who might that be?"

"None but Alexander Wedderburn."

"Wedderburn has replaced Dexter?" Sir John asked, all agog at this information.

"As I said, Sir John."

"Then has a hyena taken the place of a lapdog. When and where will this take place?"

"In a week's time at Westminster, in the Cockpit."

Having delivered his news, Lord Mansfield rose and prepared to depart. Yet Sir John would not have him leave without informing him of the latest development in this case, which seemed to grow like some evil plant whose roots spread underground in all directions only to pop up above the surface where least expected and least desired.

"What sort of development do you speak of?" asked the Lord Chief Justice.

Again, Sir John asked me to supply the details, which I did, editing them down to the bare facts of George Burkett's arrival in Robertsbridge and Ned Ferguson's death there.

"Now, who was this fellow Ferguson?" Lord Mansfield asked, addressing me direct.

"He was one of the two burglars who purloined the packet of letters," said I.

"And how did you hear where he had gone to hide?"

"His partner," said Sir John, "supplied us with that information when he surrendered to us."

"And where is he now?"

"In custody."

"Well, send him up to me at Old Bailey, and we shall at least get one of these fellows hanged."

"Let us speak of that later, shall we?"

"As you wish, Sir John. I must be getting on in any case. By the bye, do you wish me to put in for two places for you and your assistant in the gallery of the Cockpit for Franklin's appearance?"

"Do so, by all means," said Sir John. "Wouldn't miss it for the world."

. . .

The Cockpit? What could that mean? Was I to believe that members of the House of Lords and the House of Commons met there in Westminster to pursue the ancient English pastime of cockfighting? Surely that seemed beneath their dignity. (Little notion had I then how without dignity were both bodies.) During the next week I pursued the question with Sir John, yet without much satisfaction.

"What is it, sir, this place called the Cockpit?"

"Why, it is a committee room in Westminster Palace. They conduct business there."

"But why do they call it the Cockpit?"

"Well, it's . . . it's . . ." His words hung in the air for near a minute as he attempted to come forth with a proper answer to my question.

"You know, I really have no idea why it is called in such a way."

Unbeknownst to me, Clarissa heard my query to Sir John. She gave the question some thought and asked Mr. Donnelly to put it to Mr. Goldsmith, who seemed, as she said, "to know quite all about everything." The answer came back that in the time of Henry VIII, that particular room had indeed been used for cockfighting, and to this day it has retained the name, though its purpose is now altogether different. Or perhaps not quite so different as all that, for the two hours spent by Benjamin Franklin in the Cockpit had all of the drama and intensity of such a clash, even if it lacked something of the brutish nature of that sort of conflict.

Sir John feared for Franklin's safety. Upon hearing from me of the gruesome death of Isaac Kidd, he had posted an armed constable at the door of Mrs. Stevenson's house in Craven Street, in which Dr. Franklin made his home and office. During the day, there were groups of hecklers to be sent upon their way, and at night, there was always the possibility of a visit by George Burkett; and so it was young Mr. Queenan during the day, and the taciturn veteran Constable Brede at night. Only some of this I was aware of till later. I did know, however, that as time grew nearer to the hearing in the Cockpit, the magistrate grew increasingly concerned regarding the threat of George Burkett at the event and immediately afterward.

I recall quite well that Sir John had once said that if one were to murder another, it might well be best done in a great throng. I have not the words or his reasoning exact, but he felt that within a mob much may be concealed, including the killer, his weapon, and his mode of attack; and once the deed was accomplished, the mob would provide him with his means of escape, for he had but to melt into the multitude to become invisible.

Thus it was that he began making preparations as he heard news of the large crowd which was expected at Westminster. It was those who would gather outside the palace who worried him. When did a large crowd become a mob? And how? Would Lord Hillsborough have planted paid shouters in their midst to agitate against Franklin? Against all the so-called Americans? It was surprising and disturbing to me how many of those, neither upper-class nor lower but somewhere between, had united against the colonials since news of the "tea party" had come from Boston. Estimates of the size of the expected crowd were high, all the way up to a thousand. Could the constables cope with such a number? Sir John consulted with Benjamin Bailey and Mr. Perkins, as well as others, regarding what might be done. At some of these conferences I was present, and at some I was not. Yet I was sufficiently close to the planning to understand that matters might be regulated down to the last jot, yet still and all, 'twas naught but Sir John's *feeling* that Benjamin Franklin was in mortal danger at the time of the hearing that had activated this flurry of preparation. Yet, in the past, had this feeling not been enough? Often before, with little to support his certain belief, he would choose a course directly opposed to that which all logic dictated was the "right" one—and then see his choice triumph. He had instinct on his side, and Sir John's instincts had proven accurate time and again. How odd then that they should now be enlisted in this effort to protect Dr. Franklin, the very champion of logic and science.

In the end, it was fairly evident that, depending upon the size of the crowd, there was not a great deal could be done to ensure completely the safety of Dr. Franklin. If the number waiting at the great door to Westminster Palace approached a thousand, all that one could do was pray. A hundred or two hundred, even three, could be handled easily by the contingent of constables Sir John had at his disposal. But if there were many beyond that, all would depend upon the temper of the crowd. If it became an unruly mob, then the best that could be done would be to form a ring round Dr. Franklin and, with drawn cutlasses, usher him to the coach which would wait just a short distance from the entrance.

The day before the hearing was to take place Sir John dictated a letter to Benjamin Franklin in which he outlined the potential dangers to him (mentioning the murders of Isaac Kidd and Ned Ferguson, though saying nothing of the mutilation); then did he outline the precautions he had taken or was intending to take. He emphasized the importance of his cooperation and instructed him to wait there in the Cockpit and leave only with himself or "the bearer of this letter."

"I want you, Jeremy," said he to me, "to return with a firm commitment from him that he will do as I ask."

"I shall, sir."

Thus did I make a commitment, as well.

Before I could make myself known to Dr. Franklin, or to Mrs. Stevenson, I had to push my way through a small crowd in Craven Street, which had gathered at Number 10. There were less than a dozen there. They seemed curious rather than hostile. Constable Queenan seemed not to mind them, and he was most happy to see me—though less so when he learned that he and Mr. Brede would be conveying Benjamin Franklin to the hearing next day.

"Mr. Brede will drive, and you will guard Dr. Franklin," said I. "That's as Sir John wants it."

"Is that going to be as slow-going as this has been?"

"No, I give you my guaranty that tomorrow will be more interesting—cutlasses and pistols."

As we spoke thus, the door flew open and Mrs. Stevenson pulled me inside.

"Have you something for Dr. Franklin? For if you don't, then back you go whence you came."

"Yes, I—"

"I'll not have anyone bothering him while he prepares for tomorrow unless it's something important."

"A letter from Sir John Fielding."

"Oh, well, that's important. Give it here, and I'll bring it right to him."

"No, ma'am," said I firmly. "I'm to put it in his hands and wait for an answer."

"Oh . . . all right."

So saying, she turned and made her way to the stairs. Then, mounting them swiftly, she disappeared above.

As I waited, I heard a quiet mumble of voices from the first floor. All I understood of it was Sir John's name spoken loud by Mrs. Stevenson. A minute later, or perhaps less, Dr. Franklin's step sounded upon the stairs, and he appeared, a worried frown upon his face.

"Mrs. Stevenson says you have a letter for me from Sir John."

"Correct, sir," said I, taking it from my pocket and offering it to him.

Yet he did not at first accept it. "If it's a summons to another interrogation, I shall not accept it," said he. "I now have all I can do preparing for the hearing before the Privy Council."

"It is nothing of the sort. I'm to wait until you have read it and return with your message of compliance."

"Compliance, is it? Well, we shall see about that."

He then took it from me, broke the seal, and began to read the letter. He seemed notably more confident than the last time I had seen him—or, perhaps, not so much confident as determined. Yet Sir John's words persuaded him of the seriousness of the situation.

"It says here that I am to go by coach to the hearing. These two—constables Queenan and Brede—are to take me there. These are the two who have been at the door?"

"Yes sir."

"And you and Sir John will take me back to the coach when the hearing is done?"

"There will be other constables involved in your return."

"Why is Sir John doing all this for me?" He seemed quite innocently puzzled.

"Because he feels that you are in danger, sir. If you wish to know more than that, you must ask him yourself. But now, please, do I have your assurance that you will cooperate with the arrangements that have been made?"

"Oh yes," said he, "yes indeed. And please deliver to him my most profound thanks."

We in the gallery of the Cockpit were ranged round the room at a height somewhat above the thirty-six members of the Privy Council. They had their places at a single table set against the far wall. Before them were the two featured players of the drama which was about to unfold before us—Alexander Wedderburn, the new solicitor general, and Benjamin Franklin, appearing as the agent for the Colony of Massachusetts and its legislature. They sat wide apart. Wedderburn, obviously uncomfortable, twitched about awkwardly in his chair like some marionette on strings; Dr. Franklin, in the company of a barrister named Dunning, sat close and conferred with him. Those in the gallery were noisy to the point of disorder; they had come to be entertained. And, finally, the members of the Privy Council waited in silence, evidently in no mood for amusement.

The varying temper of those there in the Cockpit seemed to reflect that of others outside. Sir John and I had waited for the arrival of the rented coach which brought Dr. Franklin. As we waited, I attempted to estimate the size of the crowd. It was in no wise large. There were no more than a hundred, and probably a good deal fewer—and all rather jolly—as I told Sir John. He, for his part, cautioned me that the hundred I saw could easily grow to a thousand in the next hour or two. "I am shocked," said he, "to hear of so many here so early." Then did the coach appear, driven by Mr. Brede; he pulled the horses up as near to the great door as possible, and Dr. Franklin exited the coach, attended by Constable Queenan. Then was I surprised to hear hoots, and whistles, and hostile shouts from the crowd, which only moments before had seemed near festive in attitude. Sir John called for Constables Bailey and Rumford to go out and give young Queenan a hand. There was no more difficulty after that.

All of that had come to pass over a quarter of an hour before the commencement of the hearing. After Dr. Franklin was situated in his place, we claimed our places in the gallery. There we waited for the open places at the long table to be filled and the hearing to begin.

Lord Gower banged away with his gavel and called the hearing to order. The text of the petition which Dr. Franklin had presented was read out, for that was the nominal purpose of the hearing. Then was the text of the Hutchinson letters also read aloud, for that was the *true* purpose of the hearing: to tar Franklin for his part in the publication of the letters. Thus it began, and it swiftly proceeded from the nominal to the true. Barrister Dunning argued, as he had been coached by Dr. Franklin, that the matter of the letters did not belong in consideration with the petition because they were essentially political in nature. As it happened, Mr. Dunning was not a well man. So weak was he that he could not stand for long without showing signs of tottering, and his voice was so weakened that he could scarcely speak above a whisper. Those in the gallery round us became restive, and then unruly. There were shouts of "louder" and "speak up!" until at last Lord Gower was forced to wield his gavel once more, shouting for quiet as he sought to bring the rowdy crowd of noblemen and aristocrats under control. At last, they began to quiet down, and Mr. Dunning prepared to resume.

Before he could do so, Alexander Wedderburn leaped to his feet and began his attack. His reasoning: Since it was the Hutchinson letters which gave birth to the petition to replace the governor, then one is no less political than the other.

Yet that, reader, was the mere modicum of reasoning contained in the hour-long tirade to which he treated his audience. They had, as I said, come to be entertained, and he did entertain them. All the twitching energy I had seen in him before the hearing began, was now concentrated in this assault upon Dr. Franklin.

He talked of little but the purloined letters. He vilified Franklin as a common thief. He said, "Men will watch him with a jealous eye; they will hide their papers from him and lock up their escritoires. He will henceforth esteem it a libel to be called a man of letters."

A chorus of laughter rang out round us at that. The fact that they could find humor in such vituperation quite astonished me.

Sir John leaned toward me. "This exceeds all bounds of propriety," said he. "I have never before heard such from a member of His Majesty's government."

Nor did the solicitor general neglect to offer a reminder of what all now called the Boston Tea Party: ". . . the good men of Boston have lately held their meetings, appointed their committees, and with their usual moderation have destroyed the cargo of three British ships."

And then, sudden as it had begun, Wedderburn's attack ended. Had he exhausted the subject of Franklin's treasonous acts? Or had he simply run out of breath and bile? Whatever the answer to that, the response of Benjamin Franklin was an eloquent silence. It would not have been his nature to rail, shout, and snarl, as Wedderburn had done. Had he chosen to do so, he would have lowered himself to the level of his attacker. It was impossible not to admire him as he sat in his chair, erect and unblinking, his face set in a mask of dignity. Nor was I the only one who saw it thus. A few of those in the gallery who had come to jibe and jest at the expense of Dr. Franklin fell silent as they watched him. I discovered later that more than one newspaper, reporting upon the event, counted it a moral victory for Franklin; they also hinted that Lord North, the prime minister, was displeased with Wedderburn. It remained for Sir John to make the most telling comment—and that was made directly to Dr. Franklin himself once the business was done.

We made our way down the stairs into the cockpit, and there stood Benjamin Franklin, still silent and now alone. Even his frail barrister had withdrawn from him. I saw a man go by, almost without stopping, and squeeze Franklin's hand as he said not a word; then did he also hastily depart.

"You see how they run from me?" said Franklin to us as we approached. "As if I were a carrier of the plague."

"We know not what waits for you outside. That is why we are here to see you back to Craven Street. Now, sir, if you will just follow me and Jeremy?"

"Indeed I shall, sir, and gladly."

We set off down the long crowded hall, which led to the great door. Those passing us by gave us a wide berth, shrinking to one side, as if fearful of Franklin. He seemed to have achieved fame—of the wrong sort. Yet he seemed now to be eager to talk about the ordeal.

"The Privy Council rejected the petition," said he, talking to our backs.

"But you must have expected that," said Sir John.

"Oh, I did, but they might at least have considered it on its merits." And having said that, he launched into a presentation of what he considered to be its merits. This was, I supposed, what he would have said, had the solicitor general given him the opportunity to do so. Yet for some reason, as we approached the great door, it became increasingly difficult for Franklin to be heard—not because his voice grew weaker, but rather because there came a noise, a strange washing sound like unto that which I had heard on the beach at Deal as the tide came in; it interfered increasingly with the voice of Franklin—never truly strong under the best of conditions. Curious, I urged Sir John to pick up the pace a bit, yet he was unwilling. "We'll get there soon enough," said he. All the while, Dr. Franklin talked unconcernedly on—until we stepped through the door and he glimpsed the source of that strange noise.

"Oh, dear God!" said he.

Before us we saw a sea of faces—or, perhaps not quite so many as that, but a lake, certainly. If the pure number of people out there between us and the rented coach was impressive, the sudden roar that issued forth from them as they recognized Benjamin Franklin was much more so. It was frightening.

"Now how many would you say are here?" Sir John shouted above the tumult.

"I've no idea," I shouted in response. "Perhaps a thousand!"

"Not so many"—a new voice, that of Mr. Perkins, whom I had noticed standing now beside me. "I'd put them at not quite eight hundred."

"That's a good many."

"They're pretty well-behaved, though. They look to be shop-keepers, clerks, and the like. They're not a mob."

"Are all of us here?"

"All except Constable Brede," said Benjamin Bailey. "He had to stay with the coach. We'll have to make it through the crowd to get to him out there."

"Well and good," said Sir John. "Now, you've all done this at least once before. Cutlasses out."

There was a nasty, sharp, slithering sound as the swords left their scabbards.

"Hold the cutlasses high so they can be seen. If any in the crowd gets too close, then use the flat of the sword on him. If there is an actual attack on any of us, you may use the sharp of the sword, or shoot to wound. Form a ring round us, and remember that your first responsibility is to protect Dr. Franklin. Are you all ready?"

There was a bit of shifting about as the constables sought their places, but soon there was an affirmative chorus from them.

"All right then, let us go forward!"

Without a weapon, I felt somewhat at a loss. Yet what would I do with a cutlass? Only harm to myself, no doubt. And Sir John had forbidden me to carry a pistol into the Cockpit. ("Of course it is done," he admitted, "but it is against the law and should be. I will not have you breaking the law in my company.") And so, as a result, I was one of three protected within what Sir John had described as a "ring." In truth, it was more in the nature of a square. I walked between Benjamin Franklin on my left, and on my right, Sir John (who held lightly to my right arm). Forward on the left corner was Mr. Bailey, and to the rear on the left was Mr. Queenan; on the right forward was Mr. Perkins, with Mr. Rumford in the right rear.

(Just one more point, reader; though I have described myself as unarmed, that was not strictly so. While I had with me neither cutlass nor pistol, I did carry with me, concealed in my coat pocket, the cosh Mr. Baker had given to me so many months ago. I had taken to carrying it quite everywhere with me.)

And so, in the odd configuration which I have just described in some detail, we seven set off into the crowd. Those directly before us backed away, allowing us passage, but they did so unwillingly, even sullenly. As Mr. Perkins had said, the individuals making up this great mass of men appeared to be shopkeepers and clerks,— well-dressed, not poor, and generally law-abiding. They fell back in respect for Sir John—and also for the drawn cutlasses of the four Bow Street Runners who surrounded him.

That did not, however, prevent them from shouting abuse and invective at our troop, most of it (though not all) directed at Dr. Franklin.

"Traitor" he was called, and "Dr. Treason."

"Have you no shame?" demanded one.

"You owe the East India Company a hundred thousand pounds!" dunned another.

"The colonies must pay!"

And so on, as we marched through them.

The coach lay near seven rods away, yet I did not fix upon it. I kept scanning the crowd, looking for George Burkett, as Sir John had urged me to do. It had come to me that it would be difficult for that giant of a man to hide, even in a gathering of eight hundred; for at six feet and four or five inches in height, and eighteen stone in weight, give or take a few pounds, he would be hard to miss. The only way he could avoid towering a head above the rest would be to walk about upon his knees. And not even Burkett could keep that up for long. So it need not be difficult to see him from a distance. Yet I kept trying.

Much nearer than I had been looking, I heard something that caught my ear and kept my attention:

"Make way!"

"Make way for the veteran."

"Yes, by God! I am a veteran. I'll tell them about it."

It was close by. I could tell that. This conversation of shouts came from off to the left, not far beyond young Queenan.

"Push him up front, I say, so he can tell Franklin up close."

"Yes, I'll tell him, I will! Just let me get near him."

There was something familiar about that voice. It was . . . it was . . . no, I couldn't yet say who or what it was.

No, I could not—not until he was pushed—or propelled himself—into the front rank, coming nearer and shouting louder.

"I am a veteran of the French War, I am. Fought the French and the Hurons and lost the power of my legs there—all for these ungrateful colonials."

And then did he raise his head, displaying his face. But he did so perhaps a bit too early, for I saw him and recognized him at just about the moment that Sir John recognized his voice. "Jeremy!" he cried in alarm.

It was George Burkett, pushing himself along in a contraption which was built upon the small wheels of a child's goat cart. Had I seen something like it bearing a beggar in Covent Garden? But now it bore him straight at Dr. Franklin.

I dove forward, cosh in hand, but managed only a glancing blow at his face before he swept me off with a single swing of his huge hand. I was down on the ground, slightly dazed, when I witnessed a most singular event.

He made the mistake of attempting to jump to his feet whilst still upon the beggar's cart. He was simply too much for it—too much size, too much weight. The contraption that supported no longer supported him. It went off skittering from beneath him, leaving him flailing the air with his hands, one of which clutched in it the biggest knife I ever saw. Yet try as he may, he cannot balance himself—and he falls, dear God, how he falls, right on his belly!

I see my chance and dive upon his back that I might beat upon his head with my cosh. I hit him again, hard as I can, yet it seems to do nothing, less than nothing, for he begins to rise.

I throw my left arm round his throat and rise with him. It is like riding the back of some great fish. While I still can—for I feel myself slipping—then do I put all of the strength I have left into a single blow aimed at the base of his skull.

I fall. He falls. And that is all I remember.

TWELVE

In which Sir John
receives a letter
from Massachusetts

Though my head was concussed, I was not seriously hurt—or so
Gabriel Donnelly informed me when I was taken round to him.
True, I was briefly unconscious, yet Mr. Perkins told me that Sam-
son himself would have fallen with that first blow delivered me by
Burkett.

The wonder was, said Mr. Bailey, that having been knocked
out once, I managed to rise again and attack that huge villain from
the rear.

"It's like you put off fainting for fair till after you'd laid him low
with your cosh," said he. "Wouldn't stop beating on his head till
you'd got him proper."

I had killed George Burkett. I was in no wise sure how I felt
about that, nor would I know for years to come. Mr. Donnelly had
called it to my attention that the wounds I had inflicted were quite
like those suffered by Albert Calder at the hands of Tommy Skinner. "You quite thoroughly destroyed the back of his head, you
know," said he. "I never knew you had it in you."

He prescribed two days bedrest for my concussion. 'Twas lucky
for me that Mr. Marsden chose that as the proper time to return to
his post as clerk of the Bow Street Court, for I confess now (though
I protested otherwise to Sir John) that I was in no condition to perform the clerk's duties, as I had been doing in his stead. Had he not
resumed, Clarissa would probably have stepped forward and satisfied Sir John that she would make a better clerk than either Mr.
Marsden or I.

That, in any case, was the impression with which I was left when she came to visit me in my attic room.

"I was fully prepared," she told me, "to step in and take your place." Yet that was not all she had to say.

I recall that she entered the room very quietly, evidently fearful of waking me. But I was not asleep, and if I appeared so to her, I could only have been dozing, for my eyes flickered open the moment she came close.

"Ah," said she, "you're awake."

"Yes, it's dark out now. What time is it? Any idea?"

"Not exact, no. But Molly is preparing dinner. It must be round six."

"I should get dressed for dinner."

"You're not to come down," said she quite firmly.

"But I'm quite famished!"

"Have no fear. It will be brought to you—on a tray, by me."

"Indeed? I have not been treated so well since we visited Mrs. Keen's tearoom in Deal and were served a plate of her 'best.'"

I thought that might at least coax a smile from her—but it did nothing of the kind. She stared down at me in a manner most severe. It was then, as I recall, that she reported to me that Mr. Marsden had returned to his duties, and added that had there been any need, she would have taken the role of Sir John's clerk for as long as might have been necessary. When I said nothing to that, she lashed out angrily.

"Do you doubt I could have done it?"

"Of course I do *not*, but . . . but . . . what in the world has made you so ill-tempered?"

"All right, all right, I shall tell you. I have heard Mr. Perkins's account of what you did today, and I think two things about all that."

The girl was trembling with fury—or upset of some sort. I could not tell which.

"I think, first of all," said she, continuing, "that it was terribly brave of you. But I also think it was very foo—" Her chin trembled so that she could hardly speak. "It was very fool . . . ish of you." Then did she give in to the tears she had held back all through the last speech. She swept down upon me, and she began covering my face with kisses, "Oh, Jeremy," she wailed, "how could you? You might have been killed!"

I comforted her as best I could from my prone position, returning her kisses, hugging her to me. I struggled to rise in bed, but she would have none of that.

"No, no, you mustn't. Mr. Donnelly has said that you must rest."

"Well, I'll have to sit up in bed to eat, won't I?"

"Oh, I suppose so, but for now, you will stay in bed, won't you? I promise I'll behave better next time. I'll . . . I'll be back."

So saying, she left me.

Though Clarissa was the first to visit me during that evening and the next day or two, she was but the first of many. Mr. Donnelly appeared twice to assure me that I was responding well to his ministrations. Sir John also looked in on me twice, as did Constable Perkins. Molly made sure that I had plenty to eat, and Lady Fielding came to display proudly the new coat which she had bought me to replace the one quite ruined in my tussle with George Burkett.

Mr. Perkins brought news of great import, which Sir John confirmed: The constable had decided to take the job offered him by Peter Hollaby, magistrate of Robertsbridge. Not only that, but he explained that the move would make it possible for him to marry Bess, with whom he had been living, it seemed, for months—the two of them together above the stables.

Once I had heard the news, Sir John told how negotiations had taken place, more or less behind the scenes. Mr. Perkins had come to him and told all and made the point that the move was tied to his marriage plans. Sir John was glad to hear of it, so glad, in fact, that he offered to write the magistrate of Robertsbridge and "explain" the situation to him. In the letter, which he dictated to Clarissa, he commended Mr. Perkins to him as one of the finest, if not *the* finest of the Bow Street Runners. He declared that he would go to great lengths to keep him, yet he had heard from the constable of his desire to marry, and Robertsbridge offered much more suitable surroundings in which to begin married life and start a family. "I know, sir, that you are correct in saying that money would go farther in Robertsbridge," Sir John said in the letter. "Nevertheless, he is particularly eager to find a suitable place for him and his bride to live. Could you, in some manner, guaranty this?"

Mr. Hollaby rose to the challenge with grace and ingenuity. He admitted that he could not pay more than his original offer to meet Mr. Perkins's London pay. Still, he understood perfectly the difficulties faced by those beginning married life, and he wished to help in whatever way he could. As it happened, he had a small cottage on his property in which his son and his bride lived during the first years of their marriage. "All that it would need would be a bit of fixing up for it to be made comfortable," wrote the Robertsbridge magistrate. "This cottage can be his rent-free for as long as he wishes it."

Thus it was settled. Wedding plans were made. Banns were posted. And Oliver Perkins and his Bess were married at the earliest opportunity at a side chapel in St. Paul's, Covent Garden. 'Twas a joyous occasion attended by nearly all in Bow Street, including those constables whose duties permitted.

During Sir John's second visit, the matter of Benjamin Franklin came up. He asked if I had received a visit from him. I said I had not.

"No, I thought not," said he. "A letter? A note?"

"Nothing of the kind."

"Ah well, I hoped for better, but I can't say that I expected it. He owes you a good deal, Jeremy. You saved his life, you know."

At that I could not help but give an embarrassed chuckle. "That sounds strange to me."

"That you saved his life? Why should that strike you as strange? You've saved mine often enough. Never quite so spectacularly, however. In fairness to him, I will say that he was quite solicitous for your welfare, tut-tutting and insisting that you be taken direct to Mr. Donnelly in the rented coach. You came to your senses bouncing about upon the cobblestones."

"And what happened to Dr. Franklin? Don't tell me he took a hackney coach—surely not!"

"No, he said he would walk home. I understand that he lives quite near to Whitehall."

"Well, yes, he does, but what about the crowd? The mob?"

"What crowd? What mob? When they saw what had happened

to Burkett, they scattered in all directions. Nevertheless, I ordered Queenan and Rumford to accompany him. They made it to Craven Street without incident, in any case. That was the last we heard from him."

"What a shame, sir, that he should part from you in such a way," said I.

"And from you!" Then, with a sigh, he added, "I've a notion what now preoccupies him. He is no doubt quaking for fear that he will be charged with treason. There was some talk of that. As a matter of fact, Wedderburn's attack upon him, before the Privy Council was supposed to open the way for it. But as I understand it, Burkett's attempt upon his life, which you countered, has ended all such plans. No doubt Dr. Franklin will be returning soon to America. I would if I were he."

(As it happened, reader, Benjamin Franklin stayed on in London till sometime in 1775. He had already resigned as agent for the Massachusetts House of Representatives soon after his ordeal in the Cockpit. Yet though he was still agent for three of the North American colonies, he transacted little business on their behalf. Things simply went from bad to worse between Britain and the thirteen American colonies. Why did he remain here in London? Because, at bottom, he liked it. After all, he had spent more than half his life in London. He had friends here—the philosopher Joseph Priestley, the Earl of Chatham, and Edmund Burke, a member of Parliament, and, of course, Mrs. Stevenson. I believe he would have been happy to spend the rest of his days in Craven Street.)

On the third day, Mr. Donnelly visited, looked me over, and pronounced me fit for light duty. What that would mean, he explained, would be taking letters in dictation from Sir John and going about town to deliver them. No more than that for a while.

"Let Molly do the buying in the Garden for a while," said he. "If there are loads to be carried, I shall carry them."

"Agreed," said I. "And I'm sure she'll be glad for your assistance."

As he packed up his black bag, he took notice of something inside. He reached in for it rather carefully.

"By the bye, I've brought you something. Call it a gift, or perhaps a trophy—but it's yours."

Having said that, he brought out a large and dangerous-looking object. I recognized it as the knife wielded with such grisly results by George Burkett.

"I'm not entirely sure how it came to me," he continued. "Yet as I have supposed it, Constables Bailey and Perkins must have brought it to me along with you. Big, ugly thing, isn't it? More sword than knife. I wouldn't keep it, if I were you, but it belongs to you, more than anyone else. I'll let you decide what to do with it."

With that, he placed it carefully upon the chest of drawers, closed up his black bag, and made ready to depart. Just then—I cannot say why—it came to me to inquire after Mr. Donnelly's friend, Oliver Goldsmith.

"It's strange that you should ask," said he. "Just two nights past he had that collapse that I have so long predicted. Luckily I was present and managed to get him admitted into St. Bartholomew's Hospital."

"What is his complaint?"

"Oh, a combination of one thing and another—blood in his urine, a weak bladder, and, judging from his jaundiced complexion, a liver complaint."

"Will he recover?"

"Oh, I hope so—no, I believe so. Yet next time he may not, for unless he stops eating and drinking as he has been, there will certainly be a next time. But I must go now and visit him at St. Bart's. I'll tell him you asked after him."

"By all means do so," said I, waving good-bye to him as he disappeared through the door.

(Though Oliver Goldsmith did, in fact, recover under Mr. Donnelly's care, he was soon consuming alcohol and rich food in the same way as before. Just as his friend had predicted, another collapse came later in the year, from which Mr. Goldsmith did *not* recover. That delightful and irresponsible man died in that year of 1774.)

I worked at taking dictation and delivering letters in and around the City of London and Westminster, just as Mr. Donnelly had suggested—for Sir John would have it no other way. After a week of that, there was a letter which he dictated and directed to the City of

Liverpool in Lancashire. (I cannot now recall the matter with which it dealt.) In any case, it called for a trip to the Post Coach House, which I managed without difficulty. The man at the post window accepted the letter for Liverpool without comment, but just as I turned away, he called me back.

"Hold on," said he. "There's one here for Sir John. You've not been round for a while, and it got put aside. Give me a moment, and I'll find it for you."

He began picking, one by one, through a handful of letters.

"Where's it from?" I asked.

"Ah, here it is." He held it up and read the return. "It's from Massachusetts Colony. Should be interesting, eh?"

He pushed it across with a wink. I took it, waving my thanks, and set off for Bow Street at a run. Then, remembering Mr. Donnelly's cautions, I slowed to a fast walk and arrived just in time to catch Sir John before his court session. I burst in upon him and begged for time to read the letter to him.

"What is so important about it?" he demanded a bit suspiciously.

"It's from Massachusetts," said I. "It's from Mr. Bilbo. I'm sure of it."

"All right then, read it to me."

I broke the seal and glanced down to the signature at the bottom.

"It is from Mr. Bilbo, sir."

"Well, read it, will you?"

"Certainly! He begins, 'Sir John—'"

"Just so?"

Yet I was already reading the rest aloud:

Though this letter will be short, it has taken me a terrible long time to write. I threw away just so many as I started, which was quite a few. I'm writing to ask your forgiveness for breaking my word to you, which I know I did. It was that or hand over the woman I love, which I would not do and still would not do today. When I say I'm asking you to forgive, I mean man to man, friend to friend, for I know there's nothing can be done for me legally. And so I'll have to stay away from England. We are not likely ever to meet again in this life. It's just I would sleep better at night know-ing all was straight between us. It's a sad thing, but I'm cer-tain, and each day more certain, that there will be a war coming soon between England and America, and I know we'll be on different sides, we will, sure. There's naught can be done about that, just that those things are now all be-yond us. The lad Bunkins says he thinks often of you and Jeremy and would like to be remembered to you both. He'll never forget you, and I will not either. You accepted me for just what I was. May God bless you for that.

Having read through the body of the letter, I paused, and then added, "As I said, Sir John, it is signed 'John Bilbo.'"

"That is all, then, Jeremy?"

"That is all, sir." Then did I ask: "Do you think he is right? — About the war, I mean."

"I fear that indeed he may be," said Sir John.

AUTHOR'S NOTE

Though I am usually quite respectful of the facts of history, I admit to having taken a number of liberties in *An Experiment in Treason*. Students of American history will recognize the foundation of the story as the Affair of the Hutchinson Letters, an important milestone on the road to Bunker Hill. Because this is a work of fiction, it was necessary to fabricate murders, to cut certain corners and move a few dates forward or back; this was done, for the most part, to introduce Sir John Fielding into the plot.

Yet the facts that support the fiction are fascinating in themselves. The letters were indeed stolen—though even to this day the identity of the thief is unknown. What *is* known, however, is that Benjamin Franklin played an important role in getting the letters to certain members of the Massachusetts House of Representatives. That much he admitted in an article written by him that appeared in the *London Chronicle* and was quoted in its entirety in my text. Whether or not he did more is anybody's guess. Yet for that much he was punished in the Cockpit in the manner I have described.

All this and more I derived from various books that I had on hand:

The First American: the Life and Times of Benjamin Franklin, by H. W. Brands, New York, 2000.

The Long Fuse: How England Lost the American Colonies, by Don Cook, New York, 1995.

A Struggle for Power: The American Revolution, by Theodore Draper, New York, 1996.

Origins of the American Revolution, by John C. Miller, Boston, 1943.

Perhaps most beneficial of all to me was the Library of America's selection of *Writings* by Benjamin Franklin himself.